DAMIEN
a slater brothers novel

NEW YORK TIMES & USA TODAY BESTSELLING AUTHOR
L. A. CASEY

Damien
a slater brothers novel
Copyright © 2018 by L.A. Casey
Published by L.A. Casey
www.lacaseyauthor.com

This book is licensed for your personal enjoyment only. This book may not be re-sold or given away to other people. If you would like to share this book with another person, please purchase an additional copy for each recipient. If you're reading this book and did not purchase it, or it wasn't purchased for your use only, then please return to your favorite book retailer and purchase your own copy. Thank you for respecting the hard work of this author.

All rights reserved.

Except as permitted under S.I. No. 337/2011 – European Communities (Electronic Communications Networks and Services) (Universal Service and Users' Rights) Regulations 2011, no part of this publication may be reproduced, distributed, or transmitted in any form or by any means, or stored in a database or retrieval system, without prior written permission of the author. The scanning, uploading, and distribution of this book via the Internet or via other means without the permission of the publisher is illegal and punishable by law. Please purchase only authorized electronic editions and do not participate in or encourage electronic piracy of copyrighted materials. This is a work of fiction. Names, characters, places, brands, media, and incidents are either the product of the author's imagination or are used fictitiously. The author acknowledges the trademarked status and trademark owners of various products referenced in this work of fiction, which have been used without permission. The publication/use of these trademarks is not authorized, associated with, or sponsored by the trademark owners.

Damien / L.A. Casey – 1st ed.
ISBN-13: 978-1983725661 | ISBN-10: 1983725668

For everyone who has loved Damien and Alannah since DOMINIC, this one is for you.

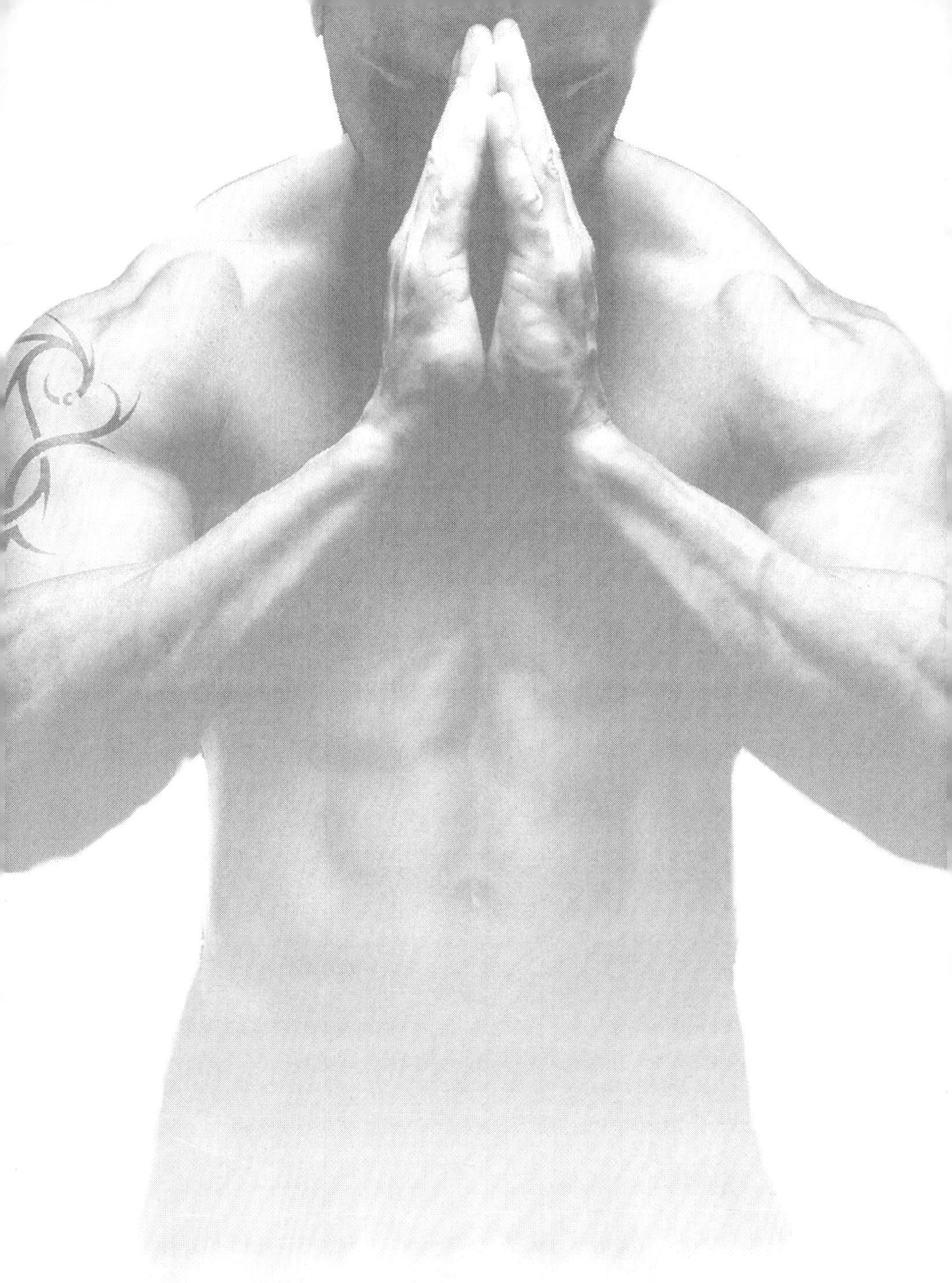

TABLE OF CONTENTS

Prologue	1
Chapter One	33
Chapter Two	37
Chapter Three	46
Chapter Four	56
Chapter Five	76
Chapter Six	90
Chapter Seven	102
Chapter Eight	117
Chapter Nine	129
Chapter Ten	136
Chapter Eleven	150
Chapter Twelve	163
Chapter Thirteen	175
Chapter Fourteen	186

Chapter Fifteen	195
Chapter Sixteen	209
Chapter Seventeen	222
Chapter Eighteen	228
Chapter Nineteen	238
Chapter Twenty	249
Chapter Twenty-One	264
Chapter Twenty-Two	274
Chapter Twenty-Three	281
Chapter Twenty-Four	290
Chapter Twenty-Five	301
Chapter Twenty-Six	307
Chapter Twenty-Seven	312
Chapter Twenty-Eight	319
Chapter Twenty-Nine	327
Chapter Thirty	333
Chapter Thirty-One	347
Chapter Thirty-Two	358
Acknowledgments	364
About the Author	366
Other Titles	367

PROLOGUE

Six Years Ago ...

Being everyone's friend sucks donkey balls.

I thought about it as I twirled the ends of my black hair around my fingers and stared up at the ceiling. The bed I was lying on suddenly dipped, pulling me from my thoughts and causing me to flinch at the disruption of my peace and quiet. I glanced at my best friend, who had one hand on her bed to balance herself while she slid her high heels on with the other.

Bronagh Murphy was my opposite in every way. When she wasn't pretending that she was invisible, she was loud, sassy, and had a solid backbone. She was funny too, and though she didn't think so, she had a *banging* body.

My pairing with Bronagh was an odd one because we hadn't always been friends. In fact, it was only over the past few weeks after Bronagh defended me from an attack by the school bully that we decided to give the friendship thing a real go. After that, we quickly found we were, in fact, BFFs and just *had* to hang out all the time.

We were a work in progress for Bronagh, though, because I wasn't exactly a social butterfly. I could make friends easily enough when I wanted to, but Bronagh couldn't. She had trust issues, so even landing a spot as her friend was a miracle. I had been in her class for the whole of secondary school and often saw her around primary school, but I never really knew her. No one did ... until Nico and Damien Slater moved to our town, got lumped into our tutor class, and quite literally, cornered her until she had no choice but to come out swinging.

Damien Slater. My mind drifted. *Where do I start with Damien Slater?*

I licked my lips.

Damien was ... my God, he was perfect. He was drop-dead gorgeous, super tall, lean with muscle, had an accent, *and* he made me laugh. He had an identical twin, but to me, he was nothing like his brother Nico. I knew from the moment I saw him on his first day in school a few months ago that I would secretly obsess over him. I just didn't know I'd be obsessing twenty-four-bloody-seven over him.

I had never had a *real* crush on a lad before Damien entered my life. I thought some lads around school and town were good looking, and hot celebrities *obviously* drew my attention like any other red-blooded teenage girl, but I had no one who I really fancied myself being with. That all changed when I first saw Damien. Even though he was very closed off, I could tell that his personality was larger than life, and as cheesy as it sounded, he looked like he was carved by angels. He was one of those perfect people you instantly knew would never even glance in your direction.

Ten seconds after I clapped eyes on him, I was imagining our wedding. My stomach somersaulted when I pictured his white blond hair standing out against his black tuxedo as we said, "I do". How his grey eyes would stare into mine as he declared his undying love for me to the world. How his plump rosy lips would feel like velvet as they claimed mine in a heated kiss. How his smile would erase my every worry and fear and replace it with hope. How his large hand would hold mine when we strolled down the street.

It took a further ten seconds for me to realise I never stood a fecking chance. Nearly every girl in our class, and probably the whole bloody school, most likely had the same thoughts as I did because they jumped to be the first one to grab and hold his attention.

It was mortifying to admit it to myself, but Damien consumed a huge part of my life, and we were *barely* even friends. If that didn't label me as pathetic, then I didn't know what would. Thankfully, no one knew about my embarrassing infatuation ... except for Bronagh, who was too attentive for her own good.

"Alannah." She bumped my leg with hers. "What're you sighin' for?"

I turned my attention to her. "Huh?"

"You keep sighin'."

I do?

"Sorry, I'm just thinkin'."

Bronagh stared at me with a perfectly shaped brow raised in question.

"About Damien?"

I felt my cheeks burn with heat. Bronagh was my best friend, but that title was new, so she didn't really know the depth of my feelings for Damien. No one did, and if I had my way, no one ever would.

"Yeah," I mumbled. "About Damien."

Bronagh simpered. "You're so cute when you blush."

'Cause that's what every eighteen-year-old girl wants to be viewed as. Cute.

I playfully kicked at her. "Leave me alone."

"Sorry," she said, amusement gleaming in her bright green eyes. "I forget how ... much of an introvert you are."

"I'm *so* not an introvert. You are."

"Me?" Bronagh gleefully laughed. "Are you serious?"

I nodded. "Which one of us kept to 'erself for *years*?"

"I was *purposely* blockin' everyone out, though; you weren't."

I didn't reply, so Bronagh raised her brow once more and stared at me, a knowing grin on her rose-coloured lips.

"Fine," I grumbled. "I'm a *little bit* of an introvert, but it suits me fine. When I try to be outgoin', it fails, so keepin' to one's self is a safe bet."

"When did it ever fail?"

When *hadn't* it failed was the real question she should have asked.

I rolled my eyes. "With Damien."

My friend frowned. "You're his friend, his *only* female friend apart from me, and that's only because I'm with his brother. If I wasn't, he'd probably try to pull me, then never talk to me again when he realised I wasn't interested."

"It's not like we're even real friends, though. I only see 'im outside of school because I'm with you all the time now, and that means I'm also with Nico. And where Nico is, Damien is."

"Alannah—"

"I don't like it when he flirts with me because I know what he wants," I cut Bronagh off, swallowing. "He is so open about not wantin' a relationship longer than a rumble under the bed sheets, but I don't want to *just* have sex with 'im. I don't want to be on his hit list. I really like 'im, and it sucks that he doesn't like me in the same way."

Bronagh reached over and placed her hand on my knee.

"Sorry, Lana. I wish he was different."

"He is great the way he is," I stressed. "But I want 'im to like *me*. I don't wanna be like Destiny or Lexi; they go through lads like it's no one's business, and I can't be like that. I can't be like them just to have his attention. I just ... I just wish I was worth more to 'im than a quick shag ... ye'know?"

Bronagh nodded. "Yeah, I know."

The mood had quickly turned melancholy, and I felt bad.

"I'm sorry, Bee. I'm bummin' you out on your big night."

She tilted her head. "Me big night?"

"Your hoo-ha has been deflowered." I deadpanned. "That means it's a *big* night."

Bronagh widened her eyes before she grabbed a pillow and hit me with it, causing me to sputter with laughter. She hit me with it again, so I squealed and laughed harder.

"You're a bitch."

I smiled wide. "You love me, though."

"Yeah," Bronagh said, sounding like she had just come to some sort of revelation. "I do."

I knew that her accepting me as a friend was a big deal for her, but I knew caring for me was an even bigger deal.

"Hey," I said, gaining her full attention. "I love you too, and that means you're stuck with me for life. Nico will have to get used to me as a third wheel."

My friend snorted. "He thinks you're gorgeous, so he won't mind."

I practically choked on air. "He does *not*!"

"He does," Bronagh tittered. "We randomly talked about it. I'm *totally* cool with you knowin' it too because I know you're the only girl at school who prefers Damien over 'im."

That was the truth.

"Mate," I cringed. "Nico is ... *ew*."

Bronagh cracked up with laughter. "Damien is his *identical twin*. They literally have the same everythin'. Well, not the same hair colour, but everythin' else is the same."

I disagreed.

"When I look at them, I see two completely different people. It's hard to explain, but they're nothin' alike to me even though they have the same everythin'. D'ye see Damien in Nico?"

Bronagh shook her head. "At first, I did, but now, I don't. Dominic has so much personality that his body can't contain it."

"Speakin' of loverboy." My lips curved upwards. "Did it, ye'know, hurt?"

Bronagh's cheeks tinged with redness as she nodded, shyly.

"At first, it pinched, then it was uncomfortable, and then everythin' changed, and it was amazin'. The pain honestly wasn't as bad as I always thought it would be, but if Dominic wasn't so focused on makin' me feel good, I think it just would have just been basic like most people's first time."

"That's good to know." I exhaled. "Maybe I won't be so wound up when I finally lose me own V-card."

"I'm a little sore *now*, but Dominic says that's normal because it was me first time. Eventually, it won't feel uncomfortable at all afterwards. That's what *he* says anyway, but he doesn't have a fanny so I don't even know why I listen to 'im."

I snickered then roamed my eyes over Bronagh as I thought about the new change in her life. She was a young woman whose life had just become very adult with her and Nico's new physical intimacy.

"You'd better go on the pill. Ye'know, just to be safe."

"I know, Branna said she'd take me to the doctor to get a monthly prescription."

"You're a slag," I teased. "Needin' the pill and an *actual* condom supply."

Bronagh's face flared with heat once more, and I momentarily wondered if the colour would ever leave her cheeks.

"Stop it. I get so embarrassed when I think of it. And I'm mortified to be on me own with Dominic again."

I raised a brow. "But he's your *fella*."

"So?" my friend questioned, her cheeks still flushed. "I love 'im, and we're in a relationship, but he just saw me *naked* and took me *virginity*. I can't help but be embarrassed."

"You're so weird, Bee."

Bronagh snorted. "That's nothin' new."

Male laughter from downstairs got my attention, and I quietened down.

"The twin's brothers," I said upon hearing them, "are *a lot* hotter than what you said they were."

"They are?"

I stared at her as if she'd just grown an extra head.

"You said they were good lookin', but babe, they're on *fire*. I've never met men quite like Ryder and Kane before. And Alec? That is too much sexiness to claim one person. Then there are the twins, who are another kind of hot. Their gene pool is bloody amazin'."

Bronagh bobbed her head in agreement. "You should have seen me when I first met them. I stared without blinkin', and I think I even drooled."

"No one would blame you if you did."

My friend laughed. "Are you ready to go?"

I sighed as I pushed myself up from the bed and got to my feet. I straightened out my dress, hoping it wasn't creased.

"I'm as ready as I'll ever be."

Bronagh hesitated. "If you'd rather stay—"

"No, I want to go out. I've never been clubbin' before; it's just ... I hope I don't get upset if Damien pulls a girl. I have no claim on 'im, but I really like 'im, so you can guarantee me emotions will kick off if he pulls. I just hope I don't cry and make a show of meself."

"Ye'know what?" my friend said, sudden confidence filling her tone. "*You* are goin' on the pull tonight. You're goin' to kiss the socks off a lad and forget about Damien Slater."

If only.

"Yeah." I whooped with fake enthusiasm. "Good idea."

Bronagh beamed, pleased with herself.

"Great. Go on down and tell the lads I'm ready. I'm gonna go get some of Branna's perfume and see if she's good to go."

I nodded and left the room. When I reached the ground floor, I turned and walked down the hallway and into the kitchen where I slammed headfirst into one of the Slater brothers. I looked up and found Alec Slater looking down at me with a shit-eating grin on his way too perfect face. He placed his large hands on my shoulders to steady me, and he left them there, which had me freaking out because he was too hot for words to be touching me for any amount of time.

"I'm so sorry," I said rapidly, the words sounding jumbled together. "I wasn't watchin' where I was goin'."

He continued to grin. "Don't worry your pretty little head, sweetheart."

I heard a groan from inside the kitchen followed by some snickering.

"She's barely eighteen, big brother."

It was Nico who spoke, and I wanted to pummel him for embarrassing me.

Alec simply winked at me before he removed his hands from my shoulders, moved around me, and ventured off down the hallway then upstairs. I inhaled and exhaled before I stepped into the kitchen. Without realising it, I turned around to the empty space Alec just vacated and stared as if he would magically reappear.

"He's so feckin' pretty."

I looked to my right when male laughter sounded, and when I found the remaining four Slater brothers staring at me, I widened my eyes.

"Did I say that out loud?"

The group nodded, and I felt blood rush up my neck to my cheeks, which prompted me to place my face in my hands.

"You're doing *much* better than Bronagh, if it's any consolation?" Nico offered. "She stared at all my brothers when she first met them. I'm sure she drooled, too."

I dropped my hands back to my sides, my cheeks still aflame.

"Speakin' of Bronagh, go and put 'er out of 'er misery."

Nico blinked. "You wanna expand on that?"

"She's mortified to see you even though you both ... *ye 'know*."

He smirked. "Yeah, *I know*."

Ryder and Kane shook their heads while Damien bumped fists with his twin as if Nico having sex with Bronagh had put him on some sort of pedestal.

"Go act normal so she can stop freakin' out 'cause when she is freaked, I have to be freaked. Best friend code."

Damien laughed even though his brothers didn't. I felt a surge of pleasure that at least *he* thought I was funny.

"I'll go take care of her," Nico said as he stood, moved past me, and left the room.

When I was alone with the remaining three brothers, I found myself rocking back and forth on my heels. I stopped moving when fear of my ankles giving way under my high heels entered my mind.

"So." I cleared my throat. "You're American."

I cringed at the shocking conversation starter that slipped from my mouth.

"And you're Irish," Kane rumbled. "Now that we've gotten the obvious out of the way, how close are you with Bronagh?"

I wasn't prepared for the question nor the tension in Kane's tone and the accusation in his glaring grey eyes. I clasped my hands together as apprehension filled me.

"Bro," Damien began, but one look from his older brother silenced him.

Kane looked back at me, awaiting my reply, but all I could do was stare at him. He was extremely intimidating. Bronagh had warned me about his appearance, and I knew that his scars wouldn't bother me because his looks didn't define him, but she failed to mention he was a bit of an arsehole.

"Close as new friends can be, I guess," I replied with a shrug of one shoulder.

Kane cocked a brow. "Has she talked to you about us?"

"Us?"

"Me. My brothers."

"Um, no." I blinked. "She told me your names, that you're from New York, and said you're all good lookin', but that's about it."

Ryder smiled and was about to speak, but Kane wasn't finished.

"Are you *gonna* ask questions about us?"

I got the feeling he didn't like me, though I wasn't sure why because he didn't know me.

I swallowed. "No, why would I?"

"Because you're curious."

"About Damien, not you."

I realised what I said the second the words left my mouth, and I wanted the ground to open and swallow me whole because I sounded sassy, and I was *rarely* sassy.

"I didn't mean that like it sounded," I spluttered. "I mean—"

"I know what you mean." Kane cut me off, leaning back in his chair as he eyed me up and down. "You aren't the first girl to be curious about him, and you won't be the last."

"Ryder," Damien grunted. "Do something."

Ryder gave him a slight shake of his head and remained quiet.

"I'm sorry, but have I done somethin' wrong on you?" I asked Kane, hating how uncomfortable he made me feel. "Because if I haven't, then I want to know what the hell your problem is and why I'm bein' interrogated for no bloody reason."

Kane raised his brows in surprise, Ryder grinned, and Damien choked on air.

"I'm just getting a feel for you," Kane replied, his eyes still locked on mine. "I don't know you, you're a stranger."

I honestly thought my heart would explode from apprehension, but I stood my ground.

"Well, you can do it in a polite way *without* the attitude. Introducin' yourself and simply bein' nice is a good way to start. I don't know what Bronagh has said about me, but I'm a nice person who can only take so much nonsense. If you don't have anythin' nice to say to me, don't say anythin' at all. I'll be more than happy to ignore you."

"Well, fuck me."

Kane and Ryder then shared at look and burst out laughing. Meanwhile, I was busy trying to control my breathing and praying to God that I didn't pass out. I didn't do confrontation, and somehow, that was just what I was involved in ... and I think I won.

"I think this conversation is over," I said and left the room in a flustered hurry.

"Thanks a lot!" Damien snapped. "Asshole!"

The laughter continued as I heard a chair scrape across the tiles, footsteps beat against the floor, and felt a presence come up behind me. I turned around just as Damien reached for me. His hand, that I'm sure was intended for my shoulder, latched onto my right breast and shock froze me to the spot.

"I did *not* mean to grab your tit," Damien said, his eyes on mine, and his hand still firmly holding my breast. "I swear."

My pulse sped up.

"It's ... okay," I squeaked. "Don't worry 'bout it."

I looked down at my chest, and when Damien realised he was still holding my breast, he dropped his hand as if it was on fire.

"Shit," he said, flustered. "I wanted to apologise for Kane's behaviour, *not* grope you."

I was so embarrassed that I considered walking out of the house without further words exchanged, but I didn't. Instead, I swallowed and forced a tight-lipped smile.

"It's whatever; he was probably just messin' with me."

"Yeah," Damien lied. "He was just playing with you."

We both knew Kane wasn't playing with me, he grilled me for a reason, but I had no idea what that reason was. I wasn't sure if I wanted to know, either.

"Forget him," Damien continued. "Don't give him a second thought."

Kane Slater wasn't someone you easily forgot.

"Already forgotten," I lied, my forced smile still in place.

Damien stared through my smile. I knew he did because his face softened. He took a step towards me and opened his mouth to speak but was interrupted when Alec jogged down the stairs. I took a step back and nodded at Alec, who moved past us with just a wink in our direction. Damien looked over his shoulder when Alec spoke, and his other brothers laughed.

The three of them then walked out of the kitchen, and Alec continued boasting.

"All I'm saying is little brother has skills that he *obviously* picked up from me. His girl called out to God more times than I could count. He was in control of that puss—"

"Finish that sentence, you slapper, and I will end you!" Bronagh snarled as she descended the stairs with Nico and Branna in tow.

Alec made the motion of sealing his lips, though I doubt he was finished teasing her and Nico about their special night. I wanted to tell him to leave her alone, but I was still shocked and felt out of place over Kane pulling a fast one on me and treating me like I was doing something wrong by being Bronagh's friend.

Damien stepped away from me without a word when Bronagh came to my side and grabbed my hand. I smiled at her and gave her hand a reassuring squeeze.

"Are you ready?"

I exhaled a deep breath as we walked out of her house and into the night.

As ready as I'll ever be.

"I should have stayed at home." Bronagh yawned and stretched. "I'm knackered."

Two hours ago, I would have jumped at the chance to chill in her room and watch a film, but now that I was tipsy and feeling the music in the club, I wasn't letting Bronagh get comfortable enough just in case she *did* fall asleep and had to be taken home.

"Have a drink and loosen up," I suggested, tipping my vodka and Coke in her direction. "This is *fun!*"

Bronagh shot me a look that would silence many people, but not me.

"We have school in the mornin', so I'm passin' on havin' a drink," she said with a raised brow. "You should just stop altogether. Otherwise, you're goin' to be dyin' with a hangover when you wake up."

I didn't want to be reminded of school or anything outside of having adult fun. This was my very first time being in a club and drinking alcohol. I wasn't eighteen yet, so I was convinced I wasn't going to gain entry to the club, but Branna knew one of the bouncers. I think she called him 'Skull', but I hoped I had heard wrong.

Once inside the club, and the drinks started flowing, I began to relax, and I wanted Bronagh to relax too. We would be finished with school in mere months, and I knew both Bronagh and I would do well on our Leaving Certificate exams, so we didn't have to worry about them. The chances of me frequently letting loose like this in the future were slim to none when I started college to pursue my passion of art, so I wanted to *enjoy* it.

"Thanks, Ma." I blew her a kiss. "I'll keep that in mind."

"Bitch!" she stated, making me laugh and her grin.

I glanced to my left and saw Branna on Ryder's lap. They were so completely wrapped up in each other that they didn't notice anyone around them. Alec, Damien, and Nico were off somewhere in the club, and Kane was still seated next to Bronagh. We hadn't spoken since he apologised to me upon entering the club, and I was happy enough to leave it at that for the night. He looked just as done with the club scene as Bronagh was, and he obviously hated being surrounded by so many people, but I refused to let his chilled demeanour rub off on me *or* Bronagh.

"Let's dance," I shouted at my friend. "Right now."

I laughed because I practically felt her sigh even though I couldn't hear it.

"Don't even *think* about sayin' no, Bronagh," I warned. "As new friends, we have to bond, and dancin' helps with that, so *c'mon*."

My friend groaned, and I feared she wasn't going to budge, so I used the only weapon in my arsenal. My eyes. My da had always told me that my eyes would be the death of him because they were big, brown, and as dangerous as a puppy's. I gave Bronagh my best pleading look, and before she even verbally agreed to dance with me, I saw her cave, so I held my hand out to her.

"Okay," she grouched and grabbed my hand. "Let's dance."

Game, set, match.

I cheered in victory, and Bronagh playfully rolled her eyes.

"We will be back later," I said to the table.

Bronagh looked back at Kane, Branna and Ryder when they gave us their attention.

"By later," she said, "she hopefully means after the *next* song."

I burst into laughter, earning a big smile from Bronagh.

"Fat chance of that." I devilishly smiled. "Now, c'mon; I *love* this song!"

I couldn't tell what song was playing, but I knew the beat, and that was enough to get me excited. I danced with Bronagh until my thighs and calves burned from overuse. My feet, that were not used to high heels in any shape or form felt like they were on fire. I was certain I had earned a few blisters too, but I knew if I took my heels off, I'd never put them back on again, so I forced it from my mind. I laughed until my throat hurt, and I tossed back drinks like it was no one's business. I wanted to tell Bronagh how much fun I was having, but I felt a hand grasping my forearm, and it distracted me. The person who had hold of me led me to the middle of the dancing crowd.

"Hey," I shouted and tried to tug my arm free. "Let go."

I looked up at the owner of the hand holding onto me, and when grey eyes and a mop of white hair became clear through my slightly drunken gaze, I beamed.

"Damien!"

I focused on him and found he was smiling down at me, his eyes gleaming with amusement. He was so tall, I had to tilt my head back just to look up at him. He placed his hands on my waist, and without a word, he tugged my body until I was flush against him, and it took my breath away. When I gathered my bearings, I placed my hands on his broad shoulders and bit my lip when I rolled my body against his. I practically felt his moan as his hands on my waist squeezed my flesh.

He said something to me. I saw his lips move, but I couldn't hear him. I got on my tiptoes and shouted, "I can't hear you."

He grabbed my hand and led me off the dance floor. When he

turned to face me, I had no idea what possessed me to do it, but I leaned back up onto my tiptoes, placed my hands on either side of his face, and tugged his head down. I moved in, and pressed my lips against his. Damien froze for a couple of seconds, but then he eagerly responded to my kiss. He wrapped his arms around my body and pulled me as close as he could get me.

"Alannah," I felt him say against my lips.

I pulled back from our kiss feeling breathless, giddy with excitement, and hot to the core.

"That was amazin'," I exhaled. "I knew it would be."

Damien squinted down at me before he grabbed my hand once more and led us over to two huge men who stood outside a door. I avoided looking at both men because they were intimidating. Instead, I silently followed Damien when the men parted and opened the door they seemed to be guarding. We stepped into a hallway, and a veil of silence descended the second the door to the club was closed.

"Me ears are ringin'," I shouted before I remembered I didn't have to.

Damien looked at me and chuckled, then silently led me down the corridor and through the last door. When we stepped into a huge living area, the first thing I spotted was the huge bed. My first reaction upon seeing it should have been uncertainty, but a boost of confidence struck me at that moment and pushed my legs to move toward the bed. When my knees knocked against it, I bent forward and ran my hand over the linen.

Silk.

"This feels good," I hummed. "It's *so* soft."

I heard a sharp intake of breath, and a rush of pleasure shot through me. I knew my dress had hiked up a little bit more than what was decent, and I knew in my bones that Damien could see everything on display.

"Heaven help me."

I stood straight, and without fixing my dress, I turned around.

"Did you say somethin'?"

Damien lifted his arm and ran his hand through his hair, and I realised it was an action I desperately wanted to repeat with my own hands.

"I said," he rumbled, "Heaven help me."

"Why do you need help?" I asked dumbly, tilting my heard. "You aren't in trouble."

"On the contrary." Damien licked his lower lip. "I think I'm in a whole heap of trouble."

I followed his tongue movement with my eyes, and my mouth ran dry.

"What trouble would that be?"

"The five-foot-five, black hair, and brown eyes kind."

Butterflies exploded in my belly.

"You think *I'm* trouble?"

"Babe." Damien chuckled. "I think you're the definition of it."

How can that be?

"I think you have me confused with someone else," I said, falling into a sitting position on the bed when I tried to take a step back. "I've never been in trouble in me whole life."

"No, I'm sure you haven't," Damien agreed, his lips twitching. "But I think you could stir up a lot of it."

"Yeah?" I questioned. "Like what?"

"Like how one kiss has me wanting to touch you in ways you've never been touched."

My heart slammed into my chest.

"H-how do ye'know what ways I've been touched?" I stammered. "I could have already been touched in every way possible."

"*Babe*," he said as his cheeks dimpled.

I felt a blush burn its way up my neck as he acknowledged my virginity with one word and a damn smirk.

"Fine." I licked my lips. "No one else has touched me, but *I've* touched me an awful lot."

The look of desire that Damien shot my way sent shivers up my spine.

"Why don't you change the former and touch me?"

His face lost all traces of amusement.

"Be careful, freckles," he warned. "I think we should just cool it and talk—"

"I don't want to talk." I cut him off. "I want to kiss you, to touch you ... I want ... I want to get into trouble with you."

"My *God*." He groaned and put his face in his hands. "You aren't a sex only girl, Lana. You're the flowers, chocolate, cuddle nights in, and steady boyfriend kind of girl. And I love that about you, but I can't give you that."

I frowned.

"Don't look at me like that," Damien said, looking flustered. "I'm trying to do right by you. I'm trying to convince myself that you don't really want me like this—"

"I do." I cut him off once more. "I know your situation, and I'm not a fool. I know it's just sex with you, but I want you so much that I'll take it."

I recalled my earlier conversation with Bronagh. I said I didn't want Damien to want me just for sex, that I didn't want to be another name on his hit list, but I had a strong desire to experience him in any capacity I could. I'd deal with the consequences later.

"This was a bad idea. I shouldn't have brought you in here." He began to pace. "I just wanted to talk to you, but *damn*, you look edible, and you smell and taste so good, it's all I can do to stay on this side of the room."

"C'mere to me," I beckoned. "Don't think about the after, think about now. If I'm angry later, it's on me. This is probably a stupid idea, but I've never needed someone like I need you. If this is a mistake, let me make it and learn from it."

"You've been drinking," Damien said flatly. "I tasted it on you."

"I've sobered up a hell of a lot since you told me I was trouble."

"You *are* trouble."

"Prove it," I challenged.

Damien took a step forward, then hesitated before he said, "Let's just chill and talk for a while. Just ... just to see if this is what you really want."

The words were hardly out of his mouth before I turned and scrambled up the bed, flopping onto my back.

"What are you doing?"

"What do you mean?" I asked, holding my position. "I'm chillin'."

Damien folded his thick arms across his broad chest, the corners of his lips quirked.

"You usually chill on a bed with your thighs parted?" he asked, a slight hint of laughter in his tone.

"This is how I lie on me bed. It's kind of ... freein'."

Damien dropped his gaze from my eyes to my parted thighs. I saw his Adam's apple bob as he swallowed. He quickly crossed the room, turned his back to me, and sat on the edge of the bed. Without turning around, he patted the spot next to him and said, "Come here and talk to me. I want to hear your voice."

I practically floated to his side, and it made Damien laugh.

"What do you want me to say?" I said, a little breathless.

Damien turned his gaze on me, and as he looked into my eyes, he said, "Say anything. I just want to hear your voice. I love your voice."

I felt as if the air had been sucked from the room.

"You do?"

Damien licked his lips. "Yeah, I hear your voice even when you aren't around."

My heart slammed against my chest.

"You do?" I repeatedly nodded for an unknown reason.

"I hear you when it's quiet," he said, dropping his gaze to my lips. "Really quiet."

I lazily dragged my tongue across my lower lip, watching Damien's pupils dilate as his eyes followed the movement.

"What do I say when you hear me voice?" I asked; my voice

sounding thick with desire.

Damien huffed a laugh. "You don't want to know, freckles."

I scrunched up my face in displeasure. "Why do you call me that?"

He lifted his hand, and with his pinkie finger, he ran the tip over my nose and underneath my eyes.

"You have a splash of freckles right here."

"If you say you think they're cute," I grunted. "I may slap you."

Damien simpered. "Cute is *not* a word I associate with you."

My pulse spiked.

"What word do you associate with me?"

"I have a few," he replied, lowering his hand from my face. "Smart, funny, hard-working ... beautiful, elegant, sexy as sin."

I gasped. "You think I'm funny?"

Damien almost instantly burst into laughter.

"Hell yes, you're funny." He shoulders shook as he laughed. "Out of all the words I said, you picked funny."

I blushed. "No one has ever said I was funny before."

"Well, you are."

I leaned in a little closer to him. "You think I'm beautiful and elegant?"

"And sexy as sin," he replied, his voice raspy. "Can't forget about that."

I smiled, and I heard a little groan come up Damien's throat like he was straining to contain it. I stood from the bed and kicked my heels off before I turned to face him. I groaned, and looked down at my feet as I wiggled my toes.

"Jesus, it feels good to take those hell blocks off."

"Hell blocks?"

"Until you've walked in high heels," I playfully glared at Damien, "you will never understand how much they hurt."

"It's a good thing I'm tall then."

"Hmmm." I licked my lower lip. "It's *definitely* a good thing that you're tall."

"You're looking at me like you want to pounce on me, freckles."

"I do."

Damien's whole body tensed. I stared down at him, and in that moment, I made the decision to freely give myself to him. I couldn't stand wanting him anymore, I needed to have him.

My body felt like it was a live wire of electricity. I wanted Damien to kiss me and touch me more than my next breath. I didn't want him to make the first move; I was too aware of him to allow that to happen. Instead, I stepped forward, parted his thighs with my knees, and stepped between them.

"Alannah, what are—"

I brought my mouth down on top of his and took what I'd wanted since the first moment I saw him. I lifted my hands, thrust them into his hair, and almost dropped to my knees with desire. His hair was thick and soft—so freaking soft. I tangled my fingers around the strands and tugged.

"You're playing a dangerous game with me, Lana," Damien said against my lips, his voice husky. "I'd walk away if I were you."

Boldness surged through me.

"That sounds like a challenge to me."

"Talking." Damien groaned into my mouth. "We're supposed to be talking."

"We are," I replied, sliding my tongue over his lower lip. "We're talkin' with our bodies."

Ursula from *The Little Mermaid* did say never to underestimate the importance of body language, and at that moment, I had never related to a Disney quote more in my entire life.

Damien broke our heated kiss and stared up at me, his expression one of shock. It was quickly replaced by one so full of heat and longing that by the time he drew me against him, I was trembling with anticipation.

"I want you so much," he breathed. "God knows I've dreamed of touching you, kissing you, tasting you."

I had to lock my knees together to keep from falling to them.

"What will you do to me if I let you touch me?" I asked, my voice thick with desire. "I need to hear it."

"I'd kiss you. Nice and slow until my lips are all you know. My hands would explore every inch of you until you only knew my touch. I'd love you so good, the feel of me would be imbedded into you for life. I'd make your body *mine*."

"Yes," I whimpered. "Please, I want that."

More than my next breath.

Damien pulled me against him and covered his mouth with mine. He growled against my lips before he stood. Hooking his hands around the back of my thighs, he picked me up as he moved. I gasped into his mouth, latching my arms around his neck and wrapping my legs around his waist.

"I love how tall you are," I panted, pulling back to gaze at him. "It makes me feel tiny."

"You *are* tiny," Damien said, pushing my dress up with one hand so he could palm my behind.

He touched his lips to mine once more, moulding them together as his tongue slid inside in a kiss so ravenous it caused my spine to arch, my heart to slam into my chest, and my skin to flush with pleasure. My thoughts were scattered with every thrust and slide of his tongue, licking against my own. Damien's kiss was so consuming I didn't know where I ended and he began.

"You're so gorgeous," I blurted against his lips. "And I love your hair. It's so feckin' pretty and soft. What conditioner do you use? Actually, never mind. I love your face. My *God,* do I love your face. Your dimples are stunnin'."

I felt Damien's laughter vibrate against my lips before he kissed down my jawline to my neck where he feathered kisses over my skin, causing goosebumps to break out over my body.

"You wouldn't *believe* the things I've dreamed of doin' to you and you doin' to me," I purred, hoping to God I sounded sultry.

Damien scraped his teeth over my sweet spot, and it caused my back to arch, which pushed my breasts against him. His hands on my behind squeezed me tightly.

"Why don't you tell me in detail what you've dreamed of us doing?" he asked. "*I* need to hear *that*."

"You used your m-mouth on me," I stammered. "And when I thought that would kill me, you added your fingers and use them both to make me scream."

Damien lightly bit my neck, encouraging me to continue.

"Your tongue." I hummed. "You'd lick, and suck, and taste me all over until I was putty in your hands"

I sucked in a sharp breath when Damien suddenly turned and dislodged my arms and legs from around him as he pushed me from his body and onto the mattress with a bounce. He rid himself of his shirt with one tug, and watching that sent a shiver up my spine.

"You're perfect," I said, staring up at him. "*Fuck*, you're perfect."

His tanned skin seemed to glow in the lighting as strands of his white hair fell forward into his eyes. He lifted a hand to push them away, and the flex of his bicep had my insides clenching with need. His broad shoulders were begging for my teeth to sink into them, and the lines of his abdominal muscles taunted my fingers to run over them.

You have no idea what you're doing to me.

"Perfect?" he repeated as he gripped the hem of my dress and pushed it up to my waist. "No, baby, that'd be you."

Without a single word, he gripped the top of my dress, pulled the straps down my shoulders, and tugged the material down until my bare breasts were free. I didn't wear a bra with my dress—I didn't need to—and if Damien's groan was anything to go by, he seemed to appreciate that. He left my dress bunched up at my waist and leaned back on his heels so he could roam his eyes over me.

"You're stunning, Lana."

My body hummed with delight as he slid his hands up my thighs, skimmed my stomach, and flattened them over my breasts.

He cupped them, giving them a gentle squeeze before he ran his thumbs over the hardened, sensitive pink tips. The tingling sensation drew a slight moan from me as heat pooled between my legs, an incessant throb growing with each tantalising touch.

I felt my cheeks burn when his gaze locked on the centre of my thighs.

"Lace?" he questioned without looking at me.

"I like pretty u-underwear."

"So do I." Damien looked up at me with fire in his eyes. "Christ, I'll never get this image of you out of my head."

I didn't want him to.

"What are you goin' to do to me?" I asked, my voice barely a whisper.

He licked his lips. "What I've wanted to do to you from the first moment I saw you."

"What's that?"

I shrieked when he gripped the hem of my underwear and yanked them from my body. If the rustled sound of fabric tearing was anything to go by, I'd say he even ripped them in the process. I could barely breathe when my thighs were parted, and Damien brought his face down to my pussy. He inhaled deeply, and I knew mortification at that moment.

"Damien!" I cried and desperately tried to shut my legs, but he didn't let me. "Why are you sniffin' me? Oh, God! Do you have a weird fetish or somethin'?"

He chuckled but didn't move a muscle other than when he stopped me from wriggling.

"No," he mused. "I'm savouring how you smell because it's damn good."

If I ever spoke to him again after this, it would be too soon.

"This is indecent!" I stated, my entire face burning. "You can't just ... Damien!"

The first flick of his hot, wet tongue was unexpected, and oh so delicious.

"Holy Mary, Mother of God."

"Pray to whoever you want, freckles. No one can save you from me now."

With that said, he began to lick and suck on my pussy lips, then he used his tongue to part them. I felt myself go cross-eyed, and it was all I could do not to buck my hips in his face. His tongue slid up the trail of slick heat until he curled it around my clit and gifted me with a sensation I never knew existed.

I reached down with my hand, tangled my fingers in his hair, and held on for dear life.

He applied pressure as he swirled his tongue around the sensitive bud, and the action sucked the air out of me. It was too much sensation—too much of a new sensation—for my body to handle. I couldn't lie still, so Damien hooked his arms around my thighs and applied heavy-handed pressure on them, which helped to keep me in place.

"*Dame, Dame, Dame, Dame*," I panted as my breathing turned irregular. "Oh!"

His response was to shake his head from side to side rapidly, flicking his tongue over my clit as he moved. It sent shocks of bliss shooting up my spine.

"Oh God!" I shouted at the new sensation of pure desire it brought. "Oh God, oh God, oh *God*!"

I screamed for only a second before I sucked in air, holding it in my lungs as mounting pleasure suddenly caused my thighs to quiver with anticipation. For a second, I felt a sharp sensation close to pain and then numbness, before a thrashing of what I could only describe as Heaven washed over me. Then a throbbing of delight exploded through me. My muscles contracted in response as if they were cheering on the sensation that curled around them.

I released the breath I was holding when my lungs demanded I do so. I didn't even realise I had closed my eyes, but I couldn't open them if I wanted to, so it didn't even matter. My limbs became lax as all traces of energy fled, and it was all I could do not to fall asleep.

"You're so beautiful, freckles." Damien's voice rasped as he parted my thighs farther apart. "I'm sorry if this is uncomfortable."

That was the only warning he gave me before my insides tensed as they were stretched and invaded. My eyes flew open, and a strangled whimper passed my lips. My hands latched onto Damien's thick arms as he stilled inside me, and my back arched as a slight pinch of pain cut through my core.

"It'll pass," he whispered, his voice hoarse. "Give it a second."

He lowered his head and kissed me with so much tenderness and care it was easy to focus on his lips instead of the discomfort. He whispered words of encouragement against my swollen lips and brushed the tip of his nose against mine, then rested his forehead on mine and stared deeply into my eyes.

We were one at that moment.

Before long, I wriggled my hips, pulling a pained groan from Damien who was trying his hardest to remain as still as a statue. I wriggled once more and only felt a slight bit of discomfort, but to my surprise, the pinch of pain had subsided completely. The second I hummed, Damien took it as a green light to move. When he withdrew slowly and thrust back in, my muscles tightened.

It didn't hurt, but it didn't exactly feel good either.

"Relax, baby," he rasped. "You're squeezing me like a vice."

"*You* relax!" I countered. "It feels like a melon is bein' shoved up me."

Damien had the nerve to chuckle, and it held my attention, but when he withdrew and thrust back into my body, I allowed my head to fall back against the bed as I moaned. He fell into a rhythm, and it took away my ability to think coherently, let alone speak.

"Christ," Damien breathed as he lowered his head and planted kisses along my neck. "You feel incredible."

I lifted my legs and wrapped them around his hips, hooking my ankles to lock them in place. I couldn't control how vocal I was, especially when every thrust sent a ripple of shivers through my body and made me hungry for more.

"Oh!" I gasped when a lick of pleasure curled around my inner muscles.

"Yeah," Damien rasped. "*Oh!*"

"Keep doin' that." I panted. "Oh, keep doin' *that*!"

"I couldn't stop if you paid me," Damien replied, sweat beading on his forehead.

Fast and hard poundings replaced the slow and gentle thrusts. I dug my fingers into Damien's flesh when the desire to bite something struck. I tried to hold back, but I couldn't. Like an animal, I leaned forward and latched my teeth onto his neck and bit down. Damien thrust into me so hard in response a resounding *slap* echoed in the room.

"*Fu...ck*! Uh, *yeah*! You're going to ruin me for any other woman."

I bloody well hoped so.

"God, I could keep you forever," he proceeded to say, his voice thick with passion.

I released him and pressed my forehead to his as I swallowed. "Will you keep me?"

"Yes." He panted, nudging my face with his. "God, yes. You're mine."

My heart thumped with delight, and a huge smile overtook my face. It was quickly wiped away when scorching heat spread over my body like butter, causing goose bumps to break out on my skin. My mouth suddenly opened in a silent scream when a rumble started in my core and kept building until an explosion of light burst from within me. The pleasure that began to ripple through my body sent small spasms rolling through my limbs and left me trembling.

When I came to, I was repeating Damien's name.

"Yes, yes," he panted as my inner walls clenched around him.

"You promise to keep me?" I asked as he pumped into me harder, faster, deeper.

"Yes," he almost shouted. "I promise. *Lana!*"

His movements became frantic then, and just as his thrusts

slowed and turned to twitches, I watched the sensations overtake his body and play out like a film on his handsome face. His eyes closed, he bit down on his lower lip; his cheeks flushed a pretty shade of pink, his brows furrowed, and his muscles tensed. Ten or so seconds later, it was like every ounce of tension that had worked its way onto his face melted away and spread over his body like a deep tissue massage.

It was the only warning I got before he fell forward.

"Damien!" I laughed as the air was knocked out of me.

All his weight was on me, and while I loved it, it was too much for my chest to handle. I nudged him, and he groaned as he used his elbows to prop himself up, taking most of his weight off me.

"Hi." I smiled up at him.

My mind, body, and heart were so content and blissful that nothing could have ruined the moment.

"I didn't mean to say that," Damien said, his eyes flashing with ... terror.

Except that.

"Say what?"

"That stuff," he said, clearing his throat. "About keeping you."

A feeling of sickness began to form in the pit of my stomach.

"Damien," I whispered. "Can you not say that while you're still *inside* me?"

He looked down at our still connected bodies and quickly pulled out of me. I winced, and he apologised. I was lying on the bed sheets, so I had nothing to cover myself except my hands. Damien disposed of the now used condom—a condom I didn't even know he'd put on—and began to dress at a shocking speed. Beginning to panic, I felt like I should do the same, so I joined him in fixing my dress until we were dressed and looking as we did when we entered the room—just a little less put together.

"I don't understand what is happenin'," I said as I slid my feet back into my high heels, they screamed in protest. "Are you okay?"

"I shouldn't have said that shit."

Striking me would have hurt less.

I flinched. "Don't say that."

"I have to; otherwise, you'll believe it."

"So, what? I'm not to believe that you said you'd keep me?" I demanded. "That you *promised* to? What the hell did you say it for then?"

"Alannah, I would have agreed to anything at that point during sex," he said, flatly. "I couldn't help it. My mind and body were both focused on the sensation, and my voice took on a role of its own."

I felt like I would throw up.

"You're ruinin' this!" I said, my lower lip wobbling. "You're ruinin' everythin' about me first time. Why are you doin' this to me?"

Damien's face blanched. "I'm sorry, but I won't lie to you."

"What's the lie?"

"When I promised to keep you."

I felt my eyes well with tears.

"Damien," I whispered.

"It's not that I *can't* keep you, Lana; it's that I don't *want* to."

He couldn't look me in the eyes as he spoke the words I knew I'd never forget. The force of it had me stumbling back a few steps as if he'd struck me. I probably had no right to feel betrayed, but I did, and it hurt more than I cared to admit.

"I'm goin' to get c-cleaned up," I stammered, trying to hold back the tears I wanted to shed.

"No." Damien frowned. "Please, we have to talk about this. What I mean is—"

"I don't think anythin' you have to say will make me feel better." I cut him off, trying my hardest to keep my emotions in check.

"Alannah—"

"It's fine."

"It's fucking *not*," he countered. "I knew this was a bad idea. Just look at how upset you are! This is why I've tried to stay away from you. You're a good girl, and I knew you'd let your emotions take centre stage. This was a mistake!"

His words were the truth, and I think that was why they pained me so much.

"You were right. This was a mistake, but I've made it." I swallowed. "And I'll learn from it, too."

Damien reached for me, but I moved farther away from him and headed towards the door I assumed led to a bathroom.

"I don't want to speak to you anymore, Damien," I said as I opened the door. "Just ... Just go away. Please."

I never wanted to speak to him again.

"Lana."

"Alannah," I said, my hold on the door handle tightening. "Me name is *Alannah*."

I entered the bathroom, closed the door behind me, and locked it. Numbly, I relieved myself and cleaned up as best as I could with small pieces of tissue paper. The evidence of blood reconfirmed that Damien had just taken my virginity, and it brought a bitter taste to my mouth. Instead of leaving the bathroom, I leaned my back against the wall and slid down it until my behind hit the floor.

I wasn't sure how long I sat there, but it was long enough for the tears that flowed from my eyes and splashed onto my cheeks to dry. Between my thighs felt strange—like a sweet tenderness I couldn't shake. I thought I heard raised voices, and when I heard a knock on the door, I flinched.

"Lana?" I heard my name being softly spoken. "It's me. Can I come in?"

Bronagh.

I stood, moved over to the door, unlocked it, and then sat on the closed lid of the toilet. Bronagh entered the bathroom and quickly closed and locked the door behind her. She kicked off her heels, bent down to her knees, and then reached forward and engulfed me in a tight hug. When I put my arms around her, I released a pain-laced sob.

At that moment, I was both hurt and mortified. I realised I had thrown myself at Damien like I had no shame, and now, shame was all that filled me. I couldn't begin to form the words to tell Bronagh how forward I behaved for fear that she would judge me, so I kept my mouth shut.

"It's goin' to be okay, Lana. You're strong and won't let an annoyin' American prick get you down, right?"

I managed a snort as I pulled back from our hug. I grabbed some tissue to wipe the snot running from my nose. I was a mess, and I knew I looked as bad as I felt.

"Ye'know somethin'?" I sniffled. "I know Nico is your fella, but I thought he was the prick and Damien was the nice one. I was so wrong. Nico is honest and has always been 'imself whether you like 'im or hate 'im. Damien, though ... he is like a snake in human form. I hate 'im."

I couldn't fault Damien for being upfront before we had sex, but the lies he spewed during and the bullshit shit excuse he had for saying them afterward angered me.

"If it makes you feel better," Bronagh interjected. "Dominic really *is* a prick, I had a huge fight with 'im before I came in 'ere."

I started laughing through my tears, but I frowned when Bronagh sat down on her behind and winced at the contact. It was a reminder that she was no longer a virgin either, but her first time had been magical, while mine had the magic sucked from me ten seconds after ending.

"I just realised we both lost our virginity tonight to the twins."

"Well ... at least we can be sore and hate them together."

I was still upset—that didn't even begin to cover it—but I laughed at Bronagh's joke, and the carefree sound helped a tiny bit. Even with my friend by my side making me laugh, I couldn't help but feel like a layer of stone had just sealed itself over my heart. I silently vowed that I would never willingly put myself in a situation where I would feel pain like this again.

Fool me once, shame on you; fool me twice, shame on me.

I called Bronagh's name when the silence surrounding us was

snatched away, and a loud thumping noise could be heard from outside. I didn't know how I knew, but I knew Damien had left the room with the door open and fled down the corridor and back into the club. Getting as far away from me as he possibly could.

The fucking coward.

Bronagh looked at me when I spoke.

"Yeah?"

"Are you ready to go back outside?" I quizzed. "I can hear 'RAMPAGE' bein' cheered now that they've stopped the music for the fight."

Things were a blur of activity as Bronagh jumped to her feet, put her heels back on, and pulled me out of the room and back down the corridor to the club. Bodies of all shapes and sizes crowded around the platform where Nico and another fighter stood. I couldn't concentrate with the noise and sea of people surrounding me, so when Bronagh broke through the crowd to reach Nico after he won the fight, I stayed just long enough to hug her when she returned to my side. The second she became solely focused on Nico, I slipped away from her and headed out of the club.

When I got outside, no one was around, not even the bouncers who had granted us entrance to the club hours before. I was glad to have a moment's solitude so I could try to wrap my head around what happened. I sat on the curb and fought off a fresh batch of tears.

This is a disaster.

There was never going to be a 'Damien and Alannah' in the way I wanted, and he made sure of that. No, *we* made damn sure of that. He took my virginity, but I was the eejit who practically begged him to take it. For that, I had no one to blame but myself ... and my godforsaken hormones.

Damien pursued our intimacy with no illusions or lies coated in pretty words—until he got what he wanted. Beforehand, he said he didn't want a relationship, he just wanted sex, and for me to feel so broken over him keeping his word was foolish. In the back of my mind, I'd silently hoped that once we had sex, Damien would want to be with me. If *that* wasn't the dumbest misconception filling the heads of teenage girls around the world, then I didn't know what was.

The pain in my chest was nothing like I had ever felt before, and I didn't know how to deal with it. I needed Bronagh. I needed my friend. I heard a noise behind me, and I wasn't sure why, but because I thought of Bronagh, I just assumed it would be her. I wanted to look around, but a sudden case of dizziness struck me, and I had trouble remaining upright. Just when I thought my head and vision were clearing, I felt a hard knock on the back of my head like someone had hit me, and it was followed by my body falling backwards.

It didn't hurt, and the first thing I thought of was that if someone hadn't hit me then I was passing out because I had drunk alcohol for the first time. I figured my emotional roller coaster had pushed my body into stress-out mode, and as a result, my mind just switched off. I was glad of it. I was glad when I found myself facing darkness because, at the current moment, darkness was a more welcoming sight than the thought of Damien Slater. But I wasn't granted that peace. Before I completely lost consciousness, the last thing I heard was his words.

It's not that I can't *keep you, Lana; it's that I don't* want *to.*

Damien didn't want me, but what hurt the most was that I knew deep down, I'd always want him no matter what happened between us. I'd never let him or anyone else know it, though. Damien might have hurt me, but I would *never* give him the opportunity to do it again.

He said he didn't want me, and for as long as I lived, I'd never forget it.

CHAPTER ONE

Present day...

I awoke with a start.

I shot upright and placed a hand on my chest, feeling my heart slam into my ribcage as it pounded erratically. My breathing was laboured, and instead of waking from a dream, it sounded like I had just completed a marathon. I closed my eyes and tried desperately to calm myself to no avail.

I hated when tears suddenly welled in my eyes, and I couldn't stop them from spilling over the brims and splashing onto my cheeks in big fat droplets. I sniffled as I carelessly wiped them away with the back of my hand. I raised my knees to my chest and hooked my arms around them, hugging them tightly.

Even in sleep, I was miserable.

Both my personal life and family life were falling apart around me, and it seemed everything I did to stop disaster from striking was only adding fuel to the fire and destroying everything I cared about faster. At the moment, my personal life was in tatters and took centre stage.

Almost every single night for the last few months, I'd relived the night I lost my virginity in detail. I hadn't dreamt about that night in a long time, but the recent appearance of *him* back in my life seemed to bring it all tumbling back down on top of me like an avalanche of emotions I couldn't escape.

I closed my eyes, and as usual, every thought switched to him. *Damien Slater.*

I didn't *want* to think about him, but it seemed I had no choice in the matter because my mind always drifted to him. To be so hung up on the boy who broke my heart in secondary school was pathetic, and I knew it was, but I couldn't seem to get over it, no matter how hard I tried. I had accepted it, of course, but I could never get over the pain I felt when I thought about him and what happened between us.

I opened my eyes and scowled at myself, like always, when I realised how much of a gobshite I was. I had lost count of the times I wished to go back in time and slap myself silly for making the stupid decision that messed up everything. I closed my eyes once more, leaned back against my headboard, and clenched my teeth when Damien's handsome face flashed across my mind.

The bastard was haunting me.

Half of the time, I didn't know where to start when I thought of him. He was in my life for such a short amount of time, yet he had such a significant impact on it. My involvement with him shaped the woman I had become. As much as I hated to give him any credit, he was the reason I'd never let another person get intimately close to me. It was because of him that I built the walls high around my bruised heart.

I hadn't always been so guarded, though. For a long time after he left me, left the poxy country, thoughts of him would consume me until I was sure all that remained was puddles of tears. That boy ... no, that *man* ... broke my heart, and I let him do it. Not only did I let him ruin me, but I also practically begged him to do so. My teenage infatuation with him went far beyond one's first heartbreak because before we became intimate, I cared for him deeper than a new friend should have.

I saw the best in Damien even when he didn't see it in himself.

Six years ago, I gave my heart and body to the new womaniser at school, and when he rebuffed my heart and only ac-cepted my body, I shouldn't have been surprised, but I was. I was devastated. I felt like I was cheated out of a magical first sexual experience because Damien became a completely different person after we had sex and didn't remain the sweet boy who promised to keep me when I asked him to. The words he spoke were lies laced around fiery passion.

Lies. Lies. Lies.

"Stupid girl," I cursed myself.

I pushed my bed covers away from my body and got to my feet. Rubbing my tired eyes as I walked forward. I ended up walking head first into my wardrobe when I misjudged the location of my bedroom door. I hissed in pain as I moved my fingers from my eyes to the now throbbing spot on my forehead. I looked over my shoulder, and through the dark, I glared at my ajar bedroom door.

The layout of my new apartment was still taking some getting used to.

I had recently moved into a spacious two-bedroom apartment in Upton thanks to one of my best friends, Aideen Collins. I had mentioned to her that I needed to move out of my old apartment due to a ridiculous rent increase, and she told me a newly furnished apartment was available in her building for the same price I had always paid in rent. I couldn't believe my luck when I found it had two large bedrooms instead of one single room, and a separate sitting room and kitchen that were both more than generous in size. The furnishings were stunning, too. I practically leapt onto the estate agent who showed me around and told her I'd take it.

That was a month ago, and I was still walking into things during the night. I put it down to my recurring dreams—no, not dreams, *nightmares*—and simply hoped that they would stop; otherwise, my friends would start to think I was secretly getting beat up if fresh bruises kept appearing on my face. I could say "I walked into my wardrobe" only so many times before they got suspicious.

I left my bedroom, flipping the light switch as I went, and headed into my bathroom where I relieved myself. After I washed and dried my hands, I heard a ping come from my bedroom. The sound had me furrowing my eyebrows as I walked over to my nightstand. I picked up my phone, removed the charging wire from its base, and pressed the home button. I sighed when I saw I had received a text, a text from a person who I didn't want to speak to.

Dante Collins.

I touched the screen to open his message and rolled my eyes as I read the text.

Booty call?

For the first time in days, I hit reply to a message.

No, thanks. Our 'booty calls' have become a problem.

The problem being that all my friends and Damien now knew about a relationship I wanted to be kept private. I sighed, sitting on the side of my bed, and kept my gaze downcast. One week ago, I was only dealing with family drama, but now, I had to add fuck buddy and ex-lover drama to the mix. I never thought I'd willingly *want* to be plagued with just the guilt of knowing my father was having an affair and doing nothing about it, but dealing with that and now the drama with Damien and my friends made me want to get into bed and stay there forever.

I lay back on my mattress, staring up at the ceiling, and thought back to a week ago.

CHAPTER TWO

Starting out like any other day, I woke up, had breakfast, and then spent most of the day flicking back and forth between sketching, painting, and designing a website for a client. My work had been the only escape from my life as of late, so I tended to immerse myself in it as often as I could, especially with the knowledge of my father's secret affair.

I was doing a good job of blocking it all out when Bronagh sent me a text message and asked me to hang out with her and Georgie. We spent the morning together, and as usual, we had fun. It all went wrong when we stopped by Ryder and Branna's house at lunchtime. Damien was there, and he was his usual friendly self. However, my past with him made me suspicious of that friendly behaviour.

He was trying with me.

I knew he was trying, but I didn't know *what* he was trying. He could have genuinely just wanted to be my friend, but in the back of my mind, I was reminded that the last time he wanted to simply be 'just my friend', I was left heartbroken and humiliated to boot. For that reason alone, I kept him at arm's length. If he walked into a room, I walked out of it. If he struck up a conversation with me, I politely shut him down. If he looked at me, I made it a point to look away and ignore him. I had been doing it since he returned home over a year ago, but a week ago, something in my attitude towards him changed.

He asked me out for lunch, and I suddenly felt like my private relationship with Dante was a noose around my neck. It was a bizarre feeling, but I felt like Damien had a right to know I wasn't available. Not because Dante and I were in a friends-with-benefits relationship, but because I didn't want him to have the false hope that something might develop between us. Not that he *had* any hope at all or wanted anything other than a real friendship, but I wanted to be as upfront with him as he had always been with me.

I knew he wouldn't disregard the warning as foolishly as I had.

"How are you goin' to get there?" Aideen had asked me when I told her about my meeting to interview a potential assistant for my graphic design business. "I know your car is at me da's garage gettin' a diesel pump repaired."

"I was goin' to walk."

"I can drop you," Damien offered, straightening up from playing with the kids. "Ry and I don't need to be back to work for an hour and thirty minutes."

I was hesitant. "I don't want to be a bother."

"You're never a bother," Damien said, his cheeks flaring with a little bit of heat. "We can get lunch or something after your interview, if you aren't busy?"

Shite. Shite. Shite.

"I can't."

"Why not?" Damien asked, crossing the room, frowning.

I avoided looking in Aideen's direction, knowing what I was about to say would set her off.

"I'm kind of seein' someone."

Everyone went deathly silent, even the kids; it was like they knew something was up.

"Who?" Bronagh asked first.

"Yeah," Damien said, his voice shockingly low. "Who?"

"It doesn't matter who—"

"It bloody well does!" Bronagh cut me off.

I looked at my friend. "I was goin' to tell you, I promise, but I knew you'd tell Aideen, and I didn't want a big deal made of it."

"Why would she tell me?" Aideen quizzed with furrowed brows. "And why would a big deal be made of it?"

I groaned and put my face in my hands.

"Oh, my God!" Bronagh suddenly gasped. "It's one of 'er brothers, isn't it?"

"What?" Aideen asked, her eyes wide. "You're goin' out with one of me brothers?"

I looked up, and instead of looking at Aideen, I looked at Damien as I said, "Yes."

Damien balled his hands into fists. "Which Collins?"

I swallowed. "Dante."

My chest constricted with pain when I saw the hurt in Damien's grey eyes.

"I have to go," he said and turned to walk out of the room.

On instinct, I grabbed his arm. "Wait. Look, we need to talk."

"No," Damien said and removed my hand from his arm. "We don't."

"Please, I don't know why I've brought this up, but we have to try—"

"I have tried with you." He angrily cut me off. "I've tried to be patient. I've tried to show you how sorry I am for what I did to you. I've tried to befriend you. I've tried to give you space ... I've tried to show you how much I care about you, but you don't want me. I see that now."

"Damien—"

"No, Alannah," he cut me off. "You're with Dante Collins, and I'm done."

"It's not a relationship," I blurted. "We aren't datin'. He is just ... there."

"What the hell does that mean?" Aideen angrily snapped.

I didn't look away from Damien's back.

"He helped me get over you—"

"*By getting* under *him?*" *he snapped.*

I winced. "That's not fair, Damien. You were gone for so long, and we weren't on good terms."

"I left for you!" Damien shouted as he spun around to face me. "When I realised how much I hurt you, when Bronagh told me the things no one else would, I made the decision to leave to better myself but also to give you time. I didn't know how to make things right back then, but I was always going to come back for you, Alannah. I would fix everything, but you've made it so hard."

A lump formed in my throat. "I ... I didn't know."

Damien shook his head. "I have to go."

He turned around and walked out of the kitchen, but I quickly followed him while everyone else stayed rooted to their spot.

"Damien, please," I pleaded, grabbing his arm again.

I could hear the kids begin to cry, most likely from all the shouting.

"Let go, Lana," Damien replied, his tone low.

"No," I stated. "We need to talk."

"What we need to do is be away from each other," Damien replied. "Go to Dante; I'm sure he'll be more than happy to comfort you."

"Damien, stop. You don't mean that."

"Alannah. Let. Go."

"No, I won't."

He turned his head in my direction and stared down at me. I could still see the hurt in his eyes, but there was anger there, too.

"Why do you want to talk all of a sudden?" Damien demanded after a few moments of tense staring. "Why not the first million times I've asked?"

"Because I'm ready to deal with all of this."

"It took you long enough!"

"Don't be nasty," I hit back. "None of this is me fault. I'm the one who was hurt and embarrassed and have been carryin' it around for years, not you."

"Not me?" Damien bellowed. *"I've carried it around since the second I did you wrong, and I fucking know it. I know what I did, and I've tried to make it right, but I can't. You've made it impossible."*

"How?"

"By being with him!" Damien roared. *"I haven't touched anyone since I touched you. I haven't kissed anyone since I kissed you. I haven't looked at another woman since I was fucking eighteen, but that ends tonight. If you have moved on, then so will I."*

I felt my mouth drop open with shock at Damien's admission, and my heart pounded against my chest, but his latter words stuck with me and held my attention.

"Fine," I hollered, but my voice cracked ever so slightly, indicating that I was going to cry. *"Go be with some bitch 'cause I won't be 'ere when you get back. You say you're done? Well, so am I!"*

Damien humourlessly laughed. *"You've been done with me for years, and you know it!"*

I scrubbed my face with my hands, reliving our fight from a few days ago that still felt too fresh to process.

Damien's reaction to my relationship with Dante was unexpected, and quite frankly, it frightened me how much I cared that I had hurt him. After Damien asked me out for lunch, I told him I couldn't go out with him because I was seeing someone, and when I revealed it was Dante, I didn't care that Aideen had reacted badly to the news, I just cared how Damien reacted to it. He reacted worse than I could have ever imagined, and *I* reacted out of fear when he walked away from me.

I tried telling myself that I *wanted* him to walk away from me, I *wanted* him to be done trying to salvage some sort of bond between us, but then when he did those exact things, I panicked.

He had tried talking to me for months about what happened between us, but I shut him down every single time. And when he walked away from me, I wasn't surprised that I was suddenly ready to talk. He had changed his mind, though; he didn't want to talk to me or have anything to do with me. He just threw Dante back in my face, told me he was done with me, and walked away. Afterwards, I immediately went home and spent the remainder of the day crying over Damien.

Something I swore a long time ago I would never do again.

I knew I had done nothing wrong. I was a single woman who could have a relationship with whoever I wanted, but for some reason, the whole situation left a bad taste in my mouth. Not because I was ashamed of hooking up with Dante, but because of his connection to the group. He was my friend's older brother, he was Kane's future brother-in-law, *and* he was Damien and Ryder's co-worker at C.A.R.—Collins Auto Repair.

I didn't want things to be awkward with Aideen, and I was afraid they would be now that she was aware I'd been sleeping with her older brother. Damien and Dante were sure to butt heads at work, too. They never liked each other much before they started working together thanks to a big fight the Slater and Collins brothers had a few years ago, so any hope of them suddenly becoming best friends after how Damien reacted to my sleeping with Dante was off the table.

"Everythin' is so messed up," I said to the empty room.

I felt like I was being punished when I just wanted to not feel so alone.

Dante was the only other person on God's green earth who I had been intimate with since Damien, but unlike Damien, I made sure *not* to form an emotional bond with him. Before, after, or during sex. It was for that reason alone that I had never kissed Dante, not even accidentally.

He knew kissing was a deal breaker for me and was more than happy to oblige that rule if it meant we could tangle between the bedsheets a couple of times a month. Dante joked about my 'using' him from time to time, but I knew he was content with our arrange-ment. He never pushed for more than I offered, and I never offered more than I wanted, and that had worked for us.

Until now.

I sat up and looked down at my phone when it pinged.

What kind of problem?

I sighed. *The kind of problem that sees us returning to being just friends.*

Barely ten seconds had passed before my phone rang, and a quick glance at my screen showed me it was Dante calling. With a groan and a shake of my head, I answered my phone, placed it against my ear, and lay back down.

"Hi."

"Shite, you actually answered. I've been tryin' to get in touch with you for *days*."

I frowned. "I'm sorry, I didn't want to speak to anyone."

"Babe, talk to *me*."

My lips twitched. "I'm not havin' phone sex with you."

Dante barked a laugh. "That'd be weird since we're *just friends* now. I mean, we *are* just friends now, right?"

"Yeah," I mumbled. "I'm goin' to need all the courage I can gather to face Aideen now that she knows. I think I'd die altogether if we continued as we were and she confronted us about it."

"Alannah." Dante chuckled. "Aideen is my *little* sister; she has no say in who I have sex with. Even if she was older, she'd still have no say. I'm an adult."

"That's such a typical brotherly response," I said with a roll of my eyes. "She doesn't care that we had sex; she cares that we did it behind 'er back. She is one of me closest friends, Dante, and she is hurtin' because I basically lied to 'er."

"How do you know she is upset?" he quizzed. "I saw 'er yesterday, and she didn't look mad to me."

"Did she speak to you?"

"Well ... no."

"Look at you?"

"For a split second ... maybe."

"Exactly. I saw it on 'er face when I told Damien I was sleepin' with you," I grumbled. "She wasn't just shocked, she was upset, and I knew it was because she was left in the dark. It was the same look Bronagh and Keela gave me. They were upset I hadn't told them. They didn't voice it, but I know."

"Alannah." Dante sighed. "You don't have to share everythin' with your friends. You're *allowed* to have a private life."

"You don't get it," I said, frustrated. "Me and the girls, we're really close. Nothin' is off limits with us."

It was one of the reasons I loved my friends so much. We could talk about anything, and until I kept my relationship with Dante from them, we had no secrets. I felt fucking awful because of that.

"D'ye want me to talk to me sister?" Dante asked on a sigh.

"It couldn't hurt. Just talk to *her,* though. Not Kane, Ryder, and *especially* not Damien."

"About that." Dante cleared his throat. "I tried to talk to Damien about it at work yesterday, and it ended ... badly."

I closed my eyes. "How badly?"

"He has a black eye, and I've a bruised jaw and busted up nose ... but that's only 'cause of Kane—"

"You fought *Kane*?" I opened my eyes, and facepalmed myself.

"He was tryin' to break up the fight, but I thought he was jumpin' me, and one thing led to another, and his cheek is a little bruised. It's nothin' ... really."

I groaned and let my head fall back.

"This wasn't supposed to happen."

Dante laughed. "Tell me about it."

"I feel like everyone is judgin' me."

"Fuck them," Dante said firmly. "You're a grown woman; you don't need permission to have a private life."

"Easier said than done when it's the older brother of me best friend who I was sleepin' with."

"Look, it's done. We've had sex, but we're not goin' to anymore ... or are we? I just need clarification on the no sex part."

I smiled. "You're such a pig."

"That's not a no on the sex."

"No more sex, *Date*." I chuckled, using his well-known nickname earned from his womanising ways.

"Okay, okay," he placated. "Don't get so down about this, okay? It's not the end of the world, sweetheart."

"I know." I sighed. "It just feels like it."

"D'ye want me to come by? You sound down, and I hate when you're sad."

"Nah, I'm fine," I said, sucking it up. "I'm goin' back to sleep. I have a feelin' Bronagh is goin' to come and kick me arse tomorrow. I've been duckin' 'er for days now, and I know she's reached 'er limit."

"Shite, good luck dealin' with that young one. That's a storm I wouldn't wish on anyone."

I laughed. "Thanks, Date."

"I love ya, gorgeous. Just because we're square now doesn't mean I don't have your back, d'ye hear?"

"Yeah." I smiled. "I hear you, and I love ya, too."

I did love Dante; I just wasn't in love with him, and I knew I never would be.

"If you ever need me, or me cock, I'm 'ere for you. Besties for life."

I laughed. "Good night, you nutter."

I hung up on a snickering Dante and felt a tonne lighter knowing that at least he and I were in a good place. Now, if I could get on the same page with everyone else in my life, things would be hunky-dory. I threw my arm over my face and groaned, knowing in mere hours, at least one of my friends would finally succeed in getting past security in my apartment building and would be banging down my door.

God only knew how I was going to weather hurricane Bronagh.

Jesus, help me.

CHAPTER THREE

"Alannah good-for-nothin' Ryan?"

I flicked my eyes towards the door of my apartment and remained unmoving. I knew who it was, and I knew she knew I could hear her. Being pregnant amplified all her senses like a crazy mama bear even though she was only a few weeks into her second pregnancy. I held my breath and hoped she couldn't smell my fear.

"You might as feckin' well open up 'cause I'm not leavin' and you can't make me."

I needed to remain strong. "Go away, Bronagh."

"Not on your life, ye'spanner," she replied swiftly.

I remained seated.

"Fine." She sighed dramatically. "Leave your *pregnant best friend* out in the corridor where any Tom, Dick, or Harry could get a piece of 'er."

I rolled my eyes but couldn't stop the corners of my lips from twitching.

"The landlord only has four tenants in the entire buildin'," I called out. "Me and Aideen are two of them, and the other two are elderly couples on the lower floors. I'm the only person on this *entire* floor. The landlord isn't in a rush to fill the apartments while most of them are still bein' furnished, so no one is around to hear you, let alone harass you."

My attention returned to the door when a thud sounded followed by the door rattling a little, which told me Bronagh gave it a little kick, and that action made me smile. She never had much patience, and it was beginning to show.

"Can you let me use the jacks at least?" she asked, her tone hopeful. "I won't even look at you. I'll go to the jacks, then I'll come back out 'ere, close the door behind me, and we can start this argument all over again. Promise."

At that, I laughed.

"You're a pain in me arse, Murphy," I grouched as I got up and walked over to the door, unlocked it, and opened it wide.

Bronagh instantly rushed by me and fled down the hallway.

"I wasn't jokin' about needin' the jacks!"

With a smile still on my face, I closed the door, and walked back over to my settee. I sat down, tucked my feet under my behind, and waited for hurricane Bronagh to roll on in. Two minutes later, she returned and went off on me like clockwork.

"You're a selfish bitch," she said as she sat across from me. "D'ye know that?"

"I'm not makin' you any tea for that remark."

Bronagh snorted. "Drinkin' tea isn't on me to-do list, but roastin' your arse is."

I decided to play dumb.

"What'd I do?"

"What'd you do?" She threw me an incredulous look. "You've been MIA for *seven* days!"

"I've been right 'ere, and ye'know that."

"That's beside the point 'cause I couldn't get in to see you no matter how much I threatened the day and night guards," she quipped. "You haven't answered or returned any of our calls since that shitstorm with Damien last week. We've all been worried sick about you. I literally puke at the thought of you now."

I cackled. "Thanks a lot."

"I'm not jokin'. Everythin' with Damien was so serious. Are you okay, babe?"

I clenched my teeth at the mention of him.

"I just needed some space, Bee."

Seven days' worth of it, and it still wasn't enough.

Bronagh folded her arms across her chest and stared at me. I resisted the urge to tease her because I knew she wasn't even close to finished with roasting my arse. If I poked the bear when she was angry, I'd most definitely lose a finger or two.

"So," I said, "is Branna still pregnant?"

"Yeah, but if she wasn't, you'd have missed the birth of the twins."

I licked my lower lip. "I'd have come out of hibernation if she was in labour."

"Sure you would."

I ignored her tone.

"I thought she was meant to be induced by now?"

"The doctor made a change in plans."

Her abrupt answers told me she was annoyed.

"Go on," I said with a wave of my hand. "Spit out whatever else you came all this way to say."

She inhaled deeply, and in one huge breath, she said, "You're shaggin' Dante Collins, and you never once thought to enlighten me with that juicy bit of information? You're the worst best friend anyone on planet Earth has ever had, and ye'don't even *care*."

I tried and failed not to laugh, which prompted Bronagh to grab a throw pillow and lob it at me. I caught it with a smile and snuggled it against my stomach.

"*Alannah*," Bronagh said, her face the picture of seriousness. "Talk to me."

I lost my smile. "I don't *want* to, Bronagh. I just wanna be on me own for a while and forget ..."

"And forget *what?*"

I looked down at the pillow, and ran my fingertips over it.

"And forget Damien exists."

She sucked in a sharp breath, and spluttered, "You *don't* mean that."

I looked her dead in the eye. "Trust me, I do."

Her lips parted slightly.

"Alannah."

I hurt her with my words, and my chest tightened because of it.

"I'm sorry," I said sincerely. "I know you're really close with 'im, but I'm cuttin' 'im out, Bronagh."

"Cuttin' 'im out of *what*?"

"Me life."

Bronagh reared back as if I had slapped her. "What happened ... it was just a misunderstandin'."

"It wasn't. It was an argument based on years' worth of tension that finally erupted."

My friend shook her head. "*Nothin'* would have erupted if you didn't randomly drop the I'm-shaggin'-Dante bomb in the middle of Branna's kitchen," she countered. "I mean, fuckin' hell, Alannah. Did you really have to out that you've been seein' someone in front of everyone when you were tellin' Damien? It was a cold thing to do."

My stomach churned.

"I didn't mean to say it then," I stressed. "I didn't plan to say it at all. I just ... I just felt like I owed it to Damien to be honest with 'im after he asked me out for lunch."

"Well." Bronagh frowned. "You were honest. Brutally honest."

"I know."

"I still can't wrap me head around this, though," Bronagh said with furrowed brows. "You're sleepin' with Dante Collins? He is *so* not your type *and* a lot older than you are. How the hell did it even happen?"

I gritted my teeth to stop myself from calling Bronagh on her shock that someone as hot as Dante would sleep with someone as homely as me, but I held back and exhaled a deep breath.

"It's only been goin' on a few months." I shrugged. "D'ye remember when I got that flat tyre a while back? Aideen told me to go to 'er da's garage, so I went, and Dante was the one who dealt with it for me. We chatted, and I don't know, we just clicked."

"I can buy that." She nodded. "I can buy that you both clicked and became friends, but fuck buddies? That is not you at all, Lana."

Alannah.

I shrugged once more. "He sent me a text one night to see what I was doin'. I was watchin' Netflix and invited 'im over. He accepted, and we—"

"Netflix and chilled?"

"Precisely."

She stared at me, and I knew exactly what she was thinking.

"You think I'm not actin' like meself, don't you?"

A blush stained her cheeks as she nodded.

I gnawed on my lower lip. "If I tell you this, please don't tell Aideen."

Bronagh crossed her finger over her heart. "Not a word."

"Dante started out as an experiment," I said in a rushed breath.

The admission took a huge weight I didn't realise I was carrying off my shoulders.

Bronagh's jaw dropped. "*Excuse* me?"

"It's not as bad as it sounds."

"Please." Bronagh waved her hand. "Explain yourself."

Where to begin?

"Okay." I exhaled. "So, Dante has a long list of women he has bedded, he doesn't do long-term relationships, he is outgoin', charmin', ridiculously attractive, carin', loyal to his family ... who does that remind you of?"

Bronagh blinked. "Any one of the brothers before they settled, but I'm goin' to go with Damien since he is your centre."

I ignored her observation of him being my centre, and focused on the mention of him.

"Bingo."

My friend furrowed her brows. "You're sleepin' with Dante because he is like Damien?"

"Exactly."

"I know there is a point to this," Bronagh said as she rubbed her temples, "but I have pregnancy brain, so go ahead and break it down for me, babe."

My lips twitched.

"I always blamed me age, cluelessness, and stupid hormones for gettin' tangled up with Damien, and I wanted to prove to meself that those trivial things really *were* the cause for how much I liked 'im. So, when the opportunity to bed Dante arose, I jumped at it, and *him*, and put me theory to the test."

"And your theory was?"

"That I could have casual no-strings-attached sex with someone like Damien and not be affected like I once was."

Bronagh raised a brow. "And how is that workin' out for you?"

"Quite well," I said proudly. "I have no romantic interest in Dante; it's purely physical."

"Your theory won't exactly prove anythin', though." Bronagh paused then said, "Well, not unless ..."

"Unless what?" I asked.

"Unless *Damien* is the person you bed and then walk away from."

I froze. "That's stupid, Bee."

She was suggesting I have *sex* with the man it took me years to get over?

Are you really over him, though?

I gritted my teeth at my thoughts as my friend deadpanned.

"You just told me you're havin' sex with Dante Collins because he is like Damien, and you want to prove you could lay 'im and leave 'im. It's great that you can have casual sex with Dante, but it proves nothin' unless you lay and leave the man who is behind this theory of yours in the first place, and that, me dear friend, is Damien Slater."

I refused to allow myself to process any of what Bronagh said.

I scowled. "I thought you said you had pregnancy brain?"

She grinned. "I have me moments."

Have them somewhere else.

"Can we *not* talk about Damien?" I almost pleaded. "I really don't want to think about 'im right now."

Bronagh watched me. "You hurt 'im, ye'know?"

The hurt that dwelled in his eyes when I told him about Dante flashed across my mind, and I tensed.

"What are you talkin' 'bout?" I asked, my tone clipped.

Bronagh didn't back down. "Damien's being tryin' with you, Lana. Ye'know he has."

Alannah.

"I don't know anythin' of the sort—"

"Keela has you drunk off your arse on video acknowledgin' that ye'know *exactly* what I'm talkin' 'bout."

I hugged the pillow in my grasp tighter. I knew damn well that Damien was tryin' to build something with me; I just didn't need everyone else telling me about something I already knew. It made staying angry with him extremely hard.

"I thought you were supposed to be *my* friend?" I demanded of Bronagh, my gaze hard.

"I *am* your friend, ye'eejit," she bit back, her own eyes narrowing. "But I'm Damien's friend too, and instead of hidin' out 'ere and feelin' sorry for yourself, you should get your arse 'round to Branna and Ryder's place and *talk* to Damien. You both got yourselves into this situation, and only the two of you can get yourselves out of it."

I shoved my pillow off my lap and angrily got to my feet.

"Maybe you should leave," I told Bronagh. "I have work to do."

"Lana—"

"Alannah," I snapped. "Me name is *Alannah.*"

"Alannah!" she snapped back, getting to her feet, too. "Don't toss me aside 'cause ye'don't like hearin' the truth, ye'gobshite. Seven days ago, you told Damien you were ready to deal with everythin' between you two, so what's changed since then?"

Everything.

"Nothin'."

"Don't bullshit me." Bronagh glared. "I know you better than ye'know yourself, so cut this act and *talk* to me."

It was *impossible* to win an argument against her!

"You were there," I said, willing myself not to get upset. "You *heard* 'im sayin' he was goin' out to 'move on'," I said using my fingers as air quotes around the words. "We both know what he meant by that. Don't pretend like ye'don't."

He was going to "move on" between the thighs of another woman. I shouldn't have cared about it, but I did, and I *hated* that.

"The farthest he got was to the Jobey where he was joined by his brothers and drank 'imself into oblivion."

My heart slammed into my chest, and I suddenly felt sick.

"He ... he didn't have sex with a random woman?"

Bronagh shook her head, and my heart leaped with the action.

"He drank 'imself sick and only got over his hangover three days ago. He's ... in a bad way, and that has nothin' to do with bein' sick from drinkin'. He got into a fight with Dante at work as well, so that hasn't helped matters."

I refused to allow myself to feel any guilt, but it was difficult.

"And everyone blames me?"

She had the decency to blush. "We're not blamin' you; you *both* are the reason for your problems."

"The *only* problem I have is the situation with me da. Other than that, I am perfectly—"

"Don't you bloody *dare* say you're fine," Bronagh cut me off. "Because you're not. Stop denyin' shite that's starin' you in the face. It makes you look thick."

I looked away from her.

"I was never in a relationship with 'im, Bronagh. It was just sex; sex that took place over *six* years ago. It's not a big deal."

"Who are you tryin' to convince, me or yourself?"

I remained mute.

"I *know* you've a lot goin' on with your parents and your job, but Damien is a huge part of why you're feelin' out of sorts."

I sighed. "What do you want me to do, Bronagh?"

"Talk to Damien," she replied. "That's all I ask. Just talk to each other."

"And if I refuse?"

"Then I'll respect your decision, but I will also tell you how dopey you would be *to* refuse. You can say ye'don't care about Damien as much as you like, but your actions say differently. Look at you, you're almost cryin' because I'm sayin' this."

I hated that my eyes stung with unshed tears.

"This is so stupid," I grumbled, and wiped my eyes before my tears had a chance to fall as I sat back down.

"Look," Bronagh said, coming over and squatting before me. "I love you, and I want to see you happy. Whether it's with Damien in or out of your life, but trust me, you will be plagued with what-ifs if you don't clear the air with 'im."

I swallowed. "I'll ... *consider* speakin' to 'im."

Bronagh winked. "Atta girl."

"That bein' said," I continued, "he couldn't get away from me quick enough last week, so he'll probably run when he sees me comin' his way."

"Probably." She grinned. "You'll just have to bide your time, pick your moment, and corner 'im when he least expects it."

"He always seems to see me before I see 'im. I won't be able to pull the wool over his watchful eyes."

"If that happens, I'll just text you when he is in me house, and I'll lock the doors so he can't leave. Simple."

That was such a Bronagh thing to say.

I shook my head. "You're crazy."

"Ye'know it," she replied and gave me a hug before she stood upright. "I've to get goin'. Dominic is downstairs in the car with Georgie. I told him if I couldn't talk sense into you in fifteen minutes, then he could come up and have a turn."

"Go." I tittered. "Before the good lookin' fucker appears, and I get arrested for attempted murder."

Bronagh left my apartment, laughing as she went. When she closed the door behind her, my smile remained on my face but only for a few moments. As much as I hated to admit it, Bronagh was right. I did need to talk to Damien. I had no clue what to say to him, but a conversation had to take place, and the thought made me extremely nervous.

I stood, then went into my bedroom and changed into black leggings, a black tank top, and a blue plaid, oversized, buttoned up shirt that I rolled up to the elbows. Each item of clothing had a stain of paint, charcoal, or ink of some kind on them, and the outfit was my go-to whenever I wanted to sketch and paint. Right now, I needed to do both.

I took my easel out of my storage press and set it up. Usually, whenever I painted, it was on paper, but today, something told me I needed to paint on canvas. I didn't have many of them. In fact, I only had six remaining from the bundle of ten that Bronagh and Nico got me for my birthday a few months ago, so I was selective about what I used them for because I didn't have the money to replace them just yet. I grabbed the biggest one, placed it on the coffee table next to my easel, and stared at it for a little while. I mulled over what paints I wanted to use, and whether I wanted it to be in colour.

I settled on dark colours to reflect my mood.

I grabbed my pencils, then settling on my settee, I crossed my legs, placed my canvas on my lap, and got to work. I hadn't decided on what to sketch until the second I touched the sharpened lead to the canvas. And when my hand automatically curved and drew the same pair of eyes I saw in my dreams every night, I realised I wasn't drawing a what.

It was a who.

CHAPTER FOUR

When I woke up the following morning, I had a plan. I decided to take Bronagh's advice from yesterday and put it to the test. I wanted to talk ... but not to Damien. I had to build up to that. The person who I wanted to speak to lived eight floors above me, and as I stood outside her apartment door, I prayed she was in a good mood. I had sent her a text to let her know I wanted to speak to her, and she acknowledged the text and told me to come up to her apartment whenever I was ready.

That was five hours ago, and I was just now finding myself in front of her door. Before I could chicken out, I lifted my arm and knocked firmly on the dark wood. Dropping my arm back to my side, I began to sweat bullets.

"I've got it."

The hollering voice belonged to none other than Kane Slater.

Out of all the Slater brothers, Kane was the one who I was least close to. We didn't do a lot of talking even though we were in each other's company a lot. It wasn't awkward because I knew how reserved he was, but my silence wasn't because I was reserved; it was because of a conversation I had with him when I was eighteen. He had asked me a bunch of questions about my friendship with Bronagh that didn't sit well with me, so I called him out on it. He had since apologised, but I never forgot that conversation, and thus remained very aware whenever I was in Kane's presence, which resulted in my silence.

I smiled politely when the door opened, and Kane gave me a welcoming nod in response.

"Alannah."

"Kane."

I could've sworn I saw his lips twitch, but I wasn't sure, so I didn't mention it. Instead, I scanned his face and focused on his bruised jaw, the one that Dante had mentioned he had when I spoke to him on the phone two nights ago. It looked worse than I thought it would have.

"Let me guess," I drawled. "The other lad looks worse?"

That earned me a grin.

"They *both* do," he replied, "but I can't take credit. Date and Damien can hold their own, which resulted in them both looking worse for wear."

I stepped inside the apartment when Kane shuffled back and gestured for me to enter.

"Just what I need," I grumbled. "Two eejits fightin' over somethin' stupid."

Kane closed the door. "You think you're something stupid?"

I turned away from him.

"They weren't fightin' over me. They were fightin' over bruised egos." He didn't reply, so I asked, "Where's Aideen? I want to get this conversation over and done with as soon as possible."

"She's in the bedroom."

I hesitated. "Is she decent?"

I had to ask. Aideen was engaged to a Slater brother, after all, and that meant if you didn't announce your presence whenever you entered a house, you were sure to get an eyeful of sweaty bodies humping one another. I'd learned that the hard way a few too many times before.

Kane snorted. "She is."

"Thanks," I said, and without another word, I walked away from

Kane and in the direction of his and Aideen's bedroom.

I knocked on the door when I was close enough to do so.

"It's me," I said, though I wasn't sure why I was announcing myself. She knew it was me because Kane sure as hell wouldn't knock on his own bedroom door and sound his name.

"Come in," Aideen called.

I took a breath, exhaled, then opened the door. I jumped with fright when a scream sounded, then I laughed. Jax, who was lying on the bed, looked up when he heard the door open and screamed with delight when he saw me.

"Hey, little man," I beamed.

I stepped into the room and held my arms out to him as he was already reaching for me, his baby language in full swing. Picking him up when I was close enough to do so, I busied myself with him for a few moments. When I peeked up at Aideen, she was staring at me as Locke slept in her arms.

"How long?"

I didn't even try to play dumb about what she was asking.

"Four months."

Aideen absorbed this. "Not since Damien came home then?"

I shook my head. "Just the past four months."

"Are you both together?"

"No," I answered. "We decided we're better at bein' friends. I love your brother but not in a romantic way. He has been me rock these past few months, and to be honest, without the relationship we shared, I may have had a meltdown sooner than a week ago. Damien bein' back has messed with me head this past year and a half, and Dante kept me sane just when I thought I might implode."

"Then I'm glad," Aideen said, surprising the hell out of me. "I'm glad he and the relationship you both shared helped you."

She didn't look all that glad, and it worried me.

"Do you hate me?"

Aideen balked. "I should smack you for even askin' that."

I leaned back just in case she got slap happy.

"No," she continued. "I do *not* hate you, and I will *never* hate you."

My shoulders sagged with relief.

"I thought you might, given who Dante is to you."

"Alannah." Aideen sighed. "I'm not jumpin' for joy that you had this secret relationship with me brother. If you had a relationship with 'im, *without* the secret part, I'd be delighted for you both. I just ... it's just ... we're friends. Since I got pregnant with Jax, we have both become really close. We're a big part of the other's life, and I truly love you. It just caught me off guard that you'd keep this from me. I know it was your decision, and you had your reasons, but I can't help but feel upset."

"I know, and I'm so sorry. I could just never pluck up the courage to tell you about it. To tell *anyone* about it, to be honest."

"I know," Aideen said, "and that's me own fault for makin' you feel that you couldn't talk to me about it, so *I'm* sorry."

I blinked and didn't know what to say, so I stayed mute.

"How are you doin'?" she asked me. "Really?"

I exhaled a deep breath and sat on the bed, letting Jax sit beside me. I kept my hand on his back for balance.

"I don't know," I answered honestly. "Me head is so messed up, and when I think of why, it pisses me off. I don't understand why Damien and I even argued. We aren't a couple, and we've never been a couple, so it was all over nothin' when you think about it."

Aideen clicked her tongue. "You both have history, you share an attraction, and dare I say you even care for one another. You're both just utterly *shite* at communicatin'."

Unexpected laughter spilled free, and it felt good to relax and shoot the shit.

"It's all just a big mess."

"Do you plan on cleanin' it up?"

I gnawed on my lower lip. "I'm goin' to talk to 'im, but God only knows how *that* will turn out."

"I don't think it'll be as bad as *you* think it will."

"You're right; it'll probably be worse."

Aideen chuckled. "You never usually talk this negatively."

"I know," I acknowledged. "I'm just a bit down lately."

"Everythin' will work out," Aideen said with confidence. "What's meant to be will be."

I kissed Jax on the crown of his head.

"You're so mellow since you had the kids."

Aideen grinned. "Only when they're quiet."

I snorted and looked down at Jax as he grabbed and played with my fingers.

"Are you goin' to stay for lunch?" my friend asked.

With my eyes still on Jax, I shook my head.

"I have to collect me car from your da's garage," I replied. "One of the lads had to replace the ruptured diesel pump. I had to wait for the part to be delivered."

Aideen whistled. "Damien is at work today. He doesn't just do roadside rescue with Ryder anymore. Me da has taken them both on as apprentices."

I looked up. "But I thought Ryder said he wasn't interested in goin' back to school?"

"He wasn't until he took an interest in engines." She shrugged. "Me da already has them set up with FAS so they get paid for workin' in the garage from me da, and get paid from FAS at the same time. The schoolin' part of it is cool, too. It takes four years to get their certificate to be approved mechanics, and they split that up between workin' in the garage and bein' in school. They're on the job eighty percent of the time, and then three months out of each year, they have their evenin' classes to prepare them for their exams. They get trainin' allowances too, so no college fees."

"That's brilliant," I praised. "Your da really did them a solid."

Aideen nodded. "He said they are as hard workin' as me brothers, so he was happy to get them on board."

"I'm happy for them."

"Are you still goin' to collect your car?"

"I have to," I said with a shrug. "Not only do I need to go shoppin' to put food in me presses, but I've also got a meetin' in town tomorrow with a lad who applied for the assistant job to help me with the business, and I'm not takin' the bus. They'll be packed because the Luas is still on strike."

"The Luas is always on bloody strike."

I snorted and looked down at Jax, who was drooling on my fingers as he chewed on them.

"You're lucky you're cute, fella."

Aideen laughed as I moved him into the centre of the bed and went to the bathroom to wash my hands. I popped my head back into her bedroom when I was finished and said, "I'll see you later, okay?"

"Let me know how it goes *and* if you have a run-in with Damien!"

I leaned my head against the door panel. "Say a prayer for me."

"I'll say two."

I grinned as I walked down the hallway.

"Bye, Kane!" I shouted as I opened the front door.

"Bye," he hollered from the sitting room.

When I left my apartment building, I thanked God it wasn't raining and started the thirty or so minute walk to C.A.R. to retrieve my vehicle. The walk did me good; it not only gave me time to think, but it allowed me to stretch my legs as well. Being holed up in my apartment for seven days straight was murder on my muscles, and the lack of use was evident as my thighs and calves burned with each step I took.

I reached the building quicker than I would have liked, but I was prepared. My plan was to get my car and be in and out of the garage before Damien or anyone else caught a glimpse of me. It was a good plan, a solid plan, a foolproof fecking plan.

I've got this.

I made it seven steps into the poxy place before I saw the back of Dante Collins. I quickly but quietly scurried my way towards the reception where I ducked out of sight so he wouldn't see me if he turned around. My heart was hammering against my chest, and my palms were sweatier than usual.

This is a shitty plan.

"Why did I think this was a good idea?" I whispered to myself.

I was in a good place with Dante, but I didn't want to stand around and shoot the shit with him knowing that Damien was on shift. I wasn't that brave. I closed the door to the reception, and I hoped to God that none of the lads walked in because I honestly had no idea what I would do if either one of them confronted me. I had all of two seconds to myself before I just about jumped out of my skin when the door to the reception opened. I swung around, and when I saw it was only Mr Collins, I placed my hand over my chest and forced myself to relax.

I was wound up tighter than a cheap watch.

"Hello, Alannah love."

"Heya, Mr Collins." I beamed. "Are you well? 'Cause you're lookin' well, sir."

"You tryin' to make an old man blush, kid?" he replied with a wink. "Have any of the lads dealt with you yet?"

I shook my head. "I just walked in."

He nodded, then glanced around the messy room.

"I really need to hire someone to organise this mess," Mr Collins scowled at the mountain of papers before he looked at me, his eyes suddenly wide and hopeful. "I don't suppose you're lookin' for a job, sweetheart?"

I giggled. "No, sir. Sorry."

"Figures." He sighed, his hands going to his hips. "I need a miracle worker to get this business organised."

"Put an advert in the paper or online," I suggested. "You'd be surprised by how many professional receptionists are out there who need a good job."

"I don't think I have any other choice," he said with a sigh. "We can't watch the reception all the time 'cause we're workin' on cars, so people who come in and wait without service get fed up and leave. In this day and age, I can't afford to lose costumers, especially since we bought the lot next door last year and had everythin' renovated into one large shop. I've so much paperwork that I consider turnin' to drink durin' tax season. I need a fairy godmother at this point in time to sort this out."

"Definitely try the advert," I encouraged. "You'll be fightin' off applicants, just you wait and see."

Mr Collins grinned before he looked over my shoulder and sighed.

"I'll be right back, love," he said. "I've to see to a customer who's bein' ignored by me lads."

I nodded. "Take your time. I'm in no rush."

Big. Fat. Lie.

I had never wanted to leave an establishment as much in my entire life. I placed my hands on the reception desk, then looked at the beautiful antique clock on the wall. It was after three p.m., and as it was a Monday, I would have my normal weekly dinner with my parents this evening at five. I hoped my da wouldn't be there; I was in no mood to sit across from him at the dinner table and pretend I didn't know he was having an affair.

I didn't have the strength for it. Not today.

The door to the reception suddenly opened and closed. Silence stretched on for a few moments, and I could have sworn I heard a snicker, which caused me to tense even more than I already was. I would just up and die if it was Damien.

"I *told* you this shite with Date was goin' to cause problems, Alannah."

My shoulders sagged as a sigh of relief escaped me.

"I know," I replied with a firm nod.

I didn't move a muscle as he moved next to me, his shadow falling over the countertop.

"Yet you ignored me words of wisdom?" he mused. "I bet you feel stupid now, huh, good lookin'?"

I turned my head, tilted it back, locked eyes with Harley Collins, then rolled them.

"I never pegged you for an 'I told you so' kind of man."

"You pegged me wrong because ... I told you so."

Harley was the only person who knew about my private relationship with Dante because the pair of them were extremely close. If either of them did something or some*one*, the other knew about it.

"Go away," I grumbled. "You're mean."

He smirked down at me.

"Date said he couldn't get hold of you and that you revoked his access to your buildin'. He was arrested when he tried to break in, ye'know?"

What the fuck?

I choked. "What?"

"Don't worry, he was released without charge thanks to the landlord of the place not pressin' charges." Harley laughed, his shoulders shaking. "The fuckin' eejit tried to use a fire escape as a back door after he was refused entry a third time. He ran from the security guards too but dropped like a fly when they tasered 'im."

"He was tasered *and* arrested?" I asked, wide-eyed.

"Fainted and everythin'." Harley cackled. "Don't tell 'im I told you that; his ego is still sore about it."

"I just spoke to 'im two nights ago, and he never mentioned anythin'."

"And you won't hear 'im speak a word. He made me and me da promise to *never* speak of it."

"Your *da*?"

"He was with me when Date called me from the garda station."

I facepalmed. "This week can't get any worse."

"Famous last words," Harley murmured.

I was mad. Steaming bloody mad.

"Where is he?"

"Now, Alannah," Harley said, raising his hands in front of his chest. "He only wanted to check on—"

I walked away from Harley, hearing him curse before he jogged to catch up with me.

"Dante Collins!" I hollered. "Where are you?"

He was across the shop, lifting a large piece of a car engine up into the air on a floor jack. He paused what he was doing, then looked over his shoulder, and when he saw me, he smiled. That smile slowly slid off his face as I approached him, and I wondered if he saw how mad I was, or if Harley was doing hand signals as he trailed along behind me.

"What in the *hell* is wrong with you?" I snapped at Dante when I came to a stop in front of him and thumped him in the chest. "Tasered and arrested? Are you naturally thick, Date, or were you born this way?"

"Born this way," JJ and Gavin called out in unison from somewhere in the shop.

Dante rolled his eyes at his brothers before looking back at me.

"I needed to see you, to talk to you ... but since you made that *impossible* before our phone call, I had to go to extreme lengths."

I scowled. "You're lucky the owner of the buildin' didn't press charges."

"The owner of the buildin' is me future—"

"Your future reason for goin' to prison if you try to break into his buildin' again," JJ all but shouted.

Dante cringed as he looked at his brother over my shoulder, before switching his gaze back to me. "What JJ said."

"I don't even want to know what you're both talkin' about," I scowled, rubbing my temple with my fingers.

"Hey," he said, stepping closer. "Everythin' is okay. There's no problem."

I scoffed.

"Sex with you has caused me *nothin'* but problems."

Dante grinned devilishly. "It was worth it, though, right?"

I hated that I tried and failed to hide a smile.

"Are you here to see me?"

I shook my head. "To collect me car."

"I finished replacin' that diesel pump this mornin' but give me five more minutes. I want to check the oil level on your car. I think it's runnin' low."

Dante jogged over to my car and popped the bonnet. I stared at him and placed my hands on my hips. I scanned my eyes around the shop, keeping watch for Damien, but there were several cars and equipment that blocked my view. The garage's extension meant the place was huge, but more space meant it had to be filled with something.

"Your body language is screamin' how uncomfortable you are," Harley murmured as he came to my side. "Relax."

"How relaxed would *you* be if the lad you have history with worked with the lad you were sleepin' with?"

Harley folded his arms over his chest. "Very uncomfortable, considerin' I'm straight."

I shoved a now laughing Harley away from me.

"You're bloody hilarious."

He came back to my side, slung his arm over my shoulder, and said, "Damien's in the back room sortin' new tools into the trolley drawers."

Harley went over to Dante then and began doing God knows what with my car engine. I looked over at the doorway that led to the back of the shop, and before I could rationally think otherwise, I walked towards it. When I entered the room, I had to walk around large tool trolleys, but when I saw Damien's white hair, my feet and my heart stopped. My eyes roamed over him. He had on black work trousers, the ones that had a million different pockets and hugged a man's arse deliciously. He was wearing thick soled boots, and a fleece jumper with the shop logo on it. It was the only matching uniform item of clothing that the men in the shop wore.

I took a breath and said, "Damien?"

Instantly, he tensed and kept his back to me.

"Can I talk to you, please?"

He remained silent, tense and unmoving.

"I know I'm probably the last person you want to see right now, but I'd be really grateful if we could talk. Please."

Nothing.

"It's okay," I said, my shoulders sagging. "I get it."

I turned around and began walking towards the exit of the back room but came to an abrupt halt when a hand gripped my forearm. In one swift motion, I was spun around and pulled against a rock-hard chest.

"Damien!"

A split second later, his mouth came crashing down on mine. Absolute bewilderment overcame my mind, but not my body. My lips acted of their own accord, and so did my hands. I ran my hands up Damien's arms, up his neck, and grabbed his thick hair tightly.

He hissed into my mouth and kissed me with the hunger of a man starving. His tongue plunged between my parted lips and danced with my own. His hands had somehow made their way to my behind, and he wasted promptly zero seconds in palming and squeezing it to the point of pain.

He didn't stop there; he ran his hands up my back, neck, and buried them in my hair. When he pulled it, as I had done to his, my mouth opened on a gasp, and he used that moment to snag my lower lip with his teeth. I groaned when he sucked my lip into his mouth and hummed.

His hands slid back down to my arse, and then, suddenly, my back was pressed against a tool trolley. I moaned, and upon hearing that sound, Damien broke our kiss, placed his lips by my ear, and growled, "*Now*, I can talk to you."

He stepped back away from me, and it was only then I realised I was trembling, and my body ached with need. My chest, like Damien's, was rising and falling rapidly. I lifted my hands to my thoroughly kiss-swollen lips, and my fingers lingered for a moment before I dropped my arm to my side. I stared at his bruised eye, and I couldn't believe how sexy he looked with it.

"Why did you do that?"

"Do what?"

What did he mean do what?

"Why did you *kiss* me?" I asked breathlessly.

That wasn't just a kiss, though, and I knew it wasn't. It was more than that; it was a claiming.

Damien's eyes were narrowed as he said, "I couldn't talk to you knowing his lips were the last to touch yours, so ... I fixed it."

"You fixed it?"

"Yep."

"You kissed me like that just because you have a stick up your arse about Dante bein' the last to kiss me?"

Damien's right eye twitched. "Something like that."

I threw my hands up in the air.

"You're un-fuckin'-believable, Damien Slater."

He surprised me when he grinned and said, "I know."

I dropped my arms and scowled. "That wasn't a compliment."

He shrugged, and repeated, "I know."

I placed my hands on my hips.

"Don't kiss me unexpectedly like that ever again."

"I can kiss you if you expect it then?"

"What? No!"

"Hey." Damien raised his hands. "I'm just making sure."

I glared at him. "No more kissin'. I don't like it."

Damien's smile dropped, and he stepped closer to me. "It's not nice to lie."

I licked my lips, shivering when I tasted him on them.

"I'm not ly—"

"You're *still* lying," he said, his voice firm as he took another step closer to me. "You kissed me like a woman possessed, freckles."

I reluctantly stepped back and realised Damien had me cornered when my back pressed against something solid. The tool trolley.

"Damien," I said, my voice sounded raspier than I would have liked. "We have to talk, remember?"

His eyes were on my lips. "I remember."

"Then back off and stop lookin' at me like I'm your prey."

He flicked his eyes to mine. "Do you feel like you're my prey?"

Hell yes.

"I do," I said, lifting my chin.

"Are you scared I'm going to eat you?" he asked, dropping his voice to a seductive whisper.

I sucked in a breath. "Stop it."

"Stop what?"

"Whatever it is that you're doin' ... I can't think."

Whenever he was close to me, all logical thought vanished.

"I make you nervous," he said, and he sounded ... pleased.

"You drive me crazy," I corrected. "You just *kissed* me."

"I know."

"Damien, you can't just kiss me."

"I had to," he said. "He kissed you last."

Dante.

"No, he didn't," I said with a sigh. "Of all the things we did, kissin' wasn't one of them."

Damien's brow furrowed together.

"What does that mean?"

"Nothin'," I answered. "I don't want to talk about Dante."

"He's part of the talk, and you know it."

I lifted my hands to my face and sighed.

"You have confused me even more than I already was," I said, dropping my hands. "I thought you wanted to be friends?"

"Do friends kiss each other the way I just kissed you?"

I licked my lips, still tasting him.

"No," I said softly.

"Then no, Alannah," he growled, "I don't want to be your friend."

My heart pounded against my chest.

"I can't offer you more than that."

"Bullshit," Damien clipped. "I felt the way you kissed me, and I see how you look at me. You want me; you're just scared."

"Just scared?" I repeated. "Damien, I'm fuckin' terrified. Me only experience with you ended in disaster."

He set his jaw. "I'm not the same person I was when I was eighteen."

I lifted my chin. "Neither am I, and *that* is thanks to you."

I turned and made for the exit, but Damien wasn't having it. He grabbed my arm again, rounded on me, and placed his large, hard body between myself and the exit.

"No," he quipped. "You're done walking away from me when we're talking."

My mouth dropped open. "You're givin' me an order?"

"You bet your perfect ass I am."

It was wrong to be so turned on by his show of dominance.

"I don't take orders from you or any other man."

"We'll see," he growled.

"We'll see nothin' because—"

"Because what?"

He was in my face again, but I couldn't think.

"I don't know!" I snapped. "I don't know anythin' when you're this close to me."

"And you say you can't give me more?" he asked on a growl. "Your body knows who it belongs to; your brain just needs to catch up."

That snapped me out of my haze.

"Me brain and body aren't the ones callin' the shots," I quipped. "The heart that you broke is!"

Damien leaned back and looked down into my eyes.

"You know I'd give anything to change how I left things with you." He placed his hands on my shoulders. "I know you know that."

He had told me as much many times over the past year, but I always put it down to his guilty conscience.

"I don't know what I know anymore," I admitted, looking down.

"Everythin' is so messed up."

Damien tipped my chin up until my gaze met his.

"We need to talk about everything. Just the two of us, babe."

Babe.

I swallowed and nodded. "When?"

"Tonight," he answered. "I'll come by tonight."

My heart pounded against my chest. "Okay."

He released his hold on me and said, "I'll walk you out."

We left the back room then, heading out to the front where my car was ready and waiting. Alec and Kane walked into the shop at that exact moment, and I looked up at the ceiling, silently asking God why he hated me so much to put me in this situation.

"Your car is good to go, good lookin'," Dante said from my right, gaining my attention.

He walked over to me, staring at me like I was the only person in the room, and before I knew it, I was staring at a person's back instead of Dante's face.

"That's far enough, asshole."

I closed my eyes the second Damien spoke, and in my heart, I knew what was about to happen.

"I'm gonna give you two seconds to step aside so I can talk to me girl real quick."

Oh, God.

"*Your* girl?" Damien snapped, stepping forward, getting in Dante's face. "She's not fucking yours, you piece of shit."

Aideen's brothers were the only men I knew to all be as tall as the Slater brothers. Even as tall as Dante was though, Damien had two or three inches on him. I rushed over to Alec and Kane, who were just watching the lads like they were having a casual conversation.

"Do somethin'!" I demanded. "Right now!"

Kane glanced at me, then up to the lads again, dismissing me without a word.

I turned to Alec. "Please!"

"Not yet," he answered without looking at me.

"I hate to break it to you, *mate*," Dante quipped from behind me. "But she sure as hell isn't yours!"

I sucked in a strangled breath as a dark cloud of what I knew was fury fell over Damien.

"Please," I begged, rushing forward and squeezing between them. "Can we all just stop and breathe for a minute? This doesn't need to end in violence."

"No violence?" Alec repeated. "That doesn't seem right."

Kane snorted but kept his eyes trained on his future brother-in-law.

"Kane, do you think this is goin' to sit well with Aideen?" I asked, hoping he would see reason. "Do you think she is goin' to be understandin' of you fightin' 'er brother? Because *you* know you're gonna fight 'im if he hits Damien."

"I'm not going to fight," he said with confidence. "I'll just break it up if it pops off."

"Mr Collins!" I hollered desperately for the only man who I knew would end this madness. "Mr Collins, sir!"

"He's gone to lunch, good lookin'."

"JJ!" I shouted, ignoring Dante. "Harley!"

"We're 'ere, Alannah," JJ answered from across the room. "But you need to move aside so they can sort out their differences, darlin'."

"Fuck you, JJ!" I snapped. "And you, Harley. Neither of you speak to me again."

"What about Gav?" Harley huffed. "He's 'ere, and he's not plannin' on stoppin' them either."

"Fuck 'im, too!"

"Thanks a lot, dickhead," Gavin grumbled to his brother. "Now she's gonna ignore me when she sees me next. She's not like Bronagh; she's doesn't hit me when I piss 'er off, she ignores me. Silence hurts way worse."

I ignored them all and focused on the Collins brother who was causing me so much trouble. I shoved Dante's chest with both of my hands, though the action didn't make him stumble back like I'd hoped it would.

"Stop this, you're eggin' 'im on for no reason."

"I have me reasons," Dante replied to me but kept his eyes over my head as he stared Damien down. "Plenty of 'em."

He was a lost cause, so I turned and looked up at Damien.

"Please," I begged. "Don't fight, Damien."

"He called you his when you're not."

"Well." Dante chuckled. "She sure as hell isn't yours, bud, or she wouldn't have had been on *my* cock otherwise."

Damien attempted to swing at Dante, but because I was directly in the middle of the pair, he stopped before I could get hurt. His eyes though ... I had never seen anger like it dwell in them before.

"Just stop!" I screamed as I pushed Damien back by his chest. "Look at *me*!"

He did; his eyes dropped to mine, and they softened almost instantly.

"Please," I begged him. "Don't do this. I *hate* fightin'."

The tension in his face slowly began to fade away.

"You better listen to 'er, Slater," Dante sneered. "Otherwise, I'll have to fuck up that pretty face of yours some more *then* talk to me girl."

Dante had the audacity to slap my behind for no other reason than to start a fight by claiming I was his. Damien's eyes hardened once more, and he moved around me so fast I barely had time to register it. I screamed as Damien and Dante collided, but thankfully, it only lasted maybe thirty or so seconds before all the lads pulled them apart. I hadn't realised I was crying until the shouting stopped, and my cries could be heard.

"I said *stop*!" I bellowed. "I don't want anyone to fight!"

Both Damien and Dante were breathing like enraged bulls and glaring at each other. Dante's nose was gushing blood, but Damien wasn't bleeding. He looked as if he faired better out of the pair of them. I wasn't even sure if they heard a word I said, but I knew the others did because I received a frown from each of them.

"Ye'know what?" I said to pair of saps, sniffling. "Kill each other for all I care. I've bigger things to worry about than your poxy egos."

I stormed forward, snatched my keys from Harley's hand without a thank you, and headed for my car.

"Alannah!" Damien shouted. "Please, wait. I'm sorry! Baby, *wait*!"

I ignored him. I got into my car, started the engine, and pulled out of the garage. Driving in the direction of my parents' house, I did nothing but cry. My chest was rising and falling rapidly, and my hands had a death grip on my steering wheel. I was furious and hurt. Always fucking hurt. When I pulled up outside my parents' house, I was glad to see my da's car wasn't in the driveway. I was a bit early for dinner, but I didn't want to go back to my apartment and sit by myself. Not after what just happened at the garage.

When I got out of my car, I locked it and headed inside my parents' house. The sound of my ma singing from the kitchen brought a small smile to my lips. She was always happy and always looked on the bright side of everything. I wished I was more like her and didn't dwell on the things that made me miserable.

"Alannah, is that you, hon?"

I hung my coat on the rack.

"Yeah, Ma, it's me."

"Brilliant," she chirped. "You can help me with dinner. I just got the veggies chopped. Da just called, and he will be joinin' us tonight. Isn't that great?"

"Yeah," I echoed. "Great."

I leaned against the wall and resisted the urge to smack my head against it. I'd already endured an awkward conversation with Dante and Damien today, as well as watch a fight between the stubborn eejits, and now I had to sit through a dinner with my parents and pretend I didn't know that my da was sleeping with

another woman.
　　Mondays fucking *sucked*.

CHAPTER FIVE

"Alannah?"

I looked up. "Huh?"

My ma smiled at me. "Hon, I'm talkin' to you."

She is?

"Sorry, Ma," I said with a forced chuckle. "I was miles away."

She came to my side and nudged me. "Is it a man who's got you thinkin' so hard?"

I looked at her, and the second I saw her devilish smirk, I laughed.

"You're such a child," I teased as I diced the chicken breasts.

"That wasn't an answer," she said, waggling her brows.

I shook my head, amused.

"Yeah, it's about a man," I said then clarified. "Two men, actually."

"*Two?*" Ma whooped. "Gerrup ow' da."

I put down the knife, leaned my head back, and laughed until my sides hurt. She rarely spoke in slang, but when she did, it cracked me up.

"It's not as excitin' as it sounds," I assured her, still chuckling. "It's actually the complete opposite."

"Tell me everythin'."

I was glad my ma was the type of mother that I *could* tell everything to, and for that reason alone, it killed me even more that I was keeping my da's affair from her. I told her everything, but I couldn't bring myself to put that on her shoulders. I'd rather it be my burden to carry than hers.

"Ye'know Damien Slater, right?"

"The little shite who took your virginity then up and fled the country when you were eighteen?"

My lips quirked. "Yup."

"What about 'im?"

"I told you that he came back from America not long before Jax was born," I added. "Right?"

"Yeah."

"Well, what I *haven't* told you is that he's been tryin' very hard to make up for what he did when we were kids. He's been really nice to me and hasn't done anythin' to upset me. He's given me space and has been an all-round gentleman."

"But?"

"But." I sighed. "I'm terrified that somethin' bad will happen again if I let 'im in. The last time, we weren't even a couple, and he really did a number on me. I'm scared that even bein' just his friend will hurt because if he got with another woman ... it'd kill me."

I couldn't deny my romantic feelings for Damien anymore, not after the kiss we shared at his job. I knew that deep down I had always harboured feelings for him, but after we fell out and he left, my mind did everything possible to cover up those feelings. I guess I believed if I denied how I truly felt about him, then I would get over him.

That clearly hadn't worked out too well.

"So, you don't want to be Damien's friend or anythin' more because you're scared of gettin' hurt, but you also don't want 'im to be with anyone else ... because that would also hurt you."

I closed my eyes. "It sounds *so* stupid when you say it out loud."

"It's not stupid, hon," Ma assured me as she wrapped her arm around my waist. "It's just unfortunate that the person you care for is the person you're also terrified can break you."

I opened my eyes.

"I wish I could click me fingers and get over everythin' ... it's just so hard. A voice in the back of me head reminds me of how hurt I once was because of our actions when we were eighteen. What if I got over everythin' and gave 'im a chance, and then everythin' went wrong? I can't imagine how much it'd hurt if I loved 'im and lost 'im. I get anxiety over it."

"I understand that, and that worry is completely valid ... but it's also no way to live your life. Worryin' about somethin' that may never happen is like takin' a sip of poison each day. Nothin' good will come from it. The only person you'll be hurtin' is yourself."

"I know." I nodded. "I know."

"What about the other lad?" Ma asked as she reached down and smacked my behind.

I yelped as she went over and sat at the kitchen table.

"The other man." I sighed. "Is Dante Collins."

"Any relation to Aideen?"

"Oh, only 'er older brother."

Ma whistled. "Well, you fucked up there, love."

I shouldn't have laughed, but I did.

"Want to know the worst part?" I quizzed. "I was with 'im in private, and no one knew about it except Dante's brother Harley 'cause they're each other's soundboard, but everyone found out when I told Damien after he asked me out for lunch last week."

"Oh, shite."

"Oh shite is right." I snorted. "I'm good with Aideen, though. I worked up the courage to speak to 'er about it this afternoon."

"That's good," Ma said. "Why 'er older brother, though?"

"Well, Dante is exactly like Damien used to be. He doesn't understand the word commitment, and he is way too handsome and charmin' for his own good." I continued to dice the food. "I wanted to see if I could have a purely physical relationship with 'im without developin' an emotional attachment."

"You did a *sex test* on the man?"

"*Ma*," I groaned. "Don't say it like that. You make it sound creepy."

"Sorry." She snorted. "Go on."

"I just wanted to prove to meself that me age was the sole reason Damien affected me the way he did."

"But you're twenty-four now, and you still feel the same hurt over Damien, and the same attraction ... right?"

I grunted. "Right."

"So, your age wasn't the problem; you just had a strong connection with the lad."

Another grunt. "I guess so."

"So, your sex test with Dante really wasn't all that necessary."

"Ma."

"What?" She chuckled. "I'm only sayin'."

I shook my head.

"About the test, though," she continued. "It wouldn't really prove anythin' unless the sexual subject was Damien. You can have sex with many men and leave them, but you wouldn't be able to prove anythin' unless you had sex with Damien and left 'im. He is the one who got you all tied up in knots in the first place, so you'd have to experiment with *him* to see if your theory was accurate."

My mouth dropped open.

"That's *exactly* what Bronagh said!"

Ma grinned. "I always said she was a bright girl."

I shook my head. "I'm not havin' sex with Damien just to prove a theory."

"Why not?" Ma quizzed. "You had sex with Dante to prove it."

She was a smartarse, but a smartarse who made total sense.

"That's enough talkin' about who I have sex with, thank you very much."

Ma laughed, and it brought a smile to my face. I loved her laugh.

"It's all so interestin', though," she continued. "Two men and only one of you."

"It's worse because Damien and Dante never really got on."

"And now they hate each other?"

"Pretty much," I said. "They fought today over me."

"Hold on," Ma said with a snap of her fingers. "So, you've be sleepin' with Aideen's older brother, and no one knew about it, but now everyone knows about it, and the man who you clearly have feelings for knows, and hates the older brother, and fought 'im over you?"

"Basically."

Ma clapped her hands together. "This is like an episode of *Maury*!"

"Ma!" I tittered. "This isn't funny."

"Of course not," she said, folding her hands on her lap. "Please, proceed."

"There is nothin' else to say." I shrugged. "Me and Dante are goin' to be just friends, and Damien wants to talk to me tonight about everythin' that's happened between us, but after seein' them both fight over me ... it's left a bad taste in me mouth."

"Two gorgeous men fightin' the other to win your heart is romantic, not tasteless."

I rolled my eyes. "You read too many romance books."

"Blame Keela," Ma countered. "She recommends all them to me."

I chuckled. "Have you read *her* book yet?"

"Yes, it's wonderful. Have you?"

"No," I answered. "She's so protective over it. She has so much self-doubt; she thinks we'll laugh at 'er if we read it. She finished it ages ago and is no closer to publishin' it."

"It's 'er baby." Ma soothed. "It's a project she has put blood, sweat, and tears into. It's normal for 'er to be scared, but she shouldn't let the fear of people dislikin' it keep 'er from publishin' it."

"Have you told *her* that?"

"Of course," Ma answered. "It'll register with 'er eventually. She just needs time. Rome wasn't built in a day, after all."

"I hope I am as wise as you when I'm older."

"Stick with me, kid." She winked. "I'll rub off on you."

I laughed. "The chicken is ready."

Together, we finished preparing dinner, taking turns cooking and seasoning the food. In the thirty minutes it took us to get everything ready, I had never laughed so much in my life, and that was a big deal, considering how often Alec Slater cracked me up. But my ma? She was on a whole other level of funny.

"Me sides are killin' me," I said as I set the table.

Ma snorted. "I think we both needed that laugh."

"I know I did."

I felt better. After the week I had, and the current day especially, it was nice to forget about everything and just laugh with my ma. She always knew what to say and do to make me feel better. We continued to tell jokes and laugh ... until the front door opened.

"I'm home, love."

I looked up at my ma and watched as a huge smile broke out across her face as my da entered the house. She quickly adjusted her apron and ruffled her hair and ran out to the hall to meet him like she was sixteen and her boyfriend just randomly stopped by for a visit. If I didn't know what a piece of shite my da was, I would have thought his relationship with my ma was perfect, but it was one-sided. My ma adored him, and he repaid that love and admiration by sleeping with another woman.

It made my blood boil.

"Alannah, love," Da beamed when he entered the room, his arms still around my ma as she hugged him tightly, her face buried against his chest. "You're 'ere early."

There was no way on God's green earth that I was telling him the real reason I was here early, and I knew my ma wouldn't either.

I shrugged. "I wanted to spend some time with Ma."

He smiled, looked down at my ma, and gave her a kiss. My fingers flexed before balling into fists. I wanted to savage the man like a wild animal for his deceit and leave nothing left for the birds to pick at, and the only reason I hadn't already done it was because of my ma. She was the *only* reason.

"Are you ready for food now?" Ma asked my da, leaning back so she could look up at him.

She was my height—five-foot-five—and my da was six-foot-four. He was super tall, and was called lanky more times than not by my ma. For some reason, my mind compared him to Damien because they were the same height. It annoyed me further because I wished that I could say that Damien would never cheat on a partner, but after witnessing my da cheating on my ma, it faulted my trust in all men.

Da nodded. "Starved."

"Perfect," Ma chirped, removing her arms from him and turning to the food. "Go wash up, and I'll dish the food."

My da didn't need to be told twice; he headed out of the room, removing his coat and suit jacket as he went, and hung them up in the hall on the coat rack. I left him to use the upstairs bathroom to wash up while I waited for my ma to finish at the sink so I could use it. I didn't want to be on my own with my da—I was afraid of what I would or wouldn't say to him if I was.

"What's that face for?"

I looked at my ma. "Huh?"

"You look like you've swallowed somethin' sour," she joked.

"Just starvin' for this dinner. It smells amazin'."

"Sit down," Ma shooed. "I'll dish your plate first."

I did as I was told and took my seat at the table. My ma put a steaming hot plate of chicken stir-fry in front of me, followed by some rice. My da re-entered the room, and she did the same for him, before joining us with her own plate of food. We bowed our heads as my ma thanked God for our meal, and when she was finished, my da echoed her amen.

I remained mute.

"How was your meetin'?" Ma asked my da, starting the conversation.

"Pretty good," Da answered, taking a bite of his food. "This quarter was better than our last, so sales are improvin' steadily."

I tuned out while they discussed business. I didn't care about my da's job, or him in general, so sitting and listening about his day was not at the top of my to-do list. However, to keep face, I had to endure it. No matter how sickly mad it made me.

"Alannah." I looked up when my name was called.

I swallowed the bite of food in my mouth.

"Huh?"

"I asked how your interview went last week," Da said. "Ye'know, the person you wanted to hire to run your graphic business online, so you could focus on the designs you needed to create."

I stared at my da for a moment, surprised he remembered my interview, or that he took an interest in my work at all. I considered telling him to fuck off, but that would only cause problems.

"I had to reschedule," I said, looking at my plate as I scooped more food onto my fork. "It's takin' place tomorrow instead."

I practically shovelled my food into my mouth, hoping that would deter either of my parents from asking me any more questions. Luckily, chatter for the remaining thirty minutes of dinner was between my parents, and I only had to give one-word answers when they threw a question my way. Afterward, I put all the dishes in the dishwasher and cleaned the kitchen, then I joined my parents in the sitting room. From the second I entered the room, I felt like something was off.

I paused by the doorway.

"Come in, hon." Ma smiled, though I could see it was strained. "Sit."

She gestured for me to sit on the settee that faced them, so with a raised brow, I did as she asked.

"Is everythin' okay?"

My parents shared a look, and instantly, I knew the answer to my question was no.

"Ma?" I prompted. "What's wrong?"

She looked at me. Her eyes were now filled with tears, and it caused my stomach to churn.

"Oh, God," I whispered. "Is it Nanny? Granda? Brogan?"

"No, no," Ma quickly said, wiping her eyes. "Everyone is okay. Nanny, Granda, and Brogan are perfectly fine."

Brogan was my cousin, and she was only six years old. She had lived with my grandparents since her parents, my auntie and uncle, passed away in a house fire when she was only a few months old. They lived in County Offaly, so we only saw them occasionally, but I was relieved to hear they were all okay.

"Then what's wrong?" I pressed. "And don't tell me nothin'. I can see it in your eyes, Ma."

My da grabbed my ma's hand when she broke down, and my heart dropped to the pit of my stomach.

"Oh God," I said to myself, gripping the settee cushion just so I had something to hold onto.

Whatever it was my parents had to tell me, it was bad.

"I'm sorry," Ma whimpered. "I don't want to be a blubberin' eejit. I promised meself I wouldn't cry."

"Hey." Da frowned at her. "You're nothin' of the sort; you can't help your emotions."

I stared at them and just about exploded.

"Tell me what is goin' on!" I demanded. "Right now."

Ma sniffled. "We need to tell you somethin', but please, don't be scared."

I looked from my ma to my da and back again.

Is this about his affair? Does she know? Are they about to tell me about it?

"Before we tell you *anythin'*," Ma said with as stern as an expression as she could muster, "I want you to sit and listen until we're finished talkin'. I don't want you to worry."

I was beyond worried.

"Tell me," I almost choked out. "Please."

Ma's lower lip wobbled, and after a pregnant pause, she said, "I'm sick."

My heart stopped.

"Sick?"

She nodded and sniffled, fresh tears splashing onto her cheeks.

"How sick?" I asked, my voice barely a whisper. "How sick are you, Ma?"

"I haven't been feelin' very well these past few weeks, so I went to my GP about it, and he advised me to go to the hospital to have some tests done after he found somethin' durin' an examination."

What'd he find?

I placed my hand over my mouth and stared at my ma with what I knew was terror in my eyes. My stomach twisted in knots, and I began to tremble.

"You're okay, though, right?" I asked, my voice cracking. "It's nothin' serious?"

She looked at my da, and her tears continued to fall as he pulled her tightly against him and wrapped his arms around her.

"Da!" I almost growled his name. "Tell me."

He locked his eyes on me, and I saw sorrow dwelling within them.

"Cancer," he rasped. "Ma has breast cancer."

The air was knocked from my lungs the second he spoke the words. Loud noise filled my ears, a pain took root in my chest, and a disgusting sensation of nausea hit me like a tonne of bricks.

"No," I whimpered. "No, she doesn't."

My ma broke away from my da and came over to me when I broke down. We wrapped our arms around each other and just held on for dear life as we cried. My ma was swaying me, trying to calm me down, when I should have been the one comforting her and assuring her that everything would be okay. The crying made her feel uneasy, so she excused herself to the bathroom to gather her bearings and clean herself up.

I had to force myself not to be sick.

"When did you both find out?"

"Last Tuesday," Da answered.

My posture went rigid. My ma had cancer, and he knew about it, and he still ... he still was cheating on her.

"It's goin' to be okay, love—"

"Don't touch me!" I slapped my da's hand away when he reached for my hand.

His mouth dropped open in shock as he looked at his hand like it was a second head.

"Love." He frowned. "What's the matter?"

"Ye'know fuckin' well, you piece of shite."

He choked on air. "Alannah!"

"I know," I said, my jaw setting.

"Ye'know *what*?" he demanded, lowering his voice and glancing at the doorway. "What are you talkin' about, Alannah?"

I wanted to thump him for looking so bemused; he had no right to pretend he was in the dark.

"I know about that tramp you're seein' behind Ma's back!"

I watched as the blood drained from my da's face, and an expression close to terror took hold.

"Yeah," I sneered. "You'd better be afraid."

"Don't tell 'er," he pleaded, his eyes darting from me to the doorway and back again. "Not now."

"You're sick," I told him. "You're lower than low."

"I know." He nodded, swallowing. "I know."

"Why?" I demanded, a lump forming in my throat. "Why would you ever want someone other than Ma? That woman worships the ground you walk on."

"I know she does," he clipped. "I know, okay? It was a moment of weakness."

I sat back, and laughed humourlessly.

"Alannah," he pleaded, his hands now shaking. "Please, don't tell your mother."

"I could kill you," I said, my fingers flexing as I balled my hands into fists. "I could kill you right 'ere and now, and I wouldn't feel a single shred of remorse."

My da stared at me, his eyes unblinking.

"Bear—"

"Don't you *dare* call me that!"

He flinched at the coldness in my tone.

"Please, baby," he croaked. "Please, I'm so sorry."

"I hate you for this," I continued. "I hate you."

His Adam's apple bobbed, his skin paled, and I could have sworn I saw his heart break right in from of me. He had to clasp his hands together to stop them from shaking.

"I'm so sorry."

I lifted my chin. "You'll never be sorry enough."

"I ended it," he quietly exclaimed. "The day I went to the hospital with your ma, and we found out she was sick, I ended it. It's taken possibly losin' your ma to make me see she is the only woman I have ever loved and will ever love. She is me first priority, and next to you, she is me entire world. She is, Alannah. I swear to you. I love 'er more than life."

I glared at him, hate flowing through my veins like blood.

"Don't tell 'er," he repeated. "I'm beggin' you."

"You don't deserve 'er."

"You're right, I don't," Da frantically agreed, flicking his eyes towards the doorway every few seconds. "But please don't say anythin'. She needs to focus on 'er upcomin' treatment and beatin' this sickness, Alannah."

Anger surged through me.

"How dare you!" I snapped. "How dare you use 'er struggle to keep me quiet!"

"Alannah!" Da almost growled. "Hate me as much as you want, but don't put your ma through any more pain than necessary."

"Me?" I whispered incredulously. "I've done nothin'! *You're* the cheatin' wanker stickin' his dick in another woman."

My da's jaw dropped. "I have *never* had sex with Olivia."

Olivia. That was the tramp's name.

"I don't believe you."

"On me life, I didn't, Alannah." He swore. "We kissed, and touched, but it never went as far as sex. It doesn't excuse anythin', and it is still a complete betrayal of your ma's trust, but your mother … she is the only woman I have ever been physically intimate with. It's been *her* since I was seventeen."

"It was *her* until you met that *tramp*."

Da's whole body slumped.

"I will forever be sorry for breakin' your ma's trust. I will, Alannah, but please, *think* about what tellin' 'er will do to 'er when we need 'er to be at 'er strongest."

I began to shake with temper.

"You're a coward," I told him. "You're a fuckin' coward."

He swallowed, his Adam's apple bobbing. "I know."

I heard footsteps descend the stairs, and I felt my da's eyes burn into me with one last plea to keep my mouth shut. I ignored him and focused on my ma as she entered the room. Her eyes were only slightly red, and she had a smile back in place on her beautiful face. She looked directly at me and found I was already staring at her. She came to my side, sat down, and placed a hand on my knee.

"We're goin' to get through this," she told me, her back straight. "There is nothin' the three of us can't beat together."

The three of us … together. *Fuck.*

When she hugged me, I looked directly at my da, and when I gave him a slight nod, he practically deflated with relief. I turned from him, closed my eyes, and focused on my ma. I would keep my da's harrowing secret from her for a little bit longer because he was right about one thing—we needed her to focus on beating her sickness, not on him breaking his vows.

"I love you so much, Mammy."

She squeezed me tightly. "I love you more, baby."

Fear wrapped itself around me.

Please God, I thought. *Don't take her from me.*

I had never known complete and utter helplessness until that moment.

CHAPTER SIX

Four hours ago, I found out my ma had breast cancer. After the initial shock, my parents explained to me that it was detected at an early stage. Treatment would start soon, and the success rate of remission was higher, too. None of that comforted me because, at the end of the day, my ma had cancer, and the only purpose of cancer was to kill its host.

That host was my mother.

I had stayed in my parents' house talking and crying as I tried to come to terms with this life-altering news. When my ma began to show signs of fatigue, I made an excuse that I had to leave so I could go home and prepare for my business interview the following day. It pleased my ma because she wanted me to carry on as normal, but from the look in my da's eyes, he knew better.

I found myself outside the front door of Bronagh and Nico's house not long after I left my parents. It wasn't very late, closing in on nine p.m. I had to park on the road because Kane's car was in the driveway next to Nico's, and Ryder's car was behind both of them, leaving no room for anyone else. Even though I had a key, I knocked on the door and waited.

Keela opened the door, and she smiled wide when she saw me, but slowly, her smile fell from her face.

"What's wrong?"

I couldn't answer her; I walked by her and heard her shut the door behind me and quickly follow me into the sitting room where everyone was. And by everyone, I mean everyone. Jax was asleep in his da's arms, and Locke was asleep in his ma's. There was no sign of Georgie, so I assumed she was already up in her bedroom asleep in her cot. Nico had her baby monitor in his hand, so he could see her and hear her if she woke up.

"Well, well," Alec announced when his playful eyes landed on mine. "Look who decided to show her face."

I didn't spare him a glance; instead, I focused on my best friend whose eyes were on me as she slowly got to her feet.

"Alannah," Bronagh said slowly, drawing to everyone's attention that I wasn't okay. "What's wrong?"

For a moment, I couldn't speak, and then, somehow, I managed to say words that I knew would plague my dreams.

"Me ma," I rasped as I prepared to say the words no child ever wants to say. "She has cancer."

Everyone sucked in shocked breaths, but that didn't surprise me. What did surprise me was that the first person to reach me, to gather me in their arms and hold me wasn't Bronagh. It was Damien, and at that moment, there was no other place I wanted to be.

I put my arms around his waist and buried my face in his chest as sobs erupted from me. I wasn't sure how long I stayed in Damien's embrace, but eventually, he moved me to a now empty settee. He sat on my left with his arm still tightly around my waist while Bronagh sat on my right. Leaning her head against mine, she hugged me.

"What happened?"

"I went around to their house for dinner, like I do every Monday." I wept. "I went early today because Dante and Damien had a fight in the garage, and I didn't want to go home and be on me own after that ... I wanted to see me ma, so I went around and helped 'er with dinner."

Damien gave me a squeeze, and I knew it was a silent apology for his fight with Dante.

"We had the best laugh we'd had together in a long time." I smiled, my lower lip wobbling. "She was takin' the piss out of me and was 'er usual happy self. That changed after dinner when 'er and me da sat me down in the sittin' room."

Another squeeze from Damien.

"I knew it was somethin' bad," I said, recalling the worried expressions on their faces. "At first, I thought somethin' might have happened to me grandparents or Brogan. Nothin' could have prepared me for what they were goin' to tell me. I wasn't expectin' them to say she had breast cancer. I had no clue. None."

Bronagh placed her hand in mine and held it tightly.

"When they told me, and me ma left the room to clean 'erself up, I just went off on me da."

Bronagh gasped. "Did you confront 'im about the affair?"

"I did; everythin' I've kept inside just boiled over." I swallowed. "I told 'im I'd savage 'im like an animal over it, too."

Silence.

Bronagh stroked her thumb over my hand. "What'd he say?"

"That he regretted it." I snorted humourlessly. "That the second he found out me ma had cancer, he ended it. That the possibility of losin' 'er made 'im realise how wrong he had been and that she is the only one he could ever love and want."

Damien murmured, "You don't believe him?"

"No," I answered. "I don't. If he loved 'er in the first place, he would have never looked at another woman, much less have a relationship with 'er. He swore to God that they never had sex, but even if they didn't, he still cheated on 'er. He broke the vows he made to 'er."

"Does your mom know?" Alec inquired.

I looked at him and shook my head, drawing a frown from him.

"He begged me not to tell 'er." I snivelled. "He said we need 'er to focus on gettin' better, and if I tell 'er, it won't help that."

"That manipulative bastard!" Aideen scowled. "He is usin' the situation to hide his mistakes."

I solemnly nodded. "I know, but as much as it pains me to admit it, he is right."

"How so?" Bronagh quizzed.

"If I tell me ma about the affair, it'll break 'er, and I don't think she'll want to beat 'er cancer."

"Of course, she will," Damien spluttered. "She'll want to live."

"You don't understand," I cried. "She adores me da. She is so in love with 'im, Damien. If I tell 'er, it'll ruin 'er."

Silence.

"Whatever you decide to do," Bronagh reassured. "We'll fully support you."

"Thanks," I acknowledged. "That means a lot."

"I'll make tea," Branna announced.

This was one situation tea couldn't make better.

"No," I quickly said, "I'm not stayin'."

She frowned at me. "But, Alannah—"

"I really just want to go home, Bran."

Branna's frown stayed in place as she nodded at me.

"I thought you were supposed to have the babies by now? On Monday, when I saw you last, you said you were gettin' induced in four days' time, but that has come and gone."

"Me doctor changed me dates last minute. I'm thirty-eight weeks now, so anytime to have them is a good time." She placed a hand on her large stomach. "I'm gettin' induced this Friday for definite if I don't go into labour before then."

I smiled. "That makes me shitty day better."

She winked at me, but she couldn't hide the worry I knew she felt for me. I didn't want to worry her further so I stood, the action causing Damien and Bronagh's arms to fall away from me. "I better get goin'."

Everyone was frowning at me, and I hated it. I didn't want anyone's pity, but I knew I received it tenfold.

Bronagh stood. "I'll walk you out."

I said goodbye to everyone, and she grabbed my hand when we reached the front door.

"What am I goin' to do?" I asked her. "I can't lose 'er, Bronagh. I can't."

"You won't," she said firmly. "There isn't a chance your ma won't beat this."

"But there is," I whimpered. "There is a chance she won't survive."

"Look at me," she ordered, and when I did, she leaned in and kissed my cheek. "She *will* be fine."

I nodded, repeating that over and over in my mind.

"I'm comin' to stay the night with you," she added. "Give me a minute to get clothes."

"No," I told her. "Stay 'ere with your family. I know I've had plenty of it, but bein' on me own when things get too much for me is just what I need."

She wasn't happy with my decision, but she didn't argue with me. He did, though.

"Excuse me, Bee."

Bronagh moved aside when Damien stepped into the hall, and I stepped back when he approached me.

"*I'm* staying the night."

I was sure my eyebrows reached my hairline.

"Excuse me?"

"You have a spare bedroom," Damien said, his eyes locked on mine. "I'm sleeping in there."

I looked at Bronagh, and she looked as shocked as I felt, but she said nothing. I turned my attention back to Damien. "I don't think that's a good idea."

He shrugged. "I'm still staying the night."

A part of me was shocked at his boldness while another part of me liked it. A week ago, if he had made such a demand, I'd have argued with him until I was blue in the face, but tonight ... I had no fight left in me. I didn't want to argue with him anymore, so I relented.

"Okay."

Bronagh almost fell over at my acceptance, but she said nothing. She stood mute as she glanced back and forth between Damien and me.

"Good," Damien said with a nod. "I don't need anything, so we can go."

Robotically, I said goodbye to Bronagh, hugging her tightly before I turned away from her, then along with Damien, I walked down the pathway and climbed into my car. I put my key in the ignition, buckled my seat belt, but before I put the car in gear, I looked at Damien in the passenger side of the car.

"Is this a good idea?"

He focused on me.

"Just for right now, forget everything that was said between us last week, and everything that happened today. I know mountains need to be moved for us to make things right, but tonight, let me be there for you. Please."

It was the first time in a long time that I didn't need to have my arm twisted to be in Damien's company.

"Thank you," I told him. "I'm not sure how I'm feelin' right now, to be honest with you, but I really appreciate you wantin' to help me."

"I've got you," he said, the promise in his words not going amiss. "You're my freckles."

Those three little words wrapped themselves around my hurt heart, and to my immense surprise, they made me feel a tiny bit better.

I looked forward, then back at Damien. "Can you drive?" I asked. "I'll put us in a ditch. Me mind is elsewhere."

We switched positions, and in a comfortable silence, he drove us to my apartment and parked my car in its designated spot. As we headed up to my home, Damien let me lead the way because he had never been in my apartment before. I knew he'd been in Kane and

Aideen's, but he'd never been on my floor, so he wasn't sure which apartment was mine.

As we neared my apartment door, I felt his eyes on me, so I glanced over my shoulder, and to my surprise, Damien's eyes were on my behind. He looked up at me, as if sensing my gaze on him, and instead of being embarrassed by being caught ogling, he simply grinned at me and shrugged his broad shoulders.

I quickly turned my gaze forward, feeling my cheeks burn. When we entered my home, I flicked on the lights and went to turn the central heating on. When I entered the kitchen, Damien already had the kettle plugged in and was filling it up with water. I left him be and went into my bedroom to change into pyjamas. I had just finished changing when, out of nowhere, I burst into tears. I covered my face with my hands and sobbed. My ma's face filled my mind, and the thought of losing her was unbearable.

It hurt.

I was so lost in worry and devastation that I didn't even flinch when the mattress dipped next to me and arms wrapped around my body. Damien went one step farther; he pulled me on his lap and cuddled me against him. I could hear him whispering words into my ear, but I couldn't make them out over my cries. He held me and I let it all out.

"I'm sorry," I wept. "I don't mean to be such a blubberin' mess."

"Hey," Damien said firmly, pressing his lips against my temple. "If you need to cry, then cry. I'm not going anywhere."

I shouldn't have been comforted by that statement, but I was.

I wasn't sure how long we stayed like that—me crying and Damien consoling me—but eventually, I sat upright and took a deep breath. I had to get it together. Whenever something went wrong in my life, my reaction was to cry and feel sorry for myself, but it was a chain that I had to break. I looked at Damien, and with the light of the hallway, I could only partly see his face. Without thought, I reached up, and tugged at his hair.

"When we were kids," I murmured, "I was convinced you bleached your hair."

When he smiled, my breath caught.

"Why?"

"Because." I shrugged, dropping my hand. "You have the same face as Nico but a different hair colour. I figured you weren't identical if your hair was really this light when his was so dark."

"Do you not think we're identical?"

I considered that then answered, "Yes and no."

"Explain."

"You both have the exact same face," I began, "but when I look at you, I don't see Nico. It sounds stupid, I know, but whenever you wore a hat in school and tried to fool other people, you could never fool me."

"Hmm," Damien mused. "I remember that. You'd always be so pleased that I couldn't trick you."

I nodded. "I'd be chuffed."

Damien gave me a squeeze, and he leaned his forehead against mine. My heart began to pound at the contact, and my body began to tremble at the small action of intimacy.

"You were perfect to me then," he whispered. "And you're perfect to me now."

I closed my eyes.

"We should go out into the sittin' room."

"Before we get in trouble?"

At the mention of the word trouble, I was brought back to our night together when I asked him to get into trouble with me just before we had sex. I sobered, opened my eyes, and got to my feet.

"Yeah," I answered. "Before we get into trouble."

Earlier today, I lost all rational thought when Damien was close to me. It resulted in a toe-curling kiss that only confused me about him even more than I already was. If I had another moment like that in a bedroom with him, trouble would *definitely* take place. I wasn't stupid enough to pretend otherwise, and I wasn't stupid enough to think I was emotionally stable to handle it.

Damien didn't object to us leaving the room. I think he needed to clear his head too, which was why he didn't fight for more to happen between us at that moment. I always thought he was level-headed, but for some reason, he seemed to give in to his instincts around me, just like I gave in to mine when I was with him.

I didn't know what to make of it.

"Do you want some tea?" he asked as we neared the kitchen. "I turned the kettle on."

I chuckled.

"What's so funny?" he asked, and I heard the smile in his voice.

I entered the kitchen, leaned against the counter, and folded my arms across my chest as I turned to face him.

"Askin' if me or the girls want some tea is somethin' you and your brothers say a lot," I mused. "I think you've all been corrupted."

"Tea calms you women down," Damien teased. "That's the only reason we offer it so much."

I smiled and shook my head, amused. I watched as Damien made me a cup of tea, and I was surprised when he added three sugars and just the right amount of milk without needing to be told. I wondered if he'd watched me make myself tea in Branna or Bronagh's house before. The idea of him observing me caused a shiver to run the length of my spine.

I grabbed some biscuits and plates while Damien made himself a cup of tea too, then carried both cups into the sitting room. Once everything was sat on my coffee table, I turned on the television and busied myself with it for something to do. I was suddenly very aware that Damien was in my apartment, and I didn't know what to think or how to feel about it. For the longest time, I had been so keen on blocking him out, but tonight, I didn't want that.

I wanted him there.

"Alannah?"

I startled. "Yeah?"

"Talk to me," Damien said, flattening his hands on his thick thighs. "You look like you're going to freak out."

"Do I?" I blinked. "I feel fine."

He raised a brow. "Don't lie."

My shoulders slumped as I raised my knees to my chest and wrapped my arms around them.

"This past week, I've been tellin' meself there was a reason we've ended up the way we have," I began. "I have to remind meself of what happened between us; otherwise, I'll do somethin' stupid."

"Something stupid ... like kissing me back when I kiss you?"

I swallowed. "Precisely."

"Alannah." Damien sighed as he leaned forward and rested his elbows on his knees. "I'm going to wait until you've had time to absorb your mom's news, but I want you to know that what happened between us *is* our past, but it *doesn't* have to be our future."

I groaned and rested my forehead atop my knees.

"What does that even mean?"

"It means," he continued, "that things change. People change. Situations change. Just because something bad happened between us before doesn't mean it'll happen again."

That was a mighty big if.

I leaned my head back, resting it on the large cushion behind my back.

"I'm scared," I said out loud.

"About your mom?"

"About everythin'," I answered. "Me ma, me business ... you. Just everythin'."

"Right now, we'll just focus on your mom. Mending things between us can happen later, and so can dealing with your job."

I closed my eyes at the mention of work.

"I have an interview with a lad who applied for me assistant job tomorrow. I blew 'im off last week, and I can't postpone the interview again because I'm worried he'll bail. He was the only person who applied, and accordin' to his previous experience, he really knows what he is talking about, and I need that. I need someone to deal with the business side of things so I can sketch and paint."

"Okay, so once you get the interview out of the way, you can breathe a little better?"

I nodded.

"Then we prep for that," he said, rubbing his palms together. "What do you need help with?"

I didn't answer. I opened my eyes and stared at the ceiling.

"Why are you 'ere, Damien?"

"I told you in the car," he answered. "You're my freckles."

"I don't know what that means."

"It means I've got you. Always."

I looked forward and found him staring at me intently.

"I don't know why," I said to him. "I have no idea why you'd want anythin' to do with me. I've been horrible to you from the moment you came back to Ireland."

"Are you kidding?"

I deadpanned. "Do I look like I'm crackin' jokes?"

"That is the dumbest thing I've ever heard you say then."

My mouth dropped open. "Excuse me?"

"To question why I'd want something to do with you doesn't make sense to me," he answered. "You weren't being horrible; you were being guarded. There is a difference."

I looked down. "I've been horribly rude to you."

"And look how upset you are knowing that," he said softly. "You aren't a mean person, freckles. You don't have a bad bone in your body, so when you resemble anything close to rude, everyone knows you have a damn good reason to behave that way."

"And you think me reason was justified?"

"And then some." Damien nodded firmly.

I rubbed my head. "I can't tell if you're lyin' or not."

"I don't lie when it comes to you."

At that, I snorted.

"Everyone lies about somethin'."

"I've told *one* lie regarding you, and it's the biggest lie I've ever told and my biggest regret."

I could hear my heartbeat in my ears.

"What was the lie?"

Damien blew out a breath. "Are you ready to hear this?"

No.

I barely managed a nod.

"The biggest lie I've ever told was that night in Darkness when I told you I didn't want to keep you."

It's not that I can't keep you, Lana; it's that I don't want to.

My heart slammed into my chest, and my mouth dried up. Words that had haunted me for years, were suddenly untrue and held no meaning. I didn't know how to process that.

"You didn't know it would span into this."

"No," he agreed, "but whether it was for days or years, I still hurt you, and I hate myself for that."

I frowned. "Well, I don't hate you."

The look of surprise on Damien's face was one I'd never forget.

"You don't?"

"Damien," I began. "If I truly hated you, then I wouldn't have been so upset over everythin' that happened between us. I've just been mad at you, at the situation. That can seem like hate sometimes, but it was just anger."

"*Was* anger or *is* anger?"

"I'm not sure." I swallowed. "I know you're sorry for everythin', you've said it enough times and showed it enough since you came back, but I just can't click me fingers and pretend everythin' is okay. I wish I could, but I can't."

"It's okay," Damien said, licking his lower lip, his eyes never once straying from mine. "I've got the time to wait for you to decide."

I blinked. "To decide what?"

"Whether you want to be with me."

CHAPTER SEVEN

The moment I opened my eyes that morning, I was aware of the events from the day and the night before. I had left my apartment after being cooped up for seven days on the trot, and in the few hours that followed, my life had once again been turned upside down. Damien had kissed me until I couldn't see straight, he fought Dante, *again*, I found out my ma had breast cancer, and Damien, of all people, was the one who stayed the night with me just so I wouldn't have to be on my own.

I was in a permanent state of confusion over that man.

I had gone from not knowing what he wanted from me to him flat out saying he would wait for me to decide if I wanted to be with him or not. To be in a steady *relationship* with him. He told me he lied when he said he didn't want me when we were eighteen. The words that haunted me day and night for years were suddenly untrue. Or at least he said they were. I was still in a state of shock over it all. I didn't know how to process what he was saying ... what he truly wanted.

It didn't feel like it was real.

Once upon a time, Damien saying he'd wait for me would have made my entire life, but I wasn't a kid anymore. I wasn't as carefree, and my heart was not new to the game. When I first met Damien, I had never been kissed, I had never had sex, and I had never come close to feeling love for another person. I was confident I didn't love Damien back when I was eighteen, but I knew I had been *falling* in love with him when everything turned south between us.

I felt something for him, something big. I wouldn't have been such a wreck over him for the past few years otherwise.

Damien left my apartment long before I woke up, and I had to admit, I was more than a little relieved. When I came into the kitchen and saw a sticky note stuck to a plate cover, I picked it up and smiled when I scanned my eyes over the scribbled words.

I'm going home to get showered before work. You needed your rest, so I didn't want to wake you, but I did make you some food. Eat it. I'll see you later – Dame x

The schoolgirl in me wanted to squeal at the kiss after Damien's name, but the woman in me kept her in check. I didn't want or need hope where Damien was concerned. I couldn't think about what he said to me; I had to focus on the bigger problem of my ma having cancer. Before I ate the breakfast Damien cooked for me, I called my ma.

"Mornin', love," she answered on the third ring.

"Mornin'," I replied. "How are you? Are you okay? Do you feel sick? I'm goin' to come by and—"

"Bear," Ma cut me off, chuckling. "I'm fine, baby."

I grunted. "No, you aren't."

"Okay," she conceded. "I'm not okay overall, but right now, at this very moment, I feel good."

I gnawed on my lower lip. "Do you promise?"

"I promise, bear."

My lips twitched at the nickname. "I'm still goin' to come by and see you later."

"After you interview that person for your assistant job?"

I nodded even though she couldn't see me.

"Yeah," I answered. "Damien helped me prep for what I want to ask the lad last night so I'm as ready as I'll ever—"

"Hold the phone." Ma cut me off again. "Damien helped you last *night?*"

I squeezed my eyes shut, mentally kicking myself for letting that slip.

"It's not a big deal, Ma."

"It bloody well is," she stated. "Weren't you 'ere just yesterday tellin' me you were sleepin' with Aideen's big brother, and Damien fought 'im over it ... and now he was with you ... at *night*time?"

I had to force myself not to laugh; my ma sounded so excited over my drama.

"Ma—"

"Did you sleep with 'im?"

"No," I said, incredulously. "What kind of woman do you think I am?"

"One with a healthy sex drive?"

At that, I did laugh.

"Nothin' happened." I chuckled. "I told everyone that you were ill, and I got a little upset, and he stayed the night with me. In the spare room, I mean. He just wanted to be there for me. He didn't give me a choice either; he just said he was stayin', and that was that."

Ma squealed. "That's *cute!*"

"Most mothers would encourage their daughter to call the guards if a man she was at odds with just stayed the night at 'er apartment without 'er askin' 'im first."

"When have I *ever* been like most mothers?"

I thought about that for a moment, then I snorted. "Never."

"Exactly," Ma said, and I just knew she had a grin on her pretty face. "Besides, if you really didn't want 'im to stay, you would have told 'im so, and from what I know of 'im, he would have listened."

I sighed. "I hate when you make sense."

"You get that from your da."

I gritted my teeth at the comparison.

"Yeah, I suppose."

"Call me after your interview."

"I'll do you one better," I said. "I'm stoppin' by."

"Alannah, I promise you, I'm feelin' fine."

"I know," I said, picking invisible lint from my pyjama trousers. "I just need to be around you. It'll make *me* feel better."

"Okay, bear," Ma said. "I'll see you in a few hours."

After we hung up, I ate my breakfast, then rinsed my plate and placed it in the dishwasher. I showered, dressed, and in an effort to be presentable for a business interview, I straightened my hair and applied makeup. I *sucked* at makeup. I had a bunch of products my friends made me buy, but I used maybe three of them when I decided to wear something on my face. I wanted to use all my goodies, but I didn't have the skill needed to apply them. I've watched thousands of YouTube tutorials, and eventually, I realised I watched those videos because I liked watching people transform their faces, rather than wanting to learn from them.

I carefully applied primer and foundation to my moisturised skin and used a little sponge to gently buff it in until it looked somewhat natural. As natural as makeup could look anyway. My hair kept falling into my face, so I pushed it back, but not before I laughed at the contrast of my hair to my skin. I had jet black hair and fair skin.

The only patch of skin that wasn't fair was the light brown freckles that sprinkled over my nose and under my eyes. Freckles that were now hidden by my foundation. I applied the setting powder and filled in my eyebrows as best as I could. After adding some mascara, a tiny bit of contour to my cheeks, and a dust of bronzer to warm my face up, I was good to go. My lips were naturally pigmented, so I never put anything other than lip balm on them.

After changing my outfit four times, I settled on wearing the only business suit I owned. It was a tight fitting grey skirt suit that my parents had bought for me a few years ago when I started looking for a job and wanted to be presentable at interviews. I was so pleased it still relatively fit.

The zipper on my torso didn't close all the way anymore, but I knew that was because I had gained a little weight over the years. If twenty-five pounds was considered 'little'. After I was ready, I stared at myself in the mirror. Tugging on the waist-length blazer, I wished it was longer to cover the shape of my hips.

I was no Bronagh Murphy.

My friend had an hourglass figure, and I didn't. I wasn't sure if there was a name for the body shape I possessed. My chest wasn't large, but not small either, and my waist was smaller than my hips but not by much. My hips were a little wide, and my thighs were "thick". That's what Nico had said when I once mentioned in his presence how much I hated the size of them.

"Thick" was apparently good, but I didn't think so.

I felt like I would be a whole lot happier with my body if I didn't have love handles. My body was a huge factor in why I almost didn't hook up with Dante considering how toned he was. I had always been insecure about it, but Dante had assured me that I was sexy, and my body was "spank bank" material.

I wasn't sure if I believed him about that, but he worshipped my body when we were together, and from the look in his eyes when he saw me bare, I knew he wasn't lying about finding me sexy. I wish I saw what he did, but I didn't. Gnawing my lip, I grabbed my phone and decided to FaceTime Bronagh for her opinion.

Nico answered, his smiling face filling my screen.

"Hello, gorgeous."

I clicked my tongue. "I'm tellin' Bee you called me that."

"Go ahead. She'd agree with me."

My lips twitched.

"Where is she? I need her opinion on me outfit."

"Is my opinion worth nothing?"

"No, 'cause you'll just tell me I look pretty."

"You are pretty."

I smiled. "Where is me mate at?"

"Bronagh!" Nico hollered. "Alannah is on the phone wanting

your opinion on her outfit."

I cringed. "You have a big mouth."

"Loud is the only language Bronagh understands."

I laughed, and not long later, Nico's handsome face was replaced with Bronagh's beautiful one.

"Hey, how are you? Are you okay? Do you want—"

"Bronagh," I cut her off, chuckling. "I'm doin' okay at the moment."

"And your ma?" she asked. "Have you spoke to 'er at all today?"

"Yeah, and she said she was okay, too."

"That's good." Bronagh nodded. "That she feels good, I mean."

"Yeah, it is."

"So?"

I grinned. "So?"

"What happened with Damien last night?" she asked, wasting no time. "Not knowin' has been killin' me."

"Nothin' happened."

"Alannah!"

"What? Literally nothin' happened. I cried all over 'im 'cause of me ma, then he helped me get questions together for me interview. He was gone when I woke up this mornin'."

Bronagh frowned. "I thought he might kiss you or ... somethin'."

I didn't want to know what the "something" was.

"He kissed me when I got me car from the garage yesterday so—"

"What?"

I jumped at the volume of her shout.

"Damien *kissed* you yesterday?" she asked incredulously.

"That's my boy!" Nico hollered in the background.

I groaned. "I called you for your opinion on what I'm wearin' to the interview, not to talk about Damien."

"Yeah, but—"

"Yo, anyone home?"

Alec.

"No, go away," Bronagh hollered. "I'm in the middle of an important conversation."

Bronagh had twisted the phone so I could partially see Alec when he entered her kitchen with Georgie in his arms. I could only see her chubby legs, but I could hear her babbling away at full volume.

"I'm returning your offspring. Her diaper is full."

"And you couldn't change it?" Nico asked, taking his child.

Bronagh shifted the phone and I could see Nico kiss all Georgie's face, making her squeal in delight.

"Could have." Alec shrugged. "Didn't want to."

"You are the Monday mornin' of people, Alec Slater." Bronagh scowled.

"Wrong!" he quipped. "I'm clearly a Friday!"

"Ha!" Bronagh's laughter taunted. "You're the furthest from a Friday!"

"Your words," Alec said, clutching his chest in mock pain. "They wound me."

My friend stalked towards him, the camera showing me her legs as her hand dropped to her side.

"*I'll* feckin' wound you!"

From the angle I could now see, Nico hooked an arm around her waist, careful to avoid her belly, and drew her against his body, grinning over her head at his older brother.

"Let me go!"

"Nope," Nico replied, popping the P. "You're pregnant, and he needs to be alive to witness the birth of his first child."

Bronagh almost growled.

"Fine," she relented, "but he won't live long enough to conceive the second."

"That's fair enough."

"Hello?" I sighed. "I'm still 'ere, ye'know?"

"Is that Lana?"

Alannah.

"Shite," Bronagh said then scrambled as she lifted the phone up so I could now see her face, and Nico's chest as he stood behind her. I could hear Georgie, but I couldn't see her. "Sorry, Alec came in and annoyed me."

I grinned. "That is his talent."

"Bite me, Ryan," Alec hollered.

I snorted as I flipped the camera on my phone and aimed it at my body-length mirror.

"Honest opinions, Bee."

"Holy shite, Alannah," she whistled. "You look like a sexy librarian."

"Shut up." I flushed. "I don't."

"She's not lying, Lana," Nico chimed in, then Alec said, "Well, fuck me sideways, you look downright sinful."

I flipped the screen back around to my face, but before I could call the lads on their bullshit, Bronagh said, "Your makeup is *so* pretty!"

My mood lightened.

"D'ye think? I tried me best with it."

"You look beautiful." My friend beamed.

I hesitated. "I don't look overdone?"

"No, you're the one interviewin' the bloke for a job. You look like the professional woman that you are."

"A professional hard-on inducing woman."

Bronagh thumped Alec for me.

"I've to go, but I'll stop by on me way home."

"You better," Bronagh warned. "We have *a lot* to talk about."

I nodded. "You got it, boss."

We said our goodbyes, and before I knew it, I was in my car and driving into town. I kept repeating what I had practiced asking over and over while glancing at the applicant's name on the front page of my papers. Morgan Allen. Then I had to repeat the name over and over so I didn't forget it when I first met him. An hour after I set off, I was sitting inside a relatively large café, sipping on a cup of tea.

I yawned for the sixth time as I waited for Morgan Allen to show up for our interview. It didn't start for another fifteen minutes, but I was hoping he'd show up early just to get the meeting over and done with. I was nervous. I had never interviewed someone to work for me before, so I was acting purely on instinct when it came to the questions I had prepared. I scanned through the questions I came up with Damien for an unknown amount of time, then I took out my travel sized pad and began sketching when a shadow fell over my table.

"Miss Ryan?"

I looked up from my sketchpad and audibly sucked in a breath when my eyes landed on the fine specimen before me. The man or god—he *really* looked like a Greek god—looked down at me with violet eyes. Logically, I knew there was no such thing as violet eyes, but this man's iris pigmentation was so light, I couldn't call it any other colour. I stared at him and his eyes for a long time, so long that he cleared his throat and reached up and awkwardly scratched his neck.

I felt my cheeks stain with heat.

"Y-yes?" I stammered.

"Hey." Violet Eyes smiled, revealing straight pearly white teeth. "I'm Morgan Allen, I'm 'ere for—"

"The interview," I finished on a nervous chuckle. "Of course, I'm so sorry for bein' weird and starin' at you; it's just ... you have really bright eyes."

"They're freaky lookin', right?"

"Freaky lookin'?" I repeated. "Try bloody cool. Are they contacts?"

Morgan shook his head.

"Nope, they're me natural eye colour, believe it or not. They're like this because there is little to no colour in me irises, so it looks like a shade of violet. It's a genetic defect. I'm pretty much a mutant."

"I wish I had a genetic defect that would give me violet eyes," I mumbled. "All I got stuck with was webbed toes."

Morgan laughed. I didn't know if he was laughing at me or not, but I didn't want to know.

"I got them fixed when I was little," I rushed. "They look just like regular toes now. No more webbiness."

"Webbiness?" Morgan quizzed, looking at me like I was that weirdly deformed dog that nobody wanted at the shelter.

"I'm sorry," I said, feeling heat spread out over my entire face. "I'm makin' an arse out of meself. Please, sit down."

"Thanks," Morgan said and sat down across from me. "And for the record, havin' a little webbiness is cool. You'd outswim me if we were ever in a situation where a shark was chasin' us and we needed to swim away. He'd get me first, and that'd be an advantage for you."

I stared at Morgan for a couple of seconds, then burst into laughter.

"Oh, my God," I tittered and covered my mouth with my hand. "You're weirder than I am!"

"Hey!" He gasped, feigning offence. "I was tryin' to make you feel better about starin' at me *and* droolin'."

"I didn't drool!"

I wiped at my chin just to make sure, and Morgan grinned. "Gotcha."

I tried not to smile as I glared at him. "You do realise I have the power *not* to give you this job, right?"

"Yeah, but then you'd have to settle for someone with regular coloured eyes, and where would be the fun in that?"

Oh, he was good.

"I suppose," I mused. "Eye colour is everythin' when workin' in design."

"You'd best snap me up quickly then 'cause I heard a *bunch* of other designers are hirin' nowadays."

I snorted.

"This is gettin' worse and worse for you," Morgan said with a shake of his head. "You stare, you drool, you once had webbed toes, and now you snort when you laugh? The list is never endin' with you, huh?"

I picked up my napkin and threw it at him. He caught it before it could hit him in the face, and he had a killer grin in place as he did so. It wasn't until that moment that I realised he was flirting with me, and I was flirting back. I didn't mean to, but his easy-going aura relaxed me. I cleared my throat, straightened up, and tapped on my papers.

"Interview time."

He sat up straight. "I'm ready."

"What made you apply for me assistant job?"

"Easy," Morgan said. "I'm a huge fan of your work, and I've been followin' you, or it, for a long time. When I saw that you were lookin' for an assistant, I jumped at the chance to apply. I can draw, too, and selfishly, I was hopin' to learn from you as well as work with you."

My lips parted. "You want to learn from *me*?"

"Definitely. Your work is inspirin'."

I felt my cheeks stain with heat.

"Thank you," I murmured before looking back down at the questions I had prepared for him. "You're aware of what your job will entail?"

When I looked back up, I found him nodding.

"Overall business management."

"And you think you can handle that?" I quizzed. "The number of job offers I've received in the past year has tripled, and I can barely read through them enough to organise and prioritise projects that interest me."

"We can devise a system," Morgan said. "Once I know what kind of projects you are drawn too, I can categorise which jobs to prioritise and which ones not to."

I nodded and looked back down to my questions.

"You said you had experience, and I've read what you've previously done, but what do you think you can bring to *my* business?"

"A strong work ethic that will achieve efficiency for your company," Morgan answered. "I will do everythin' that keeps you from sketchin' right now, and I'll make it better."

I looked up and grinned at his confidence.

"Make it better how?"

"Your work is outstandin', but as of right now, you don't market that very well."

"Job offers have tripled for me in the past year," I repeated. "That seems like marketin' is doin' just fine."

"But that is through word of mouth and referrals, correct?"

I hesitated. "I guess."

Morgan nodded. "That is fantastic, but I can market you on a higher level and reach people who don't know you from Adam. Advertisement is the key to success in graphic design. We need your work pushed into potential clients' faces. You need to be picky and aim for projects that will be successful on their platforms. I've seen your designs on book covers, but only one of those has become relatively successful."

"So, you think I should work on projects where they will be successful in their own market to draw attention to my designs?"

"Exactly." He nodded. "I'm not sayin' you shouldn't work on other projects because success can come from anywhere, but right now, you need to get *your* name known."

I nodded, finding myself agreeing with him.

"That's another thing," he said tentatively. "Your business name."

I frowned. "What's wrong with Go-to Designs?"

"It's quirky, but not somethin' that reflects your talent at first glance. You need a business name that will make people take the time to click on your website or social media pages. The name will draw 'em in, and your designs will keep 'em interested. You aren't a typical graphic designer. You don't use someone else's images to create a design; you sketch and make somethin' completely original. Your images don't look sketched unless it's a client's preference. Your designs look like photos before you scan them to a computer, and we need to market *that* talent."

I felt my ears burn at the praise.

I lifted my cup of tea and took a sip. "I'm assumin' you have some names in mind?"

Morgan's lips twitched. "A few."

"Let's hear 'em then."

"By a few, I really mean one."

I laughed. "Go on."

"Enigma Creations."

I blinked. "I ... I actually really like that."

"Brilliant." Morgan smiled. "Your designs are a mystery to me sometimes because when you draw somethin', it looks so lifelike, I have to remind meself that you hand drew it."

I bit the insides of my cheeks.

"Thanks, I think Enigma Creations is perfect."

"Glad you think so."

I went through a few more questions with Morgan, and the more he spoke, the more I wanted to stop him from talking and offer him the job completely. By the time I had asked him the last question, I was grinning like a fool. He smiled back at me.

"Does that smile mean I got the job?"

"It most definitely does."

Morgan beamed. "Deadly."

"I'm goin' to convert me spare bedroom into an office, so eventually, I'll have a place for you to come and work. I originally intended just to have you as an online manager of things, but I think havin' a work space will be much better. Does that suit you?"

"You have no idea how much."

We worked out an hourly wage and work schedule, and then we

chatted a little bit. I learned Morgan was twenty-one, and he was originally from Finglas but moved to Tallaght with his parents when he was a kid. Like me, he attended the Dublin Institute of Design and had just graduated with his BA in graphic design. He was an only child and wasn't very close to his parents. After I finished another cup of tea and Morgan drank a coffee, we stood to leave the café.

"I'll email you tomorrow, and we can go over everythin' and make the changes we discussed today."

"Sounds good, we've finished just in time for me to meet up with me girlfriend." Morgan said, fixing his bag's straps over his shoulders. "I'll speak to you tomorrow, Miss Ryan."

"Please, call me Alannah."

"Alannah," Morgan smiled and bowed his head. "Thank you for givin' me a chance, I won't let you down."

I was going to offer him a lift but decided against it. I didn't want to jump straight into a friendship with Morgan; my business came first, and he was now my employee, so I had to keep boundaries. When we parted, I watched him walk away, and I noticed that a group of girls and women stopped and focused on him as he fit his earbuds into his ears. I smiled and shook my head, wondering if he knew just how good looking he was.

As I walked to the multi-storey car park to retrieve my car, my phone rang.

"Heya, Ma," I said upon answering. "Are you okay?"

"I'm fine. I'm just callin' to say me and Da are goin' shoppin', so I won't be home if you stop by."

I frowned. "Okay, will you be home tomorrow?"

"Yep."

"I'll pop around then," I said. "I'll call you tonight before you go to sleep. What time do you think that'll be?"

"You don't have to phone me, love."

I got into my car. "I want to."

Ma chuckled. "I'm usually asleep by half nine."

"I'll call at quarter to."

"Okay," she said. "How was your interview with that lad?"

"Brilliant." I beamed. "I hired 'im, and I'm so pleased about it. I'm excited because he has some great ideas for the business."

"I'm chuffed for you, love."

"Thanks, Ma."

"I'll speak to you later."

"Okay, bye. I love you."

"I love you too, bear."

After we hung up, I drove back to Tallaght and headed straight for Bronagh's house. I was pleased to see no cars in the garden apart from Nico's because it meant no one else was in the house with them. I loved our group, but it had grown so much over the years that it was rare for Bronagh and me to hang out one on one. After I parked my car in the driveway, I headed towards the front door. I was about to knock but decided to test the handle first and was pleased to find it gave way and opened.

I didn't think to announce myself. The sitting room was empty, so the next obvious place for me to check was the kitchen.

"Hey, Bee," I said, pushing the door open. "Wait till I tell you about—OHMYGOD!"

I screamed, Bronagh screamed, and Nico laughed.

Currently, my best friend was bent over the kitchen table with her jeans and knickers around her ankles. Nico's tight bare arse was on display for all, or just me, to see, and his jeans were pushed down to his mid thighs. I had no doubt from the position he was in behind Bronagh and the grip he had on her bare hips where the *rest* of his body was.

"Oh, Jesus Christ!" I paled. "I'm *so* sorry."

CHAPTER EIGHT

I need to bleach my eyes.

That thought ran wild in my head as I pulled the kitchen door shut with a firm slam, turned and ran down the hallway, only to crash into a body of muscle when I opened the front door. I yelped and instantly fell backwards, only to be grabbed mid-air, swung around, and pressed against a hard body as I hit the ground. Or as the body I landed on hit the ground. The impact knocked the breath out of me, so when I gasped, the person under me struggled to sit us up.

"Alannah, are you okay?"

Damien.

Once I took a few breaths, I managed to get to my feet with Damien helping me as he got to his.

"I'm fine," I rasped then looked down at my skirt. "Shite, did I rip it?"

I turned around so Damien could see if I ruined my skirt, and when he didn't answer, I said, "Damien, did I ruin it?"

He cleared his throat. "It's perfect."

I blew out a relieved breath. "Thank God, this is the only suit I have."

His eyes raised to my face, and he paused. "What's with all the make up?"

"What's wrong with it?"

He squinted. "I can't see your freckles."

"So?"

"So, I like being able to see them. They're pretty, *you're* pretty without all … that."

Hearing him call me pretty caused butterflies to flutter around my stomach.

"Does that mean make up makes me ugly?"

"No!" Damien balked. "You look good. I guess I'm just used to you not wearing it. You look perfect either way, but … I like being able to see your freckles."

Those damn freckles.

"I only wore it for me interview to look put together."

I turned toward the kitchen when I could have sworn I heard a climatic moan, and my cheeks burned with heat. At the reminder of what I was running away from and caused me to crash into Damien in the first place, I cringed.

"I need to go," I said and tried to push by Damien, but he wouldn't let me.

"No," he said firmly. "Tell me what's wrong first."

I huffed. "What's wrong is I just saw me best friend takin' it like a champ, and to top it off, I saw your brother's bare arse!"

Damien stared down at me for a moment, then he laughed. Hard.

"You walked in on Dominic and Bronagh having sex?" he asked, his shoulders shaking.

I placed my hands on my burning cheeks.

"Yeah," I answered. "And I can never look either of them in the eye again."

He continued to laugh, and it was only then I realised how close we were standing to one another. I took a step back, hoping I wasn't being obvious that I wanted space, but from the clench of Damien's jaw, he noticed my intentions.

"How did your interview go?" he asked, shoving his hands into his jean pockets.

I perked up.

"It went brilliantly. Morgan is just what I need." At Damien's raised brow, I added, "He'll help me massively with the business. It'll really take a load off me."

"I'm glad," he then said. "Anything to put less weight on your shoulders is good."

I nodded in agreement but froze when the kitchen door opened.

"Is she still here?"

I closed my eyes. "Stay where you are, tight arse."

The twins laughed.

"I'm shoutin' when I enter this house in the future so this *never* happens again," I said, opening my eyes. "That is a visual I can never erase."

"Alannah, c'mere."

I moved around Damien and shielded my eyes with my hands as I walked by Nico, which the twins found hilarious. When I was inside the kitchen, I closed the door behind me, and exhaled a deep breath.

"I really should've rang the doorbell."

Bronagh chuckled. "Sorry about that."

I looked at her and grinned. "Yeah, you look real sorry."

She looked completely relaxed and satisfied with her hair a mess. She swatted my way for grinning at her then she fixed her hair, tying it up into a bun on the top of her head. I sat at the table, making a big deal of not sitting near the spot she was recently bent over, and it cracked her up.

"You look unreal," Bronagh commented, her eyes roaming over my outfit. "You pull that suit off perfectly."

I smiled. "Thanks, where's Georgie?"

"With Alec and Keela. They have 'er on and off most of the day. Keela is feelin' very maternal lately and wants to take the kids a lot. Alec is chill about it 'cause he says they need the practice for when their baby is born."

"That's cute."

Bronagh nodded in agreement.

"How was the meetin'?"

"Brilliant," I chirped. "I'm really pleased with Morgan and *so* excited to start workin' with 'im."

Bronagh raised a brow. "Is he good lookin'?"

"Why?"

"Just askin'."

"Well, yeah, he is."

"How old is he?"

"Twenty-one."

"Where is he from?"

"Finglas but moved to Tallaght when he was a kid."

"Does he have a bird?"

I laughed.

"I didn't ask 'im that, nosy hole, but yeah, he does. He brought it up in conversation."

Bronagh's lips twitched. "Okay, on to *better* conversation."

"'Ere we go."

Bronagh made us tea as she said, "Tell me everythin' and leave nothin' out."

"Bronagh, nothin'—"

"Don't even," she cut me off then lowered her voice. "You said Damien *kissed* you yesterday."

I flushed at the memory.

"He did."

"What was it like?"

I thought about that for a minute, and then I sighed. "Toe-curlin'."

Bronagh squealed. "Those are the *best* types of kisses."

"It was so unexpected. I didn't realise what was happenin', then all of a sudden, his lips and hands were on me, and I was kissin' 'im like a woman starved."

"That's *so* hot."

I licked my lips. "If he hadn't broken the kiss, I wouldn't have stopped."

"Holy shite."

She came over to the table, carrying our cups of tea. I played with the handle of mine when she placed it in front of me, before sitting across from me. I couldn't look at her while we talked about this because I was too embarrassed. Usually, our conversations about sex or kissing were primarily when Bronagh spoke and I listened.

"I lose all rational thought when he is close to me," I admitted. "It's like me mind just forgets the drama between us."

"And how do you feel about *that*?"

I grunted. "Even more confused."

"You like 'im."

It wasn't a question.

"Yes," I admitted on a whisper. "But that doesn't mean anythin' because I can't let go of the past."

Bronagh said nothing.

"It gets worse," I said.

"How?"

"He said ... he said he'd wait for me to decide whether I wanna be with 'im."

"Oh, Lana."

I felt my eyes well up.

"I know," I said, rubbing my eyes to stop any silly tears from falling. "I want to believe 'im, and I want to believe things would be different than when we were kids, but I'm just too scared. And I know you all probably think it's high time I get over it, and I agree, but it's like me heart just ... can't."

I looked up at my friend when she reached over, covered my hands with hers, and gave them a squeeze. My eyes stung, and when a few droplets splashed onto my cheeks, I quickly wiped them away. I willed no more to fall because I knew if either of the twins saw that I was crying, I wouldn't be able to leave the house without telling them why.

"I think you should try," Bronagh said softly.

"Try what?" I snivelled.

"I think you should try to see what happens between you and Damien."

I looked at her, my eyes wide.

"You'll regret it forever if you don't. I know you will."

I knew I would, too.

"I've always been so against the possibility, but hearin' 'im say he is interested changes things."

Bronagh nodded in agreement.

"Do you think he'd go slow?" I questioned. "With me ma bein' sick, and me da bein' a lyin' bastard, I can't take a full-on relationship right now. I'm not emotionally stable enough for that."

"Babe, Damien will move at a snail's pace if it means he has a chance with you."

A ghost of a smile graced my lips.

"I'll ... I'll talk to 'im about it."

Bronagh squealed and clapped her hands together merrily like a performing seal, and it made me laugh. Both of our gazes shot to the door when it suddenly opened and in walked Damien with a babbling Georgie in his arms. I sat up straight and quickly rubbed my cheeks to make sure there were no remaining tears.

"This little beauty just got home, and I think she is hungry."

Bronagh got up and moved over to the fridge where she removed a tupperware box, then took off the lid and put it in the microwave.

"I blended this up for 'er this mornin'. Will you put 'er in 'er high chair?"

"You got it."

Damien moved over towards the back door where Georgie's high chair was located, and the longer I stared at him, fixing her into the chair and tightening the straps around her, the more nervous I became about speaking to him.

"Dame."

He glanced at me, his grey eyes looking almost silver in the light.

"Hmm?"

"Can we talk ... later?"

He stilled. "Talk?"

I nodded. "Later."

He blinked a couple of times, then he slowly bobbed his head.

"Thanks," I said, exhaling a breath.

Damien cleared his throat, then he turned to Bronagh, and for some reason, I knew whatever he was about to say was to take away the apprehension that had suddenly filled the room.

"Dominic said you were making pizza for dinner."

Bronagh glanced at him as she removed Georgie's dinner from the microwave and tasted it. "I am."

He glanced around, before focusing back on her.

"I don't smell anythin'."

I snapped my attention to Bronagh's, and I watched as her eyes narrowed ever so slightly.

"I have to go to Dunnes and *get* the pizzas before I can cook them. It's still early."

"Ah," he grunted. "So, there'll be no food until *later*."

"I'd watch meself, if I were you."

Damien blinked at Bronagh. "What'd I do?"

"You're gettin' too big for your boots, askin' caveman questions," I answered on my friend's behalf. "That's what you're doin'."

Bronagh snapped her fingers when I finished speaking and said, "Exactly."

"Caveman?" Damien grinned. "If I put my foot down, does that mean you'll make me a sandwich?"

I rested my chin in my palms, watching the scene unfold before me with great amusement.

"One more word," Bronagh warned Damien with a dangerous wag of her finger. "One more word, and I won't hesitate to strangle you."

"Strangle me?" He raised a brow. "Can you even reach my neck?"

"You're a prime example!" Bronagh hissed, her hands flying to her hips.

"Of what?"

"Of a tall person bein' a feckin' arsehole!"

Damien laughed, I snorted, and Bronagh glared. I watched her go back to stirring Georgie's food, and when she remained quiet for longer than ten seconds, I said, "I thought you were goin' to strangle 'im if he said one more word? He said ten of them."

"Jesus, Lana," Damien scowled, but I knew it was playful. "Sign my death certificate, why don't you."

He fled the room the second Bronagh reached for a knife. She snorted as she blew on the pureed food, grabbing a spoon instead.

"Pussy."

I laughed, then looked at Georgie who was watching her ma, smiling.

"I love 'er so much."

Bronagh glanced at us and smiled. "Me too."

"I still can't believe you have a daughter, and now you're goin' to have *another* baby. When did we get so grown up?"

"Tell me about it." Bronagh chuckled. "It feels like just yesterday we were eighteen and in school."

Amen to that.

Bronagh moved over to Georgie and fed her before she threw a fit. We chatted some more about Morgan and the ideas he had for my business; we talked about Branna and wondered which day she'd have her and Ryder's twins, and we spoke about my ma. Both of us made sure we didn't bring my da into the conversation for obvious reasons. After Georgie was fed and wiped clean, Bronagh stood.

"I'm goin' to get some bits for dinner."

"I'll come with you," I said, making a move to stand.

"No," Bronagh said firmly. "You stay 'ere; Damien will come

in once you're on your own. He might kiss you again."

I scowled. "Bronagh."

"You're not comin' with me."

I folded my arms across my chest in annoyance, and it only caused my friend to grin. Knowing she won the argument, Bronagh unstrapped Georgie from her chair and lifted her daughter into her arms, giving her a snuggle.

"I won't be long." She winked.

I was left on my own then, and just as I was about to take a sip of my tea, I realised I was being watched. Through the glass sliding door, on the far side of the back garden, hunkered down with his belly on the ground, and his ears standing at attention was Tyson. He was deathly still, and unblinking as he stared at me.

"Stop it," I called out to him. "Stop starin' at me. I'm not doin' anythin' wrong."

He didn't move a muscle or look away from me, and I scowled at him because of it. That bloody dog held a grudge better than anyone I knew. I was notorious for not exactly watching where I walked when I was distracted, and maybe once or twice, or ten times, I stepped on Tyson during his lifetime, if that, but it was *always* an accident. I'd done it to Storm a few times over the years too, and he never held it against me.

Tyson clearly hadn't forgiven me, though, or forgotten about what I had done either … he was always watching me, waiting … and it creeped me the hell out. I turned my attention from Tyson to the kitchen doorway when I heard a familiar voice bring a smile to my face.

"You better not have my cup, Ryan!"

Alec slid into the kitchen, his eyes instantly latching onto the cup in my hands. When he saw it wasn't his prized Harry Potter cup, he relaxed.

"I thought you might be using it."

"And risk your wrath? Never."

His lips twitched. "How did your interview with that guy go?"

"Brilliantly," I exclaimed. "He is goin' to be a great addition, I know it."

"Cool." Alec smiled. "Glad to hear it."

His eyes dropped to my body then, and I sucked in a breath.

"Alec!"

His eyes moved back to mine, and when he saw how wide they were, he laughed.

"You look hot, but I wasn't checking you out. I promise."

I scowled. "What were you doin' then?"

"Looking for your sketchpad."

"Me main pad is at home."

He frowned. "Damn, I wanted to see the portrait of Keela that she said you drew."

"Have you not seen it?"

"No ... come to think of it, you're always sketching, but I never actually *see* what you're drawing."

"Sure, you do," I answered. "The majority of what I sketch goes up on me website after I'm done and I know you like lookin' through me site."

"Yeah," Alec agreed, "but that's *after* you scan it onto your computer and do all your graphic designer magical things to it. Half of the time, what you sketch doesn't look hand-drawn after you get it the way a client wants."

I grinned. "Because I'm good at me job."

"You're *awesome* at your job," he corrected. "What I'm saying is, I want to see your work in person."

I hesitated. "I'll bring the pad that had the drawin' of Keela with me tomorrow, and you can flick through it, okay?"

"Good. I look forward to it."

I raised my brow when he just openly stared at me.

"What?"

"Will you come up to the bathroom with me?"

"What, why?"

"Dominic said there is something I *have* to see in the bathroom, and I'm not going up on my own in case whatever it is ... is living."

I got to my feet, laughing.

"C'mon, princess," I said, leading him out of the room. "I'll protect you."

When we reached the bathroom on the first floor, we both pressed our ears against the door, and remained deathly silent. Neither of us heard movement, or a sound of any kind, so I reached for the door handle, and opened it.

Alec decided to become brave as he walked into the bathroom, but he sucked in a sharp breath a second later, and stumbled out of the room. I peeked into the bathroom and screamed when I saw the clown. Alec was already spirinting down the stairs, leaving me to fend for myself.

"You cowardly bastard!" I bellowed after him.

He didn't stop running.

"I'm sorry," he shouted as he exited the house. "Don't judge me!"

I walked into the bathroom, and stared at the pretty terrifying cut out of Pennywise from Stephen King's horror book, *IT,* that was chilling in the bathtub. I shook my head and placed my hands on my hips. I looked over my shoulder when side splitting laughter floated up the stairs. When Nico stumbled into the room, I shook my head, and chuckled.

"His soul is probably on its way to be with Jesus right now, I hope you realise that."

Nico didn't care, he shook with laughter.

"He told me I couldn't scare him," he tittered. "Proved that bitch wrong, didn't I?"

I left the laughing hyena, and headed outside of the house to find Alec at the end of the garden.

"It's only a cardboard cut out."

"It's evil, and I swear it blinked at me." Alec clipped, placing his hands on his hips. "I'm gonna kill Dominic."

I snorted, but looked down when my phone rang in my bag, so I quickly rooted for it. I clicked answer when I saw Gavin Collin's face flash across the screen.

"I'm not talkin' to you, Gavin Collins. Do you think I've forgotten that you just ignored me pleas to stop Damien and Dante from fightin' at the garage yesterday?"

"I'm so sorry, but please, I need to talk to you, Alannah! Can I come by? I'm in deep shite."

The urgency in his tone worried me.

"Are you okay?"

"No," he answered. "I just found out somethin' that is goin' to make me brothers and sister *kill* me."

I widened my eyes. "What'd you find out?"

"I'm goin' to be a da."

CHAPTER NINE

"I need you to explain this to me one more time, Gav."

Gavin, who was lying face down on my settee, groaned. After he phoned me, I made an excuse to Alec that I had to go, then I all but ran to my car, shouting goodbye to everyone on my way. Alec knew I was on the phone to Gavin because he heard me say his name, and I could only pray that he hadn't heard Gavin's declaration because with his big mouth, it'd get back to Aideen before Gavin could tell her the news that she would be an auntie.

"I already told you everythin' I know," he said, his voice muffled as he spoke into the settee pillow. "Please, don't make me tell you everythin' again."

"Who is she?"

"Who is who?"

I threw a pillow, smacking him in the back before it fell onto the floor, but he still didn't move.

"Who is the woman you got *pregnant*?"

"Oh." He grunted as he pushed up, then turned and sat on his behind, leaning his head back on the settee. "She's just someone I was seein'. 'Er name is Kalin, you wouldn't know 'er. She's from Kildare."

I frowned. "You never mentioned goin' out with anyone."

"We weren't goin' out; we were just—"

"Havin' sex?"

"Yeah," he replied, turning his head to look at me. "Kind of like what you and me *big brother* were doin'."

I felt my cheeks burn, and Gavin snorted before he turned his head to look at me.

"I'm sorry I didn't tell you," I said, wringing my hands together. "I was goin' to, but I hardly ever see you, and when I did, I'd chicken out ... then you found out along with everyone else before I could figure out a way to form the words."

"Don't be sorry," Gavin said. "You don't need to check in with me when you fuck someone."

I cringed. "Don't say it like that."

Gavin smiled. "Sorry, you don't need to check in with me when you have *sex* with someone."

"That's better."

He chuckled, then as if remembering why he was here, he groaned out loud. Again.

"How did this happen?"

I clasped my hands together. "Well, when a man and a woman like each other—"

"Shut up, smartarse."

I giggled. "Sorry."

He leaned forward, placing his elbows on his knees and his face in his hands. My heart went out to him, so I got up and sat next to him, putting my arm around his waist and resting my head on his shoulder.

"We'll figure this out," I said, giving him a squeeze. "Have you talked to Kalin? Has she let ye'know anythin' regardin' the baby?"

"She's keepin' it, and she's six weeks along. She's also offered a paternity test to prove the baby is mine, just in case I have any doubts. That's as much as I know."

"D'ye?" I pressed. "Have any doubts?"

"At first, loads," he admitted. "Then I couldn't remember if I wore a condom or not. We mostly got together at parties, and when we drink at one of the boss's parties, we drink *good*. I'll take the test either way, but Kalin says she's only ever had sex with me so she knows the baby is mine."

The boss he referred to was Brandon Daley, Keela's uncle. I didn't know exactly what Brandon was involved in, but I knew it wasn't legal. My friends never spoke about him around me, not even when I asked questions, so I figured they probably had no clue what he was truly into either. Gavin knew, though—not that he would tell me.

From what *I* personally knew of Mr Daley, I liked. He did a lot of business with the insurance company my da worked for, and he even bought a large canvas painting off me before. I had no idea who purchased the piece until I delivered it to his house. He was a perfect gentleman, and told me he would keep his eye on my website for other pieces that caught his eye.

"You're an eejit," I said to Gavin. "A massive one."

"I know," he said. "God, I'm *so* dead."

"You're twenty-four," I reminded him. "I don't think you can get a hidin' for gettin' a girl pregnant."

Gavin scoffed a laugh. "You don't know me brothers and sister as well as you think you do if that's the case."

"This is your responsibility, not theirs, and if they have somethin' to say, listen and then tell them to feck off."

"Can you be with me when I tell them?"

"Me? No. I'd probably die of fear on your behalf. Aideen scares the shite outta me when she's mad."

Gavin burst into laughter before he hooked his arm around my shoulder and leaned in, kissing my temple.

"We don't hang out enough."

"No," I agreed when he leaned back against the cushion, pulling me with him. "We don't, and whose fault is that?"

Gavin noted my tone and sighed. "Don't start, bear. I'm not in the mood."

Apart from my parents, Gavin was the only other person who

called me bear.

"No, I will start," I said, annoyed. "How did we go from seein' each other every day to seein' each other maybe once or twice a week, if even?"

"I'm busy," Gavin answered. "Ye'know that."

"No, I don't *know* that 'cause whenever I ask what you're doin', you don't answer me."

"Ye'*know* I can't talk about what I do when I'm with the lads," Gavin said sternly. "I told you, don't ask 'cause I'm not talkin' about it."

I shook my head. "I think you shouldn't hang around with people and do God knows what if it's takin' you away from your family and friends."

Gavin frowned at me. "I'm not bein' takin' away from you, bear."

A lump formed in my throat. "What if you're involved in somethin' one day, like somethin' you can't talk about, and it *does* take you away?"

His frown deepened, and when he saw my eyes well with tears, his lips parted.

"Please, *please*, don't cry."

Too late.

"I worry about you," I said, wiping my tears before they had a chance to splash onto my cheeks. "I know you don't trust me enough to confide in me about things—"

"You're the *first* person who popped into me head when Kalin told me she was pregnant." Gavin cut me off. "Not Aideen, not me brothers, not Bronagh. You, Alannah."

I snivelled. "I suppose."

"We've been friends a long time, and we'll always be friends," Gavin assured me, tugging me closer to him. "Just because I can't talk about work doesn't mean I don't trust you, okay?"

I nodded. "Okay."

"You're me girl." Gavin gave me a squeeze. "If I didn't love you like a sister, I'd have tried me hand in bein' your lad a *long* time ago."

I shoved him jokingly while making a face of complete disgust.

"If I didn't know any better," he teased, "I'd think you were repulsed by me."

"Only if I have to think of you sexually."

I heaved, for good measure, and Gavin laughed. He didn't need me to tell him how good looking he was because I was sure he knew it. I just couldn't ever imagine him in a sexual way; I couldn't do it with any of the Slater brothers either. Well, except *one* of those brothers.

"I have somethin' to tell you."

Gavin eyed me. "You aren't shaggin' Harley or JJ ... are you?"

I slapped his arm as he laughed at me.

"Be serious."

"Okay." He chuckled. "Proceed."

"I've two things to tell you, but I'll start with the lighter one." I exhaled a breath. "Damien kissed me yesterday in the back room of the garage before he and Dante fought, and I kissed 'im back."

Gavin whistled. "Did that fuck your head up more than it already was?"

"Yeah." I sighed. "When we spoke a little last night, he said he'd wait for me to decide if I want to try bein' with 'im, and of course, me mind thinks of everythin' that happened between us and automatically shuts it down because I'm scared of history repeatin' itself. But then I spoke to Bronagh, and she said Damien would go as slow as I needed."

"You'd *have* to go slow," Gavin pressed. "You don't know each other at this point in your lives. People can change in six years for the better or for the worse. Startin' fresh makes sense."

I nodded in agreement. "It doesn't make me any less scared, though."

Gavin patted my leg. "What's meant to be will be."

"Aideen said that to me yesterday!"

"Now I know where I got that sayin' from then." He chuckled. "What's the second thing you wanted to tell me?"

My ma flashed across my mind, and I swallowed. I clasped my hands together on my lap and focused my breathing.

"Me ma is sick."

Gavin froze, his eyes widening ever so slightly. "Sick?"

"Really sick."

His lips parted but no words or sounds escaped.

"Breast cancer," I managed to say around the lump in my throat. "It's in the early stages."

"Bear," Gavin said and reached for me, pulling me into a hug.

I took deep breaths to keep from crying all over him.

"She starts treatment soon," I said, my voice muffled. "I don't know anythin' more than that, but when I go see 'er tomorrow, I'm askin' for information on everythin' and what the course of action is."

Gavin kept his arm around my shoulder. "I'm so sorry that she is goin' through this."

"Me too, bud."

"And your da," Gavin growled. "The piece of shite."

"You don't know the half of it," I said, and then filled him in on the conversation I had with my da over his affair after the cancer bombshell was dropped on me.

"What a fuckin' arsehole!" Gavin exclaimed when I finished speaking.

"I know," I agreed, "but he is right. We need me ma to focus on beatin' 'er cancer. If she knew he cheated ... I don't want to think of how she'd react."

"That's fucked up, Alannah."

"I know."

Gavin removed his arm from my shoulder and scrubbed his face with his hands. "I thought I was in a fucked-up situation, but you've taken the cake, babe."

I smiled at him. "Your situation ends with a little baby, though."

"A baby," he repeated in awe. "I can't believe I'm goin' to have a *baby*."

"When are you goin' to tell your family?"

"No clue," he answered. "I need to absorb it first."

I stilled when Gavin looked at me, his gaze hard.

"Don't tell Bronagh."

My mouth dropped open.

"No," Gavin warned before I could object. "She'll let it slip to Nico, and he'll tell Kane, and Kane will tell Aideen, and shite will kick *off*."

I scratched my neck. "Bronagh and I don't keep secrets from each other, though. Ye'know that."

"It's only for a little while," Gavin assured me. "Just until I get me ducks in a row and get the courage to tell them."

I tilted my head back and sighed. "Fine."

"I love you, bear."

"Yeah, yeah," I said, hugging him back when he pulled me into his embrace. "I love your dumbarse, too."

CHAPTER TEN

When Gavin went home after we spoke, I was so drained from the day's events that I didn't go back to Bronagh's house as I had initially intended to. I had planned to send her a text and tell her I'd swing by the next day instead, but I couldn't find my phone. I thought of the last time I had it: after I spoke to Gavin and drove home from Bronagh's house. When I realised where it was, I groaned in annoyance.

I left my apartment and made my way to the lobby of the building, waving at Joseph, the night guard as I passed by. When I retrieved my phone from my car and locked it, I heard a soft cry. A cry that was dangerously close to that of a baby. With my heart pounding, and all my senses on high alert, I spun around, and squinted my eyes, hoping it'd help me see better.

It didn't.

I jumped when I heard the cry again, and walked briskly in the direction it came from. All sorts of scenarios were flooding through my mind. I had seen on the news plenty of times about people abandoning newborn babies and leaving them out in the open with no protection. I prayed to God that wasn't the case, but when I came across a cardboard box in-between two parked cars, my entire body tensed, and I just about died on the spot. I crept forward, and when I found the courage to peek inside the box, I nearly deflated with relief when I saw it wasn't a baby ... but then sympathy flooded me when I realised what I'd stumbled upon.

Someone had abandoned a helpless, tiny kitten.

"Oh, baby," I uttered, my hands clutched to my chest.

When the kitten cried again, I was horrified to discover how much it sounded like an infant. The poor thing looked terrified, so I carefully reached into the box and picked it up. I held it against my chest, wincing when its nails dug into my skin as it held on for dear life. I hurried back into my apartment building, walking at an angle towards the elevator so Joseph couldn't see the kitten. There was a strict no animal policy in the building, but I couldn't leave the kitten out in the cold to fend for itself.

I simply couldn't.

When I made it up to my apartment, I grabbed a smaller throw-over blanket from my settee and wrapped the kitten inside it. I set it down on the settee and stepped away. I was relieved to see the kitten didn't try to escape; it simply stayed snuggled inside the safety and warmth of the blanket. I got out my phone and phoned Alec. He worked in an animal shelter and was the only person I could think of to call.

"Alannah," he answered on the fifth ring. "Is everything okay?"

I rarely called him, and it was closing in on eight p.m., so he probably figured something was up.

"Kind of," I answered. "I found a kitten."

"You found a kitten?"

"Yeah," I answered. "Some bastard left it in a cardboard box in the car park of me buildin'."

"Is it alive?"

"Yeah." I nodded, though he couldn't see the action.

"Do you want me to come and get it?" he questioned. "I can keep it and bring it to the shelter tomorrow."

I paused. When I rang Alec, it was for help for the kitten, but at that moment, I realised I had only called him for advice. I didn't want him to take the kitten. I wasn't sure when I made the decision, but I wanted to keep the kitten myself.

"No," I answered. "I'm keepin' it."

Alec was silent.

"What?" I pressed. "What're you all quiet for?"

Alec was *never* quiet, so his silence spoke volumes.

"You ... you aren't very good at taking care of animals."

My lips parted in outrage. "I am too!"

"You step on Storm a lot when you come over to our house, and he is bigger than you. I still don't understand how you don't see him."

I would never admit it to my friends, but my eyesight wasn't the best, and with each passing year, it was obvious to me that I was going to have to bite the bullet and make an eye test appointment to get the glasses I knew I needed. It didn't help that I didn't exactly watch where I was walking when I was distracted either.

"I don't watch where I place me feet, so feckin' sue me."

"Tyson growls at you whenever he sees you because you stepped on him one too many times. He just watches you whenever you're around him now."

That bloody dog couldn't forgive and forget like Storm could.

"Listen," I stated, "every time it happened was a *total* accident."

Alec laughed.

"I'm keepin' the kitten, and that's that," I said with a huff. "Can you just tell me what I need to buy? I'm clueless."

"I can do you one better," he chirped. "I can go to Maxi Zoo before it closes and bring what you need to you since you shouldn't leave the kitten alone."

My heart warmed, and my shoulders sagged with relief.

"Thank you, Alec." I gushed. "I don't know how old it is until I bring it to a vet tomorrow, but it looks really young, so get kitten food. Bring the receipt when you come over, and I'll pay you back when you get 'ere."

After we hung up, I went and sat next to my new roommate, peeking into the blanket. The cat's fur was completely white, and from what I could see, it had one green eye and one blue eye.

"You're so gorgeous," I cooed.

The cat didn't move a muscle, so I carefully picked up the blanket and cuddled it against my chest. When the kitten eventually wriggled around, I reached in and picked it up. Quickly, I checked between its legs and discovered the kitten was a girl. I put her back inside the blanket and let her get used to whatever it was that she was sniffing and scratching.

"What, baby?" I asked when she began meowing and didn't stop.

I wondered if she was hungry, and then I wondered how old she was once more.

"You should have a cool name," I said when the kitten popped her head out of the blanket and stared at me, then looked around the room. "Oh, what about Nala? She was a cool lioness in *The Lion King*."

The kitten looked back at me and stared at me, unblinking.

"I'm takin' your silence as a no."

I pondered on a couple of unique names that sounded cool in my head, but when I said them out loud, none of them suited her. Her bored expression told me they all sucked, too. I switched on the television and selected my YouTube app. I scrolled through the videos, and when one of Barbra Streisand's music videos was suggested, I stared at her name, then looked down at the kitten.

"What about Barbara?"

The kitten meowed as if replying to me. I stared at her, took the meow as a resounding yes, then chuckled. My ma's middle name was Barbara, so I was sticking with that spelling because I knew she'd get a kick out of it.

"Barbara, it is."

I picked up my phone when it began to vibrate and answered it without looking at the screen.

"Alec said you found a kitten."

I smiled. "Hey, Bee."

"Where did you find a kitten?" She continued as if I hadn't spo-ken. "I saw Alec get into his car when I was puttin' Branna's wheelie bin out. He said you found a kitten, and he was goin' to get you some stuff for it."

I filled her in on when, where, and how I found the kitten, and she grunted. "Evil bastard whoever left it."

"*Her*."

Bronagh snorted. "Have you named 'er?"

"Yup."

"Let's hear it."

I grinned. "Barbara."

Like I knew she would, Bronagh burst into laughter.

"I'm not the *least* bit surprised," she said, amused. "If you said a trendy name, I wouldn't have believed you."

"What's funny?" I heard Nico ask in the background.

"Alannah found a kitten, and she called 'er Barbara."

I smiled when he laughed and said, "I love that woman."

Bronagh and I chatted for a while, and luckily, she didn't mention anything about Gavin, which I secretly thanked God for. I was hoping that Alec would keep my phone call with Gavin to himself because if Bronagh confronted me about it, I was scared I would break my promise to Gavin and tell her everything about him becoming a father.

We had just hung up when my apartment buzzer rang. I walked over to the door and pressed the button for Alec to enter the building. I didn't glance at the monitor to make sure it was him because Barbara was meowing like a banshee. When I eventually turned, and looked at the monitor, the entryway was empty, so I figured Alec had already entered the building. I unlocked my door for him, and went back over to the settee and gently stroked Barbara. She moved away from me when my hand initially touched her, then she seemed to relax and didn't mind me scratching her ears.

My doorbell rang, so I shouted, "It's open."

I continued to rub Barbara, and when she moved back into the safety of the blanket, I turned to greet Alec and help him with the items he brought for me. Only it wasn't Alec in my apartment, it was Damien, and he had two large carrier bags in his hands. I paused and stared at him with my lips parted in surprise.

What is he doing here?

"Where should I put these?"

I didn't know what was in the bags, but I managed to say, "Kitchen, please."

He went into the kitchen without a word, leaving me to stare after him. When he returned, he closed the front door and came into the sitting room, eyeing the blanket beside me.

"So, you found a cat?"

I nodded dumbly. "She was in a box between two cars in the car park, and I decided that we could keep one another company."

"You rescued her," Damien concluded.

"I guess so."

"That's admirable."

Blood made its way to my cheeks at his praise.

"Where is Alec?" I asked, changing the subject.

"He called me and said he needed help getting some things for you, then he dropped me off with all the stuff." He lifted his hand and scratched his neck. "I thought we could have that talk you mentioned earlier at Dominic's place."

My heart thrummed in my chest when I realised I had completely forgotten about asking him that. When Gavin phoned me, everything took a back seat in my mind, and I focused on my friend and his problem.

"O-okay."

Damien's eyes dropped to the blanket when it moved. "Did you name it?"

"*Her.*"

His lips twitched. "Sorry. Did you name her?"

"I picked Barbara."

The smile that stretched across Damien's face was transfixing.

"Does it suit her?"

"It does … I probably should have called her snowflake, like I call you."

"Why?"

"She's white all over, just like your hair."

I reached into the blanket and removed Barbara, tugging the blanket away from her paws as the fabric got snagged on her nails. I held her on my chest, careful to place her slowly against me so her nails didn't prick me like the needles they clearly were.

"Cool eyes," Damien murmured as he leaned closer to get a look at her. "One blue and one green."

I stilled as he hovered close by without any indication that he would move.

I blurted, "You're makin' me nervous."

"By being here?"

I bobbed my head.

"You said you wanted to talk to me."

"I-I do," I stammered. "I'm just … just …"

"Scared?" he finished.

I exhaled a deep breath. "Immensely."

"Do you want me to go?" he asked, frowning. "I don't want you to feel uncomfortable."

That was exactly why I was nervous—because he *didn't* make me feel uncomfortable, he made me feel … whole.

"Would you believe me if I said no?"

Damien's lips parted with surprise, but nothing came out.

"Sit down," I said to him. "It's high time that I get this off me chest."

Damien sat down on the settee across from me, and when he rested his elbows on his knees and clasped his hands together, I knew he was as nervous as I felt, which allowed me to relax a little. I put the kitten back into the blanket on the settee next to me just to busy myself for a second or so. When I looked back at Damien, I spent a moment taking him in.

He was so handsome; it seemed unfair that someone could be born that beautiful. His hair, as always, was perfectly styled. It was tightly trimmed on the sides with a sick fade blending to his neck. His hair was thick; I knew from experience of touching it. It had a little length to it, not that anyone would know because he used hair gel and a hair dryer to get that perfect blown back comb over taper.

I focused on his face, his clear skin, and the stubble that had clearly grown a little from his last shave. His eyebrows had a tinge of darkness to them. They were light but nowhere near as light as his hair, which made sense to me. My hair was black, but my brows were naturally light brown. Unlike my brows, Damien's were thick and nicely shaped. No doubt thanks to Bronagh getting her hands on them. His lashes were light and long, and they framed his stunning grey eyes that seemed to penetrate my very soul with one glance.

I knew every curve of his face, every flick of his hair, and every possible way he could smile. I saw him every single night in my dreams. I could draw him from memory alone ... I had done so enough times. This man was under my skin and had been for a long time. This conversation between us was overdue, and I could only hope I could do it justice and give him the respect he deserved.

"I want to try."

Damien tilted his head. "Try what?"

What's meant to be will be.

I exhaled a breath. "I want to try bein' with you ... if you'll have me, that is."

Silence.

Oh, God.

A long period of deafening silence.

"Damien?"

He was staring at me, long and hard, and I found, at that moment, I would have paid any price and done anything to know what was going through his mind.

"Okay," I said, rubbing my now sweaty palms on my leggings. "Now you're freakin' me out."

"Sorry," he said, unblinking. "I feel like this isn't real."

I looked down at Barbara when she meowed, then flicked my gaze back up to Damien. "It's very real."

"Are you saying ... that you want to *date* me?"

Yes. Yes. Yes. Yes.

"I am." I swallowed. "But this is where things get complicated because I'm not ready to *just* be your girlfriend. I've so much goin' on right now, but I don't want that to be another excuse as to why I should shut you out any more than I've already done for the past year. I'm takin' initiative 'ere, and followin' advice given to me by seemingly everyone. That bein' said, I want to go *slow*."

"What does *that* mean?"

"It means that we go on dates and we get to know each other because, let's be honest, we're different people than when we were eighteen. I want us to build up a trust, a better connection than we have now ... I want everythin' that couples do *before* intimacy happens."

Damien licked his lips. "You mean everything we should have done *before* we had sex when we were kids?"

Exactly.

"Is that okay?"

"Are you kidding?" he exclaimed. "You bet your ass it's okay ... but ..."

My stomach tightened. "But?"

"I want to know why you want this."

I flushed. "What kind of question is that?"

"A valid one," Damien challenged. "You've been ditching me all year, keeping me at arm's length since I came home. You've been guarded, but now, suddenly, you want to try with me. I want to know *why*."

I thought about that. Hard. Simply saying I was incredibly attracted to him didn't seem a good enough answer. Not to me. I looked at Damien and repeated his question in my mind. Why did I want to be with this man? And just like that, the answer came to me.

"Because I'm tired of bein' scared to accept that you could be *it* for me. I'm tired of worryin' what could go wrong if I accepted you back into me life," I answered, my voice tight with emotion. "I convinced meself that everythin' that happened between us was your fault … and it wasn't, Dame. I'm sorry for never admittin' that before now."

Surprise lit up his features.

"It *wasn't* my fault?"

"No, not entirely, like I've always said it was." I answered. "You were upfront and honest the whole time, and I shouldn't have used what you said during sex against you. I seduced you, even when you told me it wasn't a good idea. You told me what would happen. You said I wasn't a sex only type of girl, and you were dead right, but I didn't listen. I saw how you looked at me that night, and I used your attraction for me against you because I wanted you so badly. I was aware of what could happen, of what evidently *did* happen … but I thought I could deal with it if it came to that."

"But you couldn't?"

"No, I couldn't." I cleared my throat. "I wanted to hate you; you have no idea how much I wanted to. I tried to tell meself that I did; I made it clear to everyone else that I despised you … but I didn't. I just hated what happened between us because it hurt me so bad. But just know that it wasn't all your fault. I was more to blame, but I didn't want to admit that to anyone. Especially meself."

"Alannah," Damien murmured as he scrubbed his face with his hands. "It's hard hearing you say all this."

"Does it hurt?" I asked softly. "I never wanted to hurt you."

The look on his face when I told him about Dante flashed through my mind, and it cut me to the bone.

"Hurt *me*?" He blinked. "Baby, you look so sad telling me this, it's tearing me up inside."

Baby.

"I'm fine." I smiled, sadly. "It's just been a tryin' week."

"You'll come out on top," Damien assured me. "You always

do."

"I'm not so sure," I whispered.

"What?"

"I'm not a brave person," I said, my lower lip wobbling. "When someone or somethin' hurts me, I'm not very good at standin' tall and facin' it again because I'm scared of bein' hurt worse than before." I looked down. "I have this fear in me, Damien. It ruins everythin'."

"Alannah."

"Please," I said with a shake of my head. "Don't say I'm brave because I'm not. I'm a good-for-nothin' coward."

Damien inhaled sharply.

"I am," I continued. "I was a coward with you, makin' you believe what happened between us was all down to you when I knew bloody well it wasn't. I'm a coward with me friends; they were the voice of reason where you were concerned for a long time, and I brushed their opinions aside. I automatically assumed they were wrong, just because they disagreed with me. I'm a coward with me parents; me da has been cheatin' on me ma for God only knows how long, and I haven't even tried to tell 'er because it'll hurt me if she can't handle it. The woman has breast cancer ... *she* has cancer, not me. *She* is the one who must fight this evil in 'er body, and all I can fuckin' think about is that I don't want 'er to die, because *I* couldn't cope without 'er ... I make everythin' about *me*, and I can't stand it."

"Alannah."

"I'm spineless," I stated, angrily wiping away the tears that welled in my eyes before they had a chance to fall. "I'm a coward with no courage."

I jerked back with alarm when Damien moved, and before I knew what was happening, he kneeled before me. His hands went to either side of my face, and *his* face moved as close as could be without touching his nose to mine.

"You listen to me, Alannah Ryan," he almost growled. "You are neither of those things, and you have plenty of courage!"

I turned my eyes away from Damien, not allowing myself to believe his words.

"How can you say that, let alone believe it? I'm scared of what is goin' to happen to me ma, to 'er and me da's marriage. I'm scared me business is goin' to up and fail, and I'm absolutely terrified that things will end worse with you than they did the last time."

"And you say you have no courage?" Damien asked, his thumbs stroking my cheeks. "Real courage is acting when your terrified. You *are* brave."

"Why are you bein' so nice to me?" I whispered. "I've made your life hard."

"Don't," he warned.

"You left because of me." I snivelled. "You said so last week in Branna's kitchen."

"I said I left *for* you, not *because* of you. I left for me too. I had so much shit to work through, things that I could only figure out by myself. If I thought you did anything to wrong me, Lana, I wouldn't have tried so hard to win your trust. I wouldn't have come back at all."

I looked deep into his eyes.

"How do you manage to make me feel better over somethin' that's been plaguin' me for as long as I can remember?"

"It's a talent," he said, his lips twitching. "I learned it in school."

"With other girls?"

He snorted. "None that were important. They all just wanted my attention."

"I remember."

"Everyone wanted something from me," Damien said.

I remained silent.

He roamed his eyes over my face. "Everyone wanted something ... so what did you want from me, Alannah?"

What did I want from Damien Slater?

"I want what I've always wanted, what I *still* want."

"Which is what?" he asked, leaning towards me as if he *needed* to hear my answer.

"Your time."

"What?" Damien pulled back and looked at me with confusion.

"Havin' a single moment of your time was the best part of me day back in school, d'ye know that? Everyone always wanted your attention, your looks, to be on your arm ... but I just wanted to be around you. Nothin' more, nothin' less. I just wanted to talk to you ... I just wanted your time."

"You have it," he said, placing his forehead on mine. "You have every minute of it, every millisecond. It's yours."

I closed my eyes and placed my hands on his arms.

"Kiss me."

Damien made a sound, deep in his throat.

"You said we have to go slow," he murmured. "We *have* to. I'm not ruining this."

"One little kiss won't ruin anythin', snowflake."

"One of your kisses ruined me a long time ago, freckles."

When I opened my eyes, and smiled at Damien, his breath caught, and that was the only warning I got before he covered his mouth with mine. My hands, as I knew they would, slid straight up to Damien's hair, and my fingers tangled around the thick strands. I parted my lips, and when his tongue slid against mine, a pulse began to throb between my thighs.

Instantly, I broke the kiss.

"Trouble," I rasped. "Stop. We'll get in trouble."

Damien tensed, but he didn't attempt to kiss me again, though I knew he wanted to. I could almost *feel* how much he wanted to.

"Do you want me to go?" he asked, his eyes still on my lips.

I shook my head. "No, I don't."

"You don't want me to leave *at all*?"

"No," I answered shyly.

"You're trying to kill me." Damien groaned. "I know you are."

"I promise to be good."

He grunted.

"I'll be good," I continued. "I won't tease."

"You'll be a good girlfriend?"

My stomach flip flopped at the mention of the word.

"*Am* I your girlfriend?"

"Yes," Damien answered instantly. "I don't want to play games. We'll be dating and dating *only* each other. What's the point in not being the other's partner when we *know* that's what we'll be to each other? I'm not doing that no label bullshit. I've seen some of my brothers go down that route, and it was pointless for them. I know who I want, and that is *you*."

My stomach erupted with butterflies.

"No games?" I repeated.

Damien nodded. "No games."

"We'll have to communicate," I urged. "We lacked severely in that department before, so it *has* to be a priority if we're goin' to really be doin' this."

"We *are* doing this," Damien said, licking his lips. "You're my girlfriend."

The schoolgirl in me wanted to scream, "I'm Damien Slater's girlfriend!", and for once, the woman in me was on the same wavelength.

"I'll be the best girlfriend," I assured Damien. "I promise."

He smiled, leaned in, and brushed his lips gently against mine.

"I can't fucking *believe* you're my girlfriend."

Neither could I … my friends were going to *die*.

CHAPTER ELEVEN

I shot upright when I heard a loud bang, followed by a string of curse words. I jumped out of my bed, thankful my bed sheets didn't wrap around me like a boa constrictor and bring me to my knees. I ran out of my room and came to a skidding stop in the hallway outside of the kitchen. I winced at the brightness of the light and lifted my hand to block it. With my eyes squinted, my vision cleared, and Damien came into view.

A half-naked Damien.

"Fuck."

Damien jumped and spun to face me.

"You scared the shit out of me," he said, placing a hand on his ridiculously toned chest in surprise.

My eyes roamed over his body, and my mind began to tick things off one by one.

Nice tan? *Check.*

Killer abs? *Check.*

Drool worthy V line? *Check.*

Treasure trail? *Check.*

Wearing nothing but black boxer briefs? *Check.*

"Alannah," Damien said, his voice gruff.

I flicked my eyes up to him. "How do you maintain a tan? People get lighter 'ere, not darker."

Damien looked down at his body, then back up at me.

"I'm lighter than I was a year ago."

"Doesn't look like it to me."

When he didn't reply, I looked up at him and froze when I saw how he was looking at me.

"Stop looking at me like you want to eat me," he said, his jaw tensed. "I'm only a man, and I'm going to try to touch you if you don't stop."

I wasn't sure if I could adhere to his request, so I lifted my hand and covered my eyes completely. "Done."

When Damien's low laughter filled the room, I felt the sudden sexual tension slip away so I smiled and dropped my hand back to my side.

"I didn't mean to wake you," he said, a slight frown on his face. "The cat was crying, so I came to check on her and I walked into the table when I came in here."

I gasped. "Barbara!"

Before I could turn and run into the sitting room, Damien's voice stopped me.

"She's in her crate; she's fine."

Before we both went to bed—in separate rooms—we set up everything Alec had bought on my behalf for Barbara. There were toys, food, bowls for food and water, litter trays in different sizes for when she grows, a scratching post that took surprisingly *forever* to put together, a packet of catnip, and a little fur brush. I was confident I'd need to get more supplies for her, but for the moment, it seemed I had everything to sate her needs.

"Did she eat any food?"

Damien nodded. "There is a small dent in what we gave her."

I gnawed on my lower lip, and worried.

"I hope she isn't too young for the kitten food."

"Alec told the woman in the store that you weren't sure how old she was, but that she was small, so she gave us the food she had for kittens who have just weaned off their mother's milk."

I folded my arms across my chest.

"But what if she should still be drinkin' 'er ma's milk, and we're givin' 'er solid food?"

"You're going to the vet tomorrow and you know you'll ask then, okay? We've done all we can for now."

I sighed. "Okay."

When Damien smiled, I shifted my stance.

"What?"

"We're standing in your kitchen in the middle of the night talking about a baby kitten, and we're dating." He shook his head. "This is just not how I was expecting the night to go when you said you wanted to talk to me."

"How were you expectin' it to go?"

"Honestly?"

I nodded.

"I thought you were going to say you just wanted to be friends."

My lips parted. "Why?"

"I didn't want to give myself any hope, so I always force myself to expect the worse when it came to you … just so it'd hurt less."

My stomach churned.

"Dame." I frowned as I dropped my arms to my side and crossed the room.

He opened his arms and accepted my hug wordlessly. He hugged my body to his and stroked his hand up and down my back. It amazed me how perfectly I fit against him and how soothing I found his touch to be.

"I'm sorry I made you feel like you had to do that."

"No more apologising." He kissed the crown of my head. "We aren't focusing on the past anymore, right?"

I squeezed him. "Right."

Barbara began to make a lot of noise then, and Damien sighed. "She is singing us the song of her people."

I laughed, and together we went into the sitting room. I let Barbara out of her crate and encouraged her to eat more food and drink some water. It took a few minutes, but she did consume a little more of both and it relieved me greatly. I pushed her litter tray close to her so she could see and smell it. I tapped on the screen of my phone when a question entered my head.

"I think she has to go to the toilet, and Google says to put 'er on the litter tray after she eats and drinks to promote 'er goin' to the toilet in it."

Damien rubbed his eyes. "If Google says so, it must be right."

I looked up at him.

"Are you bein' sarcastic?" I blinked. "I'm so stressed out with the cat that I can't even tell."

He tiredly laughed, then reached out and hooked his arm around my shoulder, tugging me to his body.

"I love that I can touch you like this without worrying you'll attack me."

I slipped my arm around his bare waist, my palms becoming clammy almost instantly.

"When have I *ever* attacked you?"

"The day I knew you were the one for me," he answered. "We were eighteen, and everything had just gone to shit between us. You kicked me in the balls and told me to go to hell, and never come back."

My free hand flung to my mouth, and I laughed.

"I forgot about that!"

"Jesus, I didn't." He playfully winced. "I can still feel the blinding pain when I think about it."

"You're so full of it," I cackled.

He looked down at me when I laughed and said, "You're gorgeous."

I stopped laughing almost instantly and ducked my head.

"Don't say stuff like that; you'll embarrass me."

Damien groaned. "God, that's sexy."

I looked up at him with raised brows.

"*What* is?"

"The fact that you don't know you're gorgeous; it's such a turn-on."

I narrowed my eyes, trying to ignore my burning cheeks.

"Stop it."

Damien smiled with a devilish glint in his eyes.

"Make me."

I froze. "Nico says that to Bronagh *all the time,* and nine times out of ten, I make some excuse to leave because I know they're goin' to have sex."

"I think I have more control than my dumb twin brother has."

I snorted. "You think so, huh?"

"I *know* so."

With a grin, I turned back to Barbara to see what she was doing, and I gasped.

"Damien!" I gave his waist a squeeze. "Look."

I pointed at Barbara's litter tray, the one she was currently using.

"Good girl," Damien said, and without looking up at him, I knew he was smiling.

"I think we just imparted wisdom."

Damien snorted, then when Barbara was finished, he put her back into her crate. I felt bad about putting her in there, but Damien said that Alec said that kittens don't like large spaces that are new to them, so putting her in her crate would relax her and help her adjust. I hoped to God he was right because it broke my heart to look at her through the little barred door like she was a prisoner.

"Could you not hear her in your room earlier?"

I shook my head at Damien's question.

He huffed as he straightened to his full height of hu-fucking-mongous.

"I heard her in the spare room," he said. "There is nothing wrong with her lungs, I can tell you that much."

I reached for his hand. "Maybe you should come and sleep in me room with me then?"

His eyes snapped to mine, his surprise plain as day if his open-mouthed expression was anything to go by.

"We won't get in trouble," I assured him, seeing the question in his eyes. "We'll just sleep."

Damien looked pained, but when I tugged on his hand, he offered no resistance and walked out of the kitchen with me, flipping the light off as we went. I smiled to myself. I felt in control of something for the first time in a very long time, and it felt good. I wasn't scared to sleep in the same bed as Damien. I was *excited*.

"Do you always wear so much to bed?"

"Yeah," I answered. "I get cold easily."

My room was pitch black when we entered, and I knew where my bed was, but Damien didn't, and he walked directly into the base.

"Fuck a duck!"

I laughed as I climbed up onto the bed, pushing back the blanket.

"Think that's funny, do you?"

I screeched when the bed dipped and an arm hooked itself around me, while another hand ran up and down my side, tickling me without mercy. I screamed, laughed, and begged Damien to stop, but he didn't. He vibrated with laughter, and only stopped when I fell onto my back, and he found himself leaning over me with his hand now on my bare waist since my t-shirt rode up during the tickle assault. We both went quiet then. We couldn't see each other because the room was coated in darkness, but I was hyper aware of him.

"You smell good."

I licked my lips. "I do?"

"You do."

I could hear my heart beating.

"Damien, we can't get into trouble."

"No trouble," he murmured. "I just want to touch you. Can I touch you, please?"

The urge to beg him to do just that was overwhelming.

"But ... but ..."

"Yes, I want to touch your butt, too."

I shoved him, and he lightly chuckled.

"Relax," he whispered, lowering his face enough for me to feel his hot breath on my skin. "Let me make you feel good, baby."

Baby.

I loved hearing him call me pet names, but that aside, I was apprehensive.

"I don't think this is a good idea," I murmured. "Remember what we said about buildin' a better connection and a trust between us before we get intimate?"

"Do you trust me?"

"Heaven help me, but yeah, I do."

"Then trust me not to overstep," Damien said. "Trust me just to touch your body and give you pleasure."

"I'm scared," I admitted. "I wasn't when we walked in 'ere, but I am now."

"I know, freckles," Damien almost purred. "But letting go of that fear for a little while will help you get used to me in this capacity. We're partners now, and I have to work on getting your guard down, and this moment between us will help. I know it will."

"O-okay."

"Good girl."

I jumped when his hand slid from my waist and came down to my stomach. I froze, wondering if he would say anything about *feeling* my stomach. I knew I wasn't fat, but I didn't look like my friends. I could afford to lose the twenty-five pounds I'd gained over the last couple of years, and I was very aware of that fact with Damien's hand on me.

"Why are you so tense?"

I hesitated, then remembered our agreement to communicate with one another.

"I'm embarrassed."

"Because I want to touch you?"

"Because I'm worried you won't like what you feel."

I practically felt Damien's eyes drill a hole into my skull through the darkness.

"You think I won't like your body?" he questioned incredulously. "You can't be serious, Alannah."

I wiggled next to him, but his hand remained firmly on my stomach.

"I'm a little chubby," I mumbled. "I've gained a good bit of weight since we were last together. I'm self-conscious about me stomach, hips, and thighs. Me arse, too."

"What the hell is wrong with your ass?" Damien demanded. "Or your hips, thighs, and stomach for that matter?"

"They aren't toned," I said with a mortified groan. "I have cellulite and little rolls."

God, this is fucking embarrassing.

"Just to be clear, I love your body," he said, his thumb slowly stroking my skin. "I'm *extremely* attracted to it."

I didn't mean to laugh, but I did.

"You don't believe me?"

Before I could answer, Damien felt for my hand, grabbed it, then lifted it into the air before he moved it over something ... hard. Something that was very hard and throbbed like there was no tomorrow.

"Oh," I whispered when I realised what my hand was pressed against.

Damien grunted before moving our hands back to my stomach.

"I *dare* you to disagree with how much I like your body now," he challenged. "My cock will disagree with you and so will my mind and heart."

I was glad of the darkness when a smile broke out across my face, as it burned with heat.

"I can't help how I feel about me body."

"No," he agreed. "But you'll learn to love it, just as I do."

"You love me body?"

"Yup," he said, popping the P. "Head over heels, it's a great body. Perfect, really."

I giggled but stopped when the hand on my stomach slid lower and fitted itself under the band of my pyjamas trousers. My heart pounded as Damien gently nudged my thighs apart. A shiver danced its way up my spine when his large, rough hand slid over the inside of my thighs. He squeezed my flesh here and there, making my entire body come alive.

"Damien," I whispered.

"Lana," he murmured. "I'm going to make you feel so fucking good."

My thighs suddenly clenched together and trapped Damien's hand.

"Oh, you *want* me to touch you," he hummed. "I can feel your muscles contracting."

My body flushed with heat, and my legs slowly parted once again.

"There's my girl."

I sucked in a sharp breath when Damien's thumb ran the length of my underwear. The friction of the fabric against my clit sent shivers up my spine.

"Damien," I breathed.

He moved his body closer to me.

"Fuck," he hissed. "I love how you say my name. I've been around Irish people a long time, but your accent is the *only* one that gets me hard when you speak. I love your voice."

I remembered he had told me he loved my voice once before too, and it caused my body to shudder.

"You're killin' me, Dame."

"I haven't even warmed up yet, baby."

The whole time he spoke, he was rubbing a lone finger up and down my slit. It felt good but not good enough. It was almost like he was teasing me by not pushing the fabric aside. With courage that I didn't know I possessed, I reached down into my pyjama trousers, placed my hand on top of Damien's, and manoeuvred his fingers to push the fabric of my underwear aside. When his fingers finally brushed my clit, my back arched.

"Yes!"

Damien put his mouth next to my ear and made a sound close to a snarl.

"Demanding little thing," he said, "aren't you?"

I moaned in response as he slid a lone finger down to my entrance. He dipped it in, once, twice, then groaned.

"You feel so hot, so wet. I can feel you wrap around my finger … I can't wait for it to be my cock."

Me either.

When his finger slid back up to my clit and began to swirl around it slowly but not touching it directly, I began to lose my mind. My body began to writhe from side to side, trying to force Damien's finger onto my clit with each movement. He leaned his body against me, though, and used his weight to keep me in place as he continued his delicious torture.

"For years," he murmured into my ear, "I've stroked myself and made myself come by just imagining being with you like this."

My breathing became erratic.

"You have?"

"Hell yeah," he growled. "I remembered what it was like to touch you, taste you, to feel you wrapped around me so tight. I came hard *every single time*."

The thought of watching him touching himself sent another wave of heat through me.

"Is it true?" I suddenly asked. "What you said last week, about not touchin' or kissin' anyone since you last touched and kissed me?"

I haven't touched another woman since I touched you. I haven't kissed another woman since I kissed you.

"Every word," Damien answered, his tongue flicking against my earlobe. "You've ruined me for any other woman. You're the only one I ever want to touch again. I told you ... you're my freckles."

I cried out when his finger finally rubbed my clit.

"Yes!" I screeched. "Yes!"

"Fuck, you're so hot."

Lips brushed against my cheek, then not a second later, they covered my own, and just like that, I was lost in Damien's touch and taste. I loved kissing him. I once pretended that I never enjoyed the kisses I had once shared with him, just so I would never think about them, but kissing him now, I realised what an idiot I was to try to fool myself into thinking they weren't enjoyable.

They were toe curling.

"Can I taste you?" he asked against my lips. "Please, say yes."

"You already are."

"No." He chuckled, the sound low and rumbling. "Not your mouth, your pussy."

He slipped his finger inside my pussy just as I clenched over his words, and he growled.

"You want me to," he mused. "You want my tongue on you."

"Yes," I breathed. "Yes, please."

He moved then, and before *I* could move, the blanket was pushed to the end of the bed, and my trousers and underwear were pulled down my body and flung God only knows where in the room. Hands pressed against my knees and parted my thighs wide. I jolted with surprised when lips pressed against the inside of my thighs and slowly worked their way upwards. My eyelids fluttered shut when Damien's hands slid over my body, squeezing my flesh here and there. I moaned softly when he trailed kisses inside my thighs, his teeth nipping my skin every few seconds, making me clench with excitement.

My body bucked of its own accord when I suddenly felt his warm, wet tongue slide over my sensitive folds. I sucked in a sharp breath because I hadn't felt that sensation since Damien last put his mouth on me all those years ago. When I had sex with Dante, it was just sex—no oral, no kissing. Those acts were too intimate, too special to me, and I realised then that I only wanted to share that kind of connection with Damien.

No one else, just him.

He hummed against me, then licked up and down. He didn't directly touch my throbbing clit that ached so much I ground my teeth together. I fisted my hands at my side and focused on my breathing. My eyes crossed when he tongued around the hood of my clit, teasing me, drawing long moans from my lips. He moved his attention and skilled tongue to my labia and sucked on my lips before dipping his tongue inside me.

"Damien!"

He sucked on my pussy lips and even scraped his teeth over them, sending a shiver up my spine. He moved his tongue upwards, and *finally*, I felt hot air on my clit, followed by his talented tongue lapping at it like a man starved.

"Fu…ck … *God*!"

Damien hooked his arms around my thighs and flattened his hands on my stomach, applying pressure to keep my arse on the mattress. He inhaled a deep breath, then curled his tongue around my clit *slowly*. It felt so good that it almost hurt, but that didn't deter me from begging him not to stop. I pulsed with need, and the urge to reach down and fist my hands into Damien's thick hair became difficult to ignore. My fingers flexed against my bed sheets.

Breathe, I told myself. *Just keep breathing.*

My body twitched and jerked like a live wire with every swipe and flick of Damien's tongue. My flesh was flushed with desire, and my skin burned with need. The passion I felt was as intense as it was intoxicating. This brief escape from reality was just what I needed, and Damien was just the man I wanted—no, the man I *needed* to give it to me.

"Damien," I pleaded. "Don't st-stop."

His hands flexed against my stomach in response.

Jolts of pleasure became more constant then, and with an abundance of attention focused on my clit, my orgasm built at a rapid pace. My breathing suddenly became irregular, and I couldn't focus on anything except how good I felt. I began to lose myself to Damien's touch, and I didn't resist; I threw myself over the edge.

My thighs began to quiver like jelly, so much so that Damien used his hands to grip the insides of my thighs to keep them from knocking against his head as he tongued me. With his hands' new position, he pushed my legs farther apart, and it pushed my pussy harder against Damien's mouth. At that moment, I lost my fight against the urge to bury my hands in his hair, and the second I did that, he sucked my clit into his mouth, and my body began to convulse.

I screamed God's name before I drew in a sharp breath and held it.

For a moment, I felt a split second of numbness before an inexplicable wave of bliss started at my clit and, with each pulse, pushed the sensation outward. My eyes rolled back, my spine arched, and my lips parted in a silent scream. My lungs burned for air, so I exhaled the breath I had been holding before greedily gulping more down. My body continued to jerk uncontrollably, and Damien still sucked and lapped at my now oversensitive clit as if he was trying to pull another orgasm from me.

When I began to whimper, I think he knew that I couldn't handle any more because he released my clit, placed a chaste kiss on it, then moved up my body. I felt his hands all over me; I felt his lips kissing my thighs, my hips, my stomach, and any other section of skin his lips could reach. By the time he reached my lips, I was halfway asleep, my body completely depleted of energy.

"Good night, freckles." Damien chuckled, brushing his lips against mine. "Sweet dreams."

The last thing I was aware of wasn't Damien beside me or how satisfied I was, it was how content I felt. It seeped deep into my bones and wrapped around me like a warm blanket. I hadn't felt that way in a very long time, and I prayed there was no end in sight for it.

CHAPTER TWELVE

When I awoke, it wasn't because my body decided it was ready to, it was because something was digging into my behind that made me uncomfortable. When I opened my eyes, I intended to feel for the object I'd accidentally left on my bed, but the second a soft snore echoed in my ear and someone's hot breath blew over my neck, I knew it wasn't an object that dug into me. It was a body part.

The night before came rushing back to me in seconds.

I smiled ridiculously wide as I shifted ever so slightly, and the arm hooked around me tightened. I bit down on my lower lip when a hand flexed around my left breast. I looked down and saw that Damien had put his hand up my pyjama top and grabbed himself a handful of my breast. I resisted the urge to laugh because it felt like such a male thing for him to do, even in his sleep.

He continued to snore, and I was so pleased to find that it wasn't loud or distracting, but oddly relaxing to hear. I slowly turned to face him, his hand fell away from my breast, but remained around my waist. I swallowed when I realised I was naked from the waist down, and the reason made my stomach tighten. I recalled what Damien did to me the night before, and heat ran through me.

I had only ever had Damien's mouth on me once before, but last night was the best of the two because I still felt satisfied from the release he quite literally sucked from me. I gnawed on my lower lip as I rested my head on my pillow and stared at his sleeping face. He was stunning, and I couldn't believe we had spoken and come to the decision that we would date one another. I was still terrified things would end badly between us, but like I had said to Damien the night before, I was so fed up with letting my fear of getting hurt keep me from doing the things I wanted.

I wanted to be brave, just like Damien said I was ... and I wanted that braveness to start with giving him a good morning wake-up call.

He was right when he said that small moment of intimacy between us last night would help bring my guard down because I no longer felt *entirely* apprehensive of Damien touching me in such a way. My body issues still lingered, but I believed Damien when he said he loved my body. I just had to get my mind on the same wavelength as him, so I could love it, too.

With my eyes on his face, I told myself I could do what I was about to do and that Damien would *love* it. That courage pushed me to lick my palm, then press the back of my hand against his solid chest and run it down his torso. I licked my lips as my knuckles slid over his abs and came to the band of his boxer briefs. I snaked my fingers under the band, and the second I felt his cock, I wrapped my hand around the hardened member and gently squeezed. Damien's lips parted in his sleep, and he almost whined.

The thrill that shot through me was almost toe curling.

The lubrication of my saliva on my palm allowed my hand to slide up and down easier, and from the rise and fall of Damien's chest, I knew his body was enjoying my touch. I almost wished he'd open his eyes and come awake because of the pleasure I was giving him, but watching his features contort with bliss in his sleep turned me on.

I wanted to do more to him.

Carefully, I pushed the blanket that covered us off our bodies. I had to lift his arm from around my waist and nudge him onto his back. Once or twice, I thought he would wake up, but he didn't, and when I wiggled my way down his body and parted his thighs, I stared at the outline of his thick, erect cock. Tugging it free of his boxers, I fisted it in my hand and looked up at Damien's face just as I bent down and closed my mouth around the head.

I had never given a blow job before, so I was going off what I had seen in pornos and hoped to God that I was doing it right and that it felt good for Damien. His mouth opened, his hands balled into fists, and a loud, primal groan filled the room. I bobbed my head four times, and on the fifth, when I took him to the back of my throat and swallowed, his eyes shot open.

"Fu...ck!" He hissed, pushed himself onto his elbows, and stared down at me, his lips parted and his eyes wide. "Oh, *fuck*. Alannah. Baby, *yes*."

I smiled around his cock, and I swear his eyes rolled back a little at the sight.

I sucked him, squeezed him with my hand, and fell into a rhythm of fucking him with my mouth. A few times, his hips bucked upwards, pushing his cock to the back of my throat. I gagged twice, and saliva got everywhere, but it didn't slow me down. Things got messy as I used the saliva that dribbled down my chin and slid it over Damien's cock. He was praying out loud to God, asking him to make him last longer, but I wasn't having any of that. I wanted him to come, and come now.

I worked my mouth and hand faster, sucking harder, and swallowing right when the head of Damien's cock bumped the back of my throat. He came with a roar, and his hot cum coated my tongue. I swallowed every drop, continuing to work him as I did. Damien's hips bucked a few times, and his body was so tense, he looked to be a stiff as a board, but when I released his cock from my mouth with a pop, he sagged back onto the mattress.

His eyes were closed, and his chest was rising and falling so fast, you would think he just ran a marathon. I wiped my mouth and hand with my pyjama t-shirt, then I smiled at his limp form.

"Good mornin', Damien."

"Come," he panted, "here."

I crawled up to his side and snuggled against him, pulling the blanket back over our bodies. I leaned my head on his shoulder as his arm wrapped around me. Slinging my arm over his waist, I sighed in contentment. I was a shy person when it came to sex; I could listen to my friends talk about it, but if it was my sex life under the microscope, I became uncomfortable. I didn't like to talk about it at all … but in bed with Damien? It seemed I had no filter.

"I didn't know if I'd like that or not, but I *love* givin' you head."

"Please," he almost whimpered, "you'll make me cry."

"Cry?" I raised a brow. "Why?"

"Because I've jerked off to a fantasy of waking up to you sucking me off, and my *God*, it was better than anything my mind could conjure up."

I hummed. "Glad to hear it."

"I feel like my soul has left my body," he said, his eyes still closed. "You sucked it out of me."

I vibrated with laughter. "Did you like it?"

"Is water wet?" he countered.

I smiled and kissed his chest in response.

"You didn't have to do it though, you that know that, right?" Damien asked, squeezing me gently. "I don't want you to feel like you owed me something because I ate your pussy last night."

My cheeks burned. "I know, but I *wanted* to do it. You were right when you said last night would help bring me guard down a little. I can scarely believe how comfortable I am lyin' 'ere with you."

"It feels right, doesn't it?"

"Yeah," I said, nodding. "It does."

"I'm so happy, Alannah," Damien exhaled a deep breath. "For the first time in years, I'm genuinely happy, and it's because of you."

My heart warmed.

"I feel the same way," I answered. "I'm *still* scared shitless, but

I'm happy we're doin' this."

"Me too."

"This is random, but you came a lot," I said as I brushed my fingers over Damien's chest. "Was that a build-up of six years?"

"I've jerked off a *lot* in the past six years, but today? Jesus Christ, my cock didn't understand what was happening and didn't know when to stop. Sorry about the amount, I didn't realise."

"Why are you apologisin'?" I asked, bemused. "It was sexy. Besides … I swallowed it all."

Damien groaned. "Stop. I want to fuck you, and I know I can't, so stop."

I heeded the warning instantly and was not about to tease him when I knew it would be cruel to do so.

"I'm goin' to go check on Barbara."

He lifted an eyelid. "I can't believe you named the cat Barbara."

"Don't hate on 'er name," I warned. "It's adorable."

Damien opened his eyes fully. "You're perfect."

I ducked my head, embarrassed, and he laughed, squeezing me against him.

"Are you going to see your mom today?"

I nodded, inhaling his scent. "I want to know what's the plan of action for 'er to get better."

"What about taking Barbara to the vet?"

"I'll do that too," I said. "I don't have to work until later. Though, I need to get a move on and convert the spare room into an office for Morgan."

"Morgan?"

"Me employee," I reminded. "You helped me prep to interview 'im, remember?"

"Yeah," Damien said slowly. "But didn't you say it was an online thing?"

"Originally, yeah, but I was makin' that room an office either way, and havin' 'im 'ere every so often will make talkin' about things easier. He only works five days a week for a handful of hours each day, three of those days he will be 'ere."

Damien was silent, so I sat up and looked down at him.

"What's wrong?"

He shrugged.

"That's not an answer, Dame."

He locked eyes with me.

"We *just* started dating. I can't say what I want to say without coming across as a protective boyfriend."

I reached up and brushed my thumb over his lips.

"Talk to me," I encouraged. "Keepin' things bottled up never worked for us, so I want us to be honest. Communication, 'member?"

Damien sighed but nodded.

"I don't feel comfortable with a strange man being here with you."

A smile stretched across my face. "Dame."

"I'm jealous," he continued. "This guy could be gay, have no dick, and think a pussy is revolting, and I'd still be jealous."

My smile only grew. "Dame."

"I hate when my brothers flirt with you, and they only do it to tease, so if this guy smiles at you wrong, I'm going to lose it. I know I will."

"Dame."

He sighed. "What?"

"You're so sexy when you're jealous."

Damien's eyes sparked with desire. "Don't," he warned.

I chuckled. "Morgan is me employee, and that is it. He has no romantic interest in me, and I've none in 'im. He has a girlfriend, too. The only lad who gets me attention and me blood pumpin' is lookin' at me right now."

Damien relaxed. "I trust you, but I'm still going to be jealous."

"Oh, I'm countin' on it."

He hissed. "You get off on my turmoil?"

"What can I say? The caveman act gets me clit's attention."

Damien snapped and tried to reach his hand down to find said clit, but I clamped my thighs together and laughed so hard I got a stitch.

"No," I pleaded. "We can't. You have work soon, and I've to feed Barbara."

"You should have thought of that before you ran that sexy mouth of yours," he said, pulling me against him. "You're so brazen in bed but as timid as Barbara outside of it."

"Because it's just you and me between these sheets," I answered. "I just get a little shy around everyone else, that's all."

"I know, and I like it."

"You do?"

"Hell yeah," Damien answered. "This is a side to you only I know."

The second the words left his mouth, Damien's entire demeanour changed, and I knew why. He realised that Dante shared this bed with me, and not too long ago at that.

"Look at me," I said, and when he did I leaned in and kissed his cheek. "I was never with Dante in the way I am with you. I swear on me life. I hardly spoke, we didn't kiss, we didn't do oral either. It was *just* sex. You have me now, all of me, and that's what matters, right?"

He nodded and closed his eyes. "I want to hurt him for touching what's mine."

Hearing him claim me as his was so hot.

"He only had a tiny piece of me for a short time. You have all of me, and you have since I first met you."

When Damien's eyes opened, he reached up and pulled me against him, his lips finding mine. I hummed into his mouth, and his tongue curled around mine, but when he sucked on my tongue, I moaned out loud because it felt so good.

"Stop," I rasped. "Oh, *stop*."

Damien released me, swung his feet over the side of the bed, and stood. I fell back onto my back and glared at his back.

"Don't do that to me," I said to him. "God, it's sexy."

"Shut. Up." Damien growled. "Don't speak; don't make a sound. I'm talking myself down."

"Yourself or your cock?"

"A…lannah."

"Sorry." I giggled. "Think of Alec naked, Ryder naked, or Kane naked."

"Why not Dominic?"

I snorted. "Because he's practically you so that'd be like sayin' don't think of yourself naked."

"We aren't practically the same." Damien turned to face me, a grin in place. "My cock is bigger."

"I'll get the measurin' tape out just so we can be sure."

"Smartass."

I smiled and snuggled into the blanket with Damien's eyes on me.

"I could get used to this," he said. "Waking up next to you."

My heart thrummed inside my chest. "Me too."

I closed my eyes then, feeling exhausted, and Damien said, "Are you going back asleep?"

"No," I answered but kept my eyes closed and didn't move.

I felt the bed dip, and a kiss brushed over my lips.

"I'll go feed the cat and clean out her litter tray."

I think I grunted. I felt Damien move away from me, then felt a blanket being thrown back over me. Damien yawned, pattered about the room for a minute or two, then ventured out. I wasn't planning on going back to sleep, but when I felt the bed suddenly dip, I jolted out of my daze. I opened my eyes as Damien was climbing back into bed.

"I thought you were goin' to feed Barbara."

He grinned. "You fell asleep."

"Did not."

"Did too because I fed her, and cleaned out her litter tray an hour and a thirty minutes ago," he said with a chuckle. "I got caught up watching the game I missed last night."

"What time is it?" I quizzed.

"Just after eight."

I stretched before moving over and snuggling against Damien's side. "When do you have to leave?"

"About eight forty-five. My shift is at nine thirty, but I have to go home to shower and get clean clothes."

I frowned when I realised that I didn't want him to leave, and I let him know about it.

"I don't want you to go."

His arm came around me. "I'll come back after work."

"Promise?"

He kissed the crown of my head. "Promise."

"Bring clothes with you this time, and your toothbrush, so that way you won't have to go back home before work. You can just shower 'ere and then leave."

Damien said, "Is that your way of saying you want me to stay overnight with you?"

I stilled as doubt flooded me.

"Do you not want to?"

"Hey," Damien said and didn't speak further until I looked at him. "Don't do that."

"Do what?"

"Don't retreat into yourself when you're unsure of something; you overthink things when you do that."

I frowned. "I do?"

"Yeah," Damien said, "you do."

I nodded.

"And to answer your question, I *do* want to stay the night with you. I want to stay every night if you'll let me. I wasn't going to ask because this is all new … I didn't want to push my luck."

"You said we aren't playing a game, you said we're the other's partner, and partners sleep in the same bed together."

Damien's lips twitched. "That they do."

"I'm not askin' you to move in," I said, feeling my cheeks heat. "I just ... I've spent a long time in limbo over you, and if I'm honest ... I'm lonely."

"Lonely?" Damien repeated.

"Yeah," I mumbled. "Not friendship wise just ..."

"Boyfriend wise?"

"I guess."

"Is that why you spent time with Dante?"

I swallowed. "Yes and no."

Damien inhaled and exhaled a breath and said, "Tell me. I want to know."

"It's embarrassin'."

"It's me you're talking to, sweetheart."

Sweetheart.

"Okay," I said softly. "When ... when things started out with Dante, it was just to prove somethin' to meself."

Damien was silent, so I continued.

"I wanted to prove that I was so hung up on you because I was young and dumb ... and since Dante is so much like how you were at eighteen, I figured that if I slept with 'im and didn't get bent out of shape, then it'd prove that me age *was* a factor in how broke up over you I was."

"And was it?" Damien asked quietly.

"No, because I still feel the same way about you just as I did when I was eighteen." I sighed. "I had no romantic interest in Dante, but I've *always* had that interest in you, even when I'd deny it to meself. When you kissed me the other day, I felt it in me soul ... I know that sounds stupid, but I've never felt like that with anyone but you. Granted you're the only lad I've ever kissed, but still, everythin' is about you in me mind. It always has been. Whether it was good or bad, it was constantly you."

Damien reached his hand over and cupped my cheek.

"I'm the only man you've ever kissed?"

I bobbed my head. "Only you."

"I feel the same way," he said. "I tried to move on when I returned to New York. During a low point, I went to a few bars and told myself I was going to pick the first hot chick I saw and fuck her ... but I never did. You were on my mind constantly, and not just because I felt like shit over how things ended between us ... but because I cared about you. You're such a sweetheart, Alannah, and I've always carried you in my heart even when I was thousands of miles away."

I covered my face with my hands when tears stung my eyes.

"Stop," I pleaded. "I don't want to cry all over you again."

Damien pulled me against him. "You know we aren't like a regular boyfriend and girlfriend who're just starting out, right?"

I lowered my hands and nodded.

"We have history," Damien continued. "So, don't worry about what's right and wrong when it comes to how we should behave. If it feels right to have me next to you at night in your bed, then I'll be here ... okay?"

"Okay," I replied. "I want you 'ere with me. I've never felt so content fallin' asleep as I did last night with you beside me."

I was mortified admitting that, but Damien's smile told me I had no reason to feel that way.

"Me too," he said. "I lay awake for a while just listening to you breathe and enjoying having you in my arms."

"Dame," I murmured.

He leaned in and pressed his lips against mine, giving me a short and sweet kiss.

"You make me *very* happy," Damien whispered. "Remember that whenever you start to doubt yourself or feel scared."

"You make me happy too," I said, "and like I said, I'm *still* scared shitless, but I don't regret tryin' with you."

Bronagh was right; if I didn't try with Damien, my mind would be plagued with what-ifs for the rest of my life. As hard as it was for me to do, I had to think positive; otherwise, I would be sabotaging my relationship with Damien before it even started. This was truly out of my comfort zone; by being with him, I was going against eve-rything I had forced myself to believe for six years. My mind set wouldn't change overnight, but I was willing to try, and right now, that was the best I could do.

I prayed it would be enough.

CHAPTER THIRTEEN

"You found 'er in a cardboard box, you say?"

After Damien left my apartment to get to work on time, I got showered, dressed and phoned the closest veterinarian clinic to make an appointment for Barbara. Luckily, they had a cancelation for ten a.m., and I jumped on it. The clinic just happened to be a connection to the animal shelter where Alec worked.

As I was sitting in the waiting room to be called in by the vet, I heard two women gush about a tall, stunningly gorgeous American who was "so funny" and helped them get their dogs out of their cars as he was passing by on his way to work. I rolled my eyes playfully as the women conversed. I could envision Alec's head growing five times the size with the news.

"Yeah," I answered the vet. "She was inside the box with no blanket or anythin'."

The vet shook her head as she examined Barbara from head to toe.

"Evil bastards."

My lips twitched. "I agree wholeheartedly."

"Well, I'm glad you took the little lady in," the vet praised me. "Not many people would do that."

"I couldn't leave 'er to fend for 'erself," I said. "I'd be sick with meself if I did that."

"You've got a good heart."

I felt my cheeks flare with heat. "Thanks."

"Can I ask you a question?"

I raised a brow. "Sure."

"Why did you name 'er Barbara?"

I laughed. "Barbra Streisand was on the telly, and I asked 'er if she liked the name Barbara, she meowed, so I took it as a yes. It's also me ma's middle name so I'm changin' the spellin' to how she spells it just to give 'er a laugh."

The vet covered her mouth with her forearm as she laughed. For a moment, I wondered why she didn't use her hand, but then I realised it was because she was touching Barbara and had been touching animals all morning. She wore gloves, but yeah, I didn't blame her for not putting a hand to her mouth.

"That's the best thing I've heard all week."

"Glad I could amuse you."

With a smile, the vet then said, "About 'er age ... she's not that young, me guess would be between nine and ten weeks."

I blinked. "But she's so small."

"She's malnourished," the vet explained. "She was probably pushed aside by the mother, or simply removed from 'er care before you found 'er."

My stomach tightened. "Will she be okay?"

"She will." The vet nodded. "She'll get 'er first vaccination today, and if you want, I can give 'er a vaccine for feline leukaemia. It's not a hundred percent guarantee she won't ever contract the disease, but it'll give 'er a good chance of avoidin' it."

"Give 'er whatever she needs to keep 'er healthy, please."

The next twenty minutes were filled with my signing Barbara up for pet insurance while she received two vaccinations, a worm dose, had a microchip implanted, a full body assessment, then had her first picture with her veterinarian. I had seen on the waiting room walls that the vet had pictures of hundreds of animals in all different shapes and sizes. Most of the pictures were when a pet was young, then another was years later when the animal was older. I *loved* that; it showed how trusted the vet was for people to continue to bring their animals to her over the course of their lives.

I looked up at the door when a veterinary nurse entered the room.

"Sorry for interruptin'," she said to me, then to the vet, she said, "Cora is coverin' for me; I'm goin' to help Alec feed the dogs in the kennels."

"Okay," the vet said. "Don't be long."

The nurse left with a skip with her walk, and the vet chuckled to herself.

"That man has me entire female staff in ribbons."

Alec Slater.

"*You* know Alec?"

"*Everyone* knows Alec." The vet snickered. "He's not the type of personality one forgets, and he's easy on the eyes too."

I grinned. "Don't let 'im hear you say that; he'll get a big head."

The vet chuckled. "I'm assumin' you're acquainted with 'im."

"Only a little," I joked. "He's engaged to one of me best friends."

"Ah, Keela." The vet nodded. "He talks about 'er a lot, and by a lot, I mean *constantly*."

I grinned. "He'd be lost without 'er."

"No need to tell me, I believe it," the vet said. "He's only been workin' 'ere officially a little while; after seein' how good he is with the animals, and how hard workin' he is, I had to offer 'im a full-time job. The female staff loves 'im whether he is taken or not. He makes everyone laugh, so they all want to be around 'im."

"That sounds like Alec."

The appointment was wrapped up then. Barbara was cleared for another month until she came back in for her second and final set of vaccinations, then she would just need to come back every twelve months for her yearly booster. I said my goodbyes to the vet and left the clinic. As I was walking towards the car park, I heard a familiar voice and stopped.

"Lana." Alec beamed when he and the nurse that came into the vet's examination room briefly rounded the corner, heading towards the clinic. To the nurse, he said, "This is Alannah Ryan; she's practically my sister."

I was completely taken aback with the introduction, and for some reason, I got a lump in my throat. I swallowed it down and smiled politely at the nurse.

"Nice to meet you."

"And you." She smiled back. "I'm Tracey."

Alec focused on the crate I was holding. "Is she okay?"

"Yup." I nodded. "She got 'er vaccinations, she's wormed, microchipped and is good until she gets 'er final set next month."

Alec's lips twitched. "Tell Tracey what you named her."

I scowled at him, then to Tracey, I grinned and said, "Barbara, after Barbra Streisand."

Tracey laughed, and Alec snickered to himself as he shook his head.

"You're a hater," I told him. "Nobody likes a hater."

Alec continued to grin as he excused himself from Tracey, telling her he was going to help me with Barbara to my car. I was going to tell him it was okay, but when he took her crate from me, I sighed with relief. I rubbed my shoulder where a knot had formed.

"She weighs nothin', but the bloody crate weighs a *lot*."

"You're just weak."

I rolled my eyes. "Bite me, bitch."

We walked to my car, and when Alec got Barbara settled into the back seat—even putting a seat belt around her crate—he closed the door and focused on me. I raised my eyebrows, not understanding why he was staring at me so intently.

"I spoke to Ry this morning."

My heart stopped. "Is Branna okay?"

"She's fine, still pregnant."

I relaxed. "Thank God."

"When I spoke to him, he mentioned that Damien sent him a text to let him know he wouldn't be home because he was staying over at a certain *someone's* apartment."

My entire face heated, and Alec snapped his fingers.

"I knew it," he said. "I *told* Keela you both hooked up, but she was adamant he'd sleep in the spare room."

I tried to get into my car to get away from Alec and the conversation, but he blocked me.

"No way, red face. Talk."

I groaned. "When did you turn into Bronagh?"

"The second I realised you had your dirty way with my baby brother."

I squealed and slapped his forearm. "*Shut up!*"

Alec barked with laughter. "Come on, give. What happened?"

I placed my face in my hands and groaned, before dropping them to my side.

"He *did* stay the night ... and *not* in the spare room."

"I fucking *knew* it!"

"Hold it." I held up my hand, stopping him from speaking further. "We didn't have sex ... but we also didn't *just* sleep either."

"That's my girl," Alec said, raising his hand in the air.

I laughed as I lifted mine and clapped my palm against his.

"So, what now?" Alec pressed. "I'm confused, because haven't you been proclaiming hate for him for ... like ... ever?"

I frowned, hating how accurate that description was.

"We spoke ... we spoke about *everythin'*, and we cleared up a lot of issues we had, and while we're not out of the woods yet, that conversation did us *both* a world of good. We don't wanna play any games, and we both wanna try our hand at a relationship, so ... we're datin'. Officially. Exclusively."

"Alannah." Alec smiled so wide I was sure that his cheeks were stinging him. "I'm *so* happy for you guys."

When he hugged me, I hugged him back.

"Thanks. I'm so scared, though."

"That it'll end badly?"

When we parted, I stepped back and nodded.

"Want to know a secret?"

"Always," I answered.

"I'm *still* scared that might happen with Keela."

My jaw dropped. "Shut the front door."

"I'm serious," Alec said. "When you have your whole life riding on someone ... it's only natural to worry they won't always be around to be part of that life."

Tilting my head, I said, "But you and Keela are made for each other. I've never seen two people happier." I paused. "Unless I'm with Nico and Bronagh, Kane and Aideen ... and Ryder and Branna. All your relationships are so solid; you shouldn't be scared."

"Yet in the back of my head, there is still the fear." Alec shrugged. "All I'm saying is don't think you're the only one afraid of failure. Everyone is about something."

I considered this and found myself feeling a sense of relief.

"You're brilliant," I told him. "I feel better hearin' that. Thank you."

"You're welcome."

Alec looked over his shoulder when his name was called, then he turned back to me.

"Got to go, but I'll see you later?"

"You always do."

He kissed my cheek, then turned and jogged towards the large building on the left side of the compound that I knew to be the shelter.

"If you go to Dominic's house," Alec shouted, "do *not* touch my fucking cup."

My laughter followed him, and I wanted to ask if he loved the cup so much, why didn't he keep it at his house, but I knew the answer. He enjoyed our bickering over it too much to take it away from me ever having it, and I loved that about him.

With a smile and a new sense of relief following our conversation, I got into my car and drove towards my parents' house. When I arrived, I planned to leave Barbara in the back seat of my car after seeing she was asleep in her crate, but then the rain started to come down in buckets, and the noise was too loud for her not to get scared.

Just as I unbuckled my seat belt, my phone rang. I answered it without looking at the screen.

"Hello?"

"What did you do to my little brother?"

Ryder.

I froze. "What do you mean?"

"I mean, he hasn't stopped smiling since I picked him up from your apartment, and that was three hours ago. I'm worried his face will get stuck like this."

A giggle burst free.

"He is fine," I assured Ryder. "We worked a lot out last night … and I may have given 'im a nice wake-up call."

"I knew it!" Ryder stated then he shouted, "I *knew* you got some, you lying asshole … uh, Alannah, who else would I call to ask why your grinning like that? … No, because I'm speaking to her that's wh—Ow!"

There was commotion and spewed curses.

I smiled when Damien said, "Hello?"

God, I love his voice.

"Did you just hurt your big brother?"

"He'll be fine," he answered, and I heard the smile in his voice. "What're you doing? I miss you."

I smiled so wide that my cheeks stung.

"I just left the vet with Barbara," I answered. "And I miss you, too."

"Is everything okay with her?"

"As far as the vet can tell, she's about nine to ten weeks old. She got 'er first round of vaccinations today, and I'll go back with 'er next month to get the second round. I registered 'er and got 'er pet insurance. She is officially Barbara Ryan, and I am 'er mother."

When Damien laughed, it made me smile, and I didn't care. I knew it was probably eye rolling for anyone to see, but I was happy, and I wasn't going to apologise to anyone for feeling like that.

"Does that make me her daddy?"

"I thought you were *my* daddy."

I cringed the second the words left my mouth. I once swore on everything that was holy that I would never refer to a partner as my "daddy" because it creeped me out, yet here I was, indicating Damien was ... daddy.

"Don't," Damien warned, his voice low. "Don't you dare get me hard when I'm at work surrounded by these tools."

I had a feeling he wasn't talking about the equipment.

"I'm not tryin' to get you hard," I said, my lips twitching. "Though it appears it doesn't take much to get your cock standin' at attention."

Damien growled but said nothing, and I was thankful because I was worried if he did, I would lose this little bit of brazen assurance that had filled me. I looked around and was glad it was raining so hard. It meant I could stay in the car a little longer and ... talk.

"Go into the back room," I said to Damien, licking my lips. "I want to try somethin' with you ... over the phone, that is."

"Fuck," he grunted. "Ry, I'll be back in a minute."

I thought I heard Ryder laugh, but I ignored it and so did Damien.

"Okay," Damien said a minute later. "I'm in the room, and the door is closed."

"Good," I said, my stomach swimming with butterflies. "I want phone sex."

"A...lannah."

Confidence surged through me upon hearing the desperation in his tone.

"Don't you think it'll be fun?" I questioned softly. "I think it will be great foreplay before we actually *have* sex."

"You're killing me, gorgeous."

Gorgeous.

"I feel like I can be bold with you, so I'm steppin' out of me comfort zone by even suggestin' this. I'm embarrassed, but I don't want that to stop me from bein' a little ... naughty."

"God in Heaven, help me."

My chuckle was low.

"Are you hard?" I asked, my voice a little breathless. "Are you throbbin'?"

"Yes," Damien hissed.

"Your hand is *my* hand," I told him. "*I* want to touch you."

His heavy breathing was all I could hear, then I heard some ruffling and then a few seconds later a soft groan sounded, and I knew his hand was wrapped around his cock.

"Good boy," I praised. "Do you like it when I touch you?"

He almost hissed his, "Yes."

"Lick me palm," I purred, "then close your eyes as I fist your cock."

"Jesus," Damien groaned.

"Are you doin' what I say?"

"Yes, ma'am."

I grinned.

"I'm before you on me knees," I said, licking my lips, "strokin' you while swirlin' me tongue around the head of your cock."

Damien didn't reply; the only thing I could hear was his heavy breathing.

"Can you see me on me knees in front of you, feel me touchin' you?"

"Ye-yeah," he replied. "Fu...uck."

I hummed. "You like when I look up into your eyes when I suck your cock, don't you?"

"Alannah." He panted. "Christ."

I clenched my thighs together, forcing myself to ignore the growing ache between my thighs. My focus was on Damien, and right now, I wanted everything, all the pleasure, to be his.

"I want you to come in me mouth," I said a little forcefully. "D'ye want that? D'ye want me to swallow every salty drop?"

He grunted, then gasped.

"Alannah. *Fuck.* Yessss."

He was going to come. I knew he was.

"I'm goin' to swallow all of you," I purred. "I *love* your salty taste, I want it to coat me tongue."

"Fuck," Damien panted, his voice still low. "Oh, *fuck!*"

"Give it to me, baby," I growled. "Fuck me mouth so hard that I can't see straight."

I heard grunting, a lot of grunting, then heavy breathing and a long and satisfied groan. Confidence wrapped itself around me knowing my words and the visuals I planted in Damien's head got him to the point where he lost control.

"You're sin," Damien rasped after a few moments. "Oh God, you're pure fucking *sin*."

"That was fun," I said, ignoring my burning cheeks. "I've never done phone sex before."

Damien recited Our Father, and it made me laugh.

"You have to say three Hail Marys or God won't forgive you for gettin' off at work."

When his rumbling chuckle sounded, my lips twitched.

"I'm going to get you back for this."

"Get me back?" I blinked. "You just had an orgasm. You're welcome."

Another chuckle.

"Nuh-uh, freckles, you got me worked up *at* work, knowing good and well I told you *not* to."

I pouted. "I was just havin' some fun."

"I know," Damien replied, "but I'm still getting you back."

"I'd just prefer if you got me *on* me back," I teased. "I'd learn me lesson much quicker that way … I promise."

"Sin," Damien hissed.

I was enjoying this far too much.

"I'm an angel, and ye'know it."

"You look like one and act like one, but the second we're alone, you're sin. You're *my* definition of trouble, freckles."

I laughed. "You love it."

"You bet your fine ass I do."

I shook my head. "Go give your brother back his phone and get some work done. Slacker."

There was a pregnant pause, then Damien's muttered a curse.

"I have to clean this mess up, and then wash my hands ... and Ryder's phone case, or he'll kill me."

I laughed, and Damien growled.

"I'm *so* getting you back for this, freckles."

"Snowflake," I mused, "I look forward to it."

I hung up on him and could imagine the look on his face when he realised it, and I laughed. I felt giddy and confident. It was worlds away from feeling scared and bitter about something that once happened. I sighed and thanked God I had a best friend who gave me a kick up the arse to see sense when most would only have given a nudge.

CHAPTER FOURTEEN

I quickly hurried into my parents' house, shielding the front of Barbara's crate from the rain as best as I could.

"Ma?" I called when I entered the house.

"I'm in the kitchen, hon."

I placed Barbara's crate next to the radiator so she would be warm, then shrugged out of my jacket and went into the kitchen. My ma was washing a cup out in the sink, so I walked up behind her, slipped my arms around her waist and snuggled against her. She chuckled as she grabbed a tea towel and dried her hands so she could place them over mine.

"Are you okay?"

"Am *I* okay?" I repeated. "I'm fine, Ma. Are *you* okay?"

"Right now, I am," she replied.

I released her, and when she turned to face me, I hugged her without a word.

"Bear." She chuckled. "Honey, I'm okay."

"But you're not, Ma," I said, pulling back to look at her. "You're not okay; you have breast cancer."

Saying that and knowing it to be true was like a kick in the stomach.

"I'm not the only woman to have breast cancer, love," she said softly, placing her hands on my shoulders. "Millions upon millions have it."

"Yeah, and that's awful, but you're me ma … I can't help how worried I am about *you*."

"I know," she frown, lifting her hand to my cheek. "I'll put the kettle on, and we can talk about it, okay?"

I nodded and took a seat at the kitchen table. I clasped my hands together in front of me and waited. When the tea was ready, my ma placed my cup on my coaster, then took a seat across from me. I exhaled a deep breath.

"Tell me everythin'," I almost pleaded. "I need to hear it all."

Ma nodded. "I'll tell you every detail."

I took a sip of my tea to try to settle my now upset stomach.

"I have stage one breast cancer," Ma said, and instinctively I reached over, grabbed her hand, and squeezed it. "I'm going to explain this to you as best as I can. Your da has a better understandin' of it because I don't know what all of the big words mean."

"It's okay," I assured her. "Take your time."

"Cancer has grown in the milk duct in me left breast," she explained, her voice a little shaky. "Stage one means that cancer is present, but it is contained to the area where the first abnormal cells developed. The doctor has assured me because it has been detected in the early stages, it can be very effectively treated."

I nodded but didn't speak. I couldn't.

"The doctor said I have stage 1A, meanin' that it hasn't spread to me lymph nodes, so that is really good news."

I took her word for it.

"Within my left breast, there is a small tumour, smaller than a peanut."

Hearing the word tumour, no matter how small it was, was sickening to me and I had to bite the inside of my cheek to keep from crying.

"The treatment proposed has to start immediately," she continued. "Next week, to be exact."

My breath caught.

"Ma."

"It's okay," she said, squeezing my hand. "I'll be havin' a combination of surgery and radiation. Chemo is not recommended for this stage; that is reserved for the later stages when the cancer is tougher."

I found myself bobbing my head as she spoke.

"The surgery I will be havin' is scheduled for next Thursday, and it's called a lumpectomy. The doctor will remove the tumour and as little breast tissue as possible."

My heart thrummed wildly against my chest.

"I'll start radiation four weeks from the date of me surgery. I'll have it five days a week for five to six weeks, and after that, I'm home free until I go back for testin' after six months to make sure nothin' has returned."

I didn't realise I was trembling until my ma gripped my hand tightly.

"Honey," she said. "Please, don't be scared."

"I can't help it," I swallowed. "Bein' scared is what I'm good at."

"No, it's not," Ma said firmly. "You're a tough woman."

I didn't believe that.

"*You* are tough. You're the one goin' through this."

"We're goin' through it *together*," Ma stated. "Me, you, and your da. This is affectin' all of us, so it's okay to be scared, to feel overwhelmed. I'd be worryin' if you weren't."

I exhaled a breath. "I'm just glad that a plan is in place."

"Me too."

"I'm goin' to the hospital with you on your surgery day," I informed her. "And to all your radiation appointments."

"Okay, bear." She smiled.

I swallowed. "I wish it were me instead of you, Ma."

"Don't you ever say that!" She said with blinding fear shining in her brown eyes at the possibility of me ever being as sick as her. "I'm glad it's me and not you, d'ye hear me?"

I nodded.

"Because I have breast cancer, the chances of you havin' it has risen, so I want you to go and get a breast check yearly if you can, okay? I know it's recommended every three years for your age group, but I don't care about that. We can't be too careful."

I agreed with her.

"I'll arrange an appointment with me GP, okay?"

"Okay." She relaxed. "Good."

She froze when a meow came from the hall.

"That was a cat just then," she said, her back straightening. "Did you leave the door open?"

"No," I answered. "But I *did* bring a cat with me."

Ma's lips parted with surprise, so I quickly filled her in on how I came to have Barbara, and that she is healthy and had just received her first round of vaccinations. I got her from the hallway and carried her crate into the kitchen.

"She's white," Ma gushed as she peered into the crate. "And has one green eye and one blue eye. She's *so* cute."

"Right?"

"Hello, Barbara," Ma cooed then tittered. "I can't believe you called 'er Barbara."

"I like it." I smiled. "It suits 'er."

Ma looked from Barbara inside her crate to me, and she stared at me, and when I chuckled she pointed her index finger at me.

"What's goin' on with you?" She jokingly demanded. "Why do you seem different?"

"Different?"

"Yeah, different. You keep smilin' … like *that*! Look, you're smilin' again!"

I laughed, and shook my head.

"Tell me!"

"I *may* have sorted things out with Damien."

Ma's eyes widened. "Meanin'?"

"Meanin' we're together." I blushed. "Boyfriend and girlfriend."

"What?" Ma screeched, then lowered her voice as to not scare Barbara. "How did *that* happen?"

"We talked," I answered. "We like each other and want to be together, so we're together."

"This is such a turn of events," Ma said, placing a hand on her chest. "Wasn't he punchin' Aideen's brother the other day for sleepin' with you?"

I cringed. "Yeah ... but that's in the past."

At the mention of Dante, I made a mental note to tell him about my new relationship status. Not to rub it in his face—he mostly will be happy that I'm happy—but I wanted him to respect Damien and not throw our previous involvement in his face because that was just a low thing to do.

"I want to meet 'im," Ma announced with a bob of her head. "I want to meet this lad who fucked you over and now is your partner."

Oh, my God.

"You won't have a go at 'im, will you?"

"You gonna do anythin' about it if I do?" she challenged with a raised brow.

"Hell no, I'm not stupid."

"I'm not goin' to grill 'im." She grinned, amused by my answer. "I just wanna meet 'im. You're a grown woman who can make 'er own decisions on who she has in 'er life ... but, I *will* gut 'im if he ever hurts you. That I can't back down on, so you'll just have to accept that 'ere and now."

I chuckled. "Understood."

"Brilliant." She reached for my hand. "I'm happy for you; a new relationship is so excitin'. The beginnin' is a magical time."

"You think so?"

"I know so." She winked.

I knew she was thinking of my da then, and I had to resist the urge to ball my hands into fists.

I stayed at my parents' house for an hour, chatting with my ma before she went to bed for a nap. Along with Barbara, I drove back to my apartment. I closed all the doors once inside and let Barbara out in the sitting room. That way I wouldn't lose her if she hid somewhere. She seemed to be content with hiding under the sofa, so I went into my bedroom, tied my hair into a bun on the top of my head, then changed into my work clothes. I grabbed my sketchpad and pencil case from the spare bedroom and returned to the sitting room.

I also grabbed my laptop from the coffee table and switched it on. I emailed Morgan and gave him the password to my website and work email so he could get a head start on organising everything for me. I checked my calendar, noting the next day work began on a project for an author who wanted me to design a post-apocalyptic young adult fiction book cover. Her email had been very detailed, so I was excited to get a start on it.

After I emailed Morgan the information, I pulled my pad onto my lap and spent an hour drawing a portrait of Barbara on eight by ten paper. Once I had the initial sketch outline drawn, I used charcoal to define it, and just as I was finished, a knock sounded at my apartment door. I frowned as I stood and walked out the hallway.

"Who is it?"

"Your boyfriend."

I opened the door and beamed at Damien.

"How'd you get up here without me buzzin' you in?"

"I came by just as Kane was coming home from the store with Aideen and the boys." He shrugged, leaning against the door panel looking too hot for words. "I came up with them."

"Did they ask why you were comin' to see me?"

"Obviously." He smirked. "Aideen is so excited we're datin' that she screamed."

I snorted. "Alec high fived me when I saw 'im at the shelter."

I stepped back and gestured for Damien to come into the apartment, but he was too busy roaming his eyes on me to see it.

"You're beautiful," he said, his eyes lingering on my face.

I raised a brow. "I'm pretty sure I've charcoal on me nose."

"You do. You have some on your cheeks and forehead too." Damien nodded. "And you're still stunningly beautiful."

I flushed at the compliment, and it brought a smile to Damien's face. Not a grin or a smirk, but a real smile, and it was gorgeous.

"You've such a pretty smile."

He pushed away from the door panel, stepped forward, and brought his hands to my cheeks and cupped them, stroking his thumb over my skin.

"I'm sure I'm supposed to be the one sweet talkin' you."

"Does the Man Bible say that?"

Damien smiled wider. "It does."

"I'll shut up and let you sweet talk me then," I said, placing my hands on his waist. "Wouldn't want to feel the wrath of Nico and his trusted Man Bible."

"A wise decision," Damien murmured.

He lost his smile, and his eyes were now locked on my lips. I closed my eyes the second his lips touched mine, and before a real kiss could even begin, I thought of Barbara, pulled back, and gasped, "Close the door. Barbara is out of 'er crate!"

Damien spun and quickly closed the door as I rushed into the sitting room, dropped to my hands and knees next to my settee, and looked under it. I almost shook with relief as I sat back on my heels and said, "She's still 'ere."

Damien was standing behind me, and he looked relived but when he glanced at my sketchpad on the settee, he smiled.

"You drew Babs?"

"Babs?" I repeated.

"Everyone has a nickname, and Barbara's is Babs. Deal with it."

I snickered. "Yeah, I drew *Babs*."

"You're crazy talented, baby."

A shiver ran up my spine.

"Thanks," I replied bashfully.

"How do you make it so lifelike?" Damien asked, peering at the sketch. "It almost looks three-dimensional."

"Practice," I answered. "Lots and lots of practice."

"How did you learn to draw so well?"

"No idea," I answered. "I always doodled, and I kept at it because I loved doin' it so much. I just got better over time."

"It shows in your work because wow."

I always found it hard to take a compliment, but whenever I was praised for my work, my pride soared. I still didn't like focusing on me though, I'd rather talk about someone, or something, else.

"Do you want some lunch? How long is your break?"

"Don't do that."

I froze. "Don't do what?"

"You get embarrassed when people praise your work, and you try to change the subject."

I gnawed on my lower lip. "I'm shy."

"Shy?" Damien repeated. "You didn't seem all that shy earlier on the phone."

My cheeks turned supernova at the reminder.

"Oh, God, *don't*!" I warned. "I was brave earlier, but I'm not anymore. Please, don't talk about it. I'll die."

"I'll leave you alone ... but I'm still getting you back."

"And I'm still looking forward to it, but in the meantime, shut up."

Damien chortled and returned his gaze back to the sketch.

"Do you always prefer to just sketch?"

"Depends on my mood," I explained. "Some days I like to paint."

Damien's eyes dropped to my plaid shirt, noting the stains. "I can see."

"It can get messy sometimes."

Heat flashed in his eyes for a moment, then as quick as it appeared, it vanished.

"What kind of artist are you?"

I thought about that question. Hard.

"I'm different," I shrugged. "Some people see the world in black and white, or in a burst of colour ... I see it as a blank canvas waitin' for me to add me life *through* colour."

I smiled and looked down at my hands, noting different coloured paint dotted my skin and decorated my nails as well as some smduges of charcoal.

"I love the freedom of art. There are no rules, no right or wrong, no punishment, just self-expression. This is me centre; it's what I love doin', so I don't care that it makes me different. I like different."

"I like different, too," Damien said. "People who are different have a shot at being original. They stray from the lines instead of sticking to the script. Everything they do is an adventure."

I felt my mouth hang open.

"Exactly," I said softly. "Exactly."

"What's the shocked face for?"

"You get me," I answered. "No one has ever just ... got me before."

"Yeah, well, you never know," Damien winked. "Maybe I'm different, too."

"Yeah," I agreed, staring at him like I was seeing him for the first time all over again. "Maybe."

CHAPTER FIFTEEN

After Damien had lunch at my apartment, he went back to work, and Ryder graciously picked him up so he wouldn't be late. I got cleaned up, changed out of my work clothes, and got Barbara settled into her crate after she had food and water. I didn't want her to be in the crate outside of when I had to travel with her, but she seemed to love staying inside it. She wandered into it and stayed inside it even when the door was open. I left the door of the crate open so she had access to her food, water, and her litter tray. Then I headed to Bronagh's house. I knew that Nico was at work, so I wanted to go and keep her company with Georgie until he got home. The second I stepped into her house, my best friend tackled me in a hug, and she was ... crying.

"Bronagh?" I said, alarmed. "What's wrong?"

"You and ... D-Damien," she sobbed. "You're both a couple. Ryder told Branna and she told me and I've been cryin' ever since."

I stared at her when she pulled back from our hug.

"It makes you *cry*?"

"I'm so happy." She sniffled. "*So* happy for you both."

I smiled at her and hugged her again, knowing her hormones were back to being all over the place now that she was pregnant again.

"Put the kettle on," I said, "and I'll tell you everythin'."

We went into the kitchen, and I glanced at Georgie's buggy, noting it was empty.

"Where is Georgie?"

"Nappin'," Bronagh answered, pointing at the baby monitor on the counter before she grabbed some tissues and dabbed under her eyes. "She just went down ten minutes ago, so we've a solid hour, at least, before she stirs."

"What do you want to hear about first?" I questioned. "Me ma or Damien?"

"Your ma," Bronagh answered instantly.

I launched into the same detailed conversation my ma had with me about her cancer and her upcoming treatment. Bronagh made us tea and sat at the kitchen table with me as I explained everything. She listened, and when I finished speaking, she said, "Does havin' a plan make you feel better?"

"Yeah," I replied. "I still hate it, but knowin' there is a plan in place, and that she's not stuck in limbo is kind of reassurin'."

"I'm glad." Bronagh sipped her tea. "I'm goin' to drop by tomorrow and see 'er. I haven't stopped in for a cuppa in a while."

"She'd love that, and honestly, so would I," I admitted. "I start a new project tomorrow, and knowin' you'll see 'er for a bit will relax me a little. I feel so protective of 'er. I constantly want to be around 'er or talk to 'er."

"She'll be fine," Bronagh said. "Normalcy is what she needs. If you're hangin' out with 'er every day, it'll probably make 'er feel like she is disruptin' things."

I frowned. "She isn't, though."

"Ye'know your ma," Bronagh continued. "She doesn't like to burden anyone, even when she most definitely *isn't* a burden. All I'm sayin' is try to keep things normal for 'er. I know it'll be hard but try to rein it in just a little. She doesn't see you every single day, but now you're tryin' to see 'er as much as you can. D'ye understand what I mean?"

"Yeah," I grumbled. "I'm bein' overbearin'."

"You're a worried daughter," Bronagh corrected, "and your ma gets that. Everyone gets that, and no one is sayin' it's a bad thing because it's *not*. I just think that makin' you aware of how your sudden change in routine will probably appear to *her* will be helpful to you."

"Thanks," I said with a nod. "I didn't realise it before, but whenever I talk to 'er now or stop by, she's constantly assurin' me that she is okay. I don't want 'er to become tiresome constantly tellin' me that 'cause it means that 'er cancer is always the centre of attention. She knows she has cancer, and she doesn't need anyone else remindin' 'er of that."

"Exactly," Bronagh said, exhaling a breath. "I was worried I might offend you."

"Never," I said. "You're me best mate. Tellin' me shite that no one wants to is your job."

Bronagh grinned. "And since you're *my* best mate, your job is to dish on everythin' about you and Damien, and I mean *everythin'*!"

I felt the tip of my ears burn, and Bronagh squealed and wiggled in her seat.

"This is gonna be *good*!"

"You're crazy."

"Everyone knows that," she said. "Now, get talkin'."

"Right," I began, "so, so much has happened since I spoke to you last night. After I found Barbara—"

"I still can't *believe* you named the cat Barbara."

I raised a brow. "You got a problem with 'er name?"

"Nope," Bronagh answered with a smile plastered on her face. "It's fantastic."

My lips twitched.

"Anyway," I continued, "last night, Damien brought by all the stuff Alec got for Barbara, and we had that talk, and Bronagh, it was so … relievin'. We spoke about everythin' that happened between us. I apologised—"

"*You* apologised?" Bronagh cut me off, her eyes wide.

I nodded. "I admitted that I was the one to seduce him, so holdin' a grudge over what he told me would happen and eventually *did* happen seemed pointless. Well, it seems pointless *now*, but at the time, pretendin' I hated Damien sort of helped me push 'im away, ye'know?"

Bronagh stared at me, unblinking.

"What?" I frowned. "Why're you lookin' at me like that?"

"I've been tellin' you for years that—"

"I know." I cut her off before she launched into an "I told you so" speech. "I know, you've been the voice of reason, all of you have, but I was too stubborn to listen or to admit that what happened wasn't just down to Damien. Trust me when I say I know I've been completely unreasonable when it came to 'im, but you have to understand, it was completely out of fear."

"Fear of what?"

"Fear of possibly bein' with 'im and things goin' tits up."

"And you aren't scared of that anymore?"

I almost choked on air.

"Are you jokin'? I'm *terrified*, but I want to be brave, like Damien says I am. Me ma even said to me that not tryin' somethin' because you're scared of the outcome is a shitty way to live. I *know* it's a coward's way to live a life, and I don'*t want* to live like that, so I bit the bullet and laid everythin' out to Damien, and it resulted in us becomin' boyfriend and girlfriend. We don't want to play games; we want to be together, so we are."

Bronagh clapped her hands together.

"I'm *so* happy about this," she gushed. "You have seriously no idea."

"Me too." I smiled. "Now that I'm not forcin' meself to focus on pushin' 'im away, I'm goin' through the stages of fancyin' 'im all over again. I miss 'im even though I just saw 'im, I smile when I think of 'im, I can't wait to be near 'im again. I just … it feels like everythin' that happened before between us made me realise just how deeply I care about 'im now that we're on the same page."

"That's deep."

"I can't quite believe it's real, though. Like, I can kiss 'im whenever I want."

"*Have* you kissed 'im?"

I looked away from my friend, and she reached over and slapped my hand, resulting in me hissing at her like a cat and cradling my now stinging hand against my chest.

"What was *that* for?"

"Don't you dare get embarrassed," she warned. "We talk about *my* sex life *all* the time. I wanna hear about yours."

"*You* talk about your sex life. *I* just listen."

Bronagh narrowed her eyes at me, so I held my hands up in surrender.

"Okay, okay. Down girl."

I was about to launch into a play by play of what went down between Damien and me when Bronagh raised a finger.

"Before you say anythin', I want to ask you a question that has been botherin' me."

"Shoot."

"Do you remember when we all took pregnancy tests before we found out Aideen was pregnant with Jax? We weren't sure who it was that could be up the duff. You said, and I quote, 'there's been no tick in me clock for six months, so it's not me who's pregnant' … was that a lie?"

"Obviously." I snorted. "I didn't want you to know how pathetic I was for only havin' sex that one time with Damien."

"I'd have never thought that, and ye'know it."

"I know." I sighed. "I was just embarrassed. I mean, apart from sex a few times with Dante and that one time with Damien, I've no experience. Not like you or the girls, anyway."

"Alannah, that doesn't mean anythin'," Bronagh said with a frown. "It took me at least a year of sex with Dominic before I became confident enough to know what I was doin'. He had to teach me everythin'. He literally had to tell me how to give 'im a blowjob because I was worried I'd mess it up."

"You see, that freaks me out, because I'm inexperienced like that right now, and Damien has boatloads of experience."

"Damien also hasn't had sex in six years, so your lad is bound to be rusty."

My cheeks heat. "Not accordin' to what he did to me last night."

Bronagh leaned in, her eyes gleaming.

"What'd he do?"

"He ... went down on me."

Bronagh rested her palms under her chin. "And?"

"And what?"

"Ye'know bloody well what, how was it?"

I gnawed on my inner cheek before I said, "I think mind-blowin' is the perfect word."

Bronagh grinned. "Continue."

I relaxed into the conversation.

"He just seems to know exactly what to do to make me lose me mind," I said with a shake of my head. "I mean, he teased me. God in Heaven, he teased me to the point where I wanted to scream, then bam, an abundance of attention went to me clit, and I just about died right there on the bed."

Bronagh laughed joyfully. "Sounds to me like he can give a hell of an orgasm."

"You can say that again."

"Did you have sex afterward?"

I shook my head. "No, the oral itself was a surprise because I was clear about us goin' slow, but Damien asked me if I trusted 'im to make me feel good, and I did, so he did."

"Did you reciprocate?"

I cleared my throat.

"Yeah," I said, my voice low, "but not last night because I knocked out when he got me off."

Bronagh snorted.

"I gave 'im a nice wake-up call," I said, feeling proud when I thought of him waking up and seeing my mouth on him. "I was so nervous I'd do it wrong, but I wanted to pleasure 'im, and I did."

"Did he wake up with you suckin' on 'im, or did you just surprise 'im?"

"Woke 'im up," I answered. "You should have seen his face. He looked like he was about to die."

Bronagh laughed.

"How did he work his way into your bed?"

"He didn't," I answered. "I asked 'im to sleep with me. I wanted to sleep next to 'im and wake up with 'im by me side."

Bronagh sighed. "That's so cute."

"I think I'm in a state of shock whenever I sit and think about it because yesterday I was plannin' on just talkin' to 'im, and today, we're in an exclusive relationship. I never believed somethin' like this could happen, let alone happen so rapidly."

"Anythin' can happen at the drop of a hat." Bronagh shrugged. "There are no rules when it comes to bein' with someone. Though I know there are people out there who enjoy forcin' their opinion down people's throats. All that matters is that it feels right to you and Damien. If anyone else has a problem or thinks it's 'too fast', they can take a seat and shut the fuck up because what works for you won't work for everyone."

"Well, feck me, you've gotten your point across."

Bronagh grinned. "Good."

"I think it's funny that we are goin' out with twins. I'd have never thought this was possible when we were kids."

I daydreamed about it a lot, but never imagined it could be a reality.

"We'll never get them mixed up," she joked. "And I'm not talkin' about their hair colour."

"Right?" I said, chuckling. "I could never mistake Damien for Nico, not ever. They're *way* too different."

"Like night and day," Bronagh concluded.

We spent twenty minutes talking about everything from my new relationship, to being a cat mother, to my parents, and finally to Gavin.

"Gav's bailin' on me this past month," Bronagh commented. "He is always 'busy' whenever I phone or text 'im. I called 'im yesterday, and had to leave a fuckin' voicemail. The dickhead still hasn't phoned me back."

I felt my hands become sweaty as the information I had about Gavin weighed down on me like a tonne of bricks. At that moment, I could have smacked him silly for making me promise to keep his secret.

"I know." I cleared my throat. "I wish he wasn't workin' for Mr Daley. Whatever he does is shady."

Bronagh began to look as uncomfortable as I felt.

"What do you mean exactly when you say 'shady'?"

I shrugged. "You've heard the rumours that Mr Daley is a businessman, but the … scary kind."

"Scary kind?"

"C'mon," I said with a roll of my eyes. "I know you've heard that he's involved with the … with the mob."

I said the last part in a whisper, and it made Bronagh's lips twitch.

"Have you ever spoken to Gavin about your concerns for who his boss does business with?"

My hand went to my chest. "I'd die with fright before I could get a word out."

Bronagh laughed. "You're such a chicken."

"And proud," I said, my head held high. "I can barely watch mob films, so bein' involved with anythin' like that or havin' any connection to it … I'd just die. I wouldn't be able to stomach it. It's why I'm always so worried over Gavin."

Bronagh looked away from me suddenly.

"Yeah," she said. "I know what you mean."

The vibe between us changed then, and for some reason, I felt that there was something left unspoken between us. I felt like that a lot with my friends whenever we got into random conversation. I would say something, and they would shut down, and I'd felt like there was more to be said … but nothing further would happen, and I'd be left feeling like I was missing something. This was one of those times, and just like all the *other* times, I was too apprehensive to question it, so I pushed it to the back of my mind and pretended it was all in my head.

"I'm goin' to the jacks."

"I'll put the kettle back on," Bronagh said, jumping to her feet. "I'm hungry. Do you want some chicken stir-fry? I've loads left over from last night."

"Sounds good."

When I left the room and reached the stairs, the front door opened, and Nico walked into the house with Ryder in tow. They both stopped when they saw me, and identical grins stretched across their lips.

"Don't," I warned them. "Don't either of you think to embarrass me. I've had enough to me face burnin' like the sun to last me a lifetime."

They tittered like kids, then Nico stepped toward me, and when he leaned down and kissed my cheek, he said, "You're officially my sister now."

That did it; my face burned like lava.

"That was so cute," I whispered before I turned and fled up the stairs, the lads' laughter echoing behind me.

I didn't even get to question why either of them were home from work, and of course, since Ryder worked with Damien, I wondered where he was, too. I pondered on this as I went to the toilet. After I was finished and had washed my hands, I turned to leave the room, but on the counter, inches away from me, was the biggest spider I had ever seen in my entire twenty-four years of living.

I stared at it, and I knew it was staring back at me, challenging me ... waiting for me to make the first move. I reluctantly did when I exhaled my sucked in breath. The spider seemed to fucking glide straight for me, so I did what any normal person would do. I jumped onto the toilet and screamed bloody murder. I think roughly ten to fifteen seconds passed before the bathroom door flew open and Nico and Ryder burst in.

"It's goin' to eat me!" I screeched as I lunged at Nico with absolutely no warning.

He widened his eyes and opened his arms a split second before my body collided with his. My chest bumped his, my crotch slammed against his stomach, my legs wrapped around his waist, while my arms encircled his neck so tight, I knew I was choking him, but I couldn't let up.

"*Getoutgetoutgetout*!" I all but screamed.

Nico stumbled back into his brother as he tried to make a quick and clean exit from the bathroom. Ryder rounded on us, and the bastard was laughing. I could hear him now that I wasn't screaming.

He was really laughing.

"Shut up!" I bellowed at him. "Just kill it! My God! It's the size of me hand, Ryder, me fuckin' *hand*!"

He laughed louder.

"What is it?" Nico rasped, trying to breathe around my chokehold.

"Spider." I sobbed. "Big spider."

"You're screaming like that over a fucking *spider*?"

I remained attached to him.

"You didn't see it, Nico," I said and realised I was sobbing. "It was hu-huge."

I heard a baby's cry then, and my heart broke knowing I woke Georgie up.

"I'm sorry, baby," I called out to her but couldn't let go of her father.

Bronagh ran up the stairs, shouting, "I've got 'er, you ... continue."

Nico managed to peel my death like hold off his body, and when my feet touched the ground, he placed his hands firmly on my shoulders and stared down at me.

"A spider really made you scream like that?" he gaped. "Alannah Ryan, I am disappointed in you."

"It had fuckin' knees, Nico! *KNEES*!"

Ryder's laughter almost knocked him off his feet while I was still and brushing myself off like a madwoman. Nico looked at the cackling hyena and began snickering too, which only upset me further because I was beyond scared. I felt immense relief when Damien suddenly jogged up the stairs.

"What's going—Alannah!"

He pushed Nico aside and surged forward, planting his hands on my forearms.

"Baby, what is it?"

"A spider," I cried. "It was huge, and it was *on* me, and now I don't know where it is, but no one is helpin' me and—"

Damien scooped me up off the floor like I weighed nothing and whisked me down the stairs before I had time to comprehend what had happened. When we got into the kitchen, he put me down and helped me brush my clothing.

"It's gone," he said as he twirled me around, brushing me off all over. "It's not on you."

Sobs wracked my body, and my breathing was laboured.

"I was so s-scared."

"I know," Damien said, wrapping his arms around me. "I know you were."

I didn't let go of Damien until Bronagh came into the room and said, "Lana, are you okay? The spider is dead. Ryder killed it."

Relief filled me, but I didn't let go of Damien.

"The lads laughed at 'er," Bronagh said, her voice tight as Georgie babbled in, what I assumed was her mother's arms. "I don't think they realise how scared she is of spiders."

I was terrified of them.

I tensed when Nico and Ryder came down the stairs and entered the kitchen. I released Damien only because he nudged for me to do so. I took a tissue from Bronagh when she extended some my way. I took it with a smile, then took Georgie when she reached for me. I snuggled her against my chest and stared down at her face, delighted that I was relaxing.

"Apologise," Damien demanded of his brothers.

"For what?" Nico bristled. "We just laughed."

"She is terrified!" Damien snapped, balling his hands into fists. "Laugh at her again when she needs you, and I'll put my fist through your skull." He switched his glare to Ryder and growled, "You fucking, too."

Bronagh's mouth dropped open, Ryder raised a brow, and Nico grunted but didn't say a word.

"Damien." I sniffled, bouncing Georgie. "It's fine."

"It's not," he replied, his tone firm. "Branna is terrified of rats, and Bronagh is frightened of moths, and if I laughed at them when something they feared was scaring them, these two assholes would beat the shit out of me. And they fucking know it."

I was surprised when Ryder and Nico sort of hung their heads like they were ashamed of themselves.

"I'm sorry, Alannah," Ryder spoke first. "I didn't think you were that scared. I wouldn't have laughed otherwise."

"Me either," Nico added. "You're important to me, and to laugh while you're scared is something I would never want to do. Can you forgive me?"

"Us," Ryder corrected.

I wiped my eyes. "Of course, lads. It's really okay, I just overreacted and—"

"You have a phobia of spiders," Damien cut me off, turning to face me. "You didn't overreact."

"But Damien—"

"You. Did. Not. Overreact."

My heart thrummed in my chest.

"Okay," I said softly. "Okay."

He stepped closer to me, switching his eyes to his niece, and they softened almost instantly.

"How's my girl doing?" he asked her, touching his hand to her side, tickling her.

Her little body spasmed in my arms, so I turned her away, laughing.

"Don't tickle 'er," I warned. "She's like me; she can't handle it."

"I'll be the judge of what you can handle."

No one missed the innuendo in what Damien said.

"Shut up."

The lads snorted.

"You're on a whole other level of pretty when you're embarrassed, freckles."

I ducked my head, and Damien laughed as he put his arms around me and hugged me to him. Georgie wasted no time as she gripped his arm with her little hands, and pinched him, which had him pulling away with a yelp.

"Ow!" He frowned, and waddled his finger at her. "No. You *don't* pinch. No, not nice."

The child glared at him.

"She loves Alannah," Bronagh said. "She clearly doesn't like you touchin' 'er."

"Well." Damien stared back at his niece. "You'll have to get used to it, kid."

Georgie continued to eye Damien, and it made me chuckle.

"She's fire," I said. "Good luck to you when she's a teen, Nico."

"Jesus, I know."

We all laughed, and Georgie laughed too because of that, which we only found funnier. I handed her off to her mother, and Damien slipped his arm around my shoulder, tugging me to his side. Ryder stepped outside to take a call when his phone rang, so I focused on Damien and said, "How come you're home from work?"

"I get off work at three thirty on Tuesdays."

"Oh." I nodded. "I'll have to learn your roster."

Damien leaned his head down, and I knew his intention was to kiss me, but he paused and looked up suddenly. I followed his eyes and froze.

"What?" Damien said, his eyes flicking from Nico to Bronagh, who were staring at us. "Why're you both looking at us like that?"

"Because we've waited for fuckin' *years* to see it," Bronagh answered, a beaming smile stretching across her lips. "*That's* why, bro."

Nico smiled down at her when she called Damien bro.

"Are you all goin' to be weird about this?" I quizzed. "'Cause I *never* stare at any of you."

"None of us have been sniffing around one another as long as you and Dame have," Nico said.

"You're both me OTP."

I blinked. "What does OTP mean?"

"One true pair," she replied. "*Duh.*"

I rolled my eyes. "You're not allowed on Tumblr anymore, you're turnin' into one of those crazy people."

"Back off Tumblr, Lana."

I playfully raised my hands, and grinned before I dropped my hands to the arms around me when Damien hugged my body tightly to his.

"It's crazy for us to see you guys together." Nico said with a smile. "A good crazy."

"You'll get used to it," Damien answered. "You all will."

God, I hoped so.

I smiled up at him, but my attention was pulled to the doorway when Ryder slid into the room, his eyes wild, and his forehead shining with sweat.

"What is it?"

"Branna," he said, panicked. "Her water broke!"

CHAPTER SIXTEEN

"How did Ry get Bran to the hospital so fast?" I asked Bronagh as we jogged from the car park towards the Coombe Women & Infants University Hospital after passing by Ryder's car that was parked at a sharp angle. "We live forty minutes from 'ere, and we left at the same bleedin' time as 'im!"

"God couldn't stop that man from gettin' 'ere as fast as he could with Branna and those babies."

I could do nothing but agree with her as we jogged towards the entrance of the hospital, a stitch already forming in my side from the activity.

"I hate runnin'," I replied breathlessly.

"Since Georgie got more active and started crawlin', runnin' is all I'm good for nowadays."

I laughed, then took a much-needed breather when we slowed down upon nearing the reception desk in the lobby. I thought Bronagh was going to ask where the labour and delivery ward was situated, but when she turned left and headed towards a giant stairwell, I blindly followed her. It wasn't until we cleared the first floor that I realised Bronagh knew exactly where she was going, she *had* delivered a baby in the same hospital after all.

"Isn't the labour ward off limits to visitors?"

"Normally, yeah," Bronagh answered. "But since Branna works

'ere, and she's the patient, that means we get special privileges."

"We?" I slowed my steps. "You just said we ... as in you and *me*?"

Bronagh paused, then turned to face me.

"I hear the fear in your voice," she commented. "Push it away, 'cause we gotta focus on Branna."

My lips parted.

"But ... but ... I thought I was gonna wait in the waitin' area," I said, grasping at straws. "I can give great moral support from out 'ere, ye'know? I'll keep everyone updated. I won't leave this spot, not even to use the jacks. I'll be the best support system from a distance, I swear."

Bronagh snorted, then turned and continued walking. With a dragged-out sigh, I followed her, silently praying that a security guard or a member of staff would inform me that I had no business being in a room where a lady was about to give birth ... but no one stopped us. Not a single bloody person. I followed Bronagh towards the nurses' station, and when I spotted Ash, Branna's co-worker, behind the desk, I smiled along with Bronagh. Ash was lovely, and any time I had met him, he had always made me laugh with a dumb joke one way or the other.

"Bronagh, Alannah," he said with a bright smile when she stopped before the desk. "It's great to see you both. Which one of you is in labour so I can get you checked in?"

I snickered. "Arsehole."

He grinned at us.

"I'd jump this counter and wring your neck if I wasn't so excited," Bronagh said, bouncing from foot to foot. "Which room is Branna in?"

"Number one," Ash answered. "Sally is in there with her and so is Taylor; she's doin' beautifully. She's already dilated to eight centimetres."

Ash barely finished his sentence before Bronagh squealed excitedly and ran towards room number one at the end of the corridor. I made no move to follow her; instead, I stared at the door of the room where Bronagh just vanished.

"You look scared."

I looked back at Ash. "Just scared? Because I feel terrified."

His lips twitched. "Have you never seen a baby being born?"

"Not in person, and I avoid it on the telly whenever I can," I answered. "I wasn't expectin' to go *into* the room. I thought it would have been a private moment."

"From what Branna tells me, you're her family. You don't get any more private than that."

That made me smile.

"Yeah," I agreed. "We're a family."

"Then get in there," Ash encouraged. "The more support, the better, and it's better you than me, to be honest. Bronagh can focus on Branna, and you can focus on Ryder. The man looks like he is going to drop any second."

I nodded, swallowed, then turned and walked towards the room Bronagh disappeared into. When I reached the door, I knocked on it gently, and maybe two seconds went by before the door was pulled open, revealing a very distraught Ryder.

"Lana," he said, relieved. "Get in here."

He took my hand and pulled me into the room, closing the door behind us. Instantly, my eyes landed on Branna. She was on her hands and knees on her bed, her head down, and her hips swaying from side to side as she groaned. She was wearing a pretty pink nightdress, and her hair was pulled back into a tight French plait.

Bronagh was beside her, with her jacket and bag hung up on a rack across the room. She had her long-sleeved t-shirt rolled up to the elbows, and her hair was pushed behind her ears. Her attention was 100% on her sister as she roughly rubbed her lower spine. I noticed two women, one older and one younger, pattering around the room checking machines, checking on Branna, then chatting to one another like there wasn't a woman in excruciating pain next to them.

I assumed them to be Sally and Taylor that Ash mentioned. I

had heard Branna talking about them before, but I had never met them in person.

"You've got this, Bran," I said to her, finding my voice. "You're gonna be a mammy soon."

Branna lifted her head, and though she was sweaty and red faced, she smiled at me as best as she could.

"I'm so happy about you and Damien, honey."

My heart warmed. "Thanks, Bran."

She lowered her head, and said, "'Ere comes another one."

She moaned in pain, and Ryder, who still had hold of my hand, squeezed it.

"Hey," I said, gaining his attention. "She's goin' to make you a daddy real soon, and she is goin' to be perfectly okay."

He bobbed his head, and I knew he was repeating what I had said over in his mind. He gave my hand another squeeze, then moved over to Branna's right side. He kissed her cheek, head, then hunkered down beside her, grabbing her hand as she powered through a contraction.

She suddenly cried out in pain, and I jumped with fright.

"I really shouldn't be 'ere for this," I said to no one, my stomach tightening. "I think I'm gonna faint."

Ash snickered as he entered the room, and that frightened me as well, which told me just how wound up I was. I focused on him.

"This room is over capacity, right?"

"Yes," he answered with a twitch of his lips. "But Branna works here, so having extra people in with her is no problem."

I frowned at the man. "You were supposed to agree with me, then escort me off this ward and to a waitin' room."

Ash rumbled with laughter. "My bad."

I focused on my friend and so did Ash.

"You're doing beautifully, babe," he said to her. "You're flying along."

Branna groaned in response, and Ryder sort of glared at Ash, while Bronagh continued to rub her sister's back and spoke words of encouragement to get her through the current contraction.

"She's progressin' like lightnin'," the older woman, who I assumed to be Sally from what Branna had told me, beamed with pride. "Those twins will be 'ere within the hour, mark me words."

Ryder looked like he was about to faint.

"Isn't this happenin' too fast?" I quizzed to Ash. "Shouldn't she be in labour for hours? Me ma was in labour for twenty-seven hours before she had me, she said it's the reason I'm an only child."

"Every woman is different," Ash answered with a one-shoulder shrug. "When I came on shift this morning, the woman who had been in labour for twelve hours when I left last night was still in her room labouring while another woman came in and left an hour later after having her baby."

"Wow," I murmured. "That's insane."

"Branna's been in labour since six o'clock this morning, and she said nothing just so Ryder would go to work. She's in labour a good nine hours now," Ash explained. "She just didn't ring Ryder until her water broke an hour ago because she knew how long labouring could take, and she didn't want to worry him."

That was such a Branna thing to do. She wouldn't bother anyone, even her husband, unless she absolutely had to.

Branna suddenly cried out in pain as her contractions strengthened, and I cringed right along with her as her entire body tensed. Crossing my legs absentmindedly as I inhaled and exhaled deep breaths. I found that the actions helped me as much as it seemed to help Branna, so I kept on at it.

"Do you remember," Bronagh said to her sister with a smile, "when I was eighteen and you dropped me off at school, but I didn't wanna go inside because I didn't want to be around Dominic?"

Branna nodded, breathing heavily. "I remember."

"Do you remember laughin' at me?"

"Yeah," Branna panted, sweat running down the sides of her face. "I do."

"Do you remember that I said I would remind you of that moment when you were at the height of pain in labour?"

Branna growled. "I remember."

"This is me revenge for that moment ... does it hurt?"

Branna swiped at Bronagh, who leaned away laughing before returning to her sister's side. She resumed forcefully rubbing the base of Branna's spine, and it made Branna groan and not in pain. She seemed to like the treatment Bronagh was giving her, while I found it all to be rather ... rough.

"You won't make me see Dominic again when I don't want to, will you?" Bronagh teased.

Branna laughed, then cried out in pain again, and even though I had only been in the room for a few minutes, I could tell they were getting stronger and faster.

"It hurts," she growled. "God, it fuckin' *hurts*."

"I know," Bronagh said. "Breathe through it. You've got this, Bran."

Branna screamed through the worst of her contratcion and agony played across her face. The sound, and visual, cut me in two. I looked at Ryder who was staring at his wife with non-blinking eyes, and he looked exactly how I felt. Fucking terrified.

"What can I do, sweetness?" he almost pleaded. "I'll do anything, just tell me, and I'll do it."

"Ice," Branna groaned. "Some ice, please."

Ryder zoomed out of the room to gather some ice before Branna even finished her sentence.

I watched him go. "He is feckin' terrified."

Branna inhaled and exhaled deeply four times before she said, "There is no point in reassurin' 'im. Until the babies ... are born ... he will remain that way."

"Or until they're eighteen," I teased.

Everyone laughed just as my phone rang. I checked the screen, saw it was Damien, and answered instantly.

"Any news?"

I winced as Branna screamed and latched onto Bronagh like a

boa constrictor. Bronagh's face reddened a little, which told me just how tight of a grip her sister had on her.

"She's still in labour."

"I heard her, poor mama," Damien said, and I could picture him frowning. "Is she okay apart from her obvious pain? How is Ryder holding up?"

"Branna is doin' brilliantly." I looked at his older brother down the hallway gathering ice from the ice machine and said, "And Ryder is still conscious so I'm countin' that as a positive."

Damien snorted, and Ash grinned beside me before he said something to Taylor to make her cheeks redden. I watched as he patted her behind with his hand, and a smirk stretched across his face before he left the room. If didn't take much to see that they were more than co-workers.

"I wasn't expectin' to be *in* the room," I whispered to Damien when I refocused on our phonecall. "I feel so scared, and I keep crossin' me legs when Branna gets a pain. Bein' 'ere is such good birth control; they should make teenage girls come and experience this."

Damien's laughter relaxed me, but another cry from Branna cut the sound off. I placed my finger in my free ear so I could hear him better.

"You'll be fine," he assured me. "Think of it this way; you'll get to see our nephews come into the world."

Our nephews.

"Yeah," I said, smiling. "You're right."

Branna screamed so loud it scared the bejesus out of me, and I could do nothing but wince on her behalf.

"Gotta go," I said to Damien. "I'll phone you when I have another update."

"Okay, baby. Bye."

I bit down on my lower lip to keep from smiling like a fool. Every single time he called me baby, or some silly pet name, it reminded me that we were *really* together, and I hadn't imagined our coupling.

"Bye."

After I ended the call, I pocketed my phone. Ryder re-entered the room with a jug full of ice, instead of just a small cup, and it made me grin. I had never seen someone as big as him look so scared, but I knew he wasn't just scared for his babies. He was also terrified for his wife.

"Ye'know," I randomly said, "I keep forgettin' that you're both married, and your surname is Slater now, Bran."

She smiled through her pain.

"I know. It has a ring to it, though, doesn't it?"

"Yup," I agreed. "Bronagh Slater sounds foreign, though."

"I probably won't take Dominic's last name," Bronagh said with a shrug. "It's the twenty-first century; not *every* woman takes 'er husband's last name."

Ryder, who popped a piece of ice into Branna's mouth, looked at his sister-in-law and said, "Does Dominic know about this?"

"No."

I grinned. "Can I be there when you tell 'im?"

"Me too," Ryder and Branna said in unison, making one another laugh.

I frowned when Branna whimpered as pain consumed her once more. She tucked her head against Ryder's neck and began to cry as he leaned down to hug her. Bronagh continued to rub her back, and Ryder murmured things to Branna that made her bob her head. I sat on a chair to the left of the room as things progressed fast. One minute, Branna was breathing through her pain, and the next, her legs were parted and there was a flurry of people in the room.

A man called Doctor Harrison, Taylor, Sally and two more nurses who were on standby to take each baby when they were born filled the already crowded room.

Before I knew it, Branna was pushing. Bronagh was on her left, and Ryder was on her right, both looked like they'd swap positions with Branna in a heartbeat if they could. I, on the other hand, was focused on my breathing because I felt like my heart was about to beat out of my chest. I wouldn't have been able to swap with Branna even if I wanted to; I was too scared.

This fear, I felt was warranted, so I didn't feel any guilt for it.

During all the commotion, I took out my phone and began recording. I made sure to get the full view of Branna as she gave birth, and I noted that I would instantly delete it if she didn't want to keep it, but since no one else thought to record the moment, and I was doing nothing but hyperventilating, I figured I'd make myself useful and capture the once in a lifetime memory.

"He's crownin'," the doctor announced after minutes of pushing. Once the head was out, Branna screamed to the high heavens. "Shoulders, chest ... penis, thighs ... and Baby A is *here*."

Branna cried with relief as her son was placed on her chest, Ryder was completely in awe as he stared down at his firstborn son, and Bronagh, she was silently crying. Tears were streaming down her cheeks as a smile stretched across her lips.

"You did it, Bran," Bronagh gushed and kissed her sister's head. "You did it!"

"Thank you," Ryder said to Branna before kissing her face. "Thank you for making me a daddy. I love you so much."

"I love you too," Branna sobbed.

Together, she and Ryder stared down at her baby while Taylor silently wiped him off with a towel. Ryder kissed his son's head, and Branna quickly followed suit.

"He's perfect," Branna said in wonder. "And he looks just like you!"

"Are you kidding?" Ryder replied, his eyes glazed over with unshed tears. "He's beautiful. That's all you, sweetness."

I stared at the baby. "Am I seein' things, or does the child have white blond hair?"

"You aren't seein' things," Bronagh laughed. "Damien isn't the only fair haired lad anymore."

I got a lump in my throat as emotion overcame me, but I kept my hand steady, making sure the video I was recording wouldn't be messed up. Seven minutes later, Branna groaned in pain, and Baby A was taken to the side by Sally where he could get cleaned up, weighed, and checked over properly. I desperately wanted to go and see him, but I stayed rooted to the spot. Things then went from calm to insanity in seconds. Branna was contracting once more, and she began to push her second son out.

My vagina was in agony just looking at her, my legs were so tightly crossed I knew Damien would need to be awarded a medal if he ever managed to pry them open again.

I found myself pushing right along with Branna, as if trying to help her. Baby B, who had white blond hair also, took ten minutes longer to make his appearance into the world, making his brother seventeen minutes older, but when he did, it was with a whooping scream.

Everyone cried, mainly Branna, and a part of me thought it was because she didn't have to push another kid out at that moment. After Baby B spent a few minutes with his mammy and daddy, he was taken aside to be cleaned, weighed, and checked over just like his brother. Both babies were returned to Branna once she delivered the afterbirth, got cleaned up with a wash cloth and got settled into bed.

I had stopped recording by the time that happened, but I was taking lots of pictures, just in case Branna and Ryder wanted me to delete the video. I moved over to the twins after they were bundled in blue blankets and had tiny white hats on their heads. I gushed over them, and when Bronagh came to join me, we both hugged each other with excitement.

After the babies were handed back to Branna, Sally said, "Baby A is five pounds ten ounces and twenty inches long, and Baby B is five pounds even and twenty inches long, too. Good job, sweetie."

Branna beamed then turned her head and kissed Ryder, who was wiping tears from his cheeks. He spent minutes gazing down at the twins, then kissing Branna and thanking her for giving them to him once again. He carefully took one twin from her and cuddled him against his chest. My heart squeezed as I watched him. He was a mountain of a man, super tall, lean with muscle, and here he was, completely at the mercy of the tiny bundle in his arms.

"Pictures," I announced.

Ryder beamed at me as I took a picture of him and his son, Branna mimicked him as I snapped one of her and their other son. Ryder leaned in closer, so I could get the first photo together of them as a family.

"Can we hear their names now?" I asked, lowering my device. "I think I'm about to collapse from all the excitement; give me somethin' good to go out on."

The new parents grinned at me.

"This little man, Baby A," Branna beamed, "is Nixon Joe Slater."

Ryder partly sat on the side of Branna's bed.

"This little dude, Baby B." He smiled down at his son as he yawned, "is Jules Alec Slater."

I clutched my free hand to my chest. "Alec is gonna cry when he finds out."

"Definitely." Bronagh echoed, then to her sister, she said, "You gave Nixon his middle name after Da?"

"Of course." Branna smiled tiredly. "He's the greatest man, besides Ry, that I've ever known."

Bronagh walked over to her sister and kissed her cheek; she then silently cried again as Branna offered her Nixon to hold for the first time. Bronagh sat down on the chair provided, and when Ryder rounded the bed and handed Jules to her, too, a little sob burst free.

"Smile, Bee," I said and waited until she did as I asked before I took a picture of them.

Ryder and Branna hugged and kissed some more, but when he turned to me, he grinned. I was bouncing from foot to foot. I was so proud of them both, and I was so happy for them that I could have burst.

"You're a *daddy*!" I squealed and launched myself at Ryder, who caught me, laughed and hugged me so tight, I could have sworn I heard my bones crunch.

"I'm a daddy."

"Congratulations, I'm so happy for you both, Ry."

I scrabbled for my phone once more when he released me.

"I have to update everyone," I announced. "They'll kill me otherwise."

Ryder snorted, then moved over to Branna, who was now nibbling on a slice of toast and sipping a cup of tea Sally brought her. She didn't look like she wanted either of them, but from the look Sally shot her way, she knew arguing against it was futile.

I focused on my phone and dialled Damien's number. He answered on the second ring.

"How is she?"

"She is fabulous," I squealed, "and so are our nephews!"

"*What?*" Damien shouted. "She had them already?"

"Yup!"

"Branna had the twins!" He screamed so loudly, I had to pull my phone away from my ear, laughing. "She had them!"

"Two boys for definite," I said. "Both perfectly healthy."

Damien repeated the information I fed him, and cheers sounded in the background.

"And Branna?" he asked.

"She's brilliant," I gushed. "You should have seen 'er; she was like superwoman. I'm not even jokin'; she is literally me hero after seein' 'er go through that *twice* in the space of a few minutes."

Damien laughed. "Are *you* okay?"

"No," I answered instantly. "I thought I was about to faint five or six times, and me legs may permanently remain crossed forever after what I just witnessed."

Damien sucked in a breath. "You don't mean that."

"I just saw a woman push not one, but two humans out of 'er vagina," I said with a shake of my head. "I'm never havin' sex again. I'm sorry, it's just not happenin'."

"Alannah," Damien said ... or did he whimper. "Don't make any rash decisions, just ... just put sex from your mind and focus on those babies and Branna, okay?"

"Okay." I nodded. "Still not havin' sex, though."

"Fuck!"

"You're such a man."

"Don't tell me to calm down," Damien snapped to someone in the background. "She just said she's never having sex with me because she watched Branna give birth! How would you feel if Keela said that to you? ... Exactly! You'd fucking cry!"

Alec.

I laughed so hard everyone looked at me, so I waved them off and turned my back, trying to focus on Damien.

"I have to go," I said to him. "I'll see you later."

I hung up, noting he was still arguing with his brother to even hear me say goodbye. I jumped when my phone rang before I put it into my pocket; at first, I thought Damien was calling me back, but when a different name shot across the screen, I smiled and clicked answer.

"Hey, Morgan," I beamed.

"Hey, Alannah," came his response. "I'm just checkin' in that we're still good for me startin' tomorrow? I've logged your address into my sat-nav, so I'll make it there no problem."

"We're still on for tomorrow," I said, glancing at my friends. "I still haven't got the spare bedroom switched around yet, but we'll manage with the desk and setup I have for the time being."

"Brilliant," Morgan answered. "I've a schedule done out, and I'm buzzin' to get started."

"Well, it seems I made the right choice in hirin' you. You sound more than ready to get to work.

His chuckle practically rumbled through the receiver of my phone.

"Born ready, *boss*."

CHAPTER SEVENTEEN

It was seven p.m. when we prepared to leave the hospital so Branna and Ryder could have one-on-one time with their sons and get some well-deserved rest. Bronagh and I stayed the entire time; the rest of the tribe showed up one hour after she gave birth, and by then, she was settled in a large private room with no distractions. All of us stared at the babies in complete awe. Georgie and Jax looked at them but weren't all that bothered; the only time they showed any interest was when their parents held the twins. They didn't like that very much, and they didn't like when *I* held them either.

"I *told* you she was their favourite," Keela scowled. "They didn't cry when the rest of us held the babies."

I grinned, taking Jax from Kane after I carefully handed Jules back to his father. Jax snuggled against my chest and placed his hand on my breast. He began to play with it, and this was how I knew he was tired and that Aideen would have to nurse him soon. I glanced at his younger brother, and my lips twitched. Locke slept nearly the entire time he was in the hospital. He was brilliant at two things, eat-ing and sleeping.

"Am I the only one seeing him openly play with her tit?"

I rolled my eyes at Alec.

"Am I also the only one seeing Damien openly glare at the boy for it?"

I looked at Damien, and sure enough, his grey eyes were locked on his first-born nephew, and they were narrowed.

"I don't even think *I'm* allowed to freely play with them," Damien said, not taking his eyes off Jax. "Why should he be allowed?"

"Because he is a baby."

Damien flicked his gaze to mine. "That's no excuse."

Jax locked eyes on Damien then fully rested his hand on my breast, his palm flattened, and it caused Damien to hiss at him.

"You know damn well what you're doing, kid. I know you do."

I couldn't believe it when Jax tiredly chuckled.

"See!" Damien pointed at him. "I told you. He knows she's mine, and that touching her pisses me off."

The playful show of dominance caused a pulse to grow between my thighs.

"Stop cussing," Kane said to Damien. "He's nearly one; he'll learn the words easier if they're spoken often."

"Is damn a curse word?" Bronagh mumbled to her sister.

Branna smiled, tiredly. "Not to us, but in America? Yeah."

"What about hell?"

"It's a cuss," Nico answered his fiancée.

"That's stupid. How can it be a curse word when it's a *place*?"

"We didn't make up the rules, baby." Nico chuckled, cuddling Georgie to his chest. "We've just been raised to know they're cuss words."

"Curse, not cuss."

I rolled my eyes. "Let them have their way of sayin' it; we've a shiteload of words they have to deal with daily, and you don't hear them complain about it."

Every male in the room said, "Thank you."

I smiled and kissed Jax's head, gaining his attention.

"Do you want to have a sleepover, little man?" I cooed. "With Auntie Alannah?"

"*And* Uncle Damien."

I smiled, not taking my eyes off my nephew. "If one of you are stayin' in me bed, it's Jax."

"Damn, kid."

"Damien!"

"What? Shit, sorry."

"Don't say shit either!"

"I can't remember all these rules, Kane!"

I laughed. "I'll remind you, big man."

Damien's attention zeroed in on me. "Is that a promise, gorgeous?"

I swallowed.

"Oh." Bronagh sighed. "I can *feel* the sexual tension between you both."

Instantly, my face reddened.

"Bronagh!"

"What?" She smiled, fluttering her eyelashes. "What'd I do?"

She knew bloody well what she did.

"Stop talkin', please."

She made the motion that her lips were sealed with her fingers, but she had a shit-eating grin on her face, which caused me to shake my head as I fought off a grin of my own. I focused on Aideen and Kane, then with a nod down to Jax, I asked, "Can he sleep over?"

"Yes," they answered in unison.

Damien snorted. "Locke doesn't wake up at night; I wonder what you'll both get *up* to."

Kane smirked; Aideen deadpanned.

"We'll be *sleepin'*," she said with authority. "Don't let 'im fool you either. He'll be out cold before I am."

Kane shrugged, not denying the charges against him, which made the rest of us chuckle. We all kissed and hugged Branna and Ryder, congratulating them once again. Each of us cooed over the sleeping twins once more and mentioned how much they looked like Ryder. Everyone agreed they had to keep the different coloured bands on their ankles because none of us could tell them apart.

They were identical.

Kane and Aideen took both the kids in their car because it seemed pointless to put Jax's car seat in my car when we'd all be driving to the same building. Bronagh went home with Nico and Georgie and Alec left with Keela, which left just me and Damien to climb into my car. I was buckled up before I realised that he was in the driver's seat.

"Is this a thing now?" I said. "When did you take me keys?"

"They were hangin from your back pocket. I picked them easily."

I shook my head, smiling. "I'm datin' a thief."

"I walk on the wild side, freckles."

I tiredly chuckled, before I yawned.

"Why did you suggest taking Jax if you're tired?"

"Because I love 'im," I answered. "*And* he goes asleep pretty easily for me."

"Does he fall asleep on your chest?"

"Yeah, why?"

Damien grunted. "I'd be snug enough to sleep if I was lying on your chest for a while, too."

I snickered as he backed out of the car park. Damien beeped as we passed Nico, who was loading Georgie into her car seat. He looked over his shoulder, waved at me, then stuck his middle finger up at Damien. Damien returned the gesture without blinking.

"You're not the only twins in the family now," I said as we merged into the traffic. "How do you feel about that?"

"Awesome because they aren't mine."

My lips twitched. "Could be one day."

"Then I feel sorry for you since you'll be the one carrying them."

My heart stopped, and so did the conversation.

"Lana," Damien said, giving my knee a pinch. "Don't freak out on me, please? I didn't mean to say that out loud."

I looked at him. "But you meant it either way?"

He glanced at me, then the road.

"We shouldn't talk about this," he said. "It's *way* too early for that. I don't want you any warier than you already are about us."

"Damien," I said, tilting my head as I looked at him. "You just said I'll be carrying your babies ... that's not somethin' we should sweep under the carpet."

Damien swallowed, and his Adam's apple bobbed.

"Okay." He licked his lips. "When I think of having kids, you're automatically the person I picture as their mother."

My stomach fluttered with butterflies.

"Really?"

Damien nodded, his hands tightening on the steering wheel. "Are you freaked out?"

"No," I answered honestly. "I'm pretty touched, though, that you'd see me in such an important role."

Damien shrugged. "I told you that I want to do this for real with you. I'm not looking for a fling, or a half ass relationship. I'm looking for my wife, Alannah, and I know that's going to be you someday."

My mouth dried.

"Damien."

"It's crazy, I know," he said. "But don't you think that we could get there, even a little?"

I pondered this, but only for a moment because the answer was a no-brainer.

"I envisioned meself marryin' you a few seconds after I clapped eyes on you in school, so what *d'you* think?"

Damien looked at me, to the road, back to me, then back to the road.

"Are you serious?"

"As a heart attack," I answered.

"Fuck, baby, you've made an already incredible day so much sweeter by telling me that."

I lifted my hand, ran it up his arm, and rested it behind his neck as he drove.

"We'll get there," I said. "I know we will."

"Slowly, but surely?"

I smiled and looked out the window, the city passing by in a blur of activity.

"Slowly, but surely."

CHAPTER EIGHTEEN

"**B**abe?"

I looked up from changing Jax's nappy, and just for a moment, I had to remind myself that Damien was talking to me. Hearing him refer to me as a pet name was still very surreal, and I couldn't imagine myself getting used to it.

"Yeah?"

"I won't be back until this evening, I've to work through my lunch hour and two hours after I normally finish to pull up the slack of Ryder not being there."

"Okay," I said with a nod. "I'm gonna make a roast for dinner; do you want me to dish you a plate for later?" I paused. "Do you even *like* roast dinners? It just occurred to me that I have no idea what your food preferences are. I mean, if you're gonna be 'ere, I might as well feed you, so this is information I need to know."

"Yes, I like roast dinners," Damien ... groaned. "God, I'm already looking forward to it."

I chuckled as I focused back on Jax. After I got his nappy changed, I dressed him just in time for Damien to enter the sitting room and give him snuggles and kisses.

"I can drop him up to Aideen on my way out," he offered. "You can get to work on that project you mentioned last night."

"Oh, would you?" I relaxed. "Yes, please. Me head's all over the place. I have to read through the client's briefin' again so I can capture 'er vision for the image she wants."

"You'll do great."

I looked at Jax. "Bye-bye, buddy."

He smiled at me and made the sound of kisses, so I leaned in and kissed all over his face, to which he screamed in delight.

"What about me?" Damien said, a perfect pout in place. "Don't I get kisses?"

"I don't know," I mused. "Have you been a good boy?"

"I made you come twice last night, once on my tongue, and once on my fingers ... I think I'm a *very* good boy."

I covered Jax's ears. "The baby is present!"

Damien laughed. "Give me some sugar, gorgeous."

I leaned up on my tiptoes and pressed my lips against his in a chaste kiss.

"See you later," I whispered before sliding my tongue over his lower lip.

"Sin," Damien growled. "You're *sin*!"

I winked, then turned my attention back to Jax.

"Be good for your Mammy and Daddy, okay?"

He nodded as if he knew what I was saying.

"Just his Mom," Damien said. "Kane is busy today."

Before I could stop myself from being nosy, I asked, "Doin' what?"

Damien pointedly flicked his eyes away from me, and instantly, I knew it was because whatever he was about to say was a lie. I knew because I couldn't lie for shite either, and my friends had told me on multiple occasions that I did the exact same thing when I was being untruthful.

"Running some errands," he answered. "I'm not all that sure. I wasn't listening to him when he was talking last night. I was too busy looking at you."

When Damien looked back at me, I had a forced smile on my face, trying to hide the unease I felt at him lying to me so easily.

"Well." I cleared my throat, focusing on my nephew. "You be good for Mammy, d'ye hear?"

Jax babbled in his baby language.

"I'll take that as a yes."

Damien grinned then leaned down and kissed my cheek.

"I'll see you this evening?"

I nodded.

"Is this all of his things?" Damien asked, hiking the strap of Jax's baby bag farther up his shoulder while holding Jax against his chest with one arm.

"Yeah," I answered. "I bought the travel cot since the kids stay with me so much. You have everythin' he needs in that bag."

Another kiss and another goodbye, then I was alone with my thoughts, and from previous experience, I knew how dangerous that could be when I doubted something or someone. Damien just lied to me, I knew he did, but it was regarding whatever Kane was doing. I wasn't sure if I should have been offended or simply brush it off because really, it was none of my business where Kane went, and it wasn't Damien's job to tell me, either.

I shook my head, forcing it to the back of my mind and went ahead and got changed into my work clothes. I tidied around the whole apartment, and an hour after Damien left, the buzzer rang, and I knew straight away that it was Morgan. As I walked towards the front door, I glanced at the clock on the wall and saw he was nearly ten minutes early for work, which made me smile.

I didn't answer the call; I simply buzzed Morgan in once I saw it was him on the monitor. I put Barbara into her crate, just so she wouldn't freak out when Morgan came in because she didn't know him and was still a little flighty around me and Damien. Five minutes later, there was a knock on my door.

I opened it with a smile.

"Hi, Morgan."

Morgan beamed a smile right back at me. "Heya, how're you?"

"I'm great," I said. "Come in, come in."

Morgan whistled after we entered the kitchen.

"Nice place."

"Thanks," I chirped. "I love it."

"Are you 'ere long?"

I shook my head. "I moved in a month ago; me friend lives upstairs and told me about it."

"Nice," Morgan said, his eyes roaming around the room. "Where I live is a dive compared to this."

I chuckled. "I'm lucky, I guess."

"Yeah," Morgan agreed. "I guess you are."

"D'ye want a cuppa?"

"If you're makin' tea, I won't say no. Two sugars, please."

A man after my own heart.

"I've been thinkin' about what you said about your office." Morgan spoke as I made the tea. "And I figured between the pair of us, we could get it up and operational today to get it out of the way."

I glanced over my shoulder. "Are you sure? I don't wanna have you goin' out of your way."

"It's not out of me way," he replied. "I'm gonna be workin' 'ere, so I figure I might as well help you get the workspace together."

"That's lovely of you," I said. "Thanks."

"It's settled then," he chirped. "We can get on it when we finish our tea."

I placed his cup in front of him, and together, we sat at my kitchen table.

"Have you got somethin' to work on today?" Morgan asked, sipping his tea.

"Yeah." I nodded. "I've to start a book cover for an author; she has a pretty detailed brief about it. I need to reread it to capture 'er vision as well as combinin' it with me own to create somethin' I hope she likes."

"When is your deadline?"

"In two weeks," I answered. "It usually takes me a few days to get an outline that I'm happy with, then once it's scanned to me desktop, things move quicker. I always give meself two weeks, just in case I get a block and lose the vision."

"Has that ever happened before?"

"Once," I answered, swallowing. "Family drama sort of knocked me off track for a few days."

Learning of my da's affair did more than knock me off track; it hit me like the full force of a fucking train.

"I've no doubt whatever you create will be fantastic," Morgan said. "You've never created somethin' less than incredible."

Heat rushed to my cheeks, so I lifted my cup of tea close to my face, hoping Morgan would think the steam from the scalding liquid flushed them and not his praise.

"Are you ready to check out the office?" I cleared my throat. "I'm eager to get started."

We left our cups in the kitchen sink, then entered the soon-to-be office. Morgan scanned the room, either taking it all in or figuring out where to start first.

"Where are you goin' to put the bed?"

"I was going to take it apart, then just stand everythin' upright and lean it against the wall." I shrugged. "I can't get rid of it; it's part of the furnishin' that the landlord provided."

"These look expensive as hell," Morgan noted, "and the mattress looks like it would be heaven to lie on."

"It is," I concluded. "I have the same mattress in me bedroom, and it's incredible."

Morgan placed his hands on his hips, and eyed the flat packs in the corner of the room.

"I can help you take it apart and put it against the wall, then we can put those bookcases and your desk together. It's a sorry sight seein' a Mac Desktop with such big monitors sit on a tiny stand like that."

I glanced at the pathetic stand and sighed.

"I know," I admitted. "I'm just not very handy; I suck at puttin' things together. I was goin' to ask Damien to help, but I forgot. Me friends had twins yesterday, and it's just added to an already eventful week."

"Damien?"

"Oh, sorry." I chuckled. "Damien is me boyfriend. He's at work right now."

"Cool," Morgan said with a bob of his head. "I'm sure he'd help, but since I'm 'ere, you might as well put me to work."

My lips twitched. "You don't have to tell me twice." Together, we spent an hour taking apart the spare bed and putting the wood and mattress carefully against the wall on the far side of the room. Building the large desk was a much quicker endeavour than I could have ever imagined because Morgan seemed to know *exactly* what he was doing.

I just had to hand him the correct screw here and there, and he did the rest. When everything was put together, we both lifted the desk to its new designated spot, and I placed the bookcases where I wanted them to go. Sorting out my computer and the monitors took maybe five minutes.

When we were finished, I placed my hands on my hips and smiled.

"I love it!"

Morgan glanced around. "A few of your designs on the wall will tie everything together nicely."

I agreed and already began filing away ideas of what to paint at a later date. Morgan swiftly moved a lone chair that no one ever sat on in the sitting room into the office, so I could sit in there and sketch while he worked. It made sense instead of us shouting back and forth to one another. Once we were settled, I reread the client's brief and got to work sketching.

Morgan logged into my business email that was connected to my website and started organising the emails in a categorised list for me to choose from. He would read a brief bit of an email, then we would both decide which file it would go into. He then replied to every single email, and from what I could see, there were a *lot* of unread ones.

"What are you sayin' to the clients?" I asked as I smoothed out a rough line on a partially destroyed building that I was drawing with my thumb, creating a smoky effect.

"A pretty standard but formal response," he asked, not looking away from the monitors before him. "Not acceptin' the offer to work with them, but not turnin' it down either. I'm askin' for more information on what you will be designin', whether it's a book cover, a piece of art to hang up in a sittin' room, stuff like that. Oh, and dates they would like work to begin and to be completed so we can check if they're available." Morgan glanced over my shoulder. "Ye'know what? I'm gonna create a form askin' for all of that information then update your contact tab on your website. Everyone will have to fill the form out and email it to you to receive a response."

I raised my brows. "Where have you been all me life?"

Morgan laughed, then turned back to the monitor.

"I'm linkin' your calendar and email up with me phone, that way I can work on the go to make sure I don't come in to work and be swamped for the few hours I'm 'ere."

I paused. "I don't want you workin' outside hours, though. That's not fair since I'm payin' you just for our agreed weekly hours."

"Alannah." Morgan snorted, looking over his shoulder at me. "I'm checkin' emails; you're hardly gonna be overworkin' me."

I made a face, but he grinned and turned back to the computer. He went on to change my entire website around, renaming it, and updating my social media accounts to reflect the changes, too.

"Your price list needs a revamp."

"Too expensive?"

Morgan laughed. "More like inexpensive."

I blinked.

"An example is your author design corner. You charge a hundred for a paperback book cover and sixty-five for an ebook cover."

"Yeah—" I frowned—"but right now, only indie authors come to me, and they don't have a whole lot of money."

"I respect that," Morgan said, "I do, but you aren't puttin' a cover together with stock photos and sendin' it on to them. You *draw* it, and unless your clients specify otherwise, your work looks lifelike, like someone took a picture. You need to charge for the quality of work you provide."

I hesitated. "I mean, if you think I should …"

"I do."

"Okay." I swallowed. "Change the prices to whatever you think, but don't make them *insanely* expensive."

Morgan nodded, then returned to work. We spoke back and forth every so often over the next three hours, him asking questions, and me answering them before asking him a question of my own. It was an interesting way for me to sketch. Normally, no one was around when I drew unless I was sketching on my travel pad, but I was pleased to find I could get lost in my craft and still hold a conversation with someone should I choose to do so.

By the time one o'clock rolled around, I had the dystopian ruined city in the background of the cover drawn with minor detail added, and the characters in the foreground outlined. I rolled my neck onto my shoulders, and when my bones cracked, I knew I was done for the day. I put my things away, then moved over behind Morgan to see what he was doing. When I saw how he had changed my entire system and organised everything, I was more than impressed.

"Okay," he said when he felt my presence behind him. "I've colour tagged categories. All pendin' projects are tagged blue, yellow is for projects you'll be acceptin', red is for projects you're declinin', green is for projects completed, and orange is for works in progress."

I smiled. "Brilliant."

"Also," Morgan added, "I've changed your policy. Once you get an outline drawn and have submitted the mock image to the client for approval, changes can only be made to a sketch *once* before you scan it and get to work with your online designin'. Additional changes after they've approved the mock will be fifty Euros per edit since you'd have to erase and physically re-draw in the changes."

I nodded. "Sounds good."

"And," he continued, "I've also amended your policy that payment for a project must be paid in full upfront. There will be no deposits or holdin' fees of any kind. It'd be a nightmare tryin' to get money from people after you've already committed to their project and spent time creatin' it."

"I wanted to originally do that, but a lot of people preferred the deposit first."

"Well, if they really want your work, they'll adhere to the new policy and have no problem."

I nodded. "Yeah, you're right."

We spent another hour deciding which projects I would be accepting, and which ones I would be declining. I hated declining anyone who liked my work enough to email me, but some of the requests were so out there, I had no idea if I could create what they were asking for. By the time we were finished, Morgan had created formal email responses with an invoice attached. Each client was informed that until the invoice was paid, work would not commence, and their spot on my calendar was in jeopardy until the balance was settled.

"As soon as invoices start gettin' paid, I will update your calendar, and reflect it on the one on your website so people will see you're booked and will have to choose from later dates when fillin' out the new project form."

I shook my head, amazed.

"Thanks, Morgan. You've literally organised me entire business."

"Hey," he said, turning to face me. "That's me job. I'm really enjoyin' meself, and it's only me first day."

"Mate, I like havin' you 'ere. You're a lifesaver."

He snorted and clapped his palm against mine when I raised my hand in the air, requesting a high five.

"When you have a minute," he said, "you need to create a new logo, and I can get to work marketin' your stuff."

"I've a few ideas for it, so I'll get to sketchin' when I have the free time and come up with some ideas to choose from."

"Cool."

I glanced at the time on the monitor and said, "Work is just about finished for you."

His phone vibrated, and he sighed. "That'd be me girlfriend; she has plans for us to go to the cinema and see that new musical with Hugh Jackman and Zac Efron."

I chuckled. "Get to it then."

"You sure you're good? I can stay and help if you need me any further."

"Go on. Get goin'." I waved Morgan on. "Your missus will rip you a new one if you make 'er wait any longer."

Morgan laughed as he grabbed his bag from the floor and put his stuff inside of it.

"I'll see you tomorrow."

"You will indeed."

After Morgan left, I let Barbara out of her crate, then went back into my office and looked around with a smile on my face. I had made some shitty decisions in my life, but hiring Morgan to work for me was not one of them.

CHAPTER NINETEEN

After I changed back into regular clothes, I fed Barbara and cleaned her litter tray. I had lost count of how many times I had cleaned it out, but Barbara had yet to go to the toilet anywhere but *in* her tray, so I kept my mouth shut and got on with it. I was a mother now, so I wasn't allowed to complain. Instead, I had to drink wine when shite got too much for me.

After I took care of her needs and put the meat for my and Damien's dinner on low heat in the oven, it took all of five seconds for me to become bored. Before I locked myself away in my house for a week straight, I'd spent nearly every day around at one of my friend's houses, and now that I was no longer in a state of depression over Damien or disarray about the future of my business, I wanted to get back to my normal routine.

I grabbed my phone and thumbed Bronagh a text.

Are you home?

Barely three seconds passed before my phone pinged.

Where else would I be?

I snorted.

Be over in 15.

With my phone still in hand, I phoned my mother next.

"Hello, bear," she answered on the second ring.

"Hey, Ma," I chirped, smiling warmly. "How're you today?"

"I feel a bit under the weather."

Nausea settled over me.

"I'm comin' over."

"No," Ma said sharply. "I've been gettin' sick and feelin' lousy. Your da took the day off work and is 'ere with me. I may have a stomach bug, and I don't want you to catch it."

"What if it's *not* a bug?"

"Your da called a dub doctor to come out and see me," she said, then coughed, and it sounded like she heaved, but I couldn't hear very well so I assumed she moved the phone away from her face. "This has nothin' to do with the cancer, hon. I just feel sick. Your da felt ill a few days ago, so I must have caught it from 'im."

I lifted my hand to my face and pinched the bridge of my nose. It went against everything I was as a person not to be there for someone I cared about, and the fact that this someone was my mother made it all the harder, but I had to respect her and heed her wishes.

"You'll call me when the doctor leaves," I pressed, "and let me know how you are, right?"

"The second he leaves."

"Okay." I sighed, reluctantly giving in to her. "Get some rest, and I'll talk to you in a while. I love you."

After we hung up, I had to force myself to leave my house and head to Bronagh's. I didn't feel like leaving my apartment anymore, but I knew that if I didn't, I would have been pacing back and forth while I waited for my ma to phone me. Bronagh and Georgie would be the distraction I desperately needed.

After I pulled up and entered her house, I found my friend and her daughter dancing around the kitchen. I leaned my shoulder against the kitchen door panel and smiled as I watched them. I got a familiar sensation of butterflies when I thought of having a baby just like Georgie one day, and for the first time in my life, the daydream accompanied Damien as my future baby's father.

"Alannah!" Bronagh squealed when she caught me out of the

corner of her eyes. "I nearly died!"

"Sorry."

She handed me Georgie, who was already reaching for me. I kissed all over her face, making her scream with delight, which made her mother laugh.

"I swear she loves you more than me."

I grinned. "How are Branna and the twins?"

"Brilliant," Bronagh beamed. "I was goin' to go up this mornin' to see them, but Ryder said Bran was wiped and has slept as much as the twins. She had a very slight tear from givin' birth, and 'er blood pressure was high last night, but she's okay now and will be allowed home tomorrow."

I felt lighter knowing that.

"I can't wait to see them again," I gushed. "They're so cute I could gobble them up."

Bronagh chuckled but agreed with a bob of her head.

"Ryder said both twins are nursin' like pros, and they're perfectly perfect. Dominic brought 'im fresh clothes before work this mornin' so Ry could shower and then he brought home their washin'. I just did a load. I'm gonna go to their house tonight and clean everywhere so they just have to come home and enjoy the babies."

I paused. "Branna's house is so clean you could eat off the floor, Bee."

"I know." Bronagh's lips twitched. "But she hates dust, so I'll tidy over everythin' so she doesn't feel like she should clean, ye'know?"

I nodded. "Sister of the year."

"Please, I'm bein' selfish." she chuckled. "Dominic already knows that I'll be helpin with the twins for the first few weeks until they get into a routine. Bein' a first-time parent is like bein' thrown in a dark pit; you never know what's gonna happen. They'll have double trouble with twins."

"They're both sorted with work, right?"

"Yup." Bronagh nodded. "Ryder started his two weeks paid paternity leave yesterday, which he is still chuffed about."

"Men all around Ireland were chuffed when that law came into effect, and it's about feckin' time if you ask me."

"Amen, sister."

"What's the deal with Branna's maternity leave, though?" I quizzed. "I know, by law, she gets twenty-six weeks of paid leave and an extra sixteen weeks unpaid if she chooses, but she's been goin' to work 'er whole pregnancy. Granted not as much lately, but she's still clocked a solid thirty-hour week this entire time."

"She worked like that so she'd have more time with the twins," Bronagh answered. "She didn't want to waste 'er paid leave sittin' at home so that's why she continued goin' to work. She officially started 'er leave last Monday 'cause we thought she'd have the twins sooner than now until 'er doctor changed stuff around. She booked 'er time off about seven weeks ago."

"Smart," I said. "Very smart."

"Ryder is so happy she gets so much time off, and that she's still gettin' paid." Bronagh snorted. "Kane was the same with Aideen; they couldn't believe how good our leave is, or the fact that we get paid."

"I'll say," I said, and I turned my focus to Georgie, who was drooling as she gnawed on her closed fist. "You're the prettiest girl in the whole wide world. D'ye know that, honey?"

She smiled at me around her fist, and it made me laugh.

"Any word on your ma today?"

I sighed as I moved towards the kitchen table and sat down, resting Georgie's behind on the table top.

"She's sick today," I answered Bronagh as I straightened Georgie's little t-shirt. "A dub doctor is comin' out. She won't let me come around in case I catch whatever she has."

Bronagh frowned. "But you saw 'er the other day, so you'd probably have whatever it was already if you were gonna catch it."

"I know," I agreed, "but try to tell me ma that."

Bronagh snorted. "I can't argue with 'er; logic sometimes flees when you want to keep your kid safe."

"You're tellin' me."

I played with Georgie's chubby hands while Bronagh made us both tea.

"How are things with you and Dame?"

"Blissful," I answered, a smile tugging at my lips. "I'm in a state of permanent shock, because whenever I think about 'im, I just can't believe we're together."

"I said the same thing to Dominic last night." Bronagh chuckled from across the room. "I said that you had both spent so many years at odds and in denial, that for you to both to have moved past your issues and be together is simply wild."

"The power of communication."

"Amen." Bronagh laughed.

I placed Georgie in her playpen while Bronagh and I drank our tea at the table.

"Today was Morgan's first day at work."

"Oh, how was it?"

"Brilliant, we got so much done. He has literally reorganised me entire system and improved it tenfold."

"Nice. Does that ease some stress off your shoulders a bit?"

"Like you wouldn't believe." I nodded. "Me job and Damien have been two major factors in why I was so stressed out this past year, and now that I'm in a good place with both, it feels weird to just have my parents' drama to deal with … and me ma bein' sick, of course."

"Of course," Bronagh echoed. "You'll get there with the others; ye'know better than anyone that things just take time."

"Yeah," I quietly agreed.

It wasn't long until our trio multiplied. Aideen and Keela showed up an hour after I came by, and I hated that I instantly wanted to ask Aideen where Kane was because my earlier conversation with Damien replayed in my head, and I couldn't shut his voice off.

"Where's Kane?" I asked as nonchalantly as I could.

Aideen looked away from me and said, "Just runnin' some errands in town."

I stared at her, and like Damien, I knew she was lying. It seemed she couldn't look me in the eye either, but unlike Damien, Aideen became unsettled with my gaze on her, and I could only imagine what was running through her mind. I was a little hurt that she had lied to me, but I had to remind myself that it was none of my business where Kane was, or what he was doing. I just hoped that whatever was going on, he was okay.

Hours passed, and the time was filled with chatting, laughter, and one relieving phone call from my ma to let me know she just had a vomiting bug and nothing more sinister.

When evening time approached, and the sun began to set, I stood up for a refill of tea, and when I placed my cup, or Alec's cup, on the counter, everything went horribly wrong. I stupidly put it too close to the edge, and when Jax screamed over something, I turned to look at him, and my elbow bumped off the cup.

Time slowed down as the cup began tumbling through the air, its rapid descent kicking my heart into overdrive. I fumbled and stumbled as I made one last desperate attempt to snatch it from the clutches of my doom, but it was out of my reach, and a second after I knocked it from the counter, it hit the tiled floor and shattered into pieces. The realisation of what happened sent a sharp pain through my chest.

Silence fell upon the room until my laboured breathing could be heard.

"He's goin' to kill me."

I practically felt Keela cringe. "I agree; he is goin' to kill 'er."

Aideen inched her way towards me. "He won't, hon. It was an accident."

"Ha!" I shook my head. "He'll lynch me before I could even explain it was an accident."

"We'll get 'im a new Harry Potter cup before he comes home," Bronagh said with a snap of her fingers. "He won't know the difference."

"He'll bloody know," I grumbled, staring down at the reason for my impending murder. "He has secret marks on the stupid thing so if I ever switched it with a different cup, he'd know."

Keela laughed. I jerked my gaze to hers and glared.

"I'm sorry." She chuckled. "He is just so funny. I love 'im so much."

I rolled my eyes. "Will you love 'im so much as you're helpin' 'im bury me body?"

Keela laughed harder, so I ignored her. She was a lost cause and was already corrupted by the terror that was Alec Slater.

"I've no other choice," I said, placing my hands firmly on my hips. "I have to leave the country."

Bronagh made a sound awfully close to a laugh, and when I looked at her, she had her body turned away from me, but her shoulders were shaking.

"You *dare* laugh at me when I'm facin' murder, Bronagh Murphy?"

"You have to admit ..." She cackled, turning to face me. "He is goin' to throw the biggest bitch fit known to humankind."

Christ, I thought. *He will.*

I cleaned up the mess I'd caused, and after I emptied the shattered cup pieces in the bin, I felt sick. Alec was *definitely* going to kill me.

"I have to get out of—"

"Kitten, are you here?"

I froze and so did time itself.

"No," I whispered. "No feckin' way, *why* is he 'ere?"

"It's Wednesday," Keela answered, her eyes widening with alarm. "He finishes work early on a Wednesday. I forgot."

Before Keela could finish, I rushed over to her and stood behind her chair. Instinct told me to unlock the back door in case I had to make a run for it, so I did. We all stood still when Alec entered the room. Even the kids went quiet and stared at him. Alec's eyes darted from Keela to everyone else, then finally to me, and he narrowed them to slits.

"What did you do?"

I inched my way closer to the back door, bringing Keela's chair and her with me. When she stood up, I held her in front of me, not feeling the slightest bit ashamed to use a pregnant woman as a human shield.

"It was an accident," I stated calmly. "Remember that *before* we tell you."

"What. Did. You. Do?"

I choked on panic, and couldn't find the words.

"Keela," Bronagh murmured. "*You* tell 'im."

Alec focused on her, and when she spoke, his right eye twitched with each word.

"It was an accident, a *total* accident ... Alannah broke your Harry Potter cup. Again, by complete accident, I'll testify on 'er behalf if it's needed."

Keela pointed at the bin, and he silently walked over to it. Alec stared into the bin, and I swear to God, his eyes welled up a little bit, before fury filled them and they turned on me. From where I was standing, the lighting made his normally grey eyes seem black, and it was at that moment, I believed he was the devil incarnate.

"I knew you'd do this eventually, you cup murdering little demon."

"I didn't do it on purpose." I frantically shook my head. "I cross me heart and hope to die."

"Doesn't matter," he said shockingly calm. "You still did it, so you better get to hopping."

Jesus.

"She's pregnant with your child." I gripped Keela's waist. "You can't come at me when she's *pregnant*."

"Watch me," Alec said and began to walk towards me, his eyes unblinking and his movements calculated.

I held my ground for all of two seconds before I turned, yanked the sliding door open, and sprung out into the back garden. My eyes darted around for an escape route, but everything was blocked by damned toys. The only thing I spotted was the trampoline, and in my head, I planned to get inside it and zip up the netting which would form a barrier between myself and Alec. That plan didn't work out because when I managed to get inside of the poxy thing, Alec was hot on my heels.

"Get back here!"

I screamed with fright and scrambled away from him as he entered through the gap in the netting. He was a big man, but his towering height intimidated me even more inside the enclosed space. Trying to flee on a trampoline was nothing but a complete failure I quickly realised, and all I could think of was to jump as hard and as fast as I could to knock Alec off his feet to give me a chance to break free. He threatened me the second I started jumping, and when he advanced, I screamed louder and bounced faster. Amid my screams and Alec's threats, I could hear my so-called friends laughing like fucking hyenas.

"Stop jumping!" Alec ordered.

I jumped harder, making his legs wobble a bit more.

"This is assault!"

"I haven't even touched you yet!"

Yet.

"It'll be assault *when* you touch me then."

"It's about to be upgraded to murder if that's the case."

I screamed. "He admitted he's gonna *murder* me!"

More laughter.

"Bronagh," I pleaded. "Help me!"

"Why me?"

"Because," I screeched when Alec lunged for me but crashed into the net when I dove out of the way. "Just because!"

"What the fuck is going—is that Alannah and Alec?"

"Damien!" I hollered, relief flooding me. "Save me!"

"What happened?" he demanded. "He looks like he's going to

kill her."

"She broke his cup," Keela answered.

"Oh, shit," a chorus of male voices spoke.

I spotted the opening to the trampoline now that Alec wasn't blocking it, and I crawled to it as fast as I could. I made it halfway out of the trampoline when a hand grabbed my left ankle and held on for dear life.

"I don't fucking think so, you life ruiner!"

"That isn't even a word!"

"I don't give a shit," Alec yelled. "I'm going to tickle you until you *cry*!"

Like a horror film, I was dragged back into the trampoline all the while I was screaming for God to help me since none of the fuckers in the back garden would.

"He is like Pennywise draggin' me away to me death," I bellowed. "One of you bastards help me; I don't wanna be like Georgie!"

My niece cheered when she heard me shout her name, not realising I was talking about a fictional Georgie who was savagely murdered by a dancing fucking clown.

I couldn't see my piece of shite friends because I had flipped myself onto my back so I could track Alec's movement, but I could hear them, and they were all laughing. I could have sworn I heard Jax and Georgie squeal too, and that was just wrong. Bringing those beautiful babies to witness my demise was unforgivable.

I stared up at Alec, and the way his head tilted as he stared down at me reminded me of Damien. All the brothers looked alike, but the twins resemble Alec the most. At the mention of the fair-haired twin, I got an idea.

"Damien!"

Silence, then, "Yeah?"

"I'll go have sex with you if you get this lunatic *away* from me!"

More silence, then Alec looked up and growled, "Don't even

fucking *think* of it, you little shit."

I heard a rustle from behind me.

"Sorry, brother." Damien chuckled, sounding awful close to me. "I can't pass up on her offer. I've been dreaming of sex with her for more years than I'm willing to admit."

Hands gripped under my armpits, and I was pulled backwards, out of reach of Alec who was diving for my legs. I bent them, preventing him from grabbing them as he bounced off the trampoline and spewed curses to everyone and their dog.

"Traitor!" Alec snapped at his younger brother.

I pointed at each of the backstabbers as Damien held me against him.

"I will remember this when you need a babysitter."

Bronagh and Aideen's smiles fell from their faces, and they paled, except Keela whose face was red from laughter.

"You too," I told her. "Your demon child is *never* gettin' five-star Alannah care."

She clapped her thighs together as she laughed. Damien was laughing too as he settled me down on my feet, then he laughed harder when I pushed by him and sprinted from the house.

"I'm gonna get you, Alannah" Alec hollered, his voice sounding demonic. "And your little cat, too."

Not Barbara!

I didn't stop in my escape until I was out of the house and safely inside my locked car and speeding away. I thanked God that I lived in a secure apartment complex because God only knew what Alec Slater was going to do to me once he eventually got his hands on me.

I was *so* dead.

CHAPTER TWENTY

"We aren't really havin' sex ... ye'know that, right?"

I had forgotten about Damien when I originally fled Bronagh's house. When I realised that he wasn't with me, I swiftly turned back around and drove back to get him. I made sure to stay in my car with the doors locked until he jogged out of the house, laughing like a madman. Tears fell from his eyes when Alec chased my car on foot while I, on the other hand, screamed bloody murder until I lost sight of him in my rear-view mirror.

"You mean you were only saying what you thought I wanted to hear to enlist my help so I'd get you away from my psychotic older brother who intended to tickle you to death for breaking his favourite tea cup? I'm positively *shocked* at this turn of events."

I stared at Damien, my lips pursed.

"Well—" I blinked "—this was your first smartarse moment in our relationship."

"Should we mark it on your calendar to celebrate next year?"

"And *that*—" I rolled my eyes "—was your second. Third strike, and you're out, buddy."

Damien's devilish grin did things to my insides. Naughty, *naughty* things.

"Have you ever watched a game of baseball in your life?"

"Jesus, no." I felt myself pale. "Why would I ever do somethin' like that?"

His laughter brought a smile to my face.

"I love your laugh."

"Yeah?" he asked, his bright eyes gleaming. "I'm a little partial to yours, too."

"Sweet talker."

He helped me out of my coat, then hung it up and his own while I saw to Barbara. I opened the sitting room door carefully, and instantly, a putrid odour stung at my nostrils. I quickly glanced around and saw the used litter tray.

"Why on Earth did I leave the stupid tray in 'ere?"

I placed my hands on my hips and searched the room, coming to a stop when I found Barbara sitting on my curtain pole.

"Barbara!" I gasped. "How in Christ's name did you get up there?"

"How did she get up whe—holy shit."

I began to panic and rushed across the room until I was directly below Barbara with my hands up, ready to catch her in case she fell. She was looking down at me with a bored expression and made no move to even try and get down.

"She stinks."

"Damien, focus on *her* right now, not the stupid smell."

"Alannah, she's a cat," he said, calmly. "She won't fall, and if she does, we'll catch her."

"*We*?" I demanded. "I'm the only one standin' 'ere with me hands up."

"I can see that," he replied. "Your t-shirt has ridden up with the action ... your ass looks *so* damn fine in those jeans."

"*Damien!*"

"Right, sorry. I'll get her."

He moved to my side, and without having to really stretch, he reached up and plucked Barbara from her seated position. Her nails snagged on the curtains, so Damien gently tugged the fabric free. When he handed the cat to me, I cuddled her against my chest, then hissed when her nails dug into me.

"You little bitch, that hurt."

"Nails like needles, huh?"

"Yeah." I frowned. "I need to put water in a spray bottle to teach 'er not to climb on the curtains. Not only could she fall, but she'll also ruin the curtains with 'er nails."

Damien raised a brow. "Cats tend to scratch things like furniture a lot."

"But I got 'er a scratchin' post!"

His lips twitched. "She's still getting used to the apartment and to us. She'll learn in time."

"I guess."

I put Barbara down, and she instantly jumped onto the settee, snuggled under one of the cushions, and plopped down on her stomach as if she had just finished running a marathon. I shook my head at her, then proceeded to clean out her litter tray while Damien moved her food and water bowls into the kitchen. I put the litter tray in the corner of the room and made a mental note to clean it out a few times a day. If I kept it poop and pee free, no smell would linger. I hoped anyway.

Damien was headed to the bathroom when he glanced into the office, paused then turned and entered the room, flipping the light on as he went.

"What the hell happened in here?"

"Oh, me office." I beamed as I practically bounced into the room. "What d'ye think?"

"I think it's awesome, but baby, I would have done this for you."

"It's really okay. I did it with Morgan."

"You did *it* with Morgan?"

"Yeah," I answered. "His first day was today, and we converted the room in, like, an hour."

It took me a moment to realise that Damien was very quiet and very still. I turned my attention from my office to him and found him staring at me. His body was tense, and it didn't take a lot for me to sense that he was annoyed. I put two and two together and cringed. This was about Morgan.

"Did I not tell you that his first day was today?"

"No," Damien answered coolly. "You didn't."

His tone told me he was mad and maybe a little jealous.

"I forgot with Branna havin' the twins, findin' out me ma is sick, and then gettin' with you," I said, knotting my fingers together. "It's only been a few days since all of those things happened, and I'm still reelin', and it just slipped me mind. I'm sorry."

He nodded and looked away from me, so I stepped into his space and put my arms around his waist.

"You have no reason to be mad or jealous," I said, speaking calmly. "None. Morgan works for me, and that's *it*."

Damien slowly relaxed.

"I know." He sighed. "I trust you, I do ..."

"But?"

"But we're brand new, and another guy being around you just rubs me the wrong way. It's petty, I know, but it's just a nagging feeling."

I tilted my head. "Would it make you feel better if you met Morgan?"

"Yes," Damien answered instantly. "This guy is a stranger to me, to you, so meeting him would probably relax me."

I doubted that, but I was willing to give it a shot.

"He works for me five days a week, but we're flexible, so most the time, he might not even be 'ere. He works from ten to two when he is 'ere, and ten to three when he isn't or less if he clocks his hours before then. Twenty-seven hours a week in total is what we agreed."

Damien frowned. "I have my work scheduled set in stone for the next few weeks, and I start at nine. Mr Collins doesn't tolerate showing up late, and I can't have any days off while Ryder is on his paternity leave. Harley and JJ have four days off to check out a location for a bar they're considering buying, or something like that."

"Dame." I chuckled. "You will meet Morgan eventually; it doesn't have to be right this second."

He only nodded in response, and I knew that meeting Morgan this second was *exactly* what he wanted, but I couldn't change that, so I pushed it aside and turned back to my office.

"We have to paint or wallpaper in 'ere."

"Are you allowed?" Damien asked, his tone lighter.

"The estate agent said the landlord allows people to decorate, but it has to be tasteful and match the furniture he or she provides."

"You don't know if your landlord is a man or a woman?"

I shrugged. "They did business through the estate agent; they probably don't wanna be involved directly with their tenants. Lots of landlords do that."

"I suppose," Damien said, walking around the room. "You should create some canvas paintings and hang them up."

"Morgan suggested the same thing."

Damien didn't answer; he only checked how sturdy the bookcase and my desk were. I shook my head at him as he searched for some fault and made a mental note not to talk about Morgan around him so his emotions could stay in check. I understood where he was coming from, and he admitted he would be jealous. I didn't want to push something in his face that was really nothing to worry about.

"Are you hungry?" I asked, changing the subject. "I've had the meat for dinner cookin' on low all day. I'm gonna get the mash, roasties, croquettes, and veg ready now if you wanna help?"

"I'll help." Damien nodded. "That's a whole lot of potatoes, though."

I leaned back and looked at him like he grew an extra head.

"There's no such thing as too much. You're in Ireland, bud."

Damien smirked. "Say potato."

I deadpanned. "No."

"Say it," he pressed.

"No."

He pouted, the grown man really pouted, and it drew a sigh

from me.

"Fine, potato." I playfully rolled my eyes at Damien's snort. "But I don't even call them that."

"Do you call them ba-day-tahs like the other girls?"

I laughed at how slowly he pronounced it.

"Yeah, that's how I say it."

"I like just stick to potatoes; that way is too much of a mouthful for me."

Together, we entered the kitchen and got to work on our dinner. After we got everything prepared and ready to cook, I removed the meat and covered it with foil until it was time to slice it up. I always listened to music as I cooked the dinner, so I instinctively reached into my back pocket of my jeans, feeling for my phone. When I realised it wasn't on my person, I checked each room of the apartment.

"What are you looking for?"

"Me phone," I answered then groaned. "I think I left it in me car. I'm always doin' that!"

"I'll go and get it."

"No." I sighed. "I'll do it; you just keep an eye on Barbara."

I left my apartment and took the elevator down to the lobby. I jogged out of the building and to my car, where I scowled at my phone sitting in one of the cup holders.

"Stupid thing."

After I got my phone, locked my car, and briskly walked back into my building, I entered the elevator but had to hold it open when someone hollered for me to. I nodded in greeting to Kane as he jogged into the elevator and said, "Thanks."

"No problem."

He flashed his personal fob over the scannered then he hit the button for his floor.

"Aideen called me."

I glanced at him. "Yeah?"

"Hmm."

"Is there a reason you're tellin' me this?"

"She mentioned what you did to Alec's cup."

I felt heat climb up my neck.

"It was an accident," I stressed. "A complete and total accident."

"I also heard he tried to murder you."

"He did." I bobbed my head. "You should have seen 'im; he was like a ravin' lunatic."

Kane looked down at me, and it was obvious he was fighting off a smile.

"It's not funny!" I scowled as the elevators doors closed. "I nearly had a heart attack when he cornered me on that trampoline."

"I wish I was there to see it."

I shook my head, fighting off a grin as Kane's shoulders lightly shook. Myself and Kane rarely spoke, so I felt bloody proud of myself whenever we did because I always seemed to make him grin, smile, or laugh, and anyone who knew him knew how difficult a task that was. I looked at him and noted he had no bags or anything that he could have picked up on the errands he was running.

"What?' he asked when he noticed my eyes on him.

I shrugged. "Do anythin' fun today?"

"Errands," he answered flatly.

I narrowed my eyes a little before I looked forward.

"What was that look for?"

"Damien and Aideen looked away when they told me you were runnin' errands, and I wanted to see if you'd do the same."

"Why?"

"I wanted to see if you were going to lie to me like they did."

I felt Kane's eyes drill a hole into the side of my face.

"What do you think they lied to you about?"

"I've no clue, and I'm not gonna press the issue because what you do is none of me business."

Silence.

"I'll tell you if you want to know."

"It's okay," I said with a shake of my head. "I'm not supposed to know; Damien and Aideen wouldn't have lied to me otherwise."

"You aren't starting off your relationship with my brother with a stupid lie lingering in the back of your mind. *My* lie."

"Me relationship with your brother is with *him*," I said, feeling a little irritated. "As I said, what you do isn't me business. Forget I said anythin'."

"I can't do that."

"Suit yourself."

More silence.

"None of the girls have ever been this closed off with me."

I swallowed. "None of the other girls were interrogated by you when they were just shy of eighteen and had no backbone."

I didn't mention that I *still* didn't have much of a backbone, but Kane didn't need to know that I was sweating having this confrontation with him.

"No backbone, my ass," he quipped. "You put me in my place and don't think I've forgotten it, because I haven't."

I didn't know what to say, so I remained mute.

"You're good for my brother, and you're as good an addition to our family as when you were eighteen," Kane said after a long pause. "I'm not social, I know that, but please don't think that because I'm reserved it means that I don't care about you."

I felt my lips part with shock.

"I'm not sure what to say."

"You don't have to say anything," Kane said. "This is the most we've talked since that first conversation, and I feel like I've overwhelmed you because this space is starting to close in on me for sure."

I surprised us both when I chuckled.

"Your apartment will close in on you when you speak to Aideen."

"And why is that?"

"Because when she laughed at me when Alec was chasin' me, I told 'er I was never babysittin' again."

Kane appeared to almost choke on air as the elevator stopped on my floor. The doors opened, and I stepped out into the corridor and turned to face Kane.

"Now, Alannah. Wait just a second," he began. "You don't need to make any rash decisions when you're—"

The doors of the elevator closed before Kane could finish, and I heard his 'fuck' being shouted as the elevator brought him up to his floor, and it made me laugh. With a little spring in my step, I turned and walked down the corridor and into my apartment.

"I'm back."

The next hour and a half consisted of finishing dinner, then eating it. After we were full and content, Damien and I sat on the settee in my sitting room and turned on a film on Netflix. I leaned against him and sighed.

"I love this."

"Love what?"

"Just bein' 'ere with you."

Damien kissed the crown of my head. "Me too, freckles."

I leaned my head back on his shoulder and said, "I wanna learn you."

"You want to learn me?" he repeated. "Is this a language barrier thing because of your accent, or did you purposely mean to word it that way?"

I chuckled. "I meant to word it that way."

"You want to *learn* me?"

I nodded. "I wanna learn what makes you, *you*."

"That's cute, but I have no idea what you mean."

I snuggled against his side.

"Does it not bother you that we have this whole history together, but we don't really *know* each other?"

"We *do* know each other," Damien lightly protested. "I know every curve of your face and body, your every laugh, and how much you love tea."

I playfully rolled my eyes.

"That's lovely, but I want to know the deep stuff."

Damien stilled, and the slight tension that filled his body was enough to make me take notice.

"What do you want to know?"

"Everythin'," I answered. "I don't know anythin' about your past or your family outside of your brothers. I don't know about your homeland because you guys *never* talk about it."

Damien was silent.

"I mean, seriously, none of you ever talk about your life before Ireland, and it's all sort of been in the back of me head. Ireland is a part of who I am; you see and hear me country when you talk to me, but apart from an accent, I don't get America from you, and I think that's sad."

Damien cleared his throat.

"There's nothing to tell, really. The five of us grew up in upstate New York, nowhere near the city. We lived in a small community where everyone knew everyone else's business. My parents died when I was fifteen in a car accident—"

My gasp cut Damien off.

"I'm so sorry," I said, reaching for his hand. "Bronagh mentioned they died, but not how, and now I understand why. *Her* parents died in a car accident, so she probably didn't want to think about it in case it brought up bad memories for 'er."

Now it made sense why she brushed the lads' parents under the carpet whenever I mentioned them. It was a sore subject not only for them, but for her, too, because of how they died.

"Yeah," Damien said, as he began to play with my fingers. "We just sort of ... floated around for a few years, then we came here and put down roots."

"Why Ireland, though?"

Damien cleared his throat. Again.

"It was only supposed to be a vacation, really, but within a few weeks, we knew we wanted to stay. Ryder got us enrolled in school for our final year; we had been homeschooled up until that point."

"Well, shite," I said, shocked. "No wonder neither you or your brother could just blend in at school and get on with it without makin' a fuss. You didn't have the experience."

"Yup."

I studied his face.

"Do you not want to tell me this stuff?" I asked. "You don't seem all that interested."

"I'm interested in *you*, not my boring childhood," he said, his lips curving into a smile. "Things only got interesting when I met you."

"Puh-lease," I tittered. "Interestin' is the last word to describe me."

"Oh, it's up there," Damien said, "but I know a few words that fit you just as well."

"Like?"

"Elegant, smart, hard-working, beautiful, funny ... sexy as sin."

He had echoed those exact words to me many years before, and it brought a smile to my face knowing he still thought all those things equaled to me.

"You think I'm funny?"

Damien laughed. "Yeah, baby, I think you're funny."

I relaxed against him.

"What was your ma like?"

Damien was silent for a few moments, and just when I thought he wouldn't respond, he said, "She wasn't like your mom."

"Meanin'?"

"She wasn't maternal." Damien swallowed. "She wasn't very affectionate and was mostly cold towards my brothers and me."

My lips parted in shock. "Why?"

He snorted. "I spent my entire childhood trying to find the answer to that question, and I never found it. My mom and dad ... they just weren't very nice people, but I couldn't see that when I was a kid. I thought they were awesome."

That broke my heart.

"I'm sorry, sweetie."

Damien looked at me and smiled. "You sounded like Branna just then."

"'Cause I called you sweetie?"

He nodded. "I was pretty torn up when my parents died, more so than my brothers because I needed the affection I never got from them, so naturally, I tried to get their attention whenever possible. I didn't have to do that with Branna; she loved me and my brothers after she fell in love with Ry. She's more of a mom to me than my real mom. Ryder is more of a dad to me, too."

I swallowed past the lump that formed in my throat.

"I'm sorry you didn't have a lovin' relationship with your parents. I can't imagine me life bein' like that," I said, squeezing his hand in what I hoped was a gesture of comfort. "I'm at odds with me da right now, but I still love him. It's why hatin' 'im hurts so bad because … I still love 'im."

"He is your dad, baby," Damien said gently. "I know this will be hard to hear, but what he did to your mom was between them. He is *still* your dad."

I looked down at my lap.

"But she is me ma," I said softly. "He broke not only her trust, but mine, too. He is the man I once would measure up me future husband against in hopes I could find someone as great as 'im, and I can't do that anymore because if the man I grew up lovin' me whole life could do what he did to me ma, someone who would die for 'im, every other man was always gonna come up short for me."

"Even me?"

"I want to say no, but yeah, even you," I answered honestly. "You could say this situation added to me already lengthy list of trust issues."

I closed my eyes when Damien leaned in and kissed my head, his lips lingering for a few moments. I sighed, opened my eyes, and stared up at him. I loved his eyes. They were grey with a circle of white around each iris.

"I don't mind spending forever assuring you I'm not going anywhere, freckles."

My heart thudded.

"You shouldn't have to, though," I said. "That's not fair to you."

"Building a solid trust takes time," Damien assured me. "Rome wasn't built in a day."

"Does that mean *you* have trust issues?"

"Not so much trust issues as straight-up fear."

I sat upright and blinked.

"What are you scared of?"

"That things won't work out between us," Damien answered. "It makes me sick to think about it being a possibility, but I know it could be one, so I'm scared of it."

My jaw dropped, and Damien's lips twitched.

"Yeah, you aren't the only one terrified if things go sideways."

"You've made me feel so ... human with that admission."

"Human?"

"Yeah." I nodded. "Like I'm not bein' overdramatic and fearin' our relationship endin' isn't a legit worry when it is."

"Of course, it is," Damien said, his thumb stroking the back of my hand. "Any one of my brothers will tell you the same, and so would the girls I'm willing to bet."

After my talk with Alec, I knew they would, too.

"Thanks for sharin' that with me about your parents," I said softly. "I know that couldn't have been easy."

Damien's body relaxed. "I haven't really thought about them in a while; it's nice every now and again to reflect on things in the past, just so I can look at who I am as a person now."

I smiled. "That's a lovely way to look at it."

Damien's eyes locked on my mouth, but there was no heat in his stare.

"What is it?"

"I never meant what I said to you that night in Darkness," he said, licking his lower lip. "I know I've told you that already, but I want you to know that I only said it because I knew it would hurt you and push you away. I was terrified of how you cared for me, and how I cared about you, and my reaction was to hurt you and force you away. In a fucked up way, I thought I was protecting you."

I lifted my palm and cupped his cheek.

"I know you'll never forget it, but I hope you'll forgive me one day for saying it."

"I *do* forgive you," I said sincerely. "I hope you forgive me for how I let you believe everythin' was your fault. I'm sorry."

"Babe." He smiled softly. "You have nothing to be sorry for."

"I do," I pressed. "What I did was wrong and unjust. I was angry, and let that anger blow what happened out of proportion. Please don't make what I did seem any less horrid because we're together now."

"Okay," Damien whispered. "I forgive you now, and I forgave years ago, too."

I closed my eyes and leaned my head against his. Feeling content, happy, and so secure it was almost frightening.

"I know it's literally just been a few days, but bein' with you makes me feel safe and sound."

"Being with you makes me feel like I can let down my defences," Damien said, nuzzling his face to mine. "You're my steady place, Lana. My freckles."

I opened my eyes and smiled.

"I used to hate me freckles."

Damien sucked in a horrified breath. "Why?"

"'Cause everyone said they made me cute, and I hated that."

"You *are* cute." Damien grinned. "Sexy and sinful, too. And beautiful. Man, you're so beautiful."

I kissed him, and he smiled against my lips.

"Do you know when I first saw you, I knew you were a girl who could make me happy."

I leaned back with raised brows. "When you first saw me, I walked head first into you and knocked you on your arse."

"Yes—" Damien snickered "—but you gave me your hand to

help me up."

"And that gave you the impression that I could make you happy long term?"

"Yeah." He nodded. "I knew you'd be someone to always help me up when I'm down, no matter what. That's why I pushed you away after we were together, you were someone who I knew could reach me at that point in my life where I forced everyone out, and that scared the shit out of me. You're my ride or die, Alannah"

"That's so romantic."

"I can be more romantic."

"Proceed."

Damien chuckled. "We're endgame."

I stared up at him, bewildered.

"I have no clue what that means."

"It means," he murmured, brushing stray hairs back from my eyes. "No matter what has happened between us, or what comes next for us, at the end of the day, you'll be with me, and I'll be with you. I know it, you know it … everyone knows it."

My heart fluttered, and my stomach came alive with butterflies.

"You sound pretty confident, snowflake."

"I am, freckles."

"Since when?"

"Since you kicked me in the balls when we were eighteen and told me to go to hell."

CHAPTER TWENTY-ONE

Ten days later ...

Ten days had passed since I found out my ma had cancer, nine days had passed since Damien and I officially started dating, and eight days had passed since I found out the treatment plan my ma was signed up for to kick cancer's arse as well as Branna and Ryder's twins being born. It was Thursday, the day of her surgery to remove the peanut-size tumour from her breast, and I had never felt as sick in my entire life. I had terrible anxiety and chewed on my nails until I had none left and each of my fingers stung, while others bled.

"Alannah." Bronagh clicked her tongue, gaining my attention. "You're hurtin' yourself."

I looked at my fingers before wiping them on my leggings.

"I can't help it." I cleared my throat. "I feel so nervous I could be sick."

I looked to my right when the arm around my waist squeezed me.

"She'll be fine."

I stared up at my boyfriend and frowned. He had taken the day off work, which worried me because Mr Collins had told him his schedule for the next few weeks was on lock, but Mr Collins allowed him to take the day to be with me. I would forever be grateful to him for that, because I needed Damien by my side.

"You don't know that, Damien."

He didn't reply to that; he leaned in and kissed my cheek instead.

"When she comes out of surgery, she's going to whoop your butt for worrying so much."

I tried and failed to smile, so he squeezed me again. The gesture was comforting, but it was his and Bronagh's presence that really kept my fried nerves in check. When I woke up that morning and got ready to head to the hospital to meet my parents, Damien surprised me by telling me he got the day off work to come with me, and that we had to pick Bronagh up along the way because she was coming too. I didn't want to cry, so I hugged him with my face pressed against his chest until we had to leave.

That was three hours ago, and my ma was one hour into her surgery. The nurse I had spoken to about my ma's lumpectomy procedure said there was no time limit because it was a very careful operation. The doctor wanted to remove as little breast tissue as possible while removing the tumour, so he had to take his time. I understood that, I encouraged that, but God above knew that the longer she was in surgery, the worse I felt.

My da seemed to share my anxiety.

He hadn't sat down once since the doors to the operating theatre closed. All of us had the option to sit in a waiting room, but we chose to sit on the row of chairs lined up outside of the entrance to the operating theatre. My da had been pacing back and forth in front of the double doors from the moment my ma went through them. Every single time they opened, he jerked to attention, but each time, his shoulders sagged when he realised it wasn't my ma.

He was sick with worry too, and it was the first time since I found out that he had cheated on her that I realised he still cared for her. Still loved her. The longer I stared at him, the possibility of what he had done, of it just being one huge mistake, became clear, and I didn't know how to feel about that. I wanted to stay angry with him, it made pushing him to one side so much easier, but seeing him vulnerable as he waited on news of my ma tugged at my heartstrings.

He loved her, and I think after what he had done, he loved her even more than ever before.

"I'm makin' some tea," I said, standing up, causing Bronagh and Damien's arms to fall away from me. "Do either of you want anythin'?"

"No," they replied in unison.

I walked across the hall to the tea and coffeemaker machine, and I had just begun to make my tea when I felt a presence to my right. I flicked my eyes towards my da, not surprised to find him standing there, staring down at me. I glanced over my shoulder at Bronagh and Damien, who were watching us like hawks. I could have sworn neither of them blinked.

"What d'ye want?" I asked as I turned back to the machine.

From the corner of my eye, I noticed my da shoved his hands into the front pockets of his jeans.

"We need to talk, Alannah."

I swallowed down bile.

"I've nothin' to say to you."

"Well, I've plenty to say to you."

I couldn't bring myself to look at him, but I remained quiet, giving him the opportunity to talk if he wanted to. I stirred my teabag around my styrofoam cup with a little wooden stick painstakingly slow.

"Until the day I die," he began, "I will be sorry for cheatin' on your ma, and breakin' both *her* and your trust in me."

Tears stung the back of my eyes.

"I don't expect forgiveness," he continued, "I don't expect anythin' less than anger because it's what I deserve, but I just want you to know that I am truly sorry, and I have never regretted somethin' more in me entire life."

My lower lip wobbled upon hearing the emotion in his voice.

"You're me baby," he said, his voice cracking slightly. "I'm so sorry I ruined our relationship."

My tears fell.

"Why?" I demanded, angrily wiping away my tears with the back of my hand. "Why did you do it?"

"I've been thinkin' of the answer to that question since it all started," he answered, clearing his throat. "Nothin' I've come up with is good enough a reason. No reason is good enough for what I've done."

On that, I agreed with him.

"I'm goin' to tell your mother."

I jerked my gaze to his so quickly, my neck hurt.

"*What?*"

"After she completes 'er radiation," Da continued. "I'm goin' to come clean and own up to what I did."

I was at a loss for words.

"Will you leave 'er?"

"Christ," Da blanched. "Never. I can only pray she won't leave me, though I deserve nothin' less."

I considered his words.

"She won't leave you," I concluded. "She loves you too much."

Da's eyes glazed over with tears.

"I hate meself," he rasped, exhaling a deep breath. "I love your ma; she is me heart. I'm sick with meself that I've done this to 'er."

"Me too."

My da locked his eyes on me.

"I will never," he said, firmly, "*ever* break either of your trust again. I would rather die."

My heart pounded.

"I can't forgive you," I said, my voice thick with emotion. "Not until she does, at least."

"I'll take it," Da practically pleaded. "I'll take any chance, no matter how small, to mend what I've done. I miss you so much, Alannah. Not talkin' to you and seein' the hurt in your eyes when you look at me breaks my heart. You're me baby girl, and what I've done has hurt you. I swore when you were just born that I would protect you from everythin' in this world, I ... I just didn't realise I had to protect you from me too."

Before I realised what I was doing, I abandoned my cup of tea and stepped forward. Wrapping my arms around my da, I burst into tears when his arms came around me. He held onto me so tight, it almost crushed the air from my lungs.

"I love you," Da cried as he leaned down and pressed his face into my hair. "I'm so sorry."

"I love you too." I sobbed, squeezing him.

God knew that I hated what he had done, but I still loved him with every bone in my body, and it was the most conflicted my emotions had ever been. I wasn't sure what was going to happen with us. I wasn't sure if I would forgive him, if I could ever fully trust him again, but one thing I was certain of was that he was sorry, and that he would never do anything to hurt my ma or me again. I was also sure that I missed him just as much as I loved him, but my anger over what he had done had blocked out those emotions as I focused on the deed he committed.

Hearing him admit his faults, owning up to them and willing to accept whatever my ma or me gave him in return really made it hit home that what he had done was just a mistake. A massive one, a life changing one, but still a mistake. I believed that everyone deserved a second chance, and as I hugged my da, I knew I would give him that chance. Just like I knew my ma would when he and she spoke about his infidelity. That conversation would be the most important one we would have as a family, after learning about my ma's cancer, of course, but I knew, deep down, that we'd get through it.

My ma was right when she said there was nothing the three of us couldn't get through together.

"I'm cryin' all over you," Da said with a little laugh as we broke apart. "Bronagh and that lad you came with are smilin' at us, too."

I could imagine.

"That *lad* is me boyfriend," I said, lifting my hands to my face so I could wipe away my tears. "His name is Damien Slater."

My da quickly rid his face of tears, stood up straight, and said, "Your ma told me about 'im. I'd like to meet 'im, if that's okay?"

My ma had met Damien a few days ago, and it went off without a hitch. Damien even took it on the chin when she started teasing him over his fight with Dante, assuring him she found it all rather romantic. I was mortified, of course, but Damien thought it was hilarious. By the time we left my parents' house, he and my ma were practically best friends.

"Of course, you can meet 'im."

As we walked, I looked down at my da's hand then without a word, I took his hand in mine, and gave a squeeze as I led him over to the observant duo.

"Da," I began went we stopped in front of them, "this is Damien Slater, me boyfriend."

Damien was already on his feet with his hand extended in my da's direction.

"It's great to finally meet you, sir."

Da shook Damien's hand firmly. "And you, son."

Son. That one word made my heart melt.

"Bronagh, love." Da smiled at my friend. "You're lookin' as lovely as ever."

She snorted as she gave him a hug in greeting since she hadn't done so when she entered the hospital because he was pacing back and forth the entire time. Coming over to talk to me was the first time he took a break from his routine.

"Where were you to tell me that this mornin' when I was stuck with me head in the toilet vomitin'?"

Da grinned. "I'm sure that lad of yours had it covered."

Bronagh snorted.

"Congratulations on your pregnancy," Da continued. "I still can't believe you have Georgie, and now you'll have another little one."

"I'll have a tribe by the time I'm thirty if Dominic gets his way."

"He will," Damien and I said in chorus.

"Well—" Bronagh's lips twitched "—maybe."

I moved to Damien's side, and I watched as my da's eyes fell to my side. When I felt Damien's fingers thread through mine, my heart leaped when a smile tugged at the corner of my da's mouth. I had never thought of what my parents would think of Damien, but knowing that my ma practically loved him and my da's first encounter with him went well really relaxed me. I couldn't imagine staying with someone long term if he and my parents didn't get along, not with how family orientated I was.

"Alannah," Bronagh suddenly said. "That's your ma."

My attention was pulled to the doors of the operating theatre, and when I recognised the nurse who brought my ma in for her operation that walking by a bed that a man pushed, I knew Bronagh was right. It was my ma. My da and I quickly moved over to the bed, and we relaxed when we saw that my ma was sleeping, but she looked perfectly fine.

"She's okay," the nurse said, gaining our attention as we mutely walked. "You can come up to 'er room with us, but she may remain sleepin' for a few hours."

I didn't want to mention that we were going up to her room with her no matter what, so with a bob of our heads, we all followed the nurse and the man who pushed my ma on her hospital bed. I grabbed Damien's hand when he came to my side, and I squeezed it. My heart was pounding against my chest, and I was sweating.

"Hey," Damien said, gaining my attention. "She's okay."

I repeated that over and over in my mind until we were in my ma's private room, and we were sat around her bed, just staring at her. I kept looking at her chest, watching it rise and fall, before I'd switch my eyes to the heart monitor that she was hooked up to, keeping an eye on her heartbeat. I wanted her to wake up, just so I could ask for myself if she was okay, but I knew I had to be patient even though it was hard.

"She looks like she could be your older sister, Alannah," Bronagh said as she stared at my ma with her head tilted. "I hope I look half as good as 'er when I'm fifty."

"It's all the laughin' she does." Da smiled, rubbing his thumb over the back of her hand that he had held from the moment we entered the room. "It keeps 'er young, bein' happy."

"If that's the case, Alec Slater will never die," I commented. "He's always happy."

Bronagh and my da chuckled, but Damien remained quiet, and that drew my attention.

"Are you okay?"

He nodded. "Just thinking."

"About?"

"Where I'm goin' to take you on our first date."

I paused. "Can it be somethin' simple?"

"Simple?"

"Yeah, like goin' to the cinema, to dinner, a trail hike when it's pretty outside. Ye'know, simple."

Damien considered this. "That seems a little *too* simple."

"I'm a simple girl." I shrugged. "I don't like things that are over the top."

"I'd listen to 'er if I were you," Da chimed in. "When me and 'er mother threw 'er a twenty-first birthday party, she was so mad that we spent money on 'er that we had to listen to 'er lecturin' us about it for weeks."

"That's true." I nodded. "I did do that."

Damien's lips twitched. "A dinner and movie date it is."

"Oh, can we go and see *The Greatest Showman*?"

I had looked it up when Morgan mentioned bringing his girlfriend to see a Hugh Jackman and Zac Efron musical and had been itching to go see it ever since.

"And that would be?"

"A musical with Hugh Jackman and Zac Efron."

Damien rolled his eyes; Bronagh gasped.

"Shut up," she said. "I *love* Hugh Jackman and Zac Efron."

I snorted. "Who doesn't?"

"I'm sitting right here, woman."

I looked at Damien and grinned.

"It's Hugh Jackman and Zac Efron. Like I have a chance."

"If they saw you, you would."

I laughed. "I wish."

Bronagh snickered over Damien's scowl, but all our attention was turned to the door when a light knock sounded and in stepped the head doctor on my ma's team, the one who had just performed surgery on her.

"We'll go and get some tea," Bronagh said, getting to her feet at the same time as Damien. "Excuse us."

When they left the room, myself and my da got to our feet, and after we greeted the doctor with a handshake and nod of our heads, we waited.

"The surgery went beautifully," the doctor said in a thick accent that I couldn't detect, folding his arms across his chest. "I removed the tumour and very little breast tissue. Once she is all healed up, a small scar is all that will be left behind."

I deflated with relief. "Thank you so much."

"My pleasure." The doctor bowed his head a little. "Now, she will be a little sore when she wakes up, and her breast, as well as some of the surrounding area, will be swollen, but that is all perfectly normal."

"When can she come home?"

"Tomorrow morning," the doctor answered. "She'll be kept overnight just for observation."

I frowned. "That soon?"

"While your mother's surgery was important for her treatment plan, it was minor. Tomorrow, she will only feel discomfort and tenderness, and in a few days, she will be feeling much better."

I nodded in understanding.

"So." Da cleared his throat. "What now?"

"She is booked in to start her first radiation treatment four weeks from tomorrow, and she'll have that for five to six weeks starting at five times a week."

Again, I nodded.

"Don't look so worried." The doctor smiled at me and my da. "This is a good day; the tumour was removed with no complications. Your mother and wife's future is much brighter than it was this morning."

Until I heard the words "no evidence of disease", I didn't think I'd stop worrying about my ma. Hell, I think I'd still worry about her even *after* I heard those all-important words. That was what you did when it came to people you loved. You worried about them just as hard as you loved them. That's how you knew how important they were to you. If you couldn't imagine your life without them, they were part of the pieces that made up your heart, and I was confident that my ma made up a whole half of mine.

CHAPTER TWENTY-TWO

Five days later ...

"I thought you'd be in a better mood after seeing Hugh Jackman and Zac Efron singing and dancing their hearts out on the big screen."

I looked up from my plate of food to Damien when he spoke, and I frowned.

"Dame, I'm sorry, I'm ruinin' our first date."

"No, you aren't."

"I am." I sighed. "I keep thinkin' about me ma."

"Call her again if it will make you feel better."

"I can't," I grumbled. "She said she'd reach through the phone and strangle me if I phoned 'er again."

"Sounds to me like she's perfectly okay if she's threatening you with bodily harm."

My lips twitched.

"It's the overbearin' protector in me," I said with a small shrug. "It makes me a pain in the arse."

"Really?" Damien grinned. "I had no idea."

"Smartarse."

He chuckled. "It's been five days since her surgery, and when we saw her yesterday, you can't say she didn't look great because she did."

"She did," I agreed, "but she wouldn't tell me if she was feelin' shitty just to keep me from worryin'."

"Alannah, your mom knows you worry either way, so she wouldn't lie to you, babe."

"I guess."

I ate some more of my food then and glanced around the restaurant.

"I like it 'ere," I said happily. "I've passed by it a million times but never came inside to eat."

"I plan on bringing you here and many other places more often, so get used to it."

I turned my attention back to Damien.

"I'd be just as happy eatin' at home with you."

"Speaking of your apartment, I have to get all my laundry together to bring back to Ryder and Branna's to get it—"

"I already washed and dried it all."

Damien blinked. "Excuse me?"

"I did all the washin' this mornin'." I shrugged. "It was really windy out today, so I hung your clothes out to dry on the line I have on the balcony in me bedroom. Windy weather is great dryin' weather. Me ma always says that."

Damien continued to stare at me, and I blushed under his gaze.

"Why're you lookin' at me like that?"

"You did my laundry?"

"Yeah, so?" I raised a brow. "I did mine, too. They were dirty so I washed them ... it's not a big deal."

When Damien smiled, I couldn't understand why.

"You're bein' really weird about me doin' your washin'."

He chuckled. "It just feels a little odd. Branna usually does it for me."

"Branna is like your mammy," I teased. "I'm your girlfriend, so I've inherited the task from 'er. You're slowly becomin' me man-child."

Damien playfully rolled his eyes.

"I do it myself, too. I'm not lazy. Branna just does it before I have a chance."

"She's like me." I shrugged. "We don't let it build up. Line dryin' is a huge thing 'ere, in case you haven't noticed. When it's a nice, windy day, all the washin' is done."

"Ryder used to dry our clothes in the tumble dryer until Branna went crazy at him about how much that would cost on the bills."

"Trust me," I said. "I have no idea people didn't dry their clothes on a washin' line out their back until a few years ago when Nico said you'd put soppin' wet clothes into a dryer and just press start. That blew me mind. I put me clothes in the dryer for, like, ten minutes to soften them, and that's it."

Damien was watching with that weird look again.

"What?"

"We're on our first date, and we're talking about laundry, and the best method of drying said laundry."

"The best method is line dryin'," I pressed. "Don't argue with me on this, buddy."

Damien laughed good heartedly, and it drew attention from the group of women who were sitting a few tables over. I watched as they stared at my boyfriend and, not so discreetly, giggled and spoke to one another. Some of them looked at me. I watched as they looked me up and down and laughed, and I knew they had decided I wasn't good enough to be at dinner with Damien. I narrowed my eyes, knowing exactly what was going through their minds when they turned their gazes back to him, because it went through mine whenever I looked at Damien.

"They want to have sex with you."

Damien choked on the bite of food in his mouth.

"*Who?*" he rasped, before taking a huge gulp of his water. "What are you talking about, Alannah?"

I rolled my eyes.

"That group of women is starin' at you, and I can tell what

they're thinkin' based on how they're eye fuckin' you."

"*Eye fucking* me?" Damien's jaw dropped. "I've never heard you say that before."

I looked down at my plate of food and messed around with my steak.

"Can we go?"

"No."

I looked up at my boyfriend and frowned.

"No," he repeated. "Tell me why you want to leave."

I shook my head.

"Then we're staying right here."

I scowled. "I can leave if I want to."

"You can," Damien agreed, "but you won't, because it's our first date."

I scowled harder at him, and he only raised a brow in question and waited.

"They were givin' me dirty looks," I grumbled, looking out of the window and to the traffic on the road outside. "It's female intuition. I know they know I'm not good enough to sit 'ere with you. Women like them are."

"Women like them?" Damien repeated.

"Yeah," I sighed. "Skinny women with a nice bum, a nice pair of boobs, and a gorgeous face. Ye'know, perfect."

"Is that your vision of what perfect is?"

I didn't answer.

"Alannah."

"I don't know." I grunted. "When I think of perfect, I think of the girls."

"But Bronagh, Keela, Branna, and Aideen all have completely different body types."

I hesitated. "So?"

"So they don't all look the same, yet you think they're perfect."

"They're perfect in their own individual way."

Damien smiled. "And so are you."

I remained mute.

"I don't know what has made you so insecure about your body, but we really need to work on it because you *are* perfect. And I'm making it my personal mission to make you see that."

I looked down at my plate as a big smile plastered itself on my face.

"You're such a pain in the arse."

"When we start having sex, I *will* be a pain in your ass. Literally."

I sucked in a sharp breath and darted my eyes up to Damien's, and he laughed once more.

"Never," I stated. "We're *never* doin' that."

"What?"

"*That*!"

"What's that?"

I lowered my voice. "Anal sex."

"You might like it."

"And I might hate it," I countered. "That hole is an exit, *not* an entrance."

Damien was thoroughly amused by me, and he didn't stop smiling until we finished dinner and made our way back to my car. After we buckled ourselves in and began the drive back to my apartment, I turned my head and stared at Damien's side profile.

"Tell me something about yourself from when you were little that no one else knows."

He thought on this for a moment.

"I always wanted to be a ninja when I was a kid. A real crime fighting one."

That drew a snort from me.

"You could never be a ninja."

"I could be if I wanted to."

"No, you couldn't."

"Why not?"

"You forgot to tie your shoelaces yesterday, and you fell on your face."

Damien considered this. "Perhaps you're right."

My lips twitched. "I'm always right."

"You are indeed."

He replied way too fast for that to be an honest answer.

I glanced at him as he drove. "Man Bible?"

"Chapter three, page nineteen, line seven," Damien answered with a nod. "Always agree with a woman no matter what. The 'no matter what' part is in bold and underlined."

I laughed. "You make it sound like you have actual Man Bible copies."

"We do," Damien answered. "In paperback."

I blinked. "Paperback?"

"Yup, Dominic asked Keela about it since she knows *everything* about self-publishing, and she helped him write out the Man Bible. He got five copies, one for each brother."

I stared at Damien in disbelief. "Are you jokin'?"

"No," he answered. "Why would I lie?"

"Because that is the most outrageous thing I have ever heard."

"It's Dominic." Damien shrugged. "Nothing is impossible with that idiot."

"Do any of the other girls know about this?"

Damien hesitated. "No, but you can't tell them."

"Oh, I'm tellin' them."

"Alannah," Damien groaned. "My brothers will kick my ass. We agreed not to tell you or the other girls because you'd want to read the Man Bible, and it's not for women's eyes. It's sacred to men."

"Oh, my God," I said with a shake of my head. "You spend way too much time with Alec. That was him that just came out of your mouth just then."

Damien grinned as we neared my apartment.

"He's my big brother, so I guess I'm more like him than I thought."

"I'm still tellin' the girls."

Damien growled. "I'll have to punish you if you do."

"If you even *consider* spankin' me, I'll knock your teeth out."

A lower rumbling chuckle filled the car. "You and what army?"

"Bronagh Murphy."

"That's not fair," Damien huffed. "She is feral when she is mad."

"Exactly, so don't mess with me or me arse, buddy."

"No promises."

I grinned like a fool.

"Do you think a lot about when we're gonna have sex?"

"At *least* one hundred times a day."

I cracked up laughing, and Damien simply smiled and shook his head. I loved how he made me feel. Carefree, beautiful, and most of all, happy. I didn't think of sex with him anywhere *close* to one hundred times a day, but I found myself thinking of it all the way home, and I decided we had both waited long enough to come together.

Literally.

CHAPTER TWENTY-THREE

Four days later ...

Four whole days.

That was how long it took for Damien to break. It took four fucking days for me to seduce the man. What I thought would be an easy task turned out to be anything but. From the moment we got home from our first date, I had been dropping hints left, right, and centre that I was ready for us to be physically intimate. Damien picked up on zero of these hints, and I was too embarrassed to simply come out and ask him to have sex with me, so I upped my game. I subtly teased him whenever I got the chance, and I talked about sex, a lot. At night, I draped myself over him in bed and purposely rubbed against him, but nothing would happen.

Either he had the patience of a saint, or he just had no clue what I wanted.

I was truly beginning to believe the latter until I apparently took it one step too far in Ryder and Branna's kitchen. We were already at the house, every one of us, kids and all. Damien waited until we all had finished our meal together to get to his feet, drawing everyone's attention. He retrieved a black box with a silver ribbon tied around it from behind the kitchen door. His attention was solely on me.

"I wanted to give this to you on our first date, but it wasn't delivered until today."

I widened my eyes as Damien handed me the box.

"But it's not me birthday," I said dumbly as I accepted the gift.

"I know." He chuckled. "It just something I got for you to show you how much you mean to me."

The girls all audibly sighed, and it took everything in me not to join in with them.

"Th-thank you," I said, looking down at the gift, perplexed. "Do I open it now?"

"Yes," Bronagh and Keela said in unison.

Damien snorted. "You can open now or later. It's up to you."

"Now," I said. "I want to open it now."

I untied the pretty silver ribbon that was perfectly wrapped into a bow, and I held my breath as I lifted the lid off the box and set it down on the table. I stared into the box, not really knowing what I was looking at. There was fancy wrapping tissue covering a folder of some kind, but sitting on top of the tissue was a framed document. I carefully lifted the frame into my hand, and I read the document. When I realised what it was for, my breath caught. I scanned it twice more before I lifted my head, and locked eyes on the grey ones staring at me intently.

"You bought me a *star*?"

A beautiful smile graced Damien's face, and my heart thumped wildly against my chest.

"And," I said, looking back at the document, smiling, "you named it Freckles."

"Yeah," Damien said, pride radiating from him in waves. "That way, when I look up at the stars at night, I'll always see you."

"Omigod," Bronagh whispered, her holding on Nico tightening. "That is so romantic."

I didn't look up at Damien, but I was smiling so hard my cheeks began to hurt.

"Thank you," I said, pressing the star ownership document against my chest. "I'll treasure this always."

When I looked up at Damien, his eyes were still on me, and I stood up, not being able to help myself. I needed to be close to him. I took another step forward, completely in a trance, until Alec spoke.

"Little bastard," he said, breaking the silence and pulling me back into the moment.

Everyone looked at him.

"What?" Damien asked, frowning.

"You're a little bastard," Alec repeated.

Damien looked at Nico, then back at Alec and said, "Not understanding why I'm a bastard."

"Little bastard."

Damien's lips twitched at Alec's correction.

"Sorry, I don't understand why you're calling me a *little* bastard."

Alec scowled. "Isn't it obvious?"

"No," everyone said in unison.

"Unbelievable," Alec said with a shake of his head. "You're a little bastard because you bought the woman a star. A fucking star. How the hell can we compete with that?"

The question was put to Kane.

"Buy your girl two stars?" he suggested.

Alec scoffed. "It wouldn't be impressive since buying a star has already been done by the little bastard."

"You could buy me a black hole," Keela suggested. "I get sucked into one whenever you start talkin', so it'd be perfect."

I cracked up with laughter, and it caused Alec to glare at me. His focus on me only lasted for a moment before he looked at Damien and asked, "*Can* you buy a black hole?"

I laughed harder, and I snorted which drew a laugh from Kane. That was something I hardly ever saw unless Aideen was humouring him.

"Look at what else is in the box," Damien urged me.

I did just that.

I removed the tissue from the box and was presented with a

thick folder. Inside was another certificate, more documentation, a star map, the personal dedication of my nickname being an actual star, a colour photo of my star, the exact coordinates of my star, and a silver necklace with a heart and star pendent. I scanned my eyes over it all, before I picked up my necklace, and looked up at Damien.

"Will you put it on me?"

He smiled, took my necklace, then placed it on me when I turned and pulled my hair over my shoulder. I shuddered after Damien clasped the necklace shut because he placed a chaste kiss on my neck, but it felt intimate, way too intimate for the group of people watching us. I quickly turned to face Damien, wrapping my arms around his waist and pressing my face against his chest.

"I love it so much," I gushed. "I can't believe you bought me a star."

"Not just any star; a supernova."

I pulled back. "What's the difference?"

"A supernova is a star coming to the end of its life; it shines so brightly it can outshine an entire galaxy. It will still be in the sky for thousands of years, but I wanted a star that would outshine the others. I wanted something to represent just how much you mean to me."

My heart beat so loud and fast that I could hear it in my ears.

"Damien," I said, softly. "I'll value it always."

"I'll value *you* always."

I smiled and closed my eyes when his arms came around me, and he leaned down, resting his forehead against mine.

"I think I'm engaged to the wrong twin."

I opened my eyes and watched as a smirk plastered itself on Damien's face.

"This will be good," he mouthed, making me snicker.

"*What?*" Nico demanded of Bronagh. "Damien gives Alannah a dying star, and all of a sudden, he is the better twin? Woman, I give you *babies*."

I turned in Damien's arms, resting my back against his chest as I watched the scene unfold before us.

"Your brothers give the girls babies too," Bronagh said with a snort. "You aren't anything special."

She was teasing him; I could tell by the way her lips kept twitching.

"Nothing special?" Nico repeated. "Nothing fucking special?"

"Hey," Kane chastised. "We have an almost one-year-old at the table."

We really did. In just three weeks, Jax would turn one, just in time for Christmas.

"Shut up," Nico said to Kane without taking his eyes off Bronagh. "We're not done talking about this."

She grinned. "I look forward to you provin' how special you are at home."

"You're damn right you are."

I snickered but did my best to cover it up with a cough, but Nico caught it.

"What's so funny?"

I shrugged. "That she can manipulate you so easily."

Nico looked from me to Bronagh, then back at me.

"What are you talking about?"

"When you both go home, you're going to prove how *special* you are with sex, and that's exactly what she wants ... do you not remember how hot she was for you when she was carryin' Georgie?" I quizzed. "Jesus, I do. I felt like I needed to spray sanitiser whenever I entered your bloody house."

Everyone laughed, apart from Nico, who was now focused on a grinning Bronagh.

"You could just *tell* me you want sex."

"Where's the fun in that, big man?"

"Devil," Nico said, his own lips curving into a smile as he leaned over and kissed Bronagh, then kissed Georgie, who was asleep on her chest.

I turned back to face Damien, and a quick glance down told me he was hard, and it made me want to chuckle. Whenever he touched me, whether it was in a sexual manner or not, he got hard. It was thrilling to know that I made him react that way. Without a word, I discreetly palmed his hardened length through his jeans and smiled sweetly up at him.

That was the straw that broke the camel's back. One second, I was in the kitchen, and the next, I was thrown over Damien's shoulder as he all but sprinted out of the room and up the stairs with laughter and cheers following us.

I stumbled when my feet hit the ground in his bedroom on the third floor.

"What in God's name are you *doing*, Alannah?"

I placed my hands on either side of my head.

"I've a massive head rush."

"Sit down," Damien grunted as he led me over to his bed, before he began to pace back and forth in front of me. "Now, tell me, what the fuck are you doing?"

I blinked up at him.

"I have no idea what you're talkin' about, Dame."

He scowled at me as he continued to pace.

"Bullshit," he quipped. "You grab my dick, and smile up at me with heat in your eyes, and you tell me that you have no idea what I'm talking about?"

"Yup."

"You're a liar." He shook his head. "And you've been trying me these last few days."

"How so?"

"How so?" Damien repeated, bewildered. "How about you suddenly not wearing clothes around the apartment? How about all the unnecessary bending over you do in front of me? How about you practically straddling me in bed before we go to sleep?"

I tilted my head to the side.

"Have I been doin' all of that?"

"You damn well have, and you know it," Damien all but

growled. "What I don't know is why!"

I looked up at the ceiling and sighed.

"Men are stupid."

Silence.

"Excuse me?"

I looked at my boyfriend. "You're thick."

"Again—" he blinked "—excuse me?"

I scratched my neck. "I have been doin' all of the things you listed, and yes, on purpose."

"I *knew* it!"

"You caught me, Sherlock."

Damien paused in front of me, placed his hands on his hips, and frowned down at me.

"You've been putting me through hell, you know that, right?"

I rolled my eyes. "You've been puttin' *yourself* through hell by not touchin' me."

"Alannah." He drew his eyebrows tighter together. "You said we have to go slow, and that's exactly what I've been doing, so of course, I'm going to keep my hands to myself. I'm not doing anything to mess things up between us."

My lips curved into a smile.

"You're a sweetheart," I said to him. "But I've been bendin' over backwards, literally, tryin' to *make* you touch me."

Damien raised one brow. "I'm sorry, *what*?"

I leaned back onto my elbows and slid my tongue along my lower lip.

"I thought you would realise by now when you're bein' seduced by me."

"Seduced?" Damien choked. "You've been *seducing* me?"

"Apparently, not very well."

Damien's lips parted with shock.

"You've been playing a game with me."

My lips twitched. "Only a little one."

"We agreed on no games."

"We did—" I nodded "—but I wanted to show you that I wanted to have sex."

"And you couldn't have just come out and *told* me so? I'd have been on you in seconds."

Laughter spilled free.

"I'm sorry," I said, covering my mouth with my hand. "This isn't funny, but you look so pissed off."

"I am," Damien said, his postured rigid. "So. Pissed."

I slowly got to my feet. "I'm sorry."

"Sorry?"

I carefully moved my body around his.

"*So* sorry."

"No need, babe," he said, his voice rough. "Not when I've just made a decision."

My brows shot up.

"What decision would that be?"

"I've spent these past couple of weeks giving you space, giving you time to make up your mind." Damien said, his eyes roaming over my body. "We've been together, but I've kept you at arm's length. I've tiptoed around you because I didn't want to scare you off, but that ends now, now that I know we want the same thing. I seem to be the only one brave enough to make it happen."

I held my ground. "And what the hell does *that* mean?"

"It means," Damien said as he suddenly stalked towards me, "I'm done with the nice guy role. I'm taking what I want from now on. If you remain where you are, I'm going to kiss you and not stop. If you can't handle that right now, run away, but know that I'm coming after you, and I *will* have you. You're mine, freckles. This game you've started is over."

I'd like to say that my mother didn't raise a chicken shit, and that I stood my ground when Damien got close enough, but that didn't happen. I freaked out when I saw the possessive look in his grey eyes because I knew he wasn't talking bullshit; he was talking facts. He was going to kiss me ... to have me. I was ready for that, *so* ready, but not here, not now.

Without a second thought, I turned around and all but shot out of Damien's bedroom like the devil himself was chasing me, hearing Damien's laughter echo behind me as I went.

"Usain Bolt. I'm a huge fan, sir," Alec, the fucking comedian, said and tried to shake my hand as I sprinted by him on the stairs.

"Tonight, freckles," Damien called after me. "We will finish this tonight."

Jesus, have mercy.

CHAPTER TWENTY-FOUR

It's going to be perfect.

I kept repeating that over and over in my mind as I stared at myself in my body-length mirror. I had on the most revealing pyjamas I owned, a skimpy pair of bum shorts that left nothing to the imagination and a matching lace crop top that you could see my nipples through. They may have been labelled as pyjamas, but there was no way in hell that they were meant for sleeping in.

The lace scratched against my skin, and the shorts fit so snug, I had to resist the urge to pull them down. Apparently, being plastered to each bum cheek was exactly what they were designed to do. Or at least that was what Bronagh said when I called her on FaceTime and asked since she gifted me the stupid outfit.

My best friend was so excited that I had been seducing Damien. Unsurprisingly, he had told them what I had been doing over the past few days, and they were all proud of me for attempting to seduce Damien, knowing how much courage it took me to do it. Granted, I didn't do it very well, but it was the thought that counted.

I liked to think so, anyway.

I examined myself from head to toe and bounced a little on my heels with what I saw. I felt sexy, and I knew this would drive my man *wild*. I wanted caveman Damien, and this lace pyjama set was going to get me him ... I just needed to keep my courage and *not* chicken out. I had fled from Ryder and Branna's house two hours ago, and I had been waiting for Damien to arrive as he had promised to do. I was waiting for my buzzer to sound so I could let him into the building, but it seemed he was purposely keeping me waiting. It was driving me crazy, which was most likely what he wanted.

I busied myself with playing with Barbara and her toy mice that I dragged along behind me on a long string. I couldn't believe how much bigger she was; I only had her a couple of weeks, but she was growing steady and fattening up big time. She had declared herself as ruler of the apartment, and that Damien and I were her people. We all accepted this happily.

When Barbara had enough of me, I went into my office and start to paint without changing my clothes. I rolled my eyes when some splashed on my skin, but before I had time to clean myself up I thought I heard laughter from the hallway outside of my apartment. I quickly put Barbara in the kitchen and closed the door behind her before I scurried over to the front door where I looked out of my peephole. I couldn't see a thing, just blackness.

"What the hell?" I said aloud. "What's wrong with—"

"Nothing is wrong with it, baby, I just have my hand over it so you can't see me."

I screeched when Damien spoke, then screeched some more when the lock on my door turned by itself, and the door opened. I jumped back, placed my hands on my chest, and stared at Damien when he stepped into my apartment with my lips parted.

"You frightened the life outta me, Damien."

His smug grin vanished the second his eyes landed on me.

"Fuck."

I placed my hands on my hips. "Where did you get a key from?"

Damien's eyes trailed over me slowly.

"I got a second one cut last week," he answered. "You said you were going to get one cut, but you never did, so I did it for you."

I blinked. "And you just assumed the key was for you? Maybe it was gonna be a spare."

Damien's eyes locked on mine, and he grinned.

"Do you want it back?"

I hesitated. "No."

"Good." Damien licked his lips. "I didn't want to give it back."

Clearly.

"What are you wearing?"

I was reminded of my revealing outfit.

"Bronagh bought it for me ages ago," I said with a little curtsey. "It's matchin' pyjamas."

"Pyjamas?" Damien repeated on a cough. "*Those* are pyjamas?"

"Yup."

Damien closed the door.

"Are you wearing them for me?"

I felt my cheeks burn. "Yes."

His eyes darkened. "Because of what I said earlier?"

"Yes."

He pocketed his keys and advanced towards me.

"Is this what you want?" he asked, gripping my waist and pulling my body against his. "You want us to be together?"

"In every way imaginable."

Damien leaned his head down and brushed his lips against mine.

"We've only been dating a few weeks," he whispered. "We can still go slow if you wan—"

"I thought you said the game I started was over."

"Oh, baby, it is. I'm just given you an out if you really want one."

"I don't," I answered. "When we got together, you said we weren't a regular couple just startin' out, and you were right. I don't care if it's too fast for other people, it feels perfectly timed to me. I've never been happier than I have been these past few weeks. You've been me rock with me ma, the voice of reason to help me mend things with me da, you helped me get me arse in gear to hire Morgan so me business could be handled, and you've taken care of me and kept me safe every single night since we became partners. I want you more than me next breath, Damien."

"Alannah," he murmured. "Baby."

"You've also gone out of your way to buy and name a star after me," I said with a teasing grin. "You'd be gettin' some for that alone."

Damien's lips twitched. "In that case, my genius plan worked."

I laughed. "Oh, it most definitely did … snowflake."

His eyes dropped to my chest, and he swallowed.

"I can see your nipples."

"Well, would you look at that, you can."

Damien lifted a hand from my waist and brushed his thumb over one of the harden peaks, and I shuddered.

"You're so beautiful."

I flushed with pleasure.

"I was goin' for sexy."

Damien pinched my nipple, drawing a gasp from me.

"You're sexy, too," he said. "*So* fucking sexy."

He turned my body around without a word and roughly slapped my behind, which nudged me into a walk. With one hand on my hip, Damien applied pressure and kept me walking until I entered the bedroom. He walked me forward until my knees knocked against the base of my bed. I began climbing up onto the bed, but it wasn't quick enough for Damien. His large hands gripped my hips firmly, and he flipped me onto my back and stepped between my thighs after he pushed them apart. He leaned over me, and his eyes raked over my body like I was his next meal.

I glanced down at myself and gasped when I remember I hadn't cleaned up yet.

"I'll get paint on you."

Damien gripped my hips and pulled me against his body. Hard.

"I don't care," he rasped. "Get it all over me."

"Give me the chance and I will."

Damien swallowed. "You want me?"

"Need you," I pleaded. "I need you to kiss me, to touch, to fuck me … to love me so hard I don't know where I start and you end."

Damien closed his eyes, and when he opened them, raw hunger dwelled within. They were a lustrous colour of a polished shard of metal, they were beautiful. *He* was beautiful.

"We're doing this *my* way," he said, his voice rough. "Later, you can have me whatever way you want, but right now, I'm having you the way *I* want."

"Yes," I whispered. "Yes, please."

He covered his mouth with mine and kissed me roughly. When our kiss broke, he took a moment to suck my lower lip into his mouth. I groaned and sought his mouth again when he released my lip with a pop. He denied me his lips, and instead trailed kisses down my neck and onto my chest. I groaned when he latched onto my left nipple through the lace of my crop top and swirled his hot, wet tongue around. The friction of the fabric as well as Damien's tongue made my back arch as licks of pleasure danced up and down my spine.

"Oh, God."

Damien moved from my left nipple to my right and showered it with just as much love and attention. By the time he had finished, I was a panting, sweating mess of need.

"Damien," I pleaded. "Please, fuck me."

"Quiet," he ordered as he kissed his way down my stomach. "I'm doing this *my* way."

"Your way will bleedin' kill me."

"Then I'll make sure you go out screaming."

Christ.

Damien's large hands went to my knees, and he gripped them firmly as he pushed them as far apart as they would go without it hurting me. I swallowed when he ducked his head, and his lips pressed against the inside of my thighs, slowly working their way upwards. I couldn't focus on any one of his movements. His lips felt incredible, but so did his palms as he slid them up and down my thighs, squeezing my flesh here and there. I moaned softly when his teeth nipped my flesh making me clench with excitement.

My body bucked of its own accord when I suddenly felt his finger push aside my shorts.

"No panties?"

"I didn't think I'd need them."

"You were right."

I sucked in a sharp breath when Damien's warm, wet tongue slid over my sensitive folds. I squeezed my eyes shut and focused on Damien—or more importantly, his mouth. He hummed against me as he licked up and down but didn't directly touch my throbbing clit that ached so much I clenched my hands into fists.

I tried to focus on my breathing, just to take my mind off the devious torture, but my eyes crossed when the talented tongue curved around the hood of my clit, teasing me, drawing long moans past my lips. Damien moved his attention and skilled tongue to my labia, where he sucked on my lips before dipping his tongue insideme.

"Damien!"

He sucked on my pussy lips, and even scraped his teeth over them, sending a shiver up my spine. He moved his tongue upwards, and *finally*, I felt hot air on my clit, followed by his warm tongue lapping at it like a man starved.

"*Fuck!*"

Damien hooked his arms around my thighs and flattened his hands at the base of my stomach, applying pressure to keep my arse on the mattress. He inhaled a deep breath, then curled his tongue around my clit *slowly*. It felt so good that it almost hurt, but that didn't deter me from begging him not to stop. I pulsed with need, and the urge to reach down and fist my hands into Damien's thick hair became difficult to ignore. My fingers flexed against my bed sheets.

When he sucked on my clit, I felt myself go cross-eyed, and it was all I could do not to buck my hips in his face. He continued to suck on my clit and curl his tongue around it. He kept his attention there and gifted me pure bliss. I rolled my hips, and Damien smiled against my pussy, then sucked my clit in response.

"Yes," I hissed. "Jesus, suck it harder."

He did, and I groaned with pleasure as I reached down and tangled my fingers in his hair. I inhaled three deep breaths, then my body fell apart. My breathing suddenly became irregular, and I couldn't focus on anything except how good I felt. I began to lose myself to Damien's touch, and I didn't resist; I threw myself over the edge.

My thighs began to tremble, so much so that Damien used his hands to grip the insides of my thighs to keep them from knocking against his head as he tongued me into oblivion. With his hands' new position, he pushed my legs further apart, and it pushed my pussy harder against Damien's mouth.

At that moment, my body began to convulse as I came hard.

When I became aware of my surroundings, I could hear how laboured my breathing was, and I was also aware that Damien was now hovering over me. I blinked my eyes a few times, then I stared up at him with a lazy smile. He chuckled before he leaned down and kissed me. Tasting myself on his tongue was one of the most erotic things I had ever experienced. I hummed into his mouth and wrapped my arms around his neck, tugging his against me.

"I know you want to fuck me your way," I murmured against his lips, "but can I ride you? I've never done that before."

Damien's eyes fluttered closed for only a second before he climbed onto the bed next to me, ridding himself of his clothes as he moved. When he was naked as the day he was born and lying on his back next to me, I wasted no time in cocking my leg over him and straddling him. I reached up and rid myself of my crop top, and Damien hissed a breath before reaching up and palming my breasts.

"You're stunning, baby."

I felt stunning. I saw the lust and adoration in Damien's eyes when he looked at me, and the boost it gave to my confidence was immense.

"You are too," I said, placing my palms on his chest. "You're perfect."

"I'm not perfect, freckles."

"You are to me."

I rolled my hips, and the head of Damien's cock parted my pussy lips and slid back and forth over my clit as I moved. Damien's hands dropped to my waist, and he curled his lip up in a snarl. He looked pissed, but his eyes were locked on my movements, and I knew it felt just as good for him as it did for me.

"Alannah," he groaned. "If you don't fuck me right now, I'm going to fuck you *into* this fucking mattress."

Wordlessly, I rolled my hips forward enough to push Damien's head back to my entrance, and when I leaned back, I watched Damien's eyes the second he felt his cock slide into my pussy. His eyes rolled back, he bit down on his lower lip, and his fingers dug painfully into my flesh, but I felt too good to comment on it. I sank down onto Damien's cock, and the man beneath me trembled.

"No co-condom," he choked out. "Oh, God. You feel ... Heaven."

I was a condom girl. I had a large box of them in my nightstand, but I never wanted to use one with Damien. I wanted all of him, in every capacity that I could have him. I rose, and just as I reached the head of Damien's cock, I sunk back down, and fell into a slow rhythm of fucking him.

"A…A…lannah," Damien panted, his face contorted with pleasure. "I'm not we-wearing a co-co-ndom—*fuck*!"

I groaned as I clenched my muscles around him once more. *Fuck*, it felt good.

"I'm on birth control," I answered as I sunk down on him again. "I only ever want *you* raw."

The second the words passed my lips, Damien flipped us, and with a screech, my back bounced against the mattress as his body parted from mine. My legs were pushed so far apart, it hurt, but the second Damien relined his cock against my entrance and thrust forward, everything changed. Any pain melted away and was replaced by pleasure. Hard, rough, mind-numbing pleasure.

"Do you like that?" Damien hissed as he fucked me. "I've wanted to fuck you like this every time I've looked at you since I came home last year. I wanted to strip you bare, clamp my hand over your mouth, and fuck you so hard you'd scream."

My muscles clenched around him, and he growled.

"Your pussy," he groaned. "It's my favourite place to be."

I dug my nails into his back, and he responded by thrusting into me harder.

"Da-Damien." I choked. "Oh, God. *Yes.*"

He lowered his head, brushed his lips against mine, but pulled out of reach when I tried to kiss him. He repeated this a few times, and the teasing made my pussy clench. Damien hissed and bucked into me harder.

"Every time I wrapped my hand around my cock when I was away, I closed my eyes and imagined it was your hand, your mouth, your pussy, your asshole. You're my fantasy come to life, and fucking you is *so* much better than I remebered."

Christ in Heaven, I couldn't take any more of his words. He was killing me.

"Fu...uck me," I groaned. "*Fuckmefuckmefuckmefuckme.*"

I cried out when Damien tilted his pelvis, and each thrust sent a pulse wave of bliss up my spine.

"Look at me," Damien growled. When I managed to focus my blurring vision on his face, he said, "Tell me how good you feel."

"I can't think," I panted. "I feel ... you feel ... fuck, *so* good."

My eyes rolled back with the next thrust, and a chuckle rumbled from Damien's chest.

"Like that, do you?"

"Yes," I rasped. "Please, don't st-stop."

He kept his rhythm of fan-fucking-tastic thrusting to a fast pace, and it blew my mind that he didn't seem to be tiring.

"I'm never going to stop," he grunted, bringing his lips to my cheek, before he swiped his tongue over my skin. "Every time I want to fuck you, I'm going to fuck you. I'm going to make you crave my cock. I'm going to make you beg me to fill you."

"Yes," I hissed. "Yes, Damien."

"When you piss me off, I'm going to fuck you. When you get an attitude, I'm going to fuck you. When you smile at me, I'm going to fuck you."

An orgasm unexpectedly slammed into me, and I screamed for only a moment before ecstasy latched itself around me. I twitched and bucked against Damien as my insides burned like molten lava. This orgasm wasn't like anything I had ever experienced before; there were no pulses in my clit and no waves of bliss. Instead, I experienced a whole-body sensation of pleasure that continued to swirl around me the longer Damien continued to fuck me.

"Harder!" I screamed.

Damien fucked me harder, and it prolonged the orgasm, and when my back arched, and I felt a rush of heat slam into my pussy, I knew it had come to an end. I fell backwards into the bed, and only noticed then that Damien wasn't moving anymore. He was slumped over me, barely holding his bodyweight on his elbows. I felt a slight jerk of his hips, but it was obvious that he came at the same time as me.

"You ... came."

I couldn't move.

"Yeah." I swallowed. "Hard."

"No." He groaned as he moved his hips and slipped out of me. "I'm mean literally."

I couldn't focus on what he was saying, so I didn't even try. I closed my eyes and relaxed.

"Alannah."

I didn't answer him.

"Baby?"

I groaned in response.

"You came," he repeated.

"I know I did," I answered groggily. "I screamed for a reason."

"Freckles." He chuckled. "I mean that you squirted."

I almost collided with Damien as I shot upright.

"I did not!" I stammered. "I don't squirt. I've never done so!"

Damien lifted his hand to the back of my head and pressed on it, until my gaze was lowered, and my eyes were locked on the wet patch on the bedsheets between my parted thighs.

"Oh, my God."

I now knew what that rush of heat was, and I wasn't sure if I should be proud or embarrassed. Damien didn't give me a moment to think, he nudged my head with his, and when I looked at him, he covered his mouth with mine and pushed me back until I was laying down, and then he covered my body with his. I wrapped myself around him and hummed with delight.

"It's so sexy that you came like that," he said against my lips as he used one hand to push my now wet shorts down my legs. "So. Fucking. Sexy."

"I've never come like that before," I said, sliding my tongue over his lower lip.

Damien pressed his forehead against mine. "I'm glad it was with me."

"I'm glad everythin' is with you."

I looked down at my naked body. "You've taken everythin' off me."

"The only thing I'm not taking off you is my eyes."

I shuddered.

Damien looked deep into my eyes and said, "You mean the world to me."

I slid my hands up his back to his neck and smiled. "You *are* the world to me."

When his lips kissed me next, I lost all rational thought and my very world became Damien.

CHAPTER TWENTY-FIVE

"Alannah?"

I looked up when Morgan called my name.

"Yeah?"

He smiled at me and shook his head. "I've called you four times."

I blushed, embarrassed.

"Sorry, I was in a world of me own."

That translated into I couldn't stop thinking about Damien, but Morgan didn't need to know that.

I hadn't seen my boyfriend since yesterday, the morning after we had sex, and I couldn't stop thinking about him. He phoned me during his lunch hour and said he was helping Kane out with a few things after work, and that I shouldn't wait up for him. I did wait up for him, but he never came by my apartment. It was the first night since we became a couple that we hadn't slept in the same bed together, and I found that I could no longer sleep without Damien being by my side or hearing his soft snores surrounding me.

I tossed and turned all night, and at four a.m., I gave up on trying to sleep. I changed into an oversized t-shirt and a pair of leggings, then went into my office and began to paint. I was an artist who expressed myself in many ways, but for some reason, I only gravitated towards painting when I was sad or stressed out about something. My portrait, of course, was a perfectly sketched image of Damien that I brought to life with colour.

I glanced at the painting that was still drying on my easel in the corner of the room. I sighed as I picked up my phone and checked for the millionth time to see if Damien had messaged me. He hadn't, and that irritated me because I had messaged him, twice, asking if he was okay, and he never replied. I was worried, but if it turned out he was perfectly okay, then I was going to be pissed at him for ignoring me.

I clicked on my Facebook page, and the first post on my timeline was from Bronagh, who tagged Aideen, and checked them in at the hospital. I stared at my phone and made a noise of displeasure.

"Is everythin' okay?"

"Yeah," I said, scrolling through Bronagh's pictures. "Me friend just had another pregnancy appointment today. She told me I could go to 'er next scan, but she went with our friend instead."

"Is your friend a mother?"

"Uh-uh."

"That's probably why."

I looked up at Morgan and raised my brows.

"What?"

"You're the only one of your friends who either doesn't have a kid or isn't expectin' one." Morgan shrugged. "She probably felt like the other friend could relate to 'er more."

Is that why she didn't ask me to go with her?

"I mean, I guess that makes sense."

Morgan turned back to the computer and began typing away again.

"Are you doin' anythin' fun today?"

"No," I answered. "I'll probably go around to my parents' house or one of me friends."

Morgan chuckled. "I don't know how you do it."

"Do what?"

"Stay on the move constantly," he answered. "From what I've

gathered from you, you're always around your 'friends' gafs. You should host for a change, let them come to you."

I blinked. "I guess I've never thought about it."

"Would they not come around?" Morgan questioned. "You sound doubtful."

"No, I'm not. It's just … I've just always gone to them. They don't come to me."

"Oh."

Hearing that outlaid made my friendships sound one-sided, but I knew they weren't.

"Don't two of your friends live upstairs, though?"

I hesitated. "Yeah."

"They come by, right?"

"No, not really."

"Oh."

That was twice he'd said "oh" in the space of thirty seconds, and I found that this conversation was beginning to hurt my head.

"It's weird about your lad's brothers, though. I thought they'd drop around to check on you every so often."

My frowned deepened. "Why d'ye mean?"

"Well," he began, "from what you've told me about them … they're great lads and always are very involved with family."

"Yeah, they are."

"Then why don't they call you or drop by to see you?"

At the moment, my tongue felt like it tripled in size.

"They have jobs and babies and—"

"And no time for you?"

I stared at Morgan for a long moment before I looked down at my sketchpad that sat on my lap. I didn't know what to say to him. A huge part of me wanted to enforce that it was no big deal, but another part of me felt saddened that my friends really seemed that they *didn't* have time for me. Whenever I saw them, I was the one who had to go around and see them;; they never came to see me. I wasn't sure why I never saw this before, and I wasn't sure why my mind stressed over it so much.

"All that happened to me," Morgan continued with a shrug. "Me friend had a baby with his bird, and it took about a year, but eventually, I realised he had cut me out of his life slowly but surely."

I shook my head instantly.

"You don't know me friends," I said with confidence. "They wouldn't do that to me."

"I thought that too," he mumbled, clearly thinking of his friend and their once friendship.

"I'm sure they'll phone me and drop by when they get the chance," I pressed. "Me friends don't really know boundaries. Bronagh can show up at any time, and it'd be normal."

"I hope so," Morgan said. "It'd suck for you to lose friends that seem like family."

I wasn't sure why, but Morgan's words made me feel sick. Logically, I was confident that I didn't have anything to worry about, but a nagging voice in the back of my mind agreed with Morgan. Any one of my friends could have called or sent me a text message to see how I was or if I was okay because it wasn't normal for me to go a day without speaking to them, especially Bronagh.

With that on my mind, I dialled her number.

"Hey," I said when she answered. "What's up?"

"Nothin'," she answered. "Just chillin' with the girls. What're you doin'?"

I glanced at Morgan who was working away.

"I'm just takin' a break from workin' and figured I'd call you."

"Are you comin' by later?"

I hesitated. "Why don't *you* come 'round to *my* apartment, I'll make dinner."

"I'm too tired," Bronagh answered. "I went to me appointment today and all the waitin' around in the hospital drained me. Georgie is actin' the maggot too. Can't you just come 'round to mine? You can help me with 'er."

I frowned.

"You want me to come 'round to help with Georgie?"

"Of course." Bronagh chuckled. "You're super auntie Alannah."

My frown deepened.

"Yeah," I said. "Super auntie Alannah."

Bronagh yawned, loudly.

"So let me ask you somethin'," I said, shifting in my seat. "Do ye'know what Damien is doin' with Kane?"

Silence.

"Bronagh?"

She cleared her throat. "What d'ye mean?"

I could hear the doubt in her voice, and it made me feel ill.

"Damien was busy doin' somethin' with Kane last night, and he never came to stay over, but he won't tell me what he was doin'. I thought maybe you'd know."

"I don't know," she answered too quickly for it to be the truth. "I've no idea."

I frowned. "Okay, Bee."

"I've gotta go," she said. It was the first time I'd ever felt brushed aside by her. "Talk to you later."

"Okay, I'll—"

I cut myself off when I realised the line went dead because Bronagh hung up on me. I pulled my phone away from my ear and stared at it like it was a foreign object. She had never hung up on me before, brushed me aside so easily, or blatantly lied to me as she had just done. My mind went into overdrive, and to stop myself from creating a problem, I phoned Aideen and Keela, but they didn't an-swer me, and neither did Branna. All three of them hung up on me; I knew that because the call rang out, then suddenly cut off like they pressed the decline button. Bronagh said she was with them, so they obviously had heard her on the phone with me.

Doubt instilled itself in my mind as I thought of my friends. In-stantly, my mind separated me from them and picked apart every little thing that was different about us until I felt like I couldn't breathe.

Bronagh was the fire, Branna was the calm, Keela was the fun, Aideen was the wild, and me? I was nothing. I didn't fit in with these women. They knew it, I knew it, even the brothers knew it, but none of them seemed to mind.

I did, though.

I minded that there was always a lingering feeling in my subconscious that I was the odd one out, like they all knew something I didn't. All the hushed conversations I've had to endure, all the confusing answers I received when I asked a question about the brothers' past, the abrupt end to a sentence whenever I entered the room to now being lied to when I asked a simple question.

My 'friends' and boyfriend were keeping something from me; the only question was ... what?

CHAPTER TWENTY-SIX

"I don't think I should leave."

I looked at Morgan and tried to focus my attention on him.

"I'm fine, Morgan."

"You're not," he argued softly. "I can tell you're not."

"Okay, I'm not particularly great today, but it's nothin' I can't handle. I promise."

He hesitated. "Are you goin' to go around to your mates?"

"Probably."

"Will you talk to them about what's botherin' you?"

It was my turn to hesitate.

"You won't, will you?" he asked, seemingly shocked. "No matter how much you doubt them, you won't confront them ... will you?"

"Confront them about *what*?"

He was confusing me more than I already was. I thought he was going to answer my question, but Morgan started to laugh. Not like an amused laugh, more like a manic laugh. One that kept on building and building and had no end in sight. It frightened me. Morgan, at that moment, frightened me.

"Your shift is over," I said, reminding him he had to leave. "I don't wanna keep you any longer than necessary."

"You aren't keeping me from anything," he assured me. "*You* are why I'm here."

His voice changed slightly, and he pronounced his words clearer, which drew my brows together.

"Are you talkin' about work?"

"No, Alannah, I'm not."

Apprehension shot up my spine.

"I'm confused."

"I know." Morgan nodded. "I planned on keeping you confused and in doubt for as long as possible, but I pity you, angel."

Angel?

"Okay, Morgan, you aren't makin' any sense."

He sighed, long and deep.

"I can't keep this shit up anymore."

I stared at him, raising my brows.

"Morgan, what are you talking about?"

"My name isn't Morgan Allen, angel."

I stared at him, then I laughed.

"Ha-ha, you're hilarious." I shook my head. "Can we get back to work now if you aren't leavin'?"

"I'll gladly get back to work once we have a little chat."

I looked up from my sketchpad.

"Why are you talkin' in that accent?" I asked, perplexed. "I don't get the joke if you're makin' one."

"Alannah," he said, his lips twitching. "You're a sweetheart. Honestly, babe, a true sweetheart. I wanted to use you to hurt him, to hurt *them*, but fuck, you don't have the backbone required to stand up to the lying assholes. No matter what I say to make you doubt them, you won't confront them or leave them."

I hurriedly began to pack my supplies away.

"I've *no* bloody idea what you're talkin' about. None."

"I'm going to be straight with you, angel, because someone in your life should be."

I paused. "What's that supposed to mean?"

"It means," he pressed, "that your friends all lie to you, your boyfriend lies to you, and even your old man lied to you at one point about his affair. Your mom kept her cancer from you, but only until she and your dad decided on when to tell you. And since I'm part of your life, you should know that I lie to you, too."

What the hell is he talking about?

I swallowed. "How did ye'know me ma had cancer, and that me da had an affair? I never told you any of those things."

Morgan shrugged. "I hacked your phone."

"You … You hacked me phone?"

"Yes."

"Why?"

"To see if what I was doing was working."

I blinked. "Morgan—"

"My name is *not* Morgan Allen."

My head pounded.

"If it's not Morgan Allen, then what is it?"

"Carter Miles."

"Carter Miles?" I repeated.

"Yup." He nodded. "I'm from New York, not Dublin, that was a lie."

I frowned. "You've given me a really bad headache."

Morgan, or Carter, laughed. "Baby, we haven't even come close to the headache yet."

"Okay, *Carter*," I said, placing my hands on my hips. "If you're really who you say you are, why lie to me?"

"I knew if I told you my real name, it would pull up a red flag with the brothers."

"The brothers?"

"Yeah, the Slaters."

I had to sit back down.

"What has this got to do with the Slater brothers?"

"Fucking *everything*, angel."

I lifted my hands to my face and rubbed my eyes.

"Okay," I said tentatively. "Just tell me why you're here, and why you said you planned to keep me confused."

"The Slaters ... your boyfriend ... they're not who you think they are."

"What? They have fake names, too?"

Morgan's lips twitched, and I decided then that I would still think of him as Morgan, because calling him another name didn't feel right.

"No, smartass."

When he chuckled, I felt like he was playing some sort of massive joke on me, but then I remembered what he said about hacking my phone and the fact that he knew information about my parents that I hadn't shared with him. That put me on edge and made me very wary of Morgan and how close he was to me.

"Who are they then?"

"People with a dark past," Morgan answered. "A past they've neglected to share with you."

I raised my brows.

"You, a complete stranger, know about their past?"

"I'm not a stranger to them, angel."

"Stop callin' me that," I scowled. "And get to the point of all this."

"I knew the Slaters back in New York. I grew up in the same compound as them."

I sat back, shocked.

"You did?"

"Yes." Morgan nodded. "I did."

"Was the compound like, a street, or somethin'?"

"No, it was a compound." He shrugged. "You know, a cluster of buildings surrounded by a big wall."

"Damien said he grew up in a small community."

Morgan snorted. "The compound wasn't small and neither was the community. People came and went every day, but only a certain amount of us called the place home, though."

"I don't feel like you messin' with me anymore."

"Good, because I'm not."

Sickness swirled in my abdomen as I realised the person sitting across from me, a person I let into my home, wasn't who I thought he was.

"Are you goin' to hurt me?"

"No," he answered, and he sounded sincere. "I'd never hurt you. I'd never hurt anyone ... once upon a time I probably would have, but not now."

"Then who were you referrin' to when you said you wanted to use me to hurt *them*?"

"The brothers," Morgan answered. "I wanted to use you to get to them but not physically."

My heart pounded in my chest as fear overcame me.

"Mentally?"

"Bingo."

"But ... why?"

"Because they killed my family."

My lips parted with shock, and my breath left me in a strangled cough.

"Wh-what?"

"As I said, angel, you don't know the Slaters like you think you do."

I swallowed down the bile that rose up my throat.

"Then tell me what I don't know."

Morgan grinned, and leaned back in his chair.

"Sit back and relax, angel. Because shit is about to get *real*."

CHAPTER TWENTY-SEVEN

"I'll start from the beginning," Morgan said, clasping his hands behind his head. "Just to give you a bit of backstory."

I didn't answer him; I only waited.

"How much do you know about the mafia?"

My heart just about exploded.

"Excuse me?"

"The mafia," Morgan repeated. "How much do you know about that circle of people?"

"Absolutely *nothin'*."

Morgan snickered. "I figured as much."

"What has the mafia got to do—"

"The compound where I grew up, where the brothers grew up, was a mafia base, so to speak."

My mouth went dry.

"The boss of the compound, my uncle Marco, worked with the mafia from time to time, different drug cartels, too. Wherever business was good and there was money to be made, my uncle dabbled in it."

His uncle sounded absolutely terrifying to me.

"We ran things from drugs, weapons, underground fighting, to prostitution," Morgan continued. "These were things the Slater brothers were all directly involved in."

I lifted my hand and covered my mouth.

"I don't believe you."

"Yes," Morgan nodded. "You do."

"You could be lyin'!"

"But I'm not, and you know I'm not," he answered. "This is the reason why you're in the dark about that entire fucked-up family. They don't want you to know about their past because they don't trust you with information that could land them in prison."

"Shut up!"

"All the other women know," Morgan pressed. "Bronagh, Aideen, Branna, and Keela. They've all been directly involved with the 'brothers' past. Everyone but you ... until now, that is."

I covered my face with my hands and began to rock back and forth, trying to calm myself down.

"Morgan, listen to yourself. This doesn't sound like real life."

"To *you* it doesn't because you weren't born and raised in it, but this is the only life I've known, and I hate it."

I dropped my hands but couldn't stop them from trembling.

"You hate it?"

"More than anything." Morgan nodded. "Once I leave this country, I'm going home and starting fresh. No more drugs, weapons ... no more *anything* illegal. I want a normal life, and I'm going to have one even if it kills me."

I didn't know what to say, so I remained quiet.

"Growing up—" he then sighed "—I hung out with the twins a lot, but mostly I'd keep to myself. My older brother, Trent, loved the lifestyle, the drugs, the violence, the women. He lapped that shit up, and he was gunning to take over for Marco one day since our uncle had no kids of his own."

Morgan's eyes turned dark.

"But he never got the chance because your precious Slaters killed him and my uncle."

"They couldn't have," I stressed. "Those men ... they wouldn't take someone's life."

Morgan humourlessly laughed.

"Kane has killed more than a few people, angel. Did you think he got his scars from a steady line of work?"

My lower lip trembled. "Stop it."

"Don't you want to know the truth?"

I did. God help me, but I did.

"Yes," I answered quietly.

"Look." Morgan frowned. "I don't want to hurt you, so I'll summarise everything you need to know instead of making a story out of it, okay?"

I could only nod my head in response.

"I know Damien told you his parents died in a car accident, but they didn't. My uncle killed them both because they were traitors to our organisation. Out of all the brothers, Damien took their death the hardest. Trent was an asshole who loved to kick people when they were down, so he said some fucked-up shit to Damien about their parents deserving their faith, and a fight took place."

I gripped the arms of the chair I sat on.

"Trent had a gun he stole from our uncle, but it changed hands and ended up in Damien's. He shot Trent, and for a long time, the Slaters thought that Damien had murdered my brother. My uncle, who was a twisted son of a bitch, decided to keep Trent's living status a secret from the brothers because they offered to pay off a life debt for what Damien had done since the punishment would have been Damien's life for Trent's."

I shrunk lower into the chair.

"Each of the brothers has their own skillset that my uncle capitalised on. Dominic became his champion fighter in the underground when he was only fifteen. Ryder became his drug and weapons mule, Kane became his enforcer, and Alec became his prostitute. For a few years, they worked and worked hard. They had paid back the life debt and then some when they decided they wanted out. They came here for one last job, liked the place, and decided to settle."

I had always wondered what brought the brothers to Ireland, and now that I knew, I'd give anything to be in the dark once again.

"Now, these men made my uncle a lot of money, so when *they* decided that *they* were done working for him, you can imagine how that displeased him. He came to Ireland to ... talk the brothers into staying. That's where you come into the story."

I blanched. "Me?"

"Yes, Alannah, you."

"I've *never* been involved with—"

"You were unconscious at the time, so you wouldn't remember."

I widened my eyes. "What?"

"I came to Ireland with my brother, uncle, and some of our men, but hurting people was never my scene. I hated that shit, to be honest. I watched everything from the shadows of Darkness, and after my uncle had you, Damien, and Bronagh at his mercy, I left the club. It's a damn good thing I did because my brother died that night at the hands of the Slaters, and if I stayed, I would have, too."

"Hold on," I said, shaking my head. "How can you be sure I was there?"

"Because I was with Trent when you walked outside the nightclub and sat down on the kerb," Morgan answered. "We were told to get you as leverage in case Damien and Bronagh weren't enough to sway the brothers into keeping their jobs, and then you just walked out of the club like you were gift wrapped for us. It was too easy. Trent punched you in the back of your head, and boom, you were out like a light."

I lifted my hand and rubbed my fingers over the back of my head.

"I remember," I said softly. "I thought I just passed out from drinking."

"Nope, it was all orchestrated," Morgan replied. "Though, I did stop Trent from raping you."

I choked on air.

"*What?*"

"My brother was sick and twisted, Alannah."

I had to take deep breaths.

"He never touched you," Morgan pressed. "I carried you into the club, then I left because Trent went to collect Bronagh from one of the back rooms."

"Oh, my God," I said, wrapping my arms around my waist. "Oh, my God."

"I'm pressing on because I'm not finished yet," Morgan said.

I wasn't sure if I could handle hearing anymore.

"A few years passed by after that," Morgan continued. "I've been here the whole time, and I kept my ear to the ground once I found out Alec developed a connection with Brandy Daley. I didn't even reconnect with my uncle, though he was still alive. Everything back home started to fall apart, thanks to Brandy Daley interfering, and the feds started sniffing around, so I knew Marco would have made me do something that would get me killed."

My entire body was shaking.

"Alec killed my uncle," Morgan said, devastating me. "Word travels amongst Daley's circle, and since I know a few his men, I got information fed to me. That's how I knew Big Phil showed up a few years later, gunning for revenge for Kane killing his son, and the others for killing Marco and Trent."

"What?" I asked, my voice cracking. "What the fuck?"

"If I stop to explain every detail, your head will explode, angel."

"Stop callin' me that."

Morgan ignored me. "You know that fire your friend Aideen was in at the school? Big Phil started that to kill her. He failed and got away. But he got Branna, and bloodied her up good, judging from the reports in the news. Big Phil was the man who Kane reported to during his time working for my uncle, and when Kane didn't do what he was told, he was scarred. Kane killed Big Phil's son for attacking a kid, and the man was hell-bent on revenge. He never got it … he died; Kane killed him."

I felt like I was going to be sick.

"You'll be glad to know that's where all the killing ends."

Tears that were pooled in my eyes, fell and splashed on my cheeks when I blinked.

"Ryder was involved with the feds for a while, though I've no idea what for, but they've backed off him now, and as far as I can tell, life is as normal as can be for the Slaters. Unbeknownst to them that I'm in your life, of course."

"I should have never hired you."

"I'm glad you did," Morgan said with a snort. "Your system was a mess. I cleaned everything up for you, and you know it."

"Shut up." I sniffed. "Just stop talkin'."

"You won't be able to process all of this information, Alannah, not when you still don't believe it's true."

I focused my blurry vision on Morgan's face.

"How do ye'know I doubt you?"

"Because I can see it on your face every time I told you a Slater did something awful," he answered gently. "The men you know aren't capable of what I've described, but that's my entire point. You don't know who they are, and they were never going to tell you so *I* had to."

"I need to see them," I said. "To talk to them."

"Go ahead and call them," Morgan encouraged. "Invite them around."

I hesitated.

"Go on," he urged. "I want to see their faces when they realise that they've lost you."

With a trembling hand, I dialled Damien's number and prayed he'd answer.

"Hey babe," he answered on the fourth ring. "I just saw your messages. I'm at work."

"Da-damien?"

Things went quiet. "Alannah?"

"I need you and all your brothers to come to my apartment right now."

"What's wrong?"

"Do ye'know a Carter Miles?"

Silence.

"Damien?"

"Where did you hear that name?"

"From him," I answered, looking Morgan dead in his eyes. "He is sittin' right in front of me, and he has told me all sorts of lies about you and your brothers."

"Lock yourself in your bedroom," Damien demanded as rushed movements could be heard. "Get away from him, right now."

"He isn't goin' to hurt me. He said so."

"Alannah, listen to me. Get away from him. Now. You don't know this guy."

"But I do." I frowned, or at least I thought I once did. "He's been workin' for me for the past couple of weeks."

CHAPTER TWENTY-EIGHT

"Drink your tea."
"I'm goin' to be sick, Morgan."
He chuckled. "Why won't you call me Carter?"
"Because I only know you as Morgan."
"Fair enough."

I glanced towards my sitting room door, waiting for Damien and his brothers to burst through it any minute. I phoned them fifteen minutes ago, and I knew they were going to arrive anytime now. Morgan knew it too, that's why he moved us into the sitting room so we could sit down and relax. His words, not mine.

I tensed when he put his arm around my shoulder.
"I'm not going to hurt you."
I remained tensed. "I hope you're lying about everything."
"Trust me, angel," he snorted. "I wish I was."

I screamed when a loud shout sounded out in the hallway, and for some reason, I thought of Barbara, even though I knew that she was safe. I put her in her crate and put her in my bedroom once Morgan said we had to leave my office because the brothers were on their way. I remained as still as a statue as the sitting room door flung open, and Damien barrelled into the room, each of his brothers filing in behind him. I shrunk under their gaze because I had never seen them look so maddening before.

"Look what the cat dragged in."

"Carter," Damien all but hissed. "If you've hurt her—"

"I haven't hurt her. I won't hurt her ... I was never *going* to hurt her," Morgan said with a grunt. "I was never going to hurt any of you, not physically. I couldn't ever do that to another human. I couldn't ever take someone's life ... but you five ... you killed my family, so I had to do something to get you back."

"Your family killed our parents," Alec snapped. "Your family took our lives from us. Your family has brought nothing but pain to the women we love, and now your fucking family has touched one of the purest women I've ever known. Fuck you, and *fuck* your evil family."

"Oh, my God," I whispered, terrified. "Oh, my God."

Alec ... his eyes ... I had never seen him look at someone with so much pain and hatred.

"It's okay," Morgan said, his hand squeezing my shoulder. "It's good that you get to see them for who they really are."

Alec turned his gaze from Morgan to me, and when he saw how scared I was of him at that moment, he paled.

"Lana," he said softly. "Do *not* let this guy get in your head. You know me."

"Does she, though?" Morgan questioned. "She seemed pretty surprised when I told her all about our upbringing, how you all had special jobs because Damien killed Trent, but not really until a few years later that is. She knows Alec killed Marco, and Kane killed Big Phil. She was so surprised; I mean, just look at her. The poor girl is still in shock."

Nico took a step forward, his eyes locked on Morgan.

"Why are you doing this?"

"Simple," Morgan replied. "I wanted to hurt all of you, if I could, for what you have done. Something that would be long lasting, and when I watched from the shadows and saw how you all treated Alannah ... well, I figured what was the harm in turning her against all of you."

Damien didn't blink once as Morgan spoke.

"I know you all love her, in your own different ways, of course," Morgan continued. "She is the gem of your little group. She isn't a loud mouth bitch like Bronagh, an asshole like Keela, or annoying dogs like Aideen and Branna. I've watched you all together, and none of your women are appealing past their looks. None but Alannah, she is practically an angel, and I *knew* I could get into her sweet little mind. I barely had to try; she welcomed me with open arms."

Damien stepped towards Morgan, but when I sucked in a breath, he remained still.

"I expected to see you guys while I worked in her office from time to time, but I was amazed that none of you came by to check me out. Not a single one of you. None of you ever dropped by or called her. I could have killed her a hundred times, and none of you would have known it was me. You're shitty friends."

I looked down at my hands as I knotted my fingers together.

"I told you, angel," Morgan said softly to me. "You're expendable to them. They don't care about you, not really."

"Carter," Nico all but snarled. "Stop messing with her."

Morgan snorted but stopped talking.

"What now?" Ryder demanded. "You just wanted to air our dirty laundry, and that's it?"

"Yeah, that's it."

"You'll leave then?"

This question came from Damien.

"Why would I stick around?" Morgan questioned with a raised brow. "I did what I set out to do. I hurt you all by getting inside my little angel's head. She knows every dirty little secret there is to know about you. She knows that none of you trusted her enough to tell her anything when you had years and every fucking opportunity to do so. She won't forget about me anytime soon, or what I opened her eyes to. None of you will. Even if she forgives you, she'll know everything and how you've treated her like an outsider. That's good enough for me."

"And if you don't walk out of this apartment," Kane growled. "Will *that* be enough for you?"

"You won't kill me." Morgan smiled, completely at ease. "I've never touched a hair on anyone's head, and I never intended to. You may look like a monster, Kane, but you aren't the monster Big Phil trained you to be ... at least, I don't *think* you are."

"He's not a monster," Alec cut in, "but I am. I was the one to take Marco's life, not him."

Hearing Alec admit he murdered someone crushed me.

"Ah, but that was justified, was it not?" Morgan grinned. "You were horrendously abused because he sold you to people like a pack of cigarettes. I think anyone would say what you did was warranted and then some."

"Shut the fuck up!" Nico snapped.

Morgan chuckled. "I'm not too sure about you, Nico. I've watched your fights over the years, and for a while, I could have sworn you *enjoyed* hurting other people."

"You're wrong," Damien interjected. "He never hurt any of those fighters more than he had to ... He never would have fought anyone if it wasn't for Marco. None of my brothers would have done any of the things they had to if it wasn't for him."

"I think you're partially to blame," Morgan said. "Don't you? I mean, you didn't kill Trent, but you thought you did. You tried to ... You wouldn't have pulled the trigger otherwise. And all over a girl you knocked up."

My world crumbled around me.

I froze. "What?"

Morgan focused on me. "That's one thing I forgot to mention to you. Damien knocked up his girlfriend when he was a kid."

He sounded like he took pleasure in telling me something that hurt me to hear.

"I thought you were me friend, Morgan."

"I am," he stressed. "I've opened your eyes to what the brothers really are."

"They've done nothin' willingly from the sound of it."

"Agreed, for the most part," Morgan said. "Except they never told you about their past when all the other girls knew about it. They never told *you* that you were knocked out the night my brother died and used as a bargaining chip. They never told you because they don't trust you, angel. They never have, and they never will. Can't you see that?"

I lifted my hands to my head as it throbbed.

"Shut the fuck up!" Damien snapped, his voice sounding murderous. "*Stop* playing fucking mind games with her."

"Mind games?" Morgan repeated. "I'm telling her the *truth*, which is the least I can do considering you assholes were never going to."

I felt sick, so I crossed my arms over my stomach.

"Baby," Damien said, his focus on me and his voice softening. "You *know* me. You know my family."

"Do I?" I repeated, looking at the floor. "Do I really, Damien? Because I've just learned things about your lives, about *my* life, that I had no clue about."

"You have to believe us when we say it was for your own protection, Alannah."

It was Alec who spoke, but I didn't react. I kept my gaze on the floor.

"Me protection?" I repeated with a scowl. "Because I'm poor, helpless Alannah who can't make decisions or fend for 'erself, right?"

"No!" The brothers chorused.

I ignored them.

"I feel sick," I said, my lower lip wobbling. "I feel like everythin' has been a huge lie. I don't know any of you."

"Lana—"

"Alannah," I cut Damien off with a bellow. "Stop callin' me that. You aren't allowed to call me that anymore. None of you are."

"Touch her, Carter, and I'll break your hand."

It was Kane who spoke, and the tone of his voice terrified me.

"I want you all to leave."

"No!" Damien snapped after I spoke. "We need to talk about this."

"*Now* we need to talk?" I repeated, looking up into his grey eyes where I forced myself to ignore the turmoil in them. "You want to tell me about this mess now, when you've had years. Literally fuckin' *years* to tell me about somethin' that I was directly involved in?"

Silence.

"I feel like a fool!" I shouted, my voice breaking. "I feel like a fuckin' eejit. Did you all laugh at me behind me back because I was so clueless? Did you laugh because you knew I loved you all, and you never cared a fuckin' bit about me? Did you all get a kick out of it?"

"You're my *sister*," Ryder said, his eyes heavy with sadness. "You watched my sons come into this world. Do you think I'd have allowed that if I didn't love you?"

I looked away from his daring eyes, unable to form a coherent reply.

"Don't touch me," I said when Damien attempted to walk towards me. "Don't you *dare* touch me ever again."

"And that, my friends, sounds like a job well done to me. I'll take it as my cue to leave."

Morgan stood up, but none of the brothers moved a muscle.

"If you're going to kill me," Morgan said, not an ounce of fear in his tone. "Do it or let me leave this life and you five in my past because I'm fucking *done* with this bullshit. I've avenged my uncle and brother in *my* way. I'm at peace, and they're dead because of the life they chose."

Still, no one moved.

"Please," I said, my throat tight with emotion. "Please, just let 'im leave. I want 'im to go away and never come back."

"I'll do just that, angel."

I focused on the brothers, and one by one, though it seemed to cause them great distress, they stepped aside and allowed Morgan to walk by them. I stood up and followed him, only to be halted when a hand latched onto my arm.

"No," Damien said. "*We* are making sure he leaves here, leaves the country. You sit down."

I touched his hand with mine and removed it from my arm.

"For once," I said, not able to look him in the eye, "trust me with somethin'. I need to speak with 'im before he leaves for good."

When I walked after Morgan, no one stopped me this time. I found him standing in front of the elevator with his hands in his jeans.

"You said Marco and Trent's deaths were justified."

Morgan glanced at me and nodded as I walked towards him.

"They were. They did horrible things to the brothers."

"Then *why* have you done all this?" I demanded. "Why would you want to hurt people who rid the world of two evils?"

"Because—" Morgan sighed "—those two evils were the only family I had, and I couldn't just do *nothing*. I was raised to be loyal to my family, to protect as best as I could. If I did nothing, I wouldn't have been able to leave my past *in* the past."

"So this is really it?" I questioned. "You just wanted to get in their heads like you did mine?"

Morgan nodded. "I was never going to physically harm anyone. I'm not my brother and uncle. I thought I was once, but I'm not. This has all proved it to me, I just want to have a normal life, I don't want to be evil like they were."

"From where I'm standin', I don't see much of a difference."

"I like you, you know?" Morgan smiled sadly. "I do feel regret for tangling you up in this, if it's any consolation."

"It's not," I quipped. "You've ruined everythin'."

Morgan frowned.

"You're a sweetheart, and you're damn talented, but you're

wasting yourself by being involved with the Slaters. They're broken ... damaged goods who've been through hell and can't be repaired. Cut your ties with them before they ruin you, too. No one will blame you for wanting to protect yourself, Alannah."

"You're wrong about them, about the men I know," I said, standing with my head tall. "They're good men, and I love them, *all* of them. They've made mistakes, and even though I'm hurt and angry at them, I won't have anyone hurtin' them. They're *my* family, even if I'm not theirs. Morgan, Carter, whatever your fuckin' name is, if you *ever* try to hurt them in any way again ... *I* will kill *you*."

Morgan smiled at me, and it was a depressing one at that.

"What do you know?" he said with a tilt of his head. "Maybe it's too late for you after all ... It looks like the angel I thought you were has fallen."

"I was never an angel to begin with ... you don't know me as well as you thought you did."

"Maybe you're right." He nodded in agreement. "Goodbye, angel. You'll never see or hear from me again. I completed what I sought out to do. I'm going home and starting a new chapter of my life. I hope you find happiness in the next chapter of yours because you fucking deserve it."

Morgan's eyes trailed up and down my body, and when they landed on my face, he winked, his vibrant eyes glinting. He turned and stepped into the open elevator then, without a word, without a glance back in my direction, and only one thought ran through my mind as the doors closed.

Good riddance.

CHAPTER TWENTY-NINE

When I reentered my apartment, I went straight into the kitchen and turned the kettle on. I didn't want any tea, but it was an instinctive thing to do when I was stressed. A cup of tea usually solved everything, but not this. Nothing could resolve my newfound knowledge.

"Alannah?"

I gripped the edge of the countertops and squeezed my eyes shut.

"You need to leave, Damien."

"I won't," he said, firmly. "I won't have him fill your head with—"

"With lies?" I finished, turning to face him. "*Please* tell me it was all lies."

Damien kept eye contact with me, but I now saw the truth in them. Morgan hadn't lied about the things he had told me, though I wished to God that he had.

"We can't come back from this," I said, shaking my head. "I can't even be friends with the girls, not after this. Not after everythin' you have all kept from me."

"Alannah," Damien said, his voice wavering. "Please. Don't leave me."

"What choice do I have?" I demanded. "You and your brothers

have murdered people, Damien. *Murdered*!"

"It wasn't like that, though." He raised his voice. "You don't understand our life, Alannah."

"How could I when none of you told me *anythin'* about it," I exploded as tears fell from my eyes. "How can you expect me to even *try* to comprehend this when this mornin' none of this was even a possibility in me mind! It wasn't a possibility even in me nightmares!"

Damien said nothing; he only watched me, his pained expression cutting me in two.

"Christ, Damien," I pressed my palm to my head. "How can this be real? How can you have all been involved in such ... such horror? I hope I'm havin' a nightmare because this is too much. I can't take this ... I can't."

"Alannah, I'm begging you—"

"I'm beggin' *you* to leave," I cut him off. "Damien, I'm goin' to scream and cry, and I need to be on my own for it."

"I can't leave you," he said, his voice helpless. "You're my freckles. My world."

"When I woke up this mornin', me world started and ended with you too, but now? I feel like the man I knew is dead."

Damien reared back as if I had slapped him, but before he could reply, I closed my eyes as voices and loud footsteps approached my apartment.

"Alannah?" Bronagh shouted. "Oh, God. Is she okay, Dominic?"

"She's fine," Nico answered. "No, actually, she's not. She ... she doesn't want to see any of us."

"What?" Keela asked. "Why?"

"She knows about everything." Alec answered her. "Our past, what happened the night she was hurt in Darkness, everything."

"Oh, God," Bronagh cried. "I need to see 'er."

I pushed away from the counter, brushed by Damien, and stepped into the hall.

"What you need to do is leave, Bronagh."

My once friend spun in my direction and when she tried to run for me, I stepped back and shook my head. Pain showcased itself on Bronagh's face, but I refused to feel guilt for hurting her with my rejection. Her secrets hurt me way worse.

"Go home to your kids, all of you."

Branna wasn't with the girls, which didn't surprise me since she had two newborns to look after.

"Aideen's brothers are watching them, and Branna is with the twins," Keela said as she gripped Alec's arm. "We're 'ere for *you*."

No, they weren't; they were here for themselves.

"Let us explain," Bronagh begged. "Please, just let us explain."

"It's too late for that."

"It's not," Ryder said, firmly. "You heard Morgan give you facts; now let us tell you the reasons behind it."

"*Is* there a reason good enough for killin' people?"

"Yes," everyone answered in unison.

I lifted my hands to my face.

"I can't hear any more," I admitted. "Me head … I just can't."

"Alannah, please."

This was Aideen.

"You have a lot of fuckin' nerve, Aideen."

No one spoke as I dropped my hands and glared at her.

"You made me feel like fuckin' shite for not tellin' you about Dante. You fed me that bullshit about how close we were, and that you were hurt I'd kept it from you when all the while you knew somethin' about me life before I even *knew* you!"

Aideen had tears in her eyes.

"I'm so sorry, Alannah."

I slapped her hands away when she reached for me. She gasped, pulled her hands to her chest, and stared at me with shocked eyes. I looked around the hallway at all the faces of people who I thought were my friends. My family.

"None of you are me friends." I focused on Bronagh. "And *you* have broken me heart."

Tears were sliding down her cheeks.

"Ye'dont understand," she cried. "Ye'dont understand how what happened could mess with your head. What happened ... I still have nightmares about it sometimes. Keela suffered a lot after what had happened to 'er, and Aideen and Branna nearly died, so I can only imagine what goes through their minds. We wanted to protect you from all of that."

"That wasn't your decision to make!" I bellowed. "It was none of your decision to keep what happened to me private."

"Alannah—"

"Don't!" I cut Damien off as he approached me from my right. "You're worse than all of them."

He blanched.

"I opened up to you and told you every secret I'd ever had, and you never told me the truth. Not once."

"I wanted to protect you."

My lower lip trembled.

"By lyin' to me?"

He stepped forward, so I took a hefty step back.

"Stay away from me."

"I can't," he answered, his eyes filled with hurt. "I love you, Alannah."

I heard little gasps from the girls, and I could feel the intense stares of Damien's brothers as he made his declaration, but I didn't care. Not about any of it. Not about these people who lied to my face for years.

"If this is how you treat me when you love me," I repeated, taking another step back. "I'd dread to see what you'd do if you hated me."

"Alannah," he said, softly. "Please don't walk away from me."

The pain in my chest hurt worse than anything I'd ever felt before.

"Please," he begged. "Don't leave me."

"I can't be near any of you right now," I said. "I trust any of you, just like none of you trust me."

"We *do* trust you, Alannah," Nico pleaded. "We do."

"But not enough to be honest with me?"

Silence.

"Exactly," I said with a shake of my head. "You can all say it was to protect me, but it was only to protect yourselves and the monsters you are for not only committin' such acts, lads, but you girls for standin' by them and knowin' what they've done, too."

"Alannah—"

"I'm goin' into me bedroom, and I'm lockin' the door. I'm goin' to force meself to go to sleep, and when I wake up, every one of you better be gone, and Damien, I mean that. I'll call the guards otherwise, and you never know what I might say, ye'know, since I'm so untrustworthy."

Damien grabbed me when I turned my back and began to walk away.

"You have to let us explain," he begged. "You have to let *me* explain."

"Right now, I can't," I said, fighting back tears. "I just need to be on me own. If I want you to explain, I will ask you all to explain, but for God's sake, let me have time to process this."

"If I let you go, you won't come back to me. I know you won't."

"That's a risk you're goin' to have to take because one way or the other, I'm puttin' space between all of you and me. I don't want to be near any of you. If you don't respect me as a person to trust me with your secrets, then at least respect me decision to not want to be around you."

"I'll tell you everything," Damien said, kissing the side of my face, drawing a small cry from me. "When you want an explanation, I'll tell your everything. I swear."

He hugged me so tight, I thought I felt my bones crunch.

"I love you, freckles."

The sad thing about all of this wasn't that he told me he loved me after I found out such horror about his family; it was sad because even though I knew what horrendous acts were committed and how he lied to my face, I loved Damien, too. Despite all of that, I loved him with every fibre of my being ... and if that wasn't a travesty, then I didn't know what was.

CHAPTER THIRTY

Two weeks later...

"Alannah?"

I looked at my ma.

"Yeah?"

"Bear, I've called your name three times."

I blinked. "Sorry, Ma, I just have a lot on me mind."

A hell of a lot.

"What is goin' on?" she asked me, gently. "Please don't tell me nothin' because I know it's somethin', baby."

I bit the insides of my cheeks to keep from crying.

"I just had a big fallin' out with Damien and the others."

"Even Bronagh?"

I grunted. "Yeah, even Bronagh."

"Oh, my God," Da said from my right. "It must have been a hell of a fight for you and Bee to fall out."

"You're tellin' me."

"D'ye want to talk about it?" Ma asked, resting her hand on my shoulder. "We'll listen."

"Honestly, I just need time away from all of them," I admitted. "I'm okay, I promise; it's just somethin' I have to work through meself, ye'know?"

"Yeah, love," Da said from my left. "We know."

I glanced at him and smiled when he winked.

Things between us had gotten so much better since that day in the hospital after my ma got her surgery. A few days ago, they got even better after my parents sat me down, and my ma admitted to knowing that da was cheating on her. He had planned to wait until she finished radiation to speak to her about it, but he felt so guilty that he told her one night when they were lying in bed, and she replied with three words, "I already know."

I was blown away, and my instinct was to react with anger at her for sticking around when she knew my da was breaking their vows, their trust, but my ma explained to me that *she* knew that my da knew it was all a mistake before he even realised it himself. She told me that people make mistakes and hurt those we love, and that is what makes us human. The ability to be less than perfect.

My ma said she could have packed my da's belongings and kicked him out, but what good would that have done either of them if they gave up on their marriage without a fight. I argued that the fight was lost the second my da strayed, but once I saw how much my da regretted his actions, I realised my ma was right, and that we were all lucky she was so caring and wise.

Some things were meant to be forgotten, and others were meant to be fought for.

My ma didn't react to a situation at the drop of a hat like I did; she took a step back and considered everything, and especially the outcome. I didn't. I acted on whatever emotion I was feeling at the moment, and when I thought about that, it made me think about what happened with my friends.

Instantly, I put up a wall and shut them all out without giving them the chance to explain what Morgan had told me. I was angry and hurt. I still was, but now that I had time to sit back and think about everything, I realised I only had one side of five different stories.

I knew I had to go see the group and hear them out, but doing that was a lot harder than I thought it would be. My heart was hurt. I felt so insufficient and kept wondering if something was so untrustworthy about me that it made everyone lie to me. I had always thought I was a nice person, someone anyone, especially my friends and partner, could confide in, but I wasn't.

Bronagh and Damien's betrayal hurt the worst. Bronagh was my best friend, someone who I thought shared everything with me, as I did with her, but knowing she willingly kept what happened from me cut me deep. Damien's betrayal hurt in an entirely different way. I loved him. I loved him more than I should for the time we were together, but I couldn't change that.

What I feared happening from the very start had taken place. Damien and I had ended, and I was in more pain than I was the first time around because this time, love was shared, a deep connection was shared. I couldn't sleep, I barely ate, and when I tried to work, all I did was sketch and paint Damien's face. He was on my mind constantly ... and so were the things he and my friends had done.

Murder.

They had murdered people. Took the lives of other human beings. No matter how long I sat and thought about it, no matter what way I looked at it, I could scarcely believe it to be the truth. The people I knew were loyal and fiercely protective, they were some of the best men I had ever known, and to learn of them committing such acts of horror completely blindsided me. If I hadn't heard them admit to such deeds, I would have never truly believed Morgan.

Morgan, who had kept his word. He left my apartment and not returned. I received an email from him letting me know he was deleting his account but had transferred all my client emails to my inbox, as well as a detailed explanation on how to keep my system in order. I didn't delete the message because I knew I would need it, so I didn't fall back into my previous disorganised ways, but when I thought of Morgan, I felt so foolish. I couldn't believe I'd let a stranger into my house, someone who could have truly hurt me, and was none the wiser. I told myself what came to be was never something I could have ever imagined but being tricked by him left a sour taste in my mouth.

The whole situation did.

"Alannah?"

I looked at my ma and blinked.

"I'm sorry." I sighed. "I'm not with it at all today."

She put her arms around me and gave me a hug.

"Isn't it Jax's birthday today?"

My shoulder's slumped. "Yeah, he's one."

"Are you goin' to drop by and see 'im?"

I shrugged. "I don't want his day to be turned into a big argument, so I was goin' to go up to Kane and Aideen's apartment and leave his card and gift outside so they could give it to 'im for me."

A lump formed in my throat knowing I was goin' to miss his big day, but I kept myself in check. My parents said nothing, probably sensing my emotional mood on the subject. They quickly changed the subject back to something mundane, then two hours later, I found myself back in my apartment complex and walking up the stairs to Kane and Aideen's apartment.

I had my large gift bag in my hand that had small toys, two outfits, some sweets, a portrait I drew of Jax from a recent picture I took of him and a handmade card. When I was outside the door, I could hear the kids inside, and I heard a lot of other voices as well which almost stopped my heart.

It was after seven, so I didn't expect anyone to be still at the party that I knew Aideen and Kane were holding for Jax. I received my invite in my postbox in the lobby a week ago. I quickly put the bag down outside the door, rang the doorbell, then turned and briskly walked down the hallway, back towards the stairwell. I knew ringing the doorbell was a mistake the second I realised just how far away the stairwell was from the apartment. I heard noise from behind, then, "Alannah, wait!"

I froze and turned around in time to see Kane bend down and pick up the gift bag. When he looked at me, he smiled tentatively and said, "Come in and see the birthday boy. He misses you."

I scowled. "Usin' that baby against me is low, even for you."

Kane shrugged. "I never said I was going to play fair."

I didn't move.

"Come in and see Jax," Kane urged. "You don't have to look or talk to anyone else."

I hesitated, but the need to see Jax beat out the option to run away.

"Five minutes, then I'm leavin'."

Kane smiled as I walked toward him, then stepped back as I entered the apartment that was like mine, just way bigger.

"Living room." He gestured with his hand. "He's in there."

And so was everyone else, I found out the second I entered the room and found all eyes were on me. The first person I locked eyes on was Damien, and my knees nearly buckled when I saw the state of him. His eyes were bloodshot, his skin a little pale, and though he looked put together, he was anything but.

I dropped my eyes, and looked at no one else, until squeal and screech sounded. I smiled when the kids realised I was in the room. I silently took Georgie from her mother because she was screaming in delight for me to do so, and I did the same with Jax because he was having a nervous breakdown that I held his cousin and not him. I kissed Locke who was in his uncle JJ's arms and grinning at me like the little stud he was.

I sat on the floor with the kids and kept my focus completely on them.

"Birthday boy," I cooed to Jax as I tickled his sides. "You're one today!"

He screamed, and everyone chuckled at his response.

When he kissed my face repeatedly, Dante said, "He takes after me. *Definitely.*"

I looked up at him and said, "Shut up, you."

He grinned like a fool but did as ordered. Kane hunkered down next to me and placed my gift bag in front of Jax. Instantly, he tore into the bag, and it made me laugh for what felt like the first time in forever. I carefully took the portrait from him when he studied it closely and handed it to Kane.

"It's just somethin' I did," I mumbled. "It's nothin', really."

"Me arse it's nothin'," Gavin said from across the room. "It looks exactly like Jax. You're so bloody good at drawin', Lana."

"He's right, Alannah," Kane said. "It's beautiful. Thank you."

I shrugged and looked back at the kids as everyone fawned over Jax's portrait while he focused on the toys I got and ignored the clothes, while Georgie discreetly took his sweets, making me grin.

"You're so pretty," I told her and tugged at the pink tutu she wore. "The prettiest girl in all the world."

She smiled at me, and the tooth that had cut through her gums a few months ago was longer now and had another two for company. I sighed, leaned in and kissed her, then Jax, before I climbed back to my feet.

"I have to go," I said to no one. "I've a lot of work to do."

That was a lie. I had completed the entire month's worth of projects in the past two weeks because they distracted me from my life.

"Hey, wait a second," Gavin said, crossing the room. "Look at me."

I did and frowned. "What?"

"Are you okay?" he asked, leaning in, squinting his eyes at me. "Are you stoned?"

"I wish." I snorted. "I just haven't been sleepin' very good, that's all."

"Are you sick?" he questioned. "You look like you've lost weight since I saw you last."

I had, twenty pounds to be exact. A broken heart took away my appetite.

"I have, but I'm fine."

Gavin stared down at me until I rolled my eyes.

"What do you want me to say?"

"I want to know what's goin' on," Gavin countered. "Aideen

said you had a fallin' out with everyone, and I want to know *why*. I hate when people keep secrets."

I laughed. "You're the *last* person to talk about secrets."

Gavin froze.

"Exactly," I said, ignoring everyone's eyes one me.

"What does she mean, Gav?" Harley asked his little brother. "You have a secret?"

Gavin glanced at his brother, then back at me and groaned.

"Yeah." He nodded. "One I asked Alannah to keep even though she hated every second of it because it meant she had to keep it from you lot."

"Don't worry about them," I mumbled. "They don't share the same sentiment when it comes to secrets."

"Alannah," Bronagh said from my right, making me bristle. "Please, talk to us."

"I have to go."

"Not until Gavin says whatever it is you both know."

I focused on Gavin after Dante spoke. "Go on, tell them."

Gavin inhaled, then exhaled a deep breath and said, "I got a woman pregnant."

As sharp intakes filled the room, I laughed, clapped my hand on his shoulder, and said, "Good luck, buddy."

"I'm gonna redden your arse for this later."

I walked out of the room shaking my head, and when I heard footsteps behind me, I calmly said, "Go away, Damien."

"How'd you know it was me?"

Because I can sense you.

"Just had a feelin' it was."

He hesitated. "Please, talk to me. I miss you so much."

I closed my eyes.

"Give me more time."

"How much more time do you need?" he impatiently inquired. "Jesus, Alannah, I'm going fucking crazy without you. I know you are, too. I know you love me as much as I love you. I *know* you do, freckles."

My heart pounded in my chest.

"You've lost weight, and I can tell by your eyes that you haven't been sleeping." He continued. "I hate that you are feeling this way because of me."

"Not just you."

"It's *all* because of me," he stressed. "Everything that happened is *my* fault."

What does he mean by that?

My hands began to tremble.

"Damien, give me more time."

"Okay," he relented softly. "Okay, but please, take care of yourself if you won't let me do it for you. I love you, Alannah."

I left Kane and Aideen's apartment then and hurried down to mine. I made it inside and closed the door behind me before I broke down and fell into a mess of tears. This was killing me. Feeling so dejected and ruined was killing me. I wasn't sure how long I cried for, but when Barbara mewled from inside the kitchen, I pulled myself together and got on with my nightly routine. I fed Barbara, cleaned out her litter tray, then changed into my work clothes and got back to working on a new painting of Damien.

I had just got his inquisitive grey eyes perfect when my doorbell rang. My instinct told me it was Damien, so I put my things down and went to answer the door. I pulled it open and said, "Damien, I ... You're not Damien."

"No," Kane answered. "I'm much better lookin'."

I opened my mouth to talk but couldn't think of anything to say.

"Cat got your tongue?"

I cleared my throat. "You're the last person I expected to see."

"Does that mean you'll let me in?"

"Why?" I questioned. "D'ye want to have a starin' contest?"

His lips quirked. "No, I want to talk to you."

"Like a conversation?"

"Yeah, like a conversation."

I narrowed my eyes. "Are you capable of that?"

"Ha-ha-ha, you're hilarious."

I turned and walked into my sitting room. I knew Kane followed me the second my apartment door closed. I sat on my settee, pulled a throw blanket around my body, and switched on the television. Out of the corner of my eye, I saw Kane take a seat on the settee facing me.

"How are you holding up?"

"Surprisingly well considerin' me so called friends are a bunch of lyin' rat bastards."

Kane whistled. "You're hurtful when you're mad."

"Good," I quipped. "I hope I make you cry."

We both knew I couldn't make Kane cry, but the thought alone made me feel better.

"Alannah." He sighed. "We all love you; it's why we did what we did."

"You *love* me?" I repeated with a laugh. "Kane, you can barely tolerate me."

"That was when you were a kid," he corrected. "You came into me life at a time when I was just used to being in my brothers' company. When Dominic and Bronagh hooked up, everything changed. Ryder and Branna got together, then Alec met Keela, and I found my Aideen. I'm quiet, and I sometimes can't handle being around everyone all at once, but if I had to choose someone, apart from Aideen, to be stuck in a room with for a week flat, it'd be you."

"Why?"

"Because you're you." He shrugged. "You've never made me feel uncomfortable or made me feel like I had to strike up a conversation to keep things from being awkward. All of the other girls have made me feel like that at some point even though they don't mean to, but not you. You're easy to be around."

"Easy to manipulate and lie to, you mean."

Kane shook his head.

"No, you're a good person. You're so ... chill. I like being around you."

"I don't like bein' around you; you're a liar."

Another sigh. "I'm sorry."

I didn't respond.

"I truly am."

I looked at him, and he looked to be sincerely sorry, and that made staying angry with him very hard.

"You've all really hurt me."

"I know we have, Lana, but you have to believe us when we say it was to protect you."

I swallowed. "None of this feels real, Kane. I can't believe you have all done the things Morgan said you did."

"His name isn't Morgan."

"I know," I grumbled. "It just feels weird to call him the other name."

Kane nodded in understanding.

"I'm not going to explain what Morgan has told you," he said. "I'm just here to convince you to give the man who needs to do that the chance *to* do it."

I looked up at the ceiling.

"He's still in your apartment?"

"Yes," Kane answered. "Aideen's dad left before you arrived. Dante has taken Jax and Locke for a sleepover, Keela went home to put Georgie to bed since she and Alec are babysitting her tonight, and Ryder brought Branna home with the twins. He is back in my place."

"Why has everyone stayed?"

"We're hoping you'll give Damien a chance to talk, then hear the rest of us out."

"What if I say no?"

"I'll tell the landlord you're being a bad neighbour, and he might kick you out."

My lips parted in shock.

"You arsehole, why would you do that?"

"Because I'm tight with him."

"You … you are?"

"Extremely."

This was news to me.

"Who is he?" I demanded. "I never knew you knew 'im."

"He's, well, me."

I blinked. "Excuse me?"

"I'm the landlord."

I didn't speak.

"I am," Kane pressed. "I own this building, and four more like it throughout Dublin. I own the community centre that's being knocked down during the summer and rebuilt so I can open it as a youth centre to target kids prone to ending up in gangs and steer them away from that life so they can focus on their education and future."

My jaw practically hit my lap.

"You don't know this because it was another fucking secret, but we're done keeping them from our family, and you are our family, so you have a right to know."

Still, I couldn't speak.

"When Damien has been helping me, it was looking at other locations to build apartments. He wasn't doing anything illegal. He was just helping me and didn't tell you because I asked him not to. I'm sorry if I made you doubt him."

I closed my mouth and just stared at Kane.

"Let me have it," he said. "Scream, shout, do what you must."

I raised a brow. "I'm not goin' to scream and shout at you."

"You're aren't?"

"No, I rarely scream and shout at anyone."

"You really aren't like the other girls."

I frowned. "I know I'm nothin' like them."

"Hey." Kane frowned. "That is not a bad thing. You're a cool girl, Lana. So chill."

"You've called me chill twice."

"Because you are." He shrugged.

I looked at my fingers before I realised something and looked up at Kane with widened eyes.

"Oh, my God," I croaked. "I *knew* this apartment was too good to be true. You're rentin' it to me *way* cheaper than it's worth because I told Aideen I couldn't afford the rent increase at me old place and—"

"Hold it," Kane cut me off. "I own the building. I can rent to my tenants at whatever price I want."

"Bullshit," I snapped. "You're rentin' it to me for eight hundred a month because you pity me."

"Alannah," he deadpanned. "If that's the case, I'm renting to all of Aideen's brothers because I pity them. They're my family; *you* are my family. I give you a discount just like I give *them* a discount."

I raised a brow. "You rent apartments to all of Aideen's brothers?"

"Dante is moving into this building next week," Kane explained. "JJ and Harley, too. This place is going to become a whole lot more interesting, that's for sure."

"Do *not* put Dante or Harley on this floor," I warned. "I'd lose me mind and kill them in their sleep."

"Noted," Kane teased. "I'll keep them far away from you."

I was amused but didn't smile.

"Gavin still lives at home with his da, does that mean that he doesn't get an apartment? That wouldn't be very fair since you're givin' them away like Oprah. You get an apartment, and you, and you, and you."

Kane laughed and fighting off a smile became a whole lot harder.

"He isn't living at home anymore as of an hour ago," Kane said with a shake of his head. "After Gavin dropped the baby bombshell, Aideen demanded he moved into one of the apartments in this building so she can help him when his baby is born. I've also put his baby's mother in the apartment opposite him. Aideen got her number from her brother, phoned her, and apparently, the woman is staying at a friend's place, something about family troubles. She accepted the apartment before Aideen could finish asking her if she wanted one. Both Gavin and this woman are going to have it tough raising a kid they didn't plan, especially when they hardly know one another. I help people when I can, Alannah ... I guess I'm trying to make up for all the wrong I've done in my past."

Admiration filled me.

"I'm proud of you," I said. "Saying that when I'm angry at you tastes like vinegar."

Kane smiled, and I loved what it did to his marred but still very handsome face.

"It means a lot to hear you say that."

"It does?"

"Yes, because I know you don't know the reasons we did the horrible things you were told, so knowing you're proud of what I'm doing shows your true character. You're a good girl. A good woman. And my brother is a lucky bastard to have you."

I felt my cheeks burn with heat.

"Are still threatening to kick me out if I don't talk to said brother?"

"Yes."

"Arsehole." I scowled. "You've gone mad with power."

Kane's grey eyes lit with amusement

"Can I go and tell him you'll speak to him? Please say yes. The kid is pleading for another chance, Alannah. He loves you so much he can't function without you. Trust me, I've seen him over the past two weeks, and he is a mess. He literally needs a good woman like you."

Damien needed me just like I needed him.

"On one condition."

"Name it."

"You let me keep Barbara even though no animals are allowed in the buildin'."

Before I could overthink a reason not to, I said, "Go get 'im then." I was dreading what he was going to tell me, but I needed to hear it, and I had a feeling that whatever it was, Damien needed to say it as much as I needed to hear it. For once, I was going to push my fear of the unknown aside to do what I feared the most and face my hurt head-on. I didn't know what the outcome would be, but I could do nothing but hope and pray for the best.

What's meant to be, will be.

CHAPTER THIRTY-ONE

"Alannah?"

My heart just about stopped as apprehension filled me. "I'm in the sittin' room."

I turned my eyes from the window to Damien when he entered the room, and it took every ounce of willpower I had not to run to him. I missed him so much it hurt, but before the possibility of a reconciliation could happen, we needed to talk.

"Sit down."

He did just that on the settee facing me.

"Thank you for agreeing to talk to me," he said, clasping his hands together as he rested his elbows on his knees. "I know how hard it is for you."

"Talkin' to you isn't hard," I said. "It's one of the easiest things to do. The hardest is hearin' what you have to say."

"I know, baby."

My heart yearned for him the second he called me baby.

"I'm goin' to listen to whatever you have to say with an open-mind, so don't dilute anythin'."

"I won't," Damien answered. "I told you when you were ready that I'd tell you everything, and I'm going to do that."

I nodded and waited.

My heart thrummed in my chest.

"My parents were murdered by a man called Marco Miles," Damien said with his eyes locked on mine. "My dad was Marco's best friend and had been since they were kids. They started up their empire from scratch and grew it from the ground up. They had links to most likely every mafia family in and out of the States, every drug cartel known to man, and others that were unknown, and they had the law in their back pocket for decades."

Breathe, I told myself. *Just breathe.*

"My brothers and I grew up in a lifestyle that was *nothing* like yours. We were treated like princes and got whatever our hearts desired because of who our dad was. Escorts were servicing me and Dominic from the time we were thirteen; the first onces were actually a birthday gift from our brothers. Our lives were a blur up until my mom and dad got killed just after my and Dominic's fifteenth birthday."

Damien's leg began to bob up and down as he spoke.

"My dad crossed Marco, looking to get some extra money on a drug deal, so Marco had my dad and mom killed. They were best friends, had known each other their whole lives, but my dad's greed for money and power changed him, made him hollow… evil. My mom was no better; the only thing she loved was money and materialistic things. I didn't lie to you about that; she and my dad were cold to me and my brothers."

My heart hurt for him.

"I'm sorry," I said. "I'm sorry you were raised by loveless parents; I hurt for you knowin' that."

Damien cleared his throat. "Thank you."

I leaned back in the chair and waited.

"For a long time after my parents died"—he sighed—"I convinced myself that I didn't love my brothers."

My lips parted in shock.

"I have always been the affectionate brother," he continued. "I was always the one who craved my parents' love and attention, and when they didn't give it to me, I'd do crazy things to get it. After they were murdered, I was so lost in grief that I was terrified of losing any of my brothers, so I pretended I didn't love them. That way if I did lose them, it wouldn't hurt. I told myself I tolerated them because they were my flesh and blood. It made me a nasty son of a bitch to be around at times. Because of that, I never let anyone close. I had sex with a lot of different women because it was the only connection that I could control. I was hollow inside … until I met you."

I swallowed.

"Back on the compound, we grew up with Marco's nephews, Trent and Carter. Carter was around us a lot, but he was the opposite of Trent. He was a loner and never seemed into anything that happened in the compound. Dominic, Trent, and I were practically best friends at one point. The only difference between us was he enjoyed when people were beat up and tortured. When our dad and his uncle made us participate in punishing someone, he loved it, said it helped build character."

I curled my lip in disgust.

"We hated it too," Damien said, noting my reaction. "We didn't want the life our dad had provided for us if it came along with the things we hated. The day our parents were murdered, Dominic and I were going to tell them we wanted to leave, but after they died, I re-fused to leave. I felt connected to the place since I no longer had them."

I understood that. His grief made him latch onto the thing his parents cared about most, that poxy compound and horrid lifestyle.

"Trent was bad for me to be around when I was in the state of mind of wanting to feel no pain, the only person who glanced me out was Nala."

I exhaled a breath. "Nala?"

"My girlfriend at the time," Damien said then quickly added, "I don't want to hurt you by talking about her, but you need to hear about her to understand everything. To understand me."

"I told you, don't dilute anythin'."

Damien nodded. "I met Nala when we were ten. She had just

moved into the compound with her dad, and we hit it off straight away. She followed me and Dominic everywhere, and I never minded because I had a crush her. I asked her to date me when we were thirteen, she said yes, and we were together up until she was murdered."

My hand flung over my mouth.

"Oh, Da-Damien," I stammered. "I'm so sorry."

He clasped his hands tighter together.

"Before that happened, we were pretty inseperable, but after my parents died, I began to pull away from her, too. I loved her, or at least as much as a thirteen-year-old could love someone. She took my pulling away from her hard, and Trent was there with his shoulder for her to lean on. Two weeks after my parents died, I was having a really bad day, and Trent made the mistake of kissing Nala. I attacked him and beat the shit out of him. He became hostile and brought my parents into the fight, saying they deserved to be dead for what they had done. He wished I was dead along with them, and that caused Dominic to snap. It was the first time I saw him fight, and it scared me how hard and fast he could hit another person."

My stomach fluttered with nerves.

"I was annoyed with Dominic for stepping in to defend me when I could do it myself, so I got him off Trent and intended to whoop him on my own, but he pulled a gun. If Nala hadn't jumped on Trent's back to distract him, he would have shot me. I saw it in his eyes, he was going to do it. I got the gun from him, thanks to Nala."

He clenched his teeth together.

"When I think about that night, I can still hear Dominic plead and cry with me to throw the gun away because we weren't our dad, and I wished I had listened to him. Because what I did ruined my brothers' lives. I shot Trent, and when he hit the ground, he stopped moving. Blood was everywhere, and shit passed by in a blur after that."

I began to chew on my nails.

"I knew what I had done would mean I would have to die. That's just how it works, a life for a life. At the time, I was prepared to accept that. I felt so torn up over my parents, over the fact that I had turned out just like my dad, that I was willing to die just to escape everything. Ryder met with Marco, and I wasn't dumb as to what it was about. If Marco killed me, he knew my brothers would retaliate, so they both discussed it until they reached a decision."

"The life debt," I concluded. "Morgan said your brothers started to work for Marco to pay off your life debt."

"Yes," Damien answered. "They cut me out of the deal to protect me."

The resentment in his tone surprised me.

"You're disappointed you couldn't have a dangerous job?"

"No," he answered. "I was disappointed that my brothers put their lives on the line to protect me and didn't give me a chance to pay off the debt I brought upon us myself. That was the day I stopped being a brother."

"What do you mean?" I quizzed. "You *are* a Slater brother."

"On paper, yeah," he said, "but inside, I don't feel like one."

"Why?"

"Because they don't treat me like their equal," Damien answered. "They treat me like the baby they were stuck with and had to raise. I hate it; I always have. Dominic is four minutes older than I am, and he was clued in on everything because he had a job for Marco."

I didn't know what to say, so I remained quiet.

"Anyway." He cleared his throat. "I didn't know that Nala was dead until we moved to Ireland and my brothers wanted out of their deal with Marco because they repaid the life debt and made Marco more money than Trent ever could. Marco wanted to keep my family under his thumb, so that night in Darkness when we were together, I was attacked until I fell unconscious. You were knocked out, too. Marco used us, and Bronagh, as bait to lure my brothers into his trap. It all went sideways for him. Trent admitted that he raped and murdered Nala the day after I shot him. She came by looking for me and walked in on Trent being treated by a doctor. Marco couldn't let her live after what she saw, so he let Trent kill her. He raped her, killed her, and then buried her in the grave that was meant for himself. She was ten weeks pregnant at the time; she had told me a few days be-forehand, and I began to pull away from her because of that. I was terrified of having a baby, but it scared me more to love it in case I lost it."

I began to silently cry.

"I didn't know it when I was a kid, but I thought Nala's dad packed her up and moved because I could never find either of them when I searched. I always thought she was alive and had our baby, and I was pissed at her for not allowing me to be apart of that. My parents' death sent me into grief, but Nala kept me there, and because of her, I kept everyone at arm's length. I was so angry with her … and all the while, I never knew that both of them were dead because of me."

"Trent."

Damien blinked. "What?"

"They died because of Trent, not you." I sniffled. "You have to stop placin' blame on your shoulders when it belongs on someone else's."

"Alannah—"

"No," I cut him off. "You blame yourself for everythin' that happened, but you were a baby. Fifteen years old. You had no control over what other people did, so stop blamin' yourself. Marco tricked your family into workin' for 'im. He is to blame for all of this, and Trent is responsible for killin' Nala and your baby. *Him*, not you!"

Damien stared at me, and I knew it was difficult for him to do as I asked.

"You aren't to blame."

He blinked. "You don't blame me for everything?"

"No," I said. "And I know no one else does either."

He looked down, and I knew in the back of his mind, he didn't believe me.

"We can come back to that," Damien said, clearing his throat. "I want to keep going."

I nodded and waited.

"After all that happened. Everything with Darkness, with us, I decided to leave to better myself thanks to Bronagh."

"Bronagh?"

"Yeah." Damien nodded. "When she came by the room we were in, she was straight with me. She told me exactly how she felt, and how horrible I was for sleeping with you when I knew you liked me. She knew how much I never wanted to be like my parents, and she made me realise how I was treating girls, how I treated *you*, was wrong and something they would do. She was brutal, but no one else was going to tell me what I needed to hear. She flipped a switch in me."

"What did you do when you went back to New York?"

"I removed the headstone for Trent on Nala's grave and had a new one made for her and the baby. I know it was still inside her stomach, but it was still a baby, and I didn't want people not to know he or she didn't exist. You know?"

"Yeah, sweetheart, I know."

Damien exhaled a breath. "Do you hate me for getting Nala pregnant?"

"Of course not," I replied, shocked. "Damien, you didn't know I existed when you and Nala were together. Don't be silly."

He nodded and looked down at his hands.

"Maybe … Maybe we can buy Nala and the baby a star, just like you bought me," I suggested. "That way when we look up, we'll know they're out there watchin' over us. Would that help you in any way?"

When Damien looked at me, my heart pounded when I saw unshed tears in his eyes.

"It's okay to cry," I told him. "You're allowed to be sad and grieve who you lost. You don't need to worry about how I feel about it. I'm sad for you and for Nala and the baby, too. No one deserves what she went through."

I didn't move when Damien got up and came to my side. I wrapped my arms around him when he hugged my body to his. He put his head on mine and cried. When he cried, it almost instantly set me off. I held him, rocked him side to side, and let him release everything he had been keeping inside.

"I have more to tell you," he said, clearing his throat.

"More of your story or your brothers?"

"My brothers," Damien answered, pulling back to look at me. "Mine ended after I … after I took Trent's life."

Hearing him say that out loud didn't horrify me like I thought it would have; it gave me an incredible sense of relief and a huge sense of justice for Nala and the baby he killed.

"I'm glad," I said, taking hold of his hand. "I'm *glad*."

Damien closed his eyes and rested his forehead against mine.

"Also, I don't want to hear your brothers' stories from you. I want to hear it from *them*."

Damien nodded and kept his eyes closed.

"Are you okay?"

"I'm just enjoying this feeling of being close to you," he answered as he opened his eyes. "I've missed you so much."

"I've missed you too," I said. "It killed me to shut you all out, but I needed to. I needed to reach this frame of mind where I was able to hear you out."

"I know, freckles."

When I kissed Damien, he was so surprised that he didn't return the kiss for a few seconds, and when he did, it felt like magic. When we separated, he kept his hold on me.

"I want to talk to you about Alec," he said. "He gave me permission to tell you this. This is something only I know, and by allowing me to tell you, he wants you to know that he loves and trusts you enough to keep this secret between the three of us."

I reared back. "I don't wanna know. I don't wanna keep secrets anymore."

"This is a secret that you won't want to share," Damien assured me. "It's only to help you understand my brother and understand the level of love and trust he has for you after everything you have been through with Carter."

I inhaled a deep breath.

"Okay."

"Alec is thirty-one, and he is happy all the time." Damien began. "He makes innuendoes, he overreacts about a lot of things, he has shits and giggles about random things that pop into his head. He is different. Have you ever stopped and wondered why?"

I raised my brows. "No."

"Out of all my brothers," Damien continued. "Alec is the one who deserves to smile and laugh over dumb shit because for a very long time, the bubbly, happy man you know didn't exist. He was a shell of a person."

"What?" I whispered. "Why not?"

"He was heavily abused in his line of work." Damien swallowed. "He was a prostitute in Marco's eyes, but he considered himself to be an escort. Most of the time, he had consensual sex on the job, a lot of the time he didn't even have to kiss his dates, but some of the time … he was forced to do things that I don't want to go into detail about."

"R-rape?"

"Yes."

A cry bubbled up my throat, and I covered my mouth with my hand to contain it.

"It got bad." Damien's voice became rough. "When I was sixteen, a year after the jobs started, Alec was hurt by two men in a way I'll never be able to get over."

I felt sick.

"He always came home late, and this night, I got some midnight snacks when I heard him come in and go up the stairs. He was crying. I had never heard him cry before, so I knew whatever happened to him was bad. I followed him up the stairs after a minute or two, just to see if he was okay and ..."

My heart stopped.

"He tried to kill himself, Alannah," Damien said, a pained expression crossing his face. "He used a cable tie, threw it over one of the beams on the ceiling, and put it around his neck. What those men did to him made him want to die."

"Oh, God."

"I still don't know how I got him down or got the cable tie from around his neck. It's all a blur, but I'm just happy I was awake when he came home, and that I followed him to see if he was okay."

I cried, and Damien held me.

"He told me everything that had happened to him and made me swear never to tell the others. Not because he didn't trust them, but because he wanted to save them the pain of knowing."

"Like ... like you and the others tried to do with me."

"Yes, because some secrets are best left buried, baby."

I agreed.

"I'll never tell," I swore. "I promise, I'll never tell. I won't even speak of it to Alec."

"I know you won't."

"I can't believe he went though that."

"All of my brothers have been through hell."

I was quiet.

"It's my fault," he continued. "I ruined their lives because I couldn't keep my temper in check."

I could repeat to him over and over that it wasn't his fault, but I wasn't one of his brothers. He needed to hear it from *them* that he wasn't to blame.

"Are you *sure* he never told Keela about this, though?"

"I'm sure." He nodded. "When I came back, and when I was on my own with him, he explained that it was a part of his life he wanted to protect her from. Since he couldn't protect her from the other parts of his life that had bad implications on their relationship."

"Then why are you telling *me*?"

"Because he wants you to know just how much he does trust you. He hated how you looked at him the day Carter got in your head; it hurt him to see you scared of him. It's just... he was silent for so long, but now he has a reason to be heard. Do you understand?"

"I do." I nodded. "I really do."

When I stood up, Damien looked up at me, frowning.

"What's wrong?"

"Nothin'," I answered. "I want to go up to Kane's apartment so we can talk to everyone else."

Damien got to his feet. "Are you sure?"

"I've never been surer of anythin' in me life."

CHAPTER THIRTY-TWO

When Damien and I entered Kane's apartment, it was silent. We both entered the sitting room, and all eyes fell on us. Everyone's eyes locked on mine and Damien's hands, and they all seemed to release a breath of relief when they saw our fingers threaded together. Before anyone spoke, my eyes landed on Alec. I let go of Damien and all but crashed into him, wrapping my arms around him so tight. I knew I had to be hurting him, but he didn't complain. He put his arms around me, rested his cheek on my head, and hugged me back.

"I love you," I said, my voice muffled against his chest. "So much, you cup obsessed bastard."

Alec vibrated with laughter.

"I love you too, you cup destroying bitch. You're getting me a new one, by the way. I'm going to be a nightmare until to do."

When we separated, I wiped my eyes as I laughed. I noticed everyone was looking at the pair of us with grins. I barely had time to look at Bronagh before she embraced me just as tight as I wrapped myself around Alec.

"I love you so much," she cried. "I'm so sorry."

"Don't be sorry," I told her. "Do *not* be sorry, I understand."

I squeezed her and kissed her cheek.

"You're me best friend, and I love you so much."

She hugged me again, and when we separated, I looked around the room.

"I apologise to all of you," I said, swallowing. "I understand why you all wanted to protect me from knowin' about your past, and I'm so sorry I called you monsters. I hope you can forgive me."

"Alannah," Ryder said with a huff. "You were forgiven the second you said it, kid."

I hugged him, and then everyone else in the room, before I returned to Damien's side and slid my arm around his waist. Keela and Branna weren't present, but I would reunite with them tomorrow and be sure to hug them just as hard.

"Me and Damien have talked, a lot, and he has told me everythin' he needed to," I said. "I wanted your stories to come from each of you, and I know you're all willin' to tell me, but as of right now, I don't need to know anymore. If I do, I'll ask. At this moment in time, I just want to leave the past in the past and focus on all of our futures."

"I couldn't have said it better myself, Lana."

I looked at Nico when he spoke and smiled.

"I just need you four to help me with somethin'," I said, nodding to Ryder, Alec, Kane and Nico. "Somethin' important."

"Anything," they replied.

"I need to you tell Damien not to blame himself for all the horrible things Marco and those other people involved have put you guys through because he blames himself and doesn't believe me when I say otherwise. He doesn't feel like he is truly a brother to you lads, and it breaks me heart that he feels that way."

Damien tensed and looked down at me with his lips parted. I stepped away from him and nodded for him to talk.

"I don't know what you want me to say."

"I do," Nico said, gaining his twin's attention. "Say that you aren't to blame, and that you're my brother."

"I am to blame, though," Damien replied. "This happened, all of it, because of me. Every job you all had to do, every ounce of pain and worry your women went through, was because of me. I ruined everything."

I was shocked when Nico crossed the room, grabbed Damien by the scruff of the neck, and got in his face.

"Whatever you have done, or whatever you do, you're still my fucking brother! Realise that, and then fucking accept it. I love you to death, man. I wouldn't change a thing about my life; it's made me who I am and brought me to my family."

"But your life—"

"Wouldn't have turned out like this if our past didn't happen. I'd have never met Bronagh, the woman I'm going to marry, and she would never have given me a beautiful baby girl or be pregnant with my second baby."

Damien stared at his twin.

"But Dominic—"

"No!" Nico snapped and shook Damien. "You. Did. Not. Ruin. Our. Lives."

"Dominic—"

"Damien!" Nico shouted, his chest rising and falling rapidly. "You did *nothing* to us. So many people are responsible for the bad shit that's happened to us, but it was all because of one person and that person was Marco, not you."

Damien remained silent.

"Acknowledge it," Nico pressed. "Out loud."

Damien squeezed his eyes shut. "I can't."

An expression of pure agony stretched over Nico's features.

"Damien," he said slowly. "Acknowledge. It. Out. Loud."

I didn't realise I was crying until a hiccup escaped my throat and an arm hooked around my waist. I knew it was Bronagh without having to look at her.

"Damien." Alec spoke from behind us. "Say it because it's the truth, bro. Everything that happened to us was not your fault. *None* of it."

Hearing him say that after knowing what he had been through

made me love the man even more.

"Say it, kid," Kane urged. "You're not to blame, for fucking any of it."

Damien's eyes blinked open, and he looked from Nico, to his brothers, who were standing around the room.

"Come on, Dame," Ryder spoke last, his voice firm. "Say it. You didn't ruin out lives, Marco did."

Damien opened and closed his mouth twice before he licked his lips and said, "I ... I didn't ruin our lives ... Marco did."

I covered my mouth to conceal my whimper as Nico enveloped Damien into a bone-crushing hug that the other brothers quickly joined.

"Everyone has demons, Dame," Kane said, clapping his hand against his brother's back. "We just need to be meaner than them because you know what, bro? We *deserve* to be happy."

When the brothers finished embracing, Damien turned his misty eyes on me.

"I love you," I said for the first time, my body trembling. "I love you so much, Damien."

He stood across the way, staring at me for a good ten seconds before he snapped out of his trance and crossed the room to me in two seconds flat. His body crashed into mine, and to avoid falling backwards, my arms instantly latched around his waist, while Damien's hands gripped either side of my face. He stared down at me with such intensity it made my knees weak and knock together. I squeezed him and stared up into his big, grey eyes. A plethora of emotions burned within them, but one emotion stood out.

Love.

"I love you, Damien," I repeated, my heart slamming against my chest. "I have never come close to loving another person; it's why I've always been so scared when it came to you. I have never loved another person the way that I love you. You are me heart, and if you'll still have me, I'm yours. I've always been yours."

I choked back a sob when tears spilled over the brims of his eyes and streamed down his cheeks, like a collapsed dam.

"Love, no," I pleaded. "Please, don't cry. Please."

I leaned up and kissed his away his tears, pressing my lips all over his face, landing lastly on his plump lips.

"I love you," I said, pressing chaste kisses to his mouth. "I love you; I love you; I love you."

Damien's forehead fell against mine, his hands dropped to my waist, and he hugged my body to him so tightly, it almost stole my breath.

"Alannah," Damien rasped, his eyes staring into mine. "I've loved you since we were kids."

A sob tore free of my throat.

"Me too, I just didn't realise it." I sniffled. "God, I love you so much it terrifies me, Damien."

"Don't be scared," he said. "I've got you. For as long as you'll have me, I've got you."

"How does forever sound?"

He squeezed me. "It sounds fucking heavenly, freckles."

"Everythin' about you, Jack Frost," I told him, "is *mine*."

"Jack Frost?"

"You've just been upgraded from snowflake. Congratulations."

Damien's smile was a true thing of beauty.

"I'm yours, Lana. Only yours."

Only. Mine.

"I've never looked forward to the future as much in me life," I declared. "You're movin' in with me, and we're havin' sex every single day at *least* three times. I want to have babies, five of them, ten of them. I don't care how many. I just want babies with you. I want to get married, but you hav'ta ask me da first, otherwise he'll kill you. When I want you, I'm havin' you, and I don't want to hear a feckin' peep outta you on the matter. Are you clear on all of that?"

Damien leaned down and pressed his forehead against mine.

"Yes. Fucking. Ma'am."

"Well," Alec whooped. "It's about fucking time!"

When we kissed, it was to the cheers, hooting, clapping, and laughter of our friends ... our family. It may as well have been kissing to fireworks at midnight on New Year's Eve because it was just as sweet, just as tender, and just as perfectly perfect as a moment could be. It was the start of a beautiful forever.

Damien licked my lower lip. "Endgame, freckles?"

Joy filled me.

"Yeah, Jack Frost." I answered, rubbing the tip of my nose against his. "We're *definitely* endgame."

ACKNOWLEDGEMENTS

I have a huge smile on my face as I type the acknowledgments to *DAMIEN*. It feels crazy to have told the last Slater brother's story. When I first wrote *DOMINIC*, I never imagined that I would have a series full of characters who I loved so dearly. Even more, I never imagined I would have a series full of characters who readers would love so dearly. I can't thank everyone enough for supporting me and the Slater Brothers series. You have made my whole world spin by doing so.

Getting this book ready from start to finish was a task and a half, and it would not have been possible without any of the following people.

Editing4Indies – Jenny, there are no words. You go beyond the call of duty when it comes to editing, especially MY form of editing. Thank you, from the bottom of my heart, for taking on a project this big at a moment's notice.

Nicola Rhead – Thank you for proofing DAMIEN, and getting the job done so fast!

JT Formatting – Jules, thank you for making my words pretty.

Mayhem Cover Creations – LJ, thank you for yet another beautiful cover.

Mark Gottlieb – Thank you for being the best agent, you're awesome.

My readers – Thank you all for your support of the series. It's not over yet! We still have ALANNAH and BROTHERS to go ... then the spin-off series for Aideen's brothers called the *Collins Brothers* series, then another spin off series for the Slater kids when they're all grown up called the *Slater Legacy* series.

It looks like I'm going to be writing about this family and world I've created until I'm in my fifties, and d'ye know what, folks? That's fine by me <3

ABOUT THE AUTHOR

L.A. Casey is a *New York Times* and *USA Today* best-selling author who juggles her time between her mini-me and writing. She was born, raised and currently resides in Dublin, Ireland. She enjoys chatting with her readers, who love her humour and Irish accent as much as her books.

Casey's first book, *DOMINIC*, was independently published in 2014 and became an instant success on Amazon. She is both traditionally and independently published and is represented by Mark Gottlieb from Trident Media Group.

To read more about this author, visit her website at
www.lacaseyauthor.com

ALSO BY L.A. CASEY

Slater Brothers Series
DOMINIC
BRONAGH
ALEC
KEELA
KANE
AIDEEN
RYDER
BRANNA

Maji Series
OUT OF THE ASHES

Standalone Novels
FROZEN
UNTIL HARRY

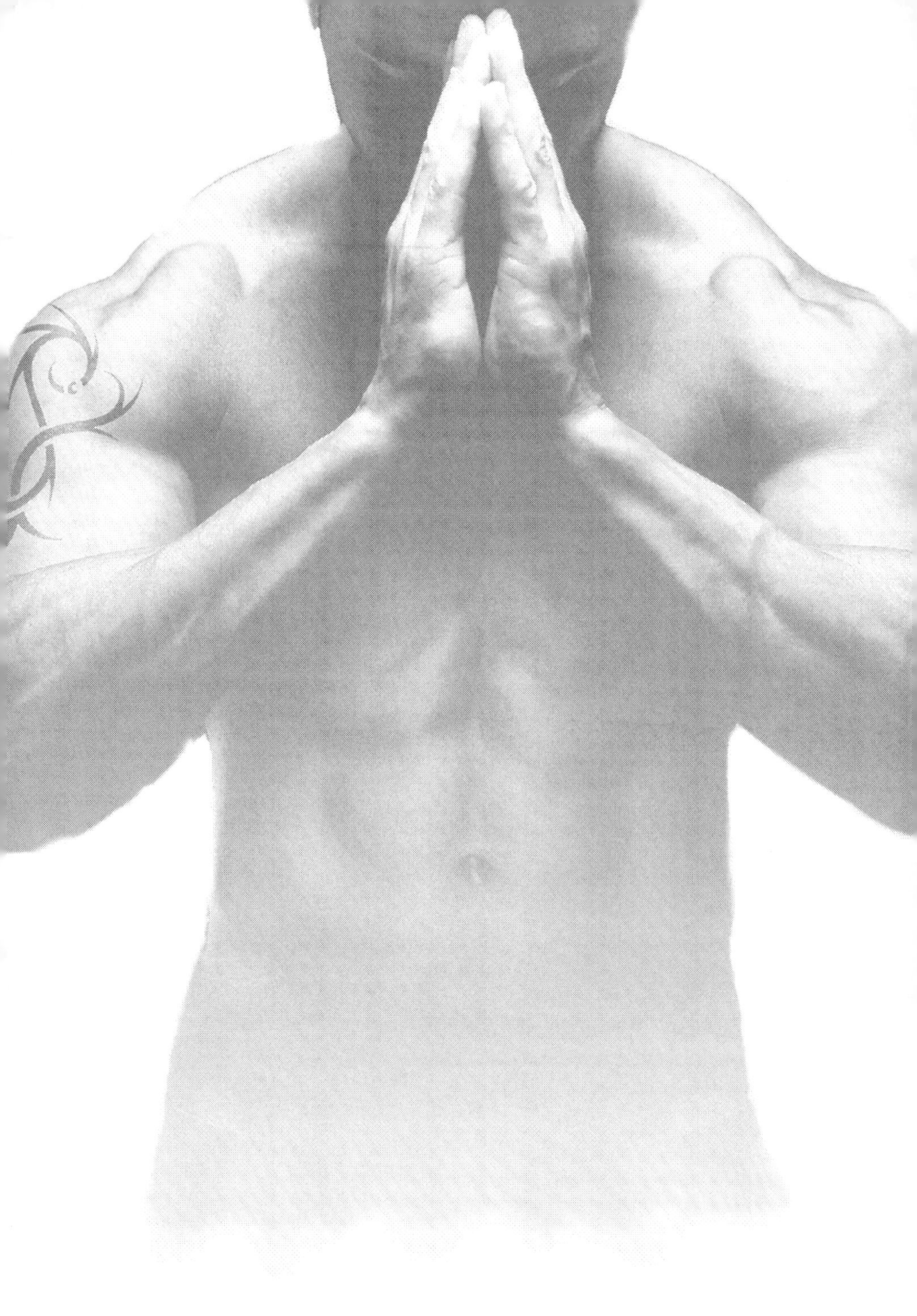

Printed in Great Britain
by Amazon